On the ground Kate Bristow anxiously watched the dogfight.

A brief burst of machine-guns fired as Spitfires and Hurricanes engaged one of the free-hunting groups of German planes. Two planes fell away while she watched. Above one, an English fighter, a parachute blossomed. The other fell in flames.

"Our man's all right!" Kate shouted. "That other one's a German plane." She always had that unworthy fear that it was Dieter. What she could not know was that the burning plane belonged to Dieter's squadron and inside it a man was dead.

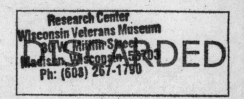

THE FIGHTERS

*A panoramic novel about
the fighter war in the West
1939-1945
by*

Colin Willock

A FAWCETT CREST BOOK

Fawcett Publications, Inc., Greenwich, Connecticut

THE FIGHTERS

THIS BOOK CONTAINS THE COMPLETE TEXT OF THE
ORIGINAL HARDCOVER EDITION.

A Fawcett Crest Book reprinted by arrangement with St. Martin's
Press, Incorporated

Library of Congress Catalog Card Number: 73-77055

Printed in the United States of America
December 1974

AUTHOR'S NOTE

Thirty years afterwards, it is impossible not to feel the strongest horror and disgust at the cause for which the German military leaders of 1939-45 fought. None was more culpable than the Supreme Commander of the Luftwaffe, Hermann Goering. Equally, it is impossible not to feel admiration for the way Goering's aircrews, and especially his fighter pilots, fought their eventually hopeless war. Their supreme commander directed their losing battle with incompetence and distrust. Almost every decision made on their behalf was the wrong one. Nevertheless, and while in no way detracting from the courage and endurance of the Allied airmen who defeated them, I believe that, as a feat of valour and arms, the struggle of the Luftwaffe fighter pilots must rank very high in military history. The story of the Allied fighter pilots has been told, and rightly so, many times. The story of the *Jagdflieger* is not nearly so well known. The fighter pilots and their families in this book are, of course, fictional. The machines they flew and the battles they fought are a matter of history, as are the actual scenes and conversations which took place among the leaders of the air war in the Third Reich. These have been recorded by those who survived. I am indebted to many sources for the facts of the case. I should like to pay particular acknowledgement to the following: *The First and the Last* by Adolf Galland; *Inside the Third Reich* by Albert Speer; *The Luftwaffe War Diaries* by Cajus Bekker; *I Flew For the Führer* by Heinz Knoke; *The Fighter Pilots* by E. H. Sims; *The Luftwaffe: A History* by J. Killen; *Air Organisation of the Third Reich* by R. J. Benda; Profile Publications for many technical details of aircraft on both sides; *Battle Over Britain* by F. K. Mason; *Horrido—Fighter Aces of the Luftwaffe* by T. J. Constable; *The Messerschmitt Bf 109* by James F. Craig; *Me 109* by Martin Caidin; as well as to many official publications. I should also like to thank John Cushman for many practical suggestions and Gerald Pollinger, air historian and ex-fighter pilot, who corrected me on several technical points on which I might have been shot down. My secretary Gillian Conway is a better researcher than she knows. My thanks to my wife, both for her secretarial help and sound criticism, go without saying but are going to be said just the same.

SUMMER, 1938

Wenn die Soldaten durch die Stadt marschieren
Öffnen die Mädchen die Fenster und die Türen ...

The lederhosened youths on the platform sang and played with enthusiasm and rich harmony. There was a fat guitarist who clowned, but only to underline the clean-limbed earnestness of the other eleven. There was a kettle-drummer who twirled his sticks with military precision, but this was only appropriate since most of their songs, even the light-hearted ones, had a military flavour. The little group glowed with health and fervour. They were without doubt a splendid and effective public relations team—so splendid that most of the sixty members of the University's International Friendship League had almost forgotten their aversion to being bottled up in hall on a hot summer's morning with the more or less enforced duty, as hosts, to listen to German marching songs.

Charles Levitson leaned forward under cover of a burst of applause and said to the slight, fair-haired undergraduate sitting directly in front of him: "You can't deny they're a fine-looking lot, Peter."

The fair boy nodded and clapped harder to hide the fact that his attention had wandered from the performance. As secretary of the Friendship League it was his duty to entertain four of the visitors for the rest of the day. Levitson, the American, had agreed to help him.

The fat guitarist had composed his features and now bent himself seriously to his instrument for the group's final song. With a nice touch of showmanship, in contrast to everything that had gone before, they sang sweetly *Roselein auf der Heide*. The singer who stepped forward to take the tenor solo was a tall, dark good-looking young man of about nineteen—the group leader.

"That's our man," Peter Bristow whispered to Levitson. "They were Teutonically efficient and sent a list of their chaps' interests. I opted for the ones that are keen on flying—this boy and three of his henchmen."

Ten minutes later the concert ended. The president of the

International Friendship League made a graceful speech, thanking the visitors for their performance and touching on the need for friendship in the difficult times that faced all European nations in the summer of 1938. He refrained from adding "especially Britain and Germany". A quarter of his members had refused to attend the concert, for the Civil War in Spain was at its height and feelings ran high in some quarters against German participation on Franco's side.

As the audience dispersed, Bristow and Levitson went to collect their four luncheon guests, who stood talking to the League president. He introduced the group leader, the youth who had sung the tenor solo. "This is Dieter Reh—our secretary Peter Bristow. And Charles Levitson here is American. Peter and Charles will be looking after you during your stay with us, Herr Reh." He moved away.

"*Guten Tag,* Herr Reh," Peter began. He had been rehearsing what little German he had. He was a law student, so it wasn't a great deal.

The German smiled and bowed. Was there the suggestion of a heel click? "Good morning, Mr. Bristow," he said. "If it does not embarrass you, we all speak English not too bad."

Levitson said: "Well, that's a hell of a relief to me. I don't have one single word."

Reh bowed again and indicated the three youths standing respectfully just behind him. "My companions would like to meet their very kind hosts. First, Gerhard Stecke. Gerhard is second in command of our *Gruppe.*" Peter saw that Stecke was the flaxen-haired, blue-eyed six-footer who had played the bass drum. Seeing him on the stage he had thought: "Adolf Hitler's ideal Aryan." Now Stecke's bow was stiff enough for a full-blown Prussian general.

The introductions continued. Heinrich Müller was of medium height but broad and obviously very strong. Peter liked the look of him; he had a humorous, thoughtful face—a gentle giant. The fourth boy was a blond and smaller version of Reh himself. "My younger brother, Jacob," he said.

The Germans stood politely waiting for the next move.

"Well," said Peter. "We thought you might like to have lunch at a typically English pub . . . er, hotel. My mother and sister are staying there, so it'll be a kind of family party in a way."

He glanced at the Germans' leather shorts. Levitson was thinking that the Germans looked like something out of the chorus of a show he had seen not so long ago, *"White Horse*

8

Inn". Peter was saying, "Er . . . perhaps you'd like to change before we go to lunch?"

"That is kind," Reh said, "but we are quite warm and comfortable. It is good we should wear *Lederhosen* during our visit to your country."

"Kind of uniform, huh?" Levitson asked.

"We are here as *Hitlerjugend*," Stecke put in stiffly.

"Let's push off and have lunch," said Peter.

They walked up the sunlit high street, the Germans pairing themselves automatically—Reh and Müller, Stecke and Reh's younger brother—falling into step at marching pace. Hands in pockets, Peter and Levitson loped along beside them, pointing out the colleges and other buildings of interest along the way.

Dieter Reh had liked both his hosts on sight, especially Peter, but he found their informality, their apparent sloppiness, strange. He had thought of the university as the centre of Britain's youth elite. He would not condemn out of hand, but he found it impossible not to compare them and the untidy students they passed in the street unfavourably with his own companions and with the young men of his own age back home in Germany. He himself came from Hamelin, a town as ancient in tradition and architecture as this city he was visiting. But in Hamelin the traditions of age were respected, while here . . . Levitson was describing how a climbing party had recently put a chamber pot on top of a college tower. He had got stuck over the interpretation of the word "chamber" and Peter was trying not to laugh at letting slip the word "jerry". The Germans missed the allusion but were perplexed by their hosts' hilarity. Stiffly they turned into the forecourt of the hotel.

Mrs Bristow and her daughter were already at the table reserved in the dining-room, and the Germans' entrance caused quite a stir. Peter's mother was a lady of formidable charm, a town councillor in the small West Country town of Axeham, a woman who prided herself on her political common sense. She thought that Hitler, though obviously undesirable in many respects, should be given the benefit of the doubt. She had been delighted when Peter in his last year at university had become secretary of the International Friendship League, for she felt ardently that if nations were to be brought together, it must be through their youth. Youth everywhere had so much in common! Now she beamed on the four young Germans a smile of welcome as golden as the suntan on the *Hitlerjugend*'s bare thighs and knees. How healthy they looked—

9

and thank goodness none of them wore a swastika armband like those awful Stormtroopers.

"Willkommen," she cried. "Welcome to a very English meal in a very English hotel." Her handsome face glowed with sincerity. As her son made the introductions, she took each German's hand in both of hers and shook it warmly, indicating where they should sit. Dieter Reh had the place of honour between herself and her daughter, Kate. When he was introduced to Peter's sister, Reh raised her hand and kissed it courteously. The girl blushed and said: "Oh, how nice! Thank you." She had often imagined how she would react when some dashing foreigner first kissed her hand, accepting the compliment in the cool, detached manner of a woman of the world. Instead she had blushed and blurted out a thank you as gauche as that of a schoolgirl.

Reh, however, found her charming. He had liked the look of Peter Bristow at first meeting, but he was captivated by the appearance of Bristow's sister, Kate. A year younger than her brother, she was as blonde as Reh was dark, tall and with a complexion that matched the roses on the table—a true Hitler *Mädchen*. She was a beautiful girl.

Mrs Bristow was the kind of hostess who believed that silence is made of lead. She was like a juggler who spins a row of plates balanced on thin poles, noting instantly when any conversational plate was in danger of slowing down or falling off and giving it an adroit twist to keep it going. By the time the melon had disappeared and the cold Scotch salmon had made its entrance, conversation had become self-supporting.

"Did the Pied Piper really steal the children of Hamelin?" Kate asked. Dieter smiled. "I think yes. All magic is possible there. Here your university city has also much magic, Miss Bristow."

"I don't live here, you know. We come from a little West Country town."

"Where you live would have magic, I think," he said gravely.

Mrs Bristow made one of her conversational cavalry charges. "I heard you mention Hamelin, Herr Reh. You young Germans have your own Pied Piper now, isn't that so?"

Dieter looked blank.

"I mean Adolf Hitler, of course. His new Germany must have great appeal to your generation."

"The Führer can give Germany back a great deal that the past has stolen from her. Yes, he has great magnetism for all of us."

"Just so long as you don't all end up in the river," said Levitson dryly. He was finding Gerhard Stecke rather hard going. *"Bitte?"* "Skip it. Have some more salad."

"Thank you. It is so good of you to provide this special dinner for us."

"Special? There's nothing all that special about it."

"But you have butter for us to eat."

"Butter? Yeah, sure. Butter comes before guns in this country, all the way."

Peter judged that it was his turn to gallop in and rescue the conversation. He raised his voice a little.

"We hear that all you chaps are keen on flying."

"Yes," Reh agreed. "We are all training as glider pilots."

"Charles and I both fly in the University Air Squadron."

"Ach so?"

"I'm just a ham-fisted learner," Levitson put in. "But Peter, here, soloed a long time ago on Avro Tutors. He's practically an ace."

"The RAF have got a display on this afternoon and we thought you all might like to come. Afterwards, I may be able to give you a flip round."

"I shall take a rest," said Mrs Bristow, "but do take Kate along with you, if it's permitted."

They drove out to the airfield in Peter's 1½ litre Lagonda. The car was his pride and joy and the Germans compared it politely with their own Mercedes.

"It is a pity," said Stecke, "that Britain does not compete with the Auto Union and Mercedes teams."

"You have the state behind you when you go motor racing. We're just a lot of blundering amateurs, but we rather like it that way."

"Your Richard Seaman was forced to drive for Germany."

"No one, that I'm aware, forced him," Peter said and put his foot down so that the acceleration caught the young German next to him off balance. "Sorry, old man." Kate, in the back between the two Rehs, with Müller and Levitson jammed on the floor of the Lagonda at their feet, said, "There's the airfield now."

An Avro 504K, a trainer that almost dated from World War One, was droning about the clear blue sky with all the sense of purpose of a hovering dragon-fly.

"I wouldn't like you to think that's all the air power they've got," Levitson explained.

The University Air Squadron was having its annual summer open day, when members of the public were admitted to

11

watch the RAF and its undergraduate assistants disport themselves. Peter led his party out on to the grass where tables and umbrellas were set out as for a garden party. A group of RAF officers with wives and girlfriends were already seated there. Peter introduced his guests to the officer who commanded the University Squadron. This squadron leader had been approached officially about the German's visit and had agreed at once. "Do them no harm to go back home and tell their chums the RAF is on its toes," he had said.

Now he greeted them. "Delighted you could come. The Glads will be over in five minutes. Then you'll see something."

"Glads?" Reh asked Peter.

"Gloster Gladiators. Single-seater fighters. They're an RAF aerobatic team."

"Do you also like flying, Fraülein Bristow?"

"Only because Peter does. My real love is horses, but I can see there are similarities in handling a horse and an aeroplane well."

"You are right, and especially a sailplane, a craft without an engine. You must come to Germany—all of you," he added quickly, "and I will take you flying in a two-seater sailplane. There is nothing quite like it."

A distant hum of engines announced that the Gladiators were arriving dead on time. The hum built up, then suddenly became a roar as three biplanes burst over the main hangar with only feet to spare, pulled up sharply and split, climbing into three separate loops at the top of which each began to emit differently coloured smoke, leaving a Prince of Wales feathers in the summer sky.

"Wunderschön," Reh exclaimed and when the three machines had finished their display of loops, rolls, spins and low-flying passes, all the young men were uniformly enthusiastic. Only Gerhard Stecke had a word of criticism. As the Gladiators taxied to a stop, lined up as if on a parade ground, he said: "Unfortunately the day of the biplane is passed."

His words were drowned in the snarl of a single Rolls-Royce Kestrel. The lovely, shining silver biplane reared over their heads, inverted, half-rolled upright at the far end of the field and pulled up, climbing vertically until it hung for a second from its shark-like nose and stalled, falling away in a spin. Five hundred feet from the ground, the pilot caught it easily, brought it beautifully under control and came back across the airfield in a series of rolls.

"Goodness, what was that?" gasped Kate.

"Hawker Fury. The RAF's standard two-gun interceptor-fighter."

"It's top speed," said Stecke, "is 272 mph."

"Say, this guy knows it all," said Levitson. "No secret weapons for him?"

The bombers next, a flight of three Hampdens droning in, their stepped-up fuselages ungainly after the grace of the Fury. They flew sedately over the centre of the field, dropped some smoke bombs into a white-washed circle and were attacked by the Hawker Fury which came in a steep dive out of the sun. As they made off towards the city, one Hampden began to emit black smoke.

A loudspeaker blared: "One of the raiding bombers has been shot down by the defending interceptor fighter."

Reh said to Peter: "Mölders says it is always the fighter's role to hunt and destroy, never to defend."

"Mölders?"

"Werner Mölders, he is the most successful fighter pilot of the Condor Legion in Spain."

"Sorry. I've not heard of him." Peter had no intention of being drawn into a discussion about the Spanish Civil War. A year ago, his tutor had gone to fight with the International Brigade there. Many students as well as dons felt strongly about German and Italian intervention on behalf of Franco. Basically Peter sympathised with them but he could not get passionate about the issue.

Stecke said, "Mölders flies the Messerschmitt Bf 109. It is the fastest fighter in the world. Only a monoplane can . . ."

The Tannoy drowned his words. "And now, the surprise of the afternoon. We are about to have a flying visit from Squadron Leader Gillan."

"Gillan?" It was Reh's turn to ask.

"He's the chap who recently flew from Edinburgh to North-olt in 44 minutes—327 miles."

"In what kind of aircraft?" Stecke was frankly disbelieving.

The question was answered a few seconds later when a dark dot appeared out of the clouds a mile away at about five thousand feet and dived steeply on the centre of the airfield. When the olive green, low-winged monoplane roared over their heads they felt flattened by the blast of its passing. Only momentary impressions were possible. The plane was sharp-nosed like the Fury, hump-backed behind the canopied cockpit. Its wheels were retracted and it had a large air scoop under the centre section, the only feature to break its clean underside.

Stecke looked stunned.

"Hawker Hurricane," Peter said, smiling.

The monoplane was now throwing itself around the sky at a speed that made the Fury's performance look like that of an elementary trainer, then made a series of rolls almost at ground level.

"It is a prototype?" Reh asked.

"Oh no. We have a squadron in service. 111 at Northolt. That's where Gillan comes from . . . ah, he's going home for tea now."

"And talking of tea," Levitson said. "How about some strawberries and cream?"

When the display was over, Peter invited Reh to fly with him. "It's our turn now. I'm allowed to take up any honoured guest who feels he'd like to risk his neck with me."

Five minutes later they had climbed into one of the University Squadron's two dual control Avro Tutors. "Just circuits and bumps. Nothing fancy," Peter said over the intercom. When he had clearance for take-off, he taxied out to the grass alongside the main runway and took off without fuss. After the second circuit of the field, he said: "Would you like to take her for a bit? I'm afraid I'll have to make the landing."

Peter loved flying. He had been a natural from the very start of his training. He could feel instantly that Reh flew with equal sympathy and understanding.

The Tutor came in so lightly that Reh hardly felt the wheels touch.

If the day had been an unqualified social success, the evening was even more so. The squadron was giving its annual summer ball. After Dieter had made sure that the rest of his group of *Hitlerjugend* were taken care of for the evening by their hosts from other colleges, he gladly accepted Peter's invitation to attend. It included his three companions.

"Kate will be delighted. Her partner has fallen through."

"Fallen through?"

"Can't come."

"I am so sorry. I may have the honour of escorting her?"

"You'd better ask her, not me."

"With your permission."

"You have it." Peter was amused at the German's formality. "What about your pals, your *Kameraden?* I can easily introduce them to some girls."

"Your mother will come?"

"Try to stop her."

"Then my companions will gladly escort Mrs Bristow."

Peter laughed: "I'll round up some girls as well."

By the time Peter and Levitson collected them at their lodgings the Germans had changed out of their *Lederhosen*. They still wore a kind of uniform—brown slacks, brown ties and shirts with a small swastika badge, backed by wings, on each breast pocket. This was their gliding proficiency insignia. Peter was a little taken aback by the swastika, but thought: "They're here to show their flag, I suppose."

Mrs Bristow greeted them in the lounge. She looked a little like a section of the Chelsea Flower Show, with just a suggestion of prize marrow for good measure. Kate, in a lime green dress topped by her blonde hair, a single slender bloom. "A lily," Dieter thought as, for the second time that day, he kissed her hand. This time she did not blush, but felt a surge of purest happiness.

The air that night was so warm and balmy one felt one could stretch out full-length and float on it. There was a full moon, a great deal of champagne and a band that made you want to dance.

The Germans all declined the fox-trots and waited for a waltz. Around midnight the band realised the visitors' preference and gave them a selection of old-fashioned waltzes which they danced with the partners Peter had organised for them. By now they were recognised guests of the squadron and received a round of applause as they whirled the last girl back to her table. Reh danced this dance, and nearly every one before, regardless of rhythm or tempo, with Kate.

Just after one o'clock Mrs Bristow announced that she was retiring. Her son offered her a ride in his Lagonda. She declined with mock horror. A taxi had been arranged to take her back to the hotel.

Seeing Kate and Dieter were so occupied together, Peter led Stecke and the younger Reh off to the mess bar to meet members of his squadron who were gliding enthusiasts. Charles Levitson found himself alone with the reserved Müller.

"Well," he asked, "what do you think of the British now you've met them in their native state?"

"I think they in many ways are like we Germans. It is strange that our two nations have ever quarrelled."

"We've had a quarrel with them, too, way back," Levitson grinned.

"It will be a tragedy if we ever quarrel again," Müller said gravely. "After this visit I think so more than ever."

"Why, sure, everyone must feel that. But, well—what about National Socialism?"

"It is a wonderful thing for Germany."

Levitson looked at the gentle giant carefully, then said, "You've maybe guessed that I have Jewish blood. What kind of future would there be for me if I lived in Nazi Germany?"

"There is a place for all people in the Führer's Third Reich." It came out quietly, with conviction.

"There is? Then what about these stories one reads about Jews being pushed around . . ."

"There is always hostile propaganda against new ideas. An historical movement must make sometimes injustices. But these will disappear."

"I surely hope so. Come on, let's find the others."

In the small hours they all went back to town in Peter's Lagonda. The Germans had taught them the words of *"Wenn die Soldaten . . ."* and they drove down the high street singing at the tops of their voices, with Stecke drumming the rhythm on a spare petrol can. It had been a wonderful evening. At that moment international friendship was a splendid reality, especially for Dieter and Kate holding hands under the motoring rug.

Next morning Mrs Bristow had her own contribution to make to international friendship. She had learned that, when the Germans' goodwill tour ended in ten days' time, Dieter Reh had been given a week's leave by the *Hitlerjugend.* He was to spend this time in Britain, enlarging his knowledge of its people and its culture while Stecke took the rest of the party home. When Peter called at her hotel after breakfast Mrs Bristow declared she had taken a great liking to young Reh and intended to invite him to spend five of his seven days at Axeham. "I shall tell him there's no better way of getting to know a typical English family than staying with us, dear," she said gaily. "And as to culture, we can show him Exeter, and Wells, and Glastonbury. He could hardly spend his time *more* culturally, could he?

"And by then, you'll be home for the summer vac, Peter, and you and Kate can help make the dear boy feel at home."

Peter looked at his sister and smiled. "I'm sure Kate will help." She turned away, reflecting his smile. He added, "It's a fine idea, mother—he's an awfully nice chap. I'm afraid there won't be a chance for any more flying, but I expect we'll find something else to do. Kate can always take him riding."

When the four young Germans came to make their farewells, the invitation was given and eagerly accepted.

Bowing stiffly, Stecke said, "We hope you will soon visit our beautiful Fatherland. We have much to be proud of there."

"Of course you have," Mrs Bristow boomed, "I have only to look at you fine young men to be perfectly sure of it."

"Then we will say *auf wiedersehen,*" Müller said softly. "We will be truly glad to greet you all in Hamelin, perhaps next summer if you come."

"*Danke schön,* dear boy," said Mrs Bristow gracefully. "And Dieter, we shall expect you the week after next. Peter has told you how to get to Exeter? We will meet the afternoon train there on, let me see, next Thursday week."

The West Country was at its midsummer best when Peter and Kate drove the Lagonda the fifteen miles from Axeham to Exeter station. As Dieter stepped off the train they saw that he had discarded his semi-uniform for an open-necked shirt and grey flannels. He could have passed for any of the British holiday visitors—almost. The qualification lay in his bearing. A pair of young Territorial Army gunners returning kitbag-laden from summer training camp tumbled out of the same compartment, but of the three, despite Dieter's civilian cloth-ing, it was he who seemed the soldier. Kate felt her pulse jump. He was quite as attractive as she had remembered. This time he didn't kiss her hand, perhaps for fear of embarrassing her in such a public place.

Peter had prayed that the weather would do its best for the Somerset countryside he loved and had grown up in. He was surprised to find how much it mattered to him that England should put on its most lovely face for his guest. He supposed that was what patriotism really was—not "Land of Hope and Glory", or standing to attention for "God Save the King" at the end of the big film at the Odeon—but just loving the land, literally the land you were born in.

Dieter was a gratifying passenger. He exclaimed with plea-sure at the red earth and at the narrow lanes whose high hawthorn hedges filled the open car with the perfume of hon-eysuckle.

The Bristows had just read *Cold Comfort Farm.* "Beware the sukebind," Peter shouted to his sister and he saw her laugh, catching the meaning of his private joke. They came down the steep, winding hill into Axeham vale and saw the grey village with its square church tower laid out below them. It was a view that Peter was never quite prepared for; it made him catch his breath even after all these years.

"There's our home." Kate pointed to a stone house lying almost directly below, between the village and the hill.

"*Wunderschön,*" Dieter cried. "This is almost as good as flying."

The high summer weather set the key to the visit. The flower-scented days enclosed the valley in a blue glass dome that effectively isolated it from the outside world. Indeed, there might not have been an outside world and whatever was going on there.

Dieter had spent many of his summers on an uncle's farm outside Hamelin, and he rode tolerably, though stiffly. Each morning Kate saddled the horses and together they rode up over the rim of the hill behind the house, dipping down into the valley after several miles to hack back along the bottom road and stop at one of the thatched vale inns. Sometimes they did not return until nearly tea time.

One afternoon the two young men went shooting rabbits. "We're infested round here and the farmers are always grateful if we thin them out a bit."

"I would like to do so very much. I shoot at home with my uncle a great deal. We have very good roebucks. My name, Reh, is German for roebuck."

"Really? Well, I'm afraid you'll find rabbits rather dull, then. Come and choose your weapon."

The weapons consisted of a Damascus barrelled 20-bore Purdey hammergun, of which Peter was very proud, a rusty single-barrelled 12-bore of the sort that is often found in the corner of a farmhouse kitchen, and a pump-action Winchester .22. Peter felt that, as host, he must offer his beloved Purdey. Dieter ran his fingers along the rich walnut stock appreciatively, broke the gun and peered expertly up the shining barrels.

"A lovely gun, but I prefer to use the rifle please. I am more used to rifles."

Peter was glad. He knew that he shot well with his little Purdey and was anxious to show himself at his best to the German.

"As long as you're happy, Dieter. I'll try to control old Rip. He's pretty good on pheasants but apt to go a bit wild on ground game. We haven't trained you very well, have we, Rip, old boy?"

The fat, liver and white English springer quivered as though handsomely complimented for reliability rather than excused for bad behaviour, and threw himself at the door, whining ecstatically.

18

"We'll try the bottom meadow first. They should be sitting out against the hedge enjoying the afternoon sun."

The rabbits were doing exactly that. Rip ran in at the first sniff of fur and sent a white scut bobbing through the tussocks. Cursing the spaniel, Peter held his fire for fear of hitting him with the wide-spread pattern of the shot gun. But the rabbit bowled over dead a yard ahead of the dog. Peter looked round in time to see Dieter eject a spent case and pump another bullet into the chamber.

"Good shot."

"So sorry. I was lucky. I did not think you would shoot because of the dog. One can be more exact with a rifle."

"You mean, you *expected* to hit that running rabbit? With a single bullet?"

"It was luck," the German insisted. "Of course we do shoot roebucks running with a rifle but they make a bigger target."

"Well, all I can say is that it was pretty impressive. I shan't let you beat me to the draw next time."

At the corner of the field Rip bolted a big buck. Remembering the curses of his master after his first wild chase, the old spaniel thought it prudent to let this one go without cornering it. Peter turned it over neatly before it was halfway back to the hedge.

"Good shot."

Peter had the impression that Dieter hadn't attempted to shoot this time, which made him all the more determined to outshoot his companion. The next rabbit that started up at his feet he missed well behind. He knew he had fired too soon. Again the .22 stopped it as it turned back towards the hedge.

"Too good for me, Dieter."

"Another lucky shot."

The next meadow produced nothing. The shooting had warned the rabbits to return to cover.

They climbed higher up the valley and worked a thick double hedge back towards the house. Soon Rip disappeared into some briars. They could hear him scuffling about yelping excitedly and saw the tops of the nettles moving. All at once, three rabbits broke cover and streaked along, parallel with the hedge. Peter shot the first, but, as he switched targets to what should have been the second, the rabbit tumbled over. The third was nearly back to the warren, some twenty yards down the bank, when the rifle killed it also.

Peter clapped the German on the back. "My God, Dieter, you're a fantastic shot. You could be an Olympic champion."

"Oh, please!"

"Well, I'm willing to give you best."

They collected the six rabbits and sat in the shade of the bank. "Better paunch them straight away."

"Paunch?"

Peter made the gesture of slitting their bellies. He took out his folding pruning knife and cut the first rabbit, spilling out its steaming intestines on to the grass.

"They keep better if you clean them at once."

Dieter was already at work, using a long dagger-like knife. Peter noticed that the Nazi emblem, the swastika, was embossed on its hilt.

Peter nicked one hind leg of each rabbit and passed the other foot through the slit, hanging all six up in a tree on a hazel stick.

The two young men lay on their backs in the warm grass looking up at the clouds sailing high above the valley rim.

"Perfect, eh?"

Dieter watched the clouds. "Only one thing would make it more perfect."

"Kate?"

He laughed. *"Natürlich.* But I was thinking of gliding. The thermals along this valley are *wunderschön.* In Germany we would have a *Hitlerjugend* gliding club here."

Peter made a face. "It would spoil the peace of the valley. I love flying but I like Axeham just as it is."

"You take flying like everything else—as a sport."

"Don't you?"

"It is a sport, yes, but a sport has a purpose: to train you for life."

"What's your purpose in life? I mean as a career?"

"In one year's time, I shall pass into the Luftwaffe training scheme."

Peter whistled. "I didn't realise you were going to be a professional airman, that's marvellous. It's the law for me, I'm afraid—only weekend flying. Look, it's clouding up a bit: we'd best be getting home."

It was true. A bank of cumulus had moved across the sun, throwing the valley into shade for the first time for several days.

It rained next morning. The break in the weather partly reconciled Kate and Peter to their mother's determination to take Dieter on a cultural tour of the West Country. Mrs Bristow drove Kate and Dieter sedately in her "Flying" Standard saloon, while Peter drove the Lagonda alone to Exeter, for Charles Levitson was coming down by train from London to stay for a few days with the Bristows. Peter was to collect him and bring him to lunch with the others at the White Hart in South Street.

Dieter was politely appreciative of the cathedral; the tower, he declared, was more impressive than anything he had seen in his own country. He stood reverently, as well anyone might, before the great carved screen. He admired the abbot's clock and compared the narrow streets and the guildhall favourably with the best of old Hamelin. Mrs Bristow boomed on good-naturedly, a cross between a forty-four gun salute and a Baedeker. Behind her mother's back, Kate made a wry, but not entirely unaffectionate tongue-out face. Peter noticed the German's response was to touch her hand reassuringly. Shortly before midday Peter was able to escape, just as the party was setting out to explore the old buildings of Southern-hay.

Lunch was almost an extension of Mrs Bristow's cultural tour, for the menu was traditional English. Despite the humid warmth of the day Dieter obediently consumed thick vegetable soup, Dover sole, steak and kidney pudding, apple charlotte and was just being instructed on how to attack a Stilton when a small red-faced man in baggy tweeds, with a thicket of pencils sprouting from a jacket pocket, crossed the dining-room to greet Mrs Bristow.

"My dear Mrs Bristow, what a pleasure to see you here. Whenever I meet you in our country town I know you're engaged on some excellent activity. What is it this time? Hospital charities? Lifeboats? Do tell me. I can always do with a paragraph for my paper."

Though the remark was jocular, it was plain that the newcomer saw Mrs Bristow as someone whose affairs were likely to be of local interest.

She bloomed, gratified by his attention. "We are just showing a friend, a German friend, a member of Herr Hitler's Youth Movement, that our beautiful West Country is something to be proud of."

The man looked at Dieter closely. "Now that does interest me. I always know there's something up when Mrs Bristow leaves Axeham Vale to grace Exeter with her presence."

"Do join us for coffee, Mr Tibbald. Mr Tibbald is a leading writer for our West Country papers." Dieter rose and bowed, Tibbald looked at the German closely, as at some rare, but possibly dangerous creature.

"I've always wanted to talk to one of Mr Hitler's young men."

"No politics, please," cried Mrs Bristow.

"But all life is politics, especially nowadays. You can't deny me the pleasure of asking our young friend some friendly questions . . . Yes, I will, dear lady, coffee would be delightful. May I sit here, Herr . . ."

"Reh. Dieter Reh." He bowed again.

Mr Tibbald sat down. "You won't mind, Herr Reh, if I ask you a frank question or two? It's not very often we get a chance to meet one of you young chaps."

"Natürlich."

"Then tell me: what does your generation think of Adolf Hitler?"

"The Führer is a great man, almost certainly a genius."

"But a hungry genius. He's already taken some large bites at Europe."

Dieter was sitting very upright. "He has only taken what was Germany's rightful property."

"And Spain? Of course, your people are fighting in Spain."

"So, I think, are yours, sir. In the International Brigade."

"Ah," said Tibbald good-humouredly. "But those are all volunteers."

"So also are the Germans."

"Like the airmen of the Condor Legion?"

"I think," declared Mrs Bristow, "that is quite enough politics. Dieter is our guest and he is here in a purely private capacity, not as German ambassador."

"Quite so," said Tibbald easily, sipping his coffee. "But one last question, if I may. Do you think Germany would go to war with Britain if we got in the way of your Mr Hitler's . . . er, demands?"

"The British are our friends. There is no wish that our countries will ever clash."

"Amen to that," Tibbald said. "But if you listen to Winston Churchill or Mr Eden, as some of us here do, you might think there was a danger."

"I do not believe so."

"You young Germans trust your leader?"

"With all our hearts." Dieter was fervent.

Tibbald rose and offered his hand. After a moment Dieter took it, then bowed and clicked his heels.

"You're a wicked man, Mr Tibbald. You promised no politics," said Mrs Bristow archly.

"Forgive me, dear lady. Once a newspaperman, always a newspaperman, I fear. But I'm sure Herr Reh's faith in his country and its leader isn't shaken by a few straight questions . . ."

The temperature fell sharply after Tibbald had left them. The German became more stiffly correct. Not even Levitson, telling stories about the effrontery of newspaper reporters back home, could restore the atmosphere of relaxed goodwill. Kate was furious with her mother. "How *could* you let that beastly little man question Dieter, as if he has a right to pester anyone he chooses."

But Mrs Bristow refused to be provoked. "Nonsense, dear, a little frank exchange of views never did anyone any harm. Now gather up your things and let's be on our way. We have other beautiful places to show you, Dieter."

They drove to Glastonbury. By the time they stepped out on to the well-tailored lawns between the broken walls of the old priory, the sun was shining and warmth had returned not only to Somerset but to the party.

There are many dark alcoves among the ruins of the great church of Glastonbury and it was in one of these that Peter, wandering alone, glimpsed Dieter and his sister. They stood together, embraced but not kissing, looking into each other's faces with a silent wonder.

It was June 1938.

Somewhere in the street outside a military band played. The August sun beat down on the glass roof of the Bahnhof. The civilians disembarking at Hamelin from the Hildesheim train picked up the beat of the band and automatically fell into marching step with it. Dieter, anxiously watching the platform at which the train from Hamburg would soon arrive, felt himself quicken to the sound of the music. A party of Stormtroopers pushed through the barrier. He was in uniform himself, that of the gliding section of the National Socialist Flying Corps. He stood aside for the SA men, who took no more notice of him than if he had been a piece of litter on the platform. But, of course, there was no litter on the platform. Though something in him resented the Stormtroopers' implied scorn of a junior, he was, in some inner way, as proud of their arrogance as he was of the spotless cleanliness of the station. It was all part of the new Germany. There was a crispness, a sense of purpose in the air which he was anxious his visitors should feel. His visitors! He had last seen Kate waving him goodbye, a slender, radiant figure against the shabby West Country terminus with its tired seaside posters, empty paper bags and shuffling holidaymakers. How lovely she had looked! What a contrast was this station of his own home town, clean, orderly, vital. The new Germany ...

A young lieutenant in Luftwaffe uniform, wearing pilot's wings low on his left breast, strode through the platform barrier. Dieter straightened to attention. The lieutenant, seeing the NSFK band and the three-gull glider proficiency insignia on his shirt, smiled in acknowledgement. The smile was faint, but it recognised that they were of the same company. Dieter felt himself blush with pleasure. And then the locomotive had arrived with a snorting and shouting that spoke power. Everything spoke power.

She was as he remembered her, blonde, flawless, the soft glow of the West Country sun her only cosmetic: a girl to be proud of in this land, at this time. He saw the Luftwaffe officer glance at her with admiration as she helped her mother from the compartment. Mrs. Bristow, in tweeds, quite unsuitable for summer traveling, looked hot and bothered but determined to command, directing Peter to hurry and find a porter. Dieter, who had already got a porter for them, waved and called a greeting. He was glad to see Peter but somehow disappointed in his appearance. He had spoken a good deal to his friends and family about his English friends and he was anxious that they make the best possible impression. Peter in his baggy grey flannel trousers and open shirt looked almost slovenly among the *Hitlerjugend* party pouring from the next coach, despite the university air squadron badge on his blazer. But Kate! Kate was perfect. Dieter seized Peter's outstretched hand and shook it warmly, but his attention was all for Kate. He bowed to Mrs Bristow.

"What an attractive boy he is," she thought. "And *what* dynamic, active people." Dieter led them into the station forecourt where he had organised a taxi, an ancient Mercedes. As they were about to put the luggage aboard, two men in the black uniform of the SS, and wearing Swastika armbands, pushed in front. The taller of the two raised his right arm. "Heil Hitler." Dieter's arm shot out in reply.

Peter heard Dieter explain that they were English tourists. The SS officer paused at the open door of the taxi, and bowed stiffly to the Bristows. "*Siche*. It's for the Party." The taxi drove off, the two officers leaning back comfortably in it without a backward glance. "I am sorry," Dieter apologised. "They are very important local officials. Their business would not wait. There is much to be accomplished in Germany ..."

"So I see," Peter said. To his mother he whispered: "Not

even the prime minister could get away with *that* in England."

"Never mind," said Mrs. Bristow, "other lands, other customs. Besides, there are plenty of bad-mannered Englishmen."

But it was twenty minutes before they could get another taxi.

Hamelin was enchanting. Dieter told the driver to take them through the oldest part of the town, and they admired everything. There was some kind of fete in progress. Flags hung from many of the timbered houses; some carried the arms of the city, but most were blood red with a black swastika in a white circle. At one point on their way through the suburbs, the taxi had to sweep wide to avoid a parked convoy of three Army scout cars and a tank. The scout cars looked remarkably like the small open tourers which Dieter had proudly pointed out as the German People's Car, the family vehicle the Führer had promised that every citizen of the Third Reich would soon own. The tank commander, wearing earphones, sat in the open hatch of the turret.

"It's one of our new *Panzers!*" Dieter explained.

"*Panzers?*"

"It is German for armour. *Panzer* is the name our army gives to its armoured forces."

"In England we hear that many of the German tanks are made of plywood, just for manoeuvres," Mrs Bristow said.

The *Panzer* had started up, its tracks clattering on the road.

"That one certainly isn't," said Peter.

The Reh house was modern and prosperous, set back off the road in a quarter acre of ground screened by lime trees. The Rehs were waiting to greet their English guests, which they did with warmth coupled with formality, expressed by a great deal of handshaking. Helmuth Reh was a neat, greying businessman in his late forties. Hs wife, Greta, was far from what Mrs Bristow thought of as a typical *Hausfrau*, being slim, dark, fashionable and, if not absolute mistress of her own house, then at least equal partner in its affairs. Peter had not thought to ask his friend what his father did for a living. An aerial photograph of a factory in the hall gave a clue. Helmuth Reh was director of a small and profitable light engineering works.

Frau Reh showed them to their rooms which were pleasantly fragrant with the smell of wood and wax polish. Mrs Bristow found it all very homely, if agreeably foreign.

Presently they sat down to a meal of rye bread, salads, cold salt beef, chilled lager. Frau Reh had little English. Her husband's was nearly as fluent as his son's, but he confined his conversation to concern for his guests' appetite and enjoyment of the meal, so much so that he seemed almost to be apologising for it. "Guns before butter" stuck in Mrs Bristow's mind, a propagandist's *canard*, no doubt, but could there be something in it? The butter was certainly not butter and the meal, though sufficient for a warm August evening, was not quite what she herself would have set before travellers at the end of a tiring journey. Nevertheless, she thought their hosts a very pleasant couple and was certain that once the ice was broken they would all get along famously. After a cup of not very good coffee—*Ersatz?*—the Bristows walked in the lime-scented garden with their hosts, Dieter and Kate a little apart, Mrs Bristow and Herr Reh together, leaving Peter to cope with his hostess, and what German he could summon. But she took his hand and led him off, laughing, to a barn a little way from the house. Proudly she held open the door. Inside was the frame of a sailplane in an advanced stage of construction.

"Marvellous! Is Dieter building this?"

She nodded, smiling with pleasure.

"Your son is very clever, Frau Reh."

"Good *Flieger*," she said delightedly.

Peter went outside. "Dieter, old boy . . ."

But Dieter and his sister were not to be seen.

Early next morning the three young people took the bus out into the country. The bus put them down at the gliding club on the green slopes of an abrupt shoulder of hills. There were already two primary training gliders in the air. As they stepped down from the bus, a slim white sailplane with the lines and grace of an albatross parted from its launching rope and soared swiftly upon the warm air rising from the slopes.

"This is the machine I am now qualified to instruct upon. I will take you both up later. Ah, here is someone you know."

Three young men were running down to meet them. Peter recognised Müller, Dieter's young brother, Jacob, and Stecke. They bowed and shook hands with the Bristows. Dieter explained: "They are all spending their vacation camping with the *HJ* here. That is why you did not meet my brother last night." Now Peter noticed for the first time the orderly rows of tents further down the valley. On a level meadow in front of them a party of youths, naked except for shorts, were doing PT. A second squad was marching and countermarching with military smartness. As they watched, a working party left the camp with shovels carried at the sloped arms position, the angles of the shafts aligned in a manner which even the Royal Marines might have applauded. Peter remembered wryly the agreeable shambles of the one University Air Squadron summer camp he had attended.

A light BMW lorry pulled them into the air. Within fifty yards they were rising like a kite pulled by a running man. Peter watched the interval between the BMW and themselves shorten as their height above the ground increased and the lorry grew smaller. Then, suddenly, they were free and still climbing. Strange to fly without the clatter of an engine and, at first, slightly vertiginous. The green field beneath them impaled itself on the tip of one slender white wing as Dieter banked sharply and turned towards the hillside, looking for an upcurrent. As they levelled and straightened, failing to find a thermal but slope-soaring along the green shoulder, Peter caught the exhilaration. This was flying, as birds flew. Why hadn't he tried gliding before? The landscape swung slowly and smoothly below. Beneath the canopy it was silent save for the faint sigh of their progress. They had climbed about eight hundred feet when Dieter pointed to port, down beyond the crest. Two grey-green monoplanes were streaking along the next valley at tree-top level. Their wings were blunt. The white-edged black crosses and the swastika in a white circle on their rudders showed clearly. They roared neck and neck with their shadows across the valley, suddenly breaking left to storm up over the hill towards the glider in a mock pass. Peter had a fractional head-on view of the low-winged silhouettes, registering the blunt propeller bosses recessed for, presumably, a cannon, and the high tail-planes supported on struts. Then the fighters had turned away on course again, leaving the glider's cockpit full of the fury of their passing.

"What were those?"

"Messerschmitt Bf 109 C1s. They should not approach us so closely."

"They were bloody fast."

"They are to become our standard fighter. They belong to JG 2, the Richthofen *Geschwader*."

As a pilot, Peter had been excited by their intrusion, but the violence of the noise alone had shattered the pure joy of the moment. Perhaps Rèh felt the same, for he pointed the sailplane's nose down towards the landing field again, explaining: "Not too good a day for soaring. No lift yet."

The day grew hotter. Dieter flew again just before midday,

and this time there was some lift. He was up for the best part of an hour, perhaps because his passenger was Kate. Kate had never flown before. Her brother just hoped that her stomach was up to it, for his own had felt decidedly queasy. When they came in to land, however, she looked pale but ecstatic. Dieter lifted her out of the cockpit and swung her round in his arms, laughing. Even her brother had to admit they were a damn good-looking pair.

Just after one o'clock, Herr Reh drove up with Mrs. Bristow in a new People's Car. On the back seat was a large wicker hamper. They picnicked by a stream, a little away from the *Hitlerjugend* camp.

Peter observed that the campers treated Herr Reh with considerable respect. They were local boys and he was plainly a local notability. The always correct Stecke addressed him as "Herr Direktor." They drank a little Rhine wine and ate a selection of garlicky cold sausages with crisp bread and salad. A single-seater sailplane hung against the blue overhead. Dieter and Kate sat a little apart from the rest of the noisy group which included Stecke, Müller, and the younger Reh. The thin-necked bottles passed freely. Four bottles of the cool, heady Rhine wine floated the party to a delightful crest from which they could look down on the world that summer's day with gaiety and relaxation. The lovers sat apart, Dieter with his arm about Kate's waist. Everyone talked at once, laughing over each other's linguistic fumblings. But with the fifth and final bottle the mood changed slightly. Possibly Herr Reh had been unwise to offer these young men even light wine on such a sun-struck day: most of them weren't used to it and it was certainly against *HJ* regulations.

As group leader the tall good-looking Stecke had given Müller and the younger Reh permission to take part in Herr Reh's picnic. Nevertheless the *HJ* were at camp and therefore, in a sense, on duty. A bronzed working party marched down the meadow carrying the inevitable polished shovels. Peter watched them idly, feeling a growing irritation at the military overtones of even the simplest camp routines. The party came smartly to a halt while the boy in charge put them through some arms drill with their shovels. Perhaps it was the wine that put an edge of criticism, almost of aggression, into Peter's voice.

"Why do your chaps have to do everything as if you're in the Brigade of Guards?"

Stecke said: "We Germans are not ashamed to be smart."

"*And* military?"

"We are a military nation. Besides we do not have rifles like you British in your officers' cadet force."

"Officers' Training Corp. O.T.C. That's just something one has to do at school."

"But you have rifles to do it with."

"A lot of broken down left-overs from the Great War. They wouldn't actually fire."

Stecke's voice was rising, "Nor would our German shovels. Your Treaty of Versailles took our arms away."

"But now, I hear, you've more than taken them back."

"Germany needs to defend herself."

"Look," said Peter, "the last thing I want is a political argument, but was your invasion of Austria last March self-defence?"

Stecke was on his feet. In his voice were echoes of another voice, already familiar from the BBC and newsreels. "Most certainly it was. Germany has taken nothing that does not belong to her. The Rhineland is hers. The Austrians and the Germans are the same people."

"I know. I've heard. *Ein Volk. Ein Reich.*"

"*Ein Führer,*" shouted Stecke, thrusting out his right arm in the salute.

Dieter had sat up and taken his arm away from Kate. "Gerhard," he said quietly, "our English friends do not want political speeches."

Peter was surprised at how greatly Stecke disturbed him. He stood up, facing Stecke.

"So where does your Hitler stop? Who's next on the list? What other European countries will your Führer consider part of his Reich? He's always talking about *Lebensraum.*"

Reh senior intervened smoothly. "Young gentlemen," he said. "Please. Let's not spoil the pleasure of the day with argument. Mr Bristow, I promise you that our two countries will never fight each other again. My son may have told you, I have some friends in high places. Only a month ago Ernst Udet visited my factory. You have heard of Udet?"

Peter nodded. "He was a famous Great War fighter ace and aerobatic pilot."

"Yes, and now made Chief of the Technical Department of the Air Ministry by Reichsmarschall Hermann Goering. As you can imagine, Herr Oberst Udet has the *Reichsmarschall's* confidence. This great man has assured me that all our defense preparations are solely directed towards the East. Communism is our enemy, as it is yours. We Germans and you British are too like each other ever to go to war again."

Stecke gave a little bow. *"Herr Direktor,* if you will excuse us now, my companions and I have gliding duties to perform. Come, Heinrich, Jacob . . ." He strode off.

The two other young Germans had got to their feet and Müller held out his hand, saying quietly: "Please understand we have great friendship for you."

Disturbed, though he was, Peter grasped the reserved Müller's hand. He felt that Müller's friendship was warm and genuine. In some ways it was even more genuine than Dieter's, for Müller was less military, more obviously the eternal civilian pushed into a military mould. Dieter, for all his outstanding qualities, was exactly that—outstanding, plainly of the officer class; at Sandhurst he would have won the sword of honour.

Jacob Reh had said nothing, but followed Stecke with military stride. The English family and their host watched the young men go, then Herr Reh said: "They are proud boys—they take all things seriously. Now let us continue our pleasant afternoon with a visit to my factory. Yes?"

"That would be delightful," said Mrs Bristow, who had been quite at a loss during the young men's confrontation. "What does your factory make?"

Herr Reh smiled and helped her to her feet. "Oh, it is too technical to explain. It is parts for the fuel injection system of fighter planes such as were flying this morning. But to be interested in the factory it is not necessary to understand the process."

The rest of the week passed pleasantly enough. Dieter and Kate were constantly together, although the young German did not forget his duties to his other guests. At dawn one morning he took Peter roe-deer stalking in the forests bordering his uncle's farm. Peter felt little sympathy with Dieter's bolt-actioned .280 Männlicher deer rifle and missed the feel of his own beloved shotguns. After a long, exhausting crawl, they got within 100 yards of a buck with a deformed horn which Dieter said must be killed for it was bad breeding stock; the strain must be kept pure. Like people, Peter mused uneasily, as he lined up the buck in the crosswires. Perhaps the thought spoilt his concentration because he missed high, chipping a branch from a tree above the buck's shoulders. The animal stood for a second and then sprang across the forest ride. It had only two yards to go to safety when it jack-knifed in the air and fell dead against the bole of a tree. Peter looked round to see Dieter extracting the spent cartridge from his Männlicher.

"You're a wonderful shot, Dieter."

"I have quite some practice. Also, I know the roebuck's habits well. My name means roe, remember?"

At the end of the week, both families were sorry to say goodbye. Each felt they had formed a solid friendship, based on an understanding of each other's way of life. At the station, when the Bristows left, Dieter and Kate clung to each other. He kissed her unselfconsciously before she boarded the train and watched it as it grew small in the distance.

Only one incident marred the journey back to England. In a Hamburg street a man was being forced to sweep the gutter by a group of Stormtroopers. He was middle-aged and humble; his face was white and wet with fear. On his back he wore the placard: *Jude*. Like everyone else on the street, the Bristows hurried past; but, although they said little, the ugly memory remained with them.

During the North Sea crossing, Kate found her brother alone on the boat deck. They had always been close to each other and usually found little difficulty in exchanging confidences, but they had hardly spoken since the boat sailed. Now she put her arm through his.

"Did you enjoy yourself, Peter?"

"Yes. No need to ask whether you did!"

He meant it affectionately, but it sounded slightly accusatory. The hold on his arm tightened.

"Don't tell mother, Peter, but Dieter and I are engaged."

He pulled away from her, surprised by the violence of his reaction.

"You must be crazy."

"Crazy? Oh Peter, what's so crazy about falling in love? Don't you like Dieter? I thought you admired him very much."

"I do, but . . ."

"But what? You mean he's a German?"

Reluctantly he said: "That's nothing against him. He's a fine chap. But how often will you be able to see him? *When* could you see him? If you marry him, you'll have to go and live in Germany."

"Englishwomen have been known to marry foreigners. Besides, you said yourself, they're very like us."

"Dieter may be . . ." The memory of the Jew sweeping the Hamburg gutter snapped off the rest of the sentence.

"You're just being typically British. Typically insular. Anyway, it's an unofficial engagement. We'll wait to see how we both feel by next spring when I go and visit him again. He's going to ask his parents to invite me."

"By then he'll be in the German Air Force."

"Would you complain if a German girl fell in love with an RAF officer?"

"It's not the same," was all Peter could say.

That was the way things were in August 1938. And then, in September, Neville Chamberlain went to Munich and brought back peace for our time. Some people in Britain took this at its face value; but in the RAF Auxiliary Squadron the same evening Peter applied for enrolment.

"Join us by all means, old boy," the adjutant said cheerfully. "Got a couple of chaps from your university squadron with us already. If you make the grade, you'll be flying Furies, though we hope to get Hurricanes within a year. Bags of flying at weekends, but, after the PM's excursion today, it doesn't look as though you'll ever see a shot fired in anger."

1939

In January 1939, Dieter Reh reported to No 11 Flying Training Regiment at Schönwalde near Berlin for basic instruction. He found that his ambition to fly a fighter aircraft, to serve Reich and Führer, was unlikely to be achieved until he had stamped his feet numb over acres of parade ground, until he could goose-step like the Kaiser's Prussian guard, until he could accept almost any insult from a drill sergeant. Recruit Reh moaned, as is any recruit's right, and yet he accepted all the repetitive drudgery his English counterpart might have failed to do, almost masochistically. Romantically, he saw himself as being tested in the crucible and believed that he would emerge better equipped to serve his country. What he learned those first three months had nothing to do with flying.

In early May, he was ordered to report to the Military Academy, the *Kriegsschule*, for training as an officer candidate. In the words of his commanding officer "he was to be forged like Krupp's steel". But first he was given a fortnight's leave. It was then that Kate received a letter inviting her to revisit the Rehs' home in Hamelin.

There were misgivings in the Bristow household when Dieter's letter arrived. Mrs Bristow misgave less than her son. She took the view that the young people had better get it out of their systems, that Germany had calmed down since she had engulfed Czechoslovakia, that on the whole there was nothing to worry about. Peter, now articled to a city solicitor and flying Hawker Furies every weekend at Hendon, was violently opposed to her going. Contact with his Auxiliary Squadron companions and with the RAF officers who trained them had convinced him that it was only a question of time before he would be called upon to fire many shots in anger. The thought of his sister further entangling herself with a member of the opposition, no matter how pleasant he might be personally, was one that appalled him and he told her so.

Kate's was not a temperament to flare up. She looked at her brother as if he simply did not understand life and told him

33

that deep personal feelings were not affected by international crises.

"Deep!" Peter said scornfully. "How can it be deep? You're simply infatuated, that's all."

"Then I shall go to Hamelin to find out if you're right."

"And if I'm wrong?"

"I shall probably marry him."

"Thank God, you're a minor."

She said, as she had said so many times over the last months, "I thought you liked him."

"I do. But that doesn't alter the fact that we could be trying to kill each other before the year's out."

To meet her at Hamelin station Dieter wore the uniform of an officer candidate. Although Kate had been expecting this, it came nevertheless as a shock. She was far less politically conscious than her brother, but during the last six months, since what the papers called the Rape of Czechoslovakia, it had been impossible not to feel that there was something both comic and sinister about a German in uniform. The comic aspect was supplied by the cartoons of David Low with his two ludicrous, bemedalled dictators, "Hit and Muss". It was fed by the smooth voices of the Gaumont-British newsreels with their facetious commentaries on goose-stepping Stormtroopers at Nazi rallies. But the sinister dread was felt deep in her heart, and Kate was not entirely shielded from it even in the sleepy Vale of Axeham. She rationalised it, in Dieter's case, by telling herself that he was simply a professional soldier, like the soldier of any other nation including her own, and that in any case, as a professional, he was excluded from the evident evils of the Nazi party.

Because he was in uniform, he was especially correct in his greeting, clicking his heels and bowing. She felt a little chill at this, wondering if he would at least kiss her hand as at their first meeting. But he made no move. His father's People's Car was waiting in the station yard and they drove, silent as total strangers, towards the suburbs. There were more uniforms than civilian clothes in the streets of Hamelin now. Dieter explained, not without pride, that the Wehrmacht was holding spring exercises in the area.

Once they had cleared the busy streets, however, Dieter reached for her hand, and at once Kate felt the old current start to flow. Herr Direktor Reh and his wife greeted Kate warmly. He told his son with a wink that, since he had important business at the factory that afternoon, he would not need the car. Dieter might therefore borrow it.

After lunch Dieter took off his uniform and changed into riding breeches. "I have a surprise for you, *Liebchen*. I have been taking riding lessons at the *Kriegsschule* and I am now not too bad in the saddle. That will please you? I have arranged two horses for this afternoon, and we will ride beside the Weser." Kate was happy. The Dieter she remembered was re-emerging. His military training had made him stiffer, more correct—more, she admitted, German, but essentially he was the same attractive, honest person that she remembered. His military bearing suited him. If anything, he was even more good-looking.

The riding school horses had little spirit compared with her own hunter, Gayboy; they were just good steady hacks. Dieter had learned something about horsemanship, but he still sat his mount as if he had been placed on it by a drill sergeant, which indeed he had. He was not one with the horse as Kate was.

"Don't you think my riding is improved?"

"Much improved," she laughed.

He laughed, too, knowing that she was mocking him. "I'm afraid I don't have the skill for horses as I have for aeroplanes."

They rode slowly beside the river. Where a series of small islands split the flow, a company of army engineers was building a pontoon bridge. Tanks, covered in camouflage nets, waited hidden beneath the trees for the engineers to complete the bridge so that they could cross.

"War games," he said. She looked away and shuddered.

"I don't like them all the same."

He leaned across and laid his hand against her cheek. "Don't worry, *Liebchen*, our two countries will never fight. We respect each other too much."

Respect? She thought of Hit and Muss and of how Hitler had treated Chamberlain at Munich.

Presently they tethered the horses to a tree and lay down in the sweet spring grass beside the river. As he kissed her, a small plane droned across the sky. She liked being kissed, but she wanted to take things more slowly so that she could be sure of every step along the way. To divert him, she asked: "What kind of plane is that?"

He moved away and looked up. "A Fieseler Storch. *Storch* means stork. It can hover like a stork, very slowly. It is an army plane for observation."

"Do you think the pilot is observing us?"

"I doubt it, *Liebchen,* but I will test his eyesight for him."

He began to kiss her again and this time her attention was not distracted until, fearful of the mounting passion that possessed them, she pushed him away. He obeyed at once.

As they ate cream with fresh strawberry jam at a little restaurant beside the Weser, he talked enthusiastically about his military training. The disciplinary school had been hell, but necessary. The *Kriegsschule* was a great improvement, and soon he would go solo on a Henschel biplane trainer. After that he hoped to be selected for the fighter arm and, with luck, would convert to flying Messerschmitts by the end of the year.

"Peter's squadron will soon be getting Hurricanes," she said.

"So. Our Bf 109 is the finest fighter aeroplane in the world," he told her. "It already holds the world speed record."

She listened dutifully, but felt a pang of disloyalty—disloyalty to Dieter. It was a disquieting, paradoxical sensation.

All that week the weather was perfect. The Rhine wine they drank was perfect. The accordion and guitar music they danced to in the restaurants were perfect. Everything was perfect. But the war games all around them continued and it seemed they could go nowhere without seeing the grey uniforms. This was the one thing that was not perfect. It seemed determined to remind her that something terrible could happen to them all to take her happiness away.

On their last night, in a pine wood above the river, Kate Bristow lost her virginity. She had not intended to do anything of the kind. They had dined in a favourite restaurant, and as they left, a radio in an open window was blaring out an hysterical voice that Kate had learned to recognise and dread.

Dieter stood to attention. "The Führer."

"I know."

At that moment she heard the word *England* flung in a furious crescendo of what could only be vituperation or accusation.

"Let's walk up the hill," she said quickly, pulling his sleeve.

Dieter was surprisingly anxious to agree. What he had heard had not been exactly a message of international goodwill. They were both secretly shaken by the experience.

They sat down under the trees and kissed as they had done many times before. But now they clung to each other with passion made fierce by the coming parting and sudden fear for the future. It was thus she ceased to be a virgin. She was frightened afterwards but Dieter treated her with such loving tenderness that she could not regret it.

Next day, before the Reh family saw her off on to the train for England, Dieter and Kate announced that they had become officially engaged. The Rehs received the news calmly. They liked the English girl. With her classic blonde looks she could hardly have been more Aryan, she would make their son an excellent wife. As an industrialist riding on the nation's armament boom, Herr Reh felt nothing but buoyancy about the future. The aeroplane engines he was helping to make were intended for defence against the Fatherland's arch-enemy in the East; he was confident they would never see service against England. He and his wife kissed Kate fondly and wished her well.

Long before she reached Axeham, Kate had determined to announce her engagement in the most open and matter-of-fact way. All things considered, her mother took it remarkably well. Though Mrs Bristow refused to believe the alarmists who declared that war with Germany was inevitable, even she had been shaken when Hitler followed his dismemberment of Czechoslovakia with a demand for Memel—instantly granted by the Lithuanians—and a determined growl at Danzig and the Polish corridor. She consoled herself with two thoughts: her daughter was still a minor, and the English Channel lay between the lovers. To Kate she said: "That's what an engagement's for, dear. To see how the pair of you stand up to the strain of being separated—and other things."

"What other things, mother?"

"Well, the international situation."

"Dieter says that Germany has only taken back what rightfully belongs to her. Hitler believes that Germany and England will never go to war."

"Mr Chamberlain's a peace-loving man but he has given our pledge to protect Poland."

"Dieter and I love each other, mother."

Mrs Bristow patted her daughter's hand. "Well, darling, that's very important in these troubled times."

Peter Bristow wasn't flying that weekend; the squadron's Furies were being exchanged for the new Hurricanes. So he came home for a rare visit to Axeham.

When Kate told him her news he said flatly, "You need your head examined. Germany and England are on a collision course."

For Dieter, Hamelin and his home were empty once Kate had left. With five days of his leave still to go, he was burning to get back to the *Kriegsschule*. His enthusiasm for his military career, the heady feeling that Germany under the Führer was destined for a glorious future, both did a great deal to fill the vacuum left by Kate's departure. He wrote to her every day and took her photograph constantly from his wallet, remembering their love-making and the trust with which she had given herself to him. As each day dragged by he longed for the numbing all-consuming routine of the officers' training barracks that would drive his longing for her out of his mind. Then on the last day of his leave, something unprecedented happened.

At breakfast his father ordered him to put on his best uniform and come with him. A most important personage was visiting the Reh factory that day, to observe progress on a new type of fuel injection pump for use in the Luftwaffe's new "wonder bomber", the Ju 88. Even the *Herr Direktor* was excited as they drove out to the airport.

Promptly, at eleven o'clock, a small red Siebel monoplane appeared over the field. Obviously the monoplane had special clearance from the control tower, for it roared low over the runway at high speed, performed two faultless slow rolls, climbed away in a graceful Immelmann and came in to land, side-slipping to kiss the tarmac with a lightness that barely raised the dust, then taxied round until it was a few feet away from the Rehs' car. Several airport officials hurried out of the control tower to greet the pilot, but the short, jolly-looking officer who jumped from the cockpit wearing the uniform of a full colonel waved them away with a good-natured shout. Dieter recognised him at once. It was Ernst Udet, former World War One fighter ace, international aerobatic pilot, and, at Goering's and the Führer's insistence, back in uniform as Head of the Technical Office of the Luftwaffe.

Dieter drew himself up and threw out his arm in salute. What an honour!

Instead of returning the salute, the principal architect of the newborn German air force threw his arms round the two Rehs.

"Ah, so this is our future fighter ace? I hear great things of you."

Overwhelmed, Dieter wondered how this was possible. Yet the great man had such charm that he could make it seem likely that he knew every detail of the young man's career, even though it could hardly be said yet to have started.

"Your son is an officer candidate at . . . ?"

"At the *Kriegsschule, Herr Oberst.*"

"*Natürlich.* That's where I heard good reports from his commanding officer. Perhaps you will make a dive-bomber pilot?"

"I wish to be a fighter pilot, *Herr Oberst.*"

"A fine ambition. I have tried it and survived."

"Sixty-two victories on the Western Front, *Herr Oberst.*"

Udet laughed. "You've studied your lessons well. But the dive-bomber is the weapon of the future. The dive-bomber will win the Reich its victories . . . should it ever become necessary to fight for them, eh? Let us hope not. Now, Helmuth, let's look at what your technicians have been doing for my dive-bombers. I'm expecting great things with this new fuel pump."

On the way to the factory, Dieter might not have existed, nor did he expect to. He thought of Kate, wondering whether she would feel proud that he had been recognised by one of the most powerful men in the armed forces of the Reich. When they reached the factory he was prepared to wait forgotten in the car, but Udet turned to him: "Come, Officer Candidate Reh, you shall be my ADC for the day. My *aides* never understand the technicalities I discuss on these visits, and you'll probably understand more than most. Your father is an old colleague of mine, I like to visit in person all the factories helping to forge our air force, and as often as I can."

Udet kept up his light and easy tone even with the technicians in the drawing-office and the foreman on the works floor, but Dieter could see that he was learning what he needed to know about the progress of the fuel injection pump. At the end of his tour he left everyone with a feeling that not only could they congratulate themselves on their progress so far, but that they must, and would, willingly work harder to achieve the perfection the Reich demanded. It was a masterly display of both showmanship and leadership.

Afterwards, as Udet relaxed and drank coffee and *schnapps* at the Reh home, Reh senior mentioned that his son was keen on rifles and was a passable shot. Nothing would do then but that the visitor challenge Dieter to a test of marksmanship. They competed with deer rifles, standing at the twenty-five-yard range that Dieter had built in the garden for zeroing his Männlichers. Dieter's target had nine shots in the bull and one inner. Ernst Udet's were all in the bull.

"Very good, young Reh," he said. "Perhaps you'll make a fighter pilot after all. Ninety per cent of being a good *Jagd-flieger* is marksmanship. The rest is flying."

They drove the great man to the airport.

"What a man," Dieter said, as the small red Siebel took off and disappeared in a steep climb towards Berlin.

"What a man," his father echoed. "But a man of action. I shall not receive one word in writing about the decisions we have made today. Organisation is not the *Herr Oberst*'s strongest point."

The *Kriegsschule* was a marked improvement on No 11 Flying Training School. The main improvement was that the officer cadets actually began to fly. Throughout June and July, Dieter received dual instruction on obsolete service biplanes such as the Heinkel 45. Here he suffered a severe disappointment. Both he and his instructors were surprised to find that he did not progress as fast as many of the other cadets. After the featherweight touch needed in an advanced sailplane, he found the lumbering powered aircraft brutally heavy, and heavily is how he flew them. As more and more of his class went solo while he remained doing circuits and bumps with his instructor, he began to worry increasingly about his lack of ability. He saw his dearest ambition—to fly a Bf 109—receding fast. At this rate he would be lucky if they made him a transport pilot. Salt was rubbed into his wounds when Stecke, who had been posted to the *Kriegsschule* a month after his own arrival, soloed in almost record time. Stecke, it was widely rumoured among the cadets, was destined for one of Reichsmarschall Goering's elite squadrons, the *Zerstörers*—the Destroyers, the twin-engined Messerschmitt 110s.

Dieter's instructor was puzzled. A man with a natural affinity for aeroplanes, plus a proven talent as a glider pilot, simply could not fail to fly well in a powered aircraft. However, the commandant reserved judgement. His task was to turn out what would eventually become the perfect Luftwaffe officer, and he was prepared to give Reh another fortnight of dual instruction. If he did not solo and show promise after that, then he would have to go into some other branch of the service.

The day after the commandant had give this ruling, Dieter was once again practising landings and take-offs. As he made his fifth circuit round the airfield, his instructor could almost feel the tension through the dual controls. He had thought about Reh a great deal. The lad was potentially first-class material. His trouble, he was sure, was that he was trying too hard. It was in his pupil's nature to worry disproportionately about failure, perhaps because he had seldom known it. The instructor, a veteran of Lufthansa and a former World War

One fighter pilot, had met cases like that before. Often the mere presence of an instructor breathing down their necks compounded and aggravated the mental blockage. He decided to take a chance. As they rolled to a stop after a landing made at least four feet too high, the instructor climbed slowly out of his cockpit. Dieter sat waiting for the inevitable blast. Instead the instructor said. "Remember when you're up there on your own, a landing made two feet above the ground is far better than one made two feet beneath it. Off you go. Relax. Imagine it's a sailplane and good luck." Then, he added the traditional good wishes of one experienced pilot to another: *"Hals und Beinbruch"*—break your neck and legs.

This greeting did more for Dieter than anything else. It made him already almost one of the elite—almost. Alone in the cockpit he felt for the first time the sort of calm he experienced in a glider. He called up the tower and got clearance to take off after a waiting Bücker Jungmeister. He opened the throttle to taxiing speed and found his place on the apron. When the Jungmeister had cleared the runway, he pushed the throttle smoothly forward, corrected a tendency to swing right-handed with just enough rudder, felt the tail lift at exactly the right moment and was into a steady climb almost before he knew it. To his amazement, it all felt perfectly natural. The green of the airfield boundary appeared through the struts as he made the turn at the correct point, keeping the Heinkel's nose up as if his instructor had been at the controls. Elation filled him. Powered flight was wonderful, after all. Even his landing, made only a foot too high, did not discourage him.

The voice from the tower was his instructor's: "Good, Reh. Now go round and do it again."

He did it again, and again, and a fourth time. He had relaxed entirely. The clumsy biplane had become part of him and he of it.

In the mess that evening, Stecke congratulated him. "Now," he said, "we'll be able to serve the Führer and the Reich together. What took you so long to go solo? Something troubling you—the English Fräulein, perhaps? Dieter, in friendship, let me suggest to you that you should perhaps look nearer home . . ."

Dieter turned stiffly away. "Thank you, Gerhard. Please excuse me, I have some studying to do."

Alone in the barrack room that he shared with five other candidates, Dieter soon put aside his air navigation books and began to write to Kate. Stecke should have minded his own business, but he had revealed something to Dieter about himself which he had not suspected. His inability to fly well enough to go solo had been, to some extent, concerned with Kate. The possibility that England might soon make the mistake of opposing Germany's legitimate territorial aspirations had lately become more widely discussed at the *Kriegsschule*, even if not taken very seriously. Only that day they had been given lectures on the flying and fighting capabilities of the new British monoplane fighters, the Hurricane and Spitfire. For the first time, Dieter recognised that a growing anxiety had clamped its hand on the controls as he struggled to learn, as if trying to hold him back from a career that could lead to having to fight, to kill, Kate's people, English people. Of course, the thought of war with Great Britain was ridiculous. The Führer firmly believed that England would never fight and the Führer had been right every time so far.

Now that he recognised where his mental blockage had lain, he could deal with it, even dismiss it. Soldiers had no business to let personal feelings divert them from their careers, let alone from their national duty. Now that he had discovered for himself the joys of flying behind an engine, he knew he would not look back. England and Germany would not fight. There had been war scares before. And if Kate would consent to come to Germany and marry him once he had qualified as a pilot, all problems would be resolved. She had said that she would be willing to share his life in Germany. He began to write proposing that they get married at the end of the year. By then he would have earned his pilot's wings.

The letter reached Axeham on the last day of June, a month after Kate's return to England. The build-up of international tension had taken place slowly at first, but with increasing pace as the result of Chamberlain's pledge to Poland the previous March. Kate herself felt the inevitability of the dangers but her heart persuaded her, irrationally, that war could not come. She had even secretly hoped that their one love-making had made her pregnant, for if she were going to have a baby then, she thought with almost childish oversimplification, her family would insist that Dieter marry her, which was what she longed for more than anything else in the world. But the month that had passed had just assured her that this hope had foundered. Now came Dieter's proposal to marry—in the New Year, at the latest. She would still need her mother's consent.

Mrs Bristow's reaction was unexpectedly practical. "Are you going to have a baby?" she asked.

Kate blushed: "Don't be ridiculous, mother."

"Then you certainly mustn't rush things. The international situation . . ."

"I thought you believed that personal relationships come first?"

"I do, dear, but even I can no longer deny that things don't look very good in Europe."

"I shall go to him in the New Year whatever anyone says."

"Kate, dear, you still need my consent."

Her brother put it more brutally. "You must be out of your mind. Dieter or no Dieter, why don't you wake up to what's happening?"

She wrote back to Dieter telling him that she needed her mother's consent, but by the New Year, when the international situation must have cooled down again, she was certain she would have it. Mother was, basically, on their side.

Throughout July, Dieter flew with growing assurance and polish. Kate's acceptance had enabled him to put the anxiety about their future out of his mind. The physical routine of the school was extremely severe. Add to this the mental exhaustion caused by learning so many new facts and techniques, and there was little energy left for contemplating any life outside the *Kriegsschule*. Indoctrination filled every vacant crevice in the mind, indoctrination that was entirely military, for the Nazi party had no official place in the life of the academy. The instructors continually emphasised: that a soldier's duty was to serve his country and therefore the government of his country. The Führer knew what was best for Germany and virtually *was* Germany's government. As future officers, therefore, they must serve him and his ideals to the last drop of their blood. But, at the school, the traditions they must concern themselves with were those of the German armed forces. Those traditions were hammered home both physically and mentally, off parade and on. This appeal to military pride found an echo in Dieter's mind and heart. He revelled in the fact that he could watch himself being forged into Krupp's steel, just as the commandant had forecast. He would not have believed only a few weeks before that his beloved Kate could exist, however temporarily, only on the periphery of his consciousness.

Towards the end of July, Peter Bristow was called up for

summer camp with his auxiliary squadron. The official period of training was a fortnight.

"When will we expect you back, Mr Bristow?" the chief clerk asked.

"Officially, the sixteenth of August, but you'd better ask Adolf what plans he has." As Peter folded away his papers in the dusty sunlight of the solicitor's office, he could not guess that he would never see them, or it, or Benson the chief clerk, ever again.

He put in ten hours on Hurricanes that fortnight. His squadron leader had hoped for a great deal more, but there were only three serviceable machines available during most of the training period. Most of Peter's ten hours in the delightfully responsive Hurricane were spent practising flying in the classic "Vic", the three-plane V-formation which would take the squadron into battle, if the battle came.

Dieter Reh would have been amazed at the apparent informality of the mess, the Christian name terms, the silk scarves worn with open-necked flying overalls, the general air of casual improvisation. How could these seemingly easy-going young men ever turn into professional fighters?

"The V-formation as flown by the Royal Air Force, the French and the Poles has been made completely out of date by our experience in Spain."

The speaker was a dark-haired, lean, good-looking lieutenant. For most of the candidates, his lecture would remain the highlight of their course, for the lieutenant's name was Mölders, Werner Mölders. As a "volunteer" fighter pilot with the Condor Legion in Spain he had become the Civil War's top-scoring ace with fourteen victories, all made in the new Messerschmitt Bf 109. But he was much more than a successful pilot and his reputation was far greater and wider than his rank or youth suggested. Since his return late in 1938 it was rumoured that his combat record had made him one of Goering's favourites.

As he listened, Dieter could sense that there was much more to the man than temporary success. Mölders had great depth and personal magnetism. He spoke of air fighting without disguising the strain, and often fear, of combat. He did not romanticise the elation which had accompanied his own successes. But the most impressive thing about him was that there was no hate in him. The enemy was the enemy and had to be beaten because he *was* the enemy, not because he was a man of certain beliefs or nationality. To beat him, one had to be master of one's machine, of tactics and, most of all, of one-self. It was air tactics of which he mainly spoke, for Mölders in one short year had revolutionised fighter tactics for all time.

In Spain his No 3 Fighter Squadron had found the V-formation hopelessly inflexible. Just keeping formation demand-ed too much of a pilot's energy and concentration, concentra-tion that should be entirely focused on spotting the enemy be-fore he spotted you. By flying in close formation, three planes automatically blotted out with their wings and fuselage a great deal of sky that might hide an enemy aircraft. The classic V invented by the great German pilots of World War One, such as Boelke and Richthofen, robbed modern fighter pilots of their main attribute—initiative. There was no longer any need to fly wingtip to wingtip to keep in touch: R/T did that.

In Spain, Mölders had taught his men to fly in pairs—*Rot-ten*. In each *Rotte*, one pilot was the attacker, the killer: the other, his wingman, was there to stick with him and protect his tail from attack. Holding his outspread fingers aloft, Mölders demonstrated how two *Rotten* formed a *Schwarm*, no two aircraft flying in the same horizontal plane. When four aircraft flew as a *Schwarm* one pair assumed the attacking role, the second *Rotte* protecting the first against surprise.

The new formation, the young officer explained, swept a far larger area of sky. It gave fighter pilots the sense of freedom that was essential to their kind of hunting.

"If other air forces insist on clinging to the old ideas," he concluded, "we shall easily outclass them."

After the lecture was over, Mölders stayed to chat infor-mally with the cadets. He had something personal for many of them. Typically, he had done his homework thoroughly with the instructors first, so that he knew something about a handful of pupils. To Dieter he said: "I hear you had difficul-ty solo-ing. Don't worry. So did I. I was always sick when I first flew. The other thing I hear is that you are an excellent shot. That's the one quality that can make the outstanding *Jagdflieger*."

Only after he had gone did Dieter realise that everything Mölders had said took for granted that they would soon be called upon to prove themselves and their new skills in action.

August was a month of anguish for Kate Bristow. That she was in love with Dieter she did not doubt. Why else would she have given herself to him? Her mind was drugged with love as only a young girl's can be in the turmoil of her first affair, but her intelligence told her that the situation between their two countries had drastically deteriorated; that Britain, perhaps too late, had decided to stand firm on the defence of Poland, no matter what the outcome.

Early in August she had gone so far as to pack an overnight bag, draw fifty pounds from her Post Office account and decide that she would take the night boat and elope to Germany. But the following day she had looked out of her bedroom window at the smiling Vale of Axeham, watched her mother carrying some carrots across the yard to give Gayboy in his stable and her determination had evaporated. She had thrown herself on her bed and cried. Mrs Bristow, hearing her sobs, had wisely left her alone. Later, she had found the packed bag and, without saying a word, had unpacked it and put the things away.

On August 16 a telegram came from Peter saying that his training period was being extended. He was part of something called a mobilisation cadre.

A week later the commandant of the *Kriegsschule* interviewed his officer candidates individually. Their training at the academy had reached the halfway mark. Those who had failed to make the required standard were dealt with first. Three were told they would be transferred to *Flak* regiments, due to their lack of flying ability. One cadet was remustered to the infantry, because in the academy's view he lacked the necessary initiative and drive. When it came to Dieter's turn, the adjutant read out his record. "Discipline: good. Leadership qualities: above average. Flying ability: above average. Marksmanship: excellent. Technical knowledge: good."

"Reh."

"*Ja, Herr Oberst.*"

"Your record is good. If you continue this way during the second half of your training here, you should make a very satisfactory officer."

The commandant hesitated as if about to dismiss him. Then he cleared his throat and said: "You are content here at the *Kriegsschule?*"

"*Jawohl, Herr Oberst.*"

"No personal problems? Our country may be facing a period of hard struggle. It is important that we all give our full attention to the part we may have to play."

Dieter remained rigid with his thumbs pressed to the seams

of his trousers, staring at the Führer's stern features on the wall behind the desk.

"No personal problems? Good. I ask all my cadets this. It is my experience that in times of crisis young soldiers have a tendency to rush into alliances that are not so easily broken as are some international alliances."

Was there a faint hint of scorn in the colonel's voice? Herr Ribbentrop had just returned in triumph from Moscow with the German-Soviet non-aggression pact. Until that moment, the German Army had always assumed that Russia was its eventual enemy.

The commandant was speaking again. "In any case, any candidate who wishes to contract such an alliance would need my approval of his application. Do I make myself clear?"

Dieter's heart knocked beneath his best uniform blouse. Was this a warning the commandant gave to all students or had someone talked to him about Kate? Stecke? It would be like Stecke to do so. Bloody fanatic! But the *Kriegsschule* was always astonishingly well-informed about its pupils, finding out everything about their family and background.

The sun cut squares on the commandant's carpet. A bee buzzed on the window pane and, beyond, an Arado trainer buzzed bee-like across the flawless summer sky. The eyes of the Führer bored down into Dieter's consciousness. Kate, lovely Kate, at that moment existed in a world as remote as a far planet.

The commandant was speaking again.

"Any requests, Reh?"

"Yes, *Herr Oberst*. I wish to become a fighter pilot."

"Request noted. The rest is up to you. Dismiss."

The feeling that war was inevitable grew—war with Poland. Everyone in the barrack rooms, including Dieter, was affected and disturbed by the continual reports of Polish atrocities against the Germans living in the Polish corridor and the "free" city of Danzig. All this had once been German territory. Reports spoke of hundreds massacred, of German refugees streaming back across the frontiers. Dieter was forced to agree with Stecke.

"The reports are dreadful," he said. He had been brought up to believe that everything in the newspapers was true.

Stecke's face was grim. "The Führer must surely call in the armed forces to protect our people."

"Perhaps the Poles will listen to reason as the Austrians and the Czechs did."

"Let us hope so, for their sake."

"And if they don't, will England and France fight for them?"

"Does it matter?" Stecke said. "You heard Mölders speak. We shall beat them in the air."

"It matters to me, Gerhard."

"You must put personal considerations out of your mind at a time like this. My only fear is that it will all be over before we've finished our training."

"If England and France come in, you'll have no need to worry about that."

"France may, perhaps. But England has no wish to fight with us."

The commandant's words were with Dieter continually. He had always been so clear-headed, he would not have believed that his loyalties could have been so split. He was the more troubled because he knew which way the choice must go, since events would almost certainly decide the issue for him.

They had now begun their cross-country navigational training. That day it had been his turn to work out the course for his crew. He had again found concentration difficult and, on the final leg back to base, he had made an error of five degrees that took them twenty miles to the north. The sergeant-instructor was scathing, telling him that if he had been on a bombing mission he would probably have attacked friendly troops, while as for flying a fighter with such carelessness, twenty miles could mean a crash-landing for lack of fuel. The Reich was not troubled about the loss of incompetent idiots, but it could not afford to lose aircraft. Dieter stood to attention, wooden-faced. He knew the blast was deserved. He also knew the error would go down on his conduct sheet.

That evening he sat down to write to Kate.

"Liebchen," he wrote, "You'll know that my love for you is unchanged, but our commandant has told me that I must have military permission to marry and in present circumstances this is not likely to be given. As a future German officer I must give my full loyalty to the armed forces and to my country. This is beyond question, as your brother would give his. An equal sense of duty compels me to tell you, darling Kate, that you must feel yourself released from our engagement to marry until happier times return and we are free to act as we both would wish. I shall not expect a reply to this letter for I know it will cause you grief. It breaks my heart to write as I

do, *Liebchen,* but honour demands that I now do so." He hesitated to sign himself "with love" and wrote instead "Your Dieter," adding his military title and address at the foot of the letter.

There were tears in his eyes as he sealed the envelope; he was cutting away a vital part of his life. But when he had posted it, he felt a weight lift from him.

The military censor read the letter and made a note to tell the commandant. There was certainly nothing to object to in the contents. He stamped the envelope to pass it. The date stamp was 26 August.

The letter arrived at Axeham on 28 August. The postman delivered it as Kate and her mother returned from a trip to Exeter. The sense of national emergency had penetrated even the summer sleepiness of the country town. Soldiers were building sandbag barricades outside the town hall, sections of corrugated iron Anderson air-raid shelters were being loaded on to lorries in the station yard; one or two Civil Defence workers were even slung about with rectangular cardboard boxes containing gasmasks. For Mrs Bristow, burning to offer her services in some form or other, it was all rather exciting. For Kate it was like the end of her world.

Kate had been expecting and dreading a letter from Germany. She saw the censor's stamp and took the letter silently, running upstairs with it to her room.

She read the words, her eyes taking them in but her mind refusing to accept their meaning. At last she knew that she had understood. Her body no longer seemed to belong to her. She stood staring out of the window. She knew, just knew that he still felt the same about her as she did about him. A yellow training plane crawled slowly across the sky.

She whispered: "Whatever happens, Dieter, we are still engaged."

Later her mother watched her saddle Gayboy and ride away up the valley.

"Poor darling," she thought. "Thank God she isn't pregnant."

When Kate returned after tea she was calm and withdrawn. Her mother still did not press her, but of her own accord Kate said: "Whatever he says we *are* still engaged, mother. One day we shall marry."

"Of course, dear. Perhaps there won't be a war after all."

That week, they were set several tactical problems. The lieu-

49

tenant who instructed them warned them that none of the answers were positively known. Not even Spain had given the Luftwaffe enough operational experience to be certain whether Stukas—dive-bombers—should be sent in to attack before medium bombers such as the Dornier 17 and the Heinkel 111. It was possible that one type of attack would create smoke that would obscure the target for the other. These things were still being argued by staff officers. Only time, possibly now only a very short time, would provide the answers. So the officer candidates had a chance to air their own theories, which might even be as good as those of the generals themselves. The instructor got his hoped-for laugh.

Then the problem was set: Given a *Staffel* each—nine planes—of Do 17s, Ju 87s and Messerschmitt 109s, draw up an operational order for a surprise attack—made without more than a few hours' previous declaration of hostilities—on an enemy airfield twenty miles inside his frontiers. Dieter's solution depended on a split-second time-table. Taking off at first light, Stukas were to attack hangars and installations to cause maximum demoralisation by using their dive-sirens. They would be followed at one-minute intervals by medium bombers dropping slightly delayed action bombs from very low level. Finally fighters would come in to shoot up such aircraft and ground personnel as remained. They would then re-form with the bombers to escort them home.

As they left the class-room, the radio announced over the public address system that there had been further mass murders of German citizens in Poland.

Many things happened on 31 August:

In Berlin, the man who should have been most confident in the power of the weapon he had so lovingly forged talked desperately with a Swedish business man called Birgen Dahlerus. Dahlerus had industrial connections with both Britain and Germany. Hermann Goering, leader of the Luftwaffe, the second most powerful man in the Reich, now harassed and depressed, was trying to use the Swede as mediator to persuade important British industrialists that there need not be war if only Britain would give Germany a free hand in Poland . . .

At Hendon aerodrome, Peter Bristow was also bitterly depressed. The two serviceable Hawker Hurricanes on which he and his fellow auxiliary squadron pilots had slowly been accumulating flying hours had been collected by two RAF flight lieutenants and ferried away to join 111 Squadron at Northolt. Peter and two of his companions were ordered to report to Uxbridge, though no one could say what would happen to them there . . .

That day, Dieter Reh flew in a Bücker Jungman for his first lesson in aerobatics. He found it exhilarating and almost second nature to him in contrast to his early flying failures . . .

On that day, too, Mrs Bristow stormed into Exeter and demanded to be taken on by the WVS. She met with no resistance and was given the job of supervising black-out precautions in Axeham and its neighbouring village of Axeham St Mary . . .

Kate Bristow rode listlessly all day, praying that the first bomb, if it came, should be a direct hit on her personally and no one else, especially not on Gayboy . . .

That evening a man with a name later to become synonymous with evil faked an attack on the German radio station at Gleiwitz close to the Polish frontier. SS men, acting on the orders of Reinhard Heydrich, "seized" the station, broadcast a short proclamation in Polish, fired a few random pistol shots in the air, left behind them the bodies of a dozen convicts dressed in German uniform. The bodies were full of bullet holes, supposedly fired by the savage Poles, but in reality made by Heydrich's men after the criminals had first been executed by lethal injection.

At dawn the next morning, the Luftwaffe above, the Wehrmacht below, the German forces roared over the frontier to avenge this unprovoked aggression. Dieter Reh heard the news over the loudspeakers as he marched with his class to breakfast in the fresh early morning air of 1 September. It was going to be another beautiful day.

September the third should have been a beautiful day, too. The sun shone. The news from Poland was excellent. A million and a half German troops were fighting their way steadily forward behind a creeping aerial barrage provided by over 300 Stukas of Wolfram von Richthofen's—a cousin of the great World War One ace—*Fliegerkorps* VIII. The Stuka, the dive-bomber in whose miracle qualities Goering and Udet had placed such faith, was more than justifying their confidence. Practically unopposed by fighters, it was reducing bridges, factories, road junctions to smoking rubble.

The tactical instructors of the *Kriegsschule* analysed each battle report that reached them, emphasising that history was being made with every bomb dropped. No air force had ever before wielded such power or used it so masterfully in co-operation with ground troops. Dieter came in for special praise for the tactical exercise he had written a few days before; it seemed that the pattern of Stuka, low-level medium bomber, fighter attack that he had outlined was almost exactly that used successfully on several occasions in the opening phase of the Polish campaign.

The war was going so fast—already the term *Blitzkrieg* was in circulation—that once again the officer candidates feared that it would all be over long before they had a chance to prove themselves. They need not have worried. By midday it had ceased to be a beautiful day for many people, including many Germans, some in high places. When Hermann Goering heard Chamberlain's sad broadcast that "a state of war exists" he is reported to have said: "If we lose this war, then God help us."

Dieter heard the news on the public address system scarcely able to believe that it had happened at last. England and France were at war with Germany. From now on he must forget everything but his training as a pilot. Until that moment, Dieter, like many Germans, including Goering, had refused to believe that Britain would take the plunge. Even now it was possible to hope that the period of hostilities would be short.

With Britain's declaration of war, the Germans expected an immediate onslaught by the bombers of the RAF. Instead, there were only weak probing attacks by British Blenheims and Wellingtons on the German fleet at Wilhelmshaven and Brunsbuettel. The Luftwaffe was heavily committed to its victorious campaign against Poland which, by 27 September, was over. Warsaw surrendered. The Polish Air Force had been crushed in exactly eighteen days, although in that time its obsolete fighters had nevertheless accounted for 126 German aircraft. But what was this out of a front line strength of nearly 2,000 aeroplanes? Now, after a pause for breath, the Luftwaffe would surely leap on Britain before the bad winter weather set in.

In early October Dieter was given a few days' leave. He found Hamelin little changed by the war except that there was an atmosphere of overwhelming confidence in Reich and Führer. Even his mother had caught the war fever, wanting to show him off in his uniform to all their friends whose sons had not yet been called up. Dieter sensed that she did this in the certainty that the war would be won before he was called upon to fight. He noted, too, with growing irritation how throughout the four days of his leave she tried to bring him

52

into contact with suitable girls. After one such encounter he said: "Mother, you must realise that I'm still in love with Kate."

"Of course, dear, but after all she's your enemy now."

"She is not mine. Nor can I believe that I am hers."

"Your first duty, Dieter . . ."

"Mother, please don't tell me where my duty lies. And please don't keep pushing our friends' daughters at me."

Frau Reh was surprised at her son's anger—it was not like Dieter.

His father avoided the issue of Kate. He was absorbed in his own affairs, seeing a rosy personal and national future ahead. His factory was working to capacity and already the *Luftfahrtministerium* was talking about the need for expansion. They wanted him to go into production with the fuel system of the Luftwaffe's new "wonder bomber", the Junkers 88. The Ju 88 had hardly been tried out in Poland. Like every other bomber in the German air force it had to conform to the Udet-Goering formula of being able to dive with its bomb-load, and it had been suggested that a second Reh plant should be opened up to make the 88's dive-brake mechanism. Helmuth Reh's fear was the same as that of many of his son's comrades, though for different reasons—that the war would be won before he would reap its full benefits.

Herr Reh was so preoccupied with business matters that he scarcely saw his son except to say good morning and good night. But on the last day of Dieter's leave he asked him to have lunch in his office. As Herr Reh left in the morning, he had paused at the front door and said: "Wear your uniform, my boy. It will be good for the morale of the men in the factory. They're proud of our boys." Then he had done an unexpected thing, he threw out his arm and said crisply: *"Heil Hitler."* Such a gesture had never been made before inside the Reh house. Automatically Dieter gave a military salute in reply, but he later reflected on his father's change. Perhaps it was as well that civilians, even his own parents, should openly ally themselves with the great forward surge of history that was the Third Reich.

Officer Candidate Dieter made a suitable impression on the shop floor. Mechanics and foremen who had known him since he was a boy asked him flattering questions: What did he think of the Bf 109, the latest of the Messerschmitt single-seater fighters, many of which carried Reh Fabrik fuel injection pumps? Had he shot down an enemy plane yet? Had he heard the *Reichsmarschall's* latest jest? Goering had declared that if a single enemy bomber got through to the Ruhr his friends could call him Meier. The foreman thought it necessary to explain the joke. "Meier is a Jewish name, you understand, sir. Imagine the creator of our air force, a Jew! A good joke, eh?"

Lunch was served by Herr Reh's secretary, a quiet, dark-haired girl with boyish figure.

"She's new, isn't she?" Dieter asked when she had gone.

"Yes, that's Liese. She's only been here a month. Quiet but efficient. I need two secretaries now to cope with all this added production work, my boy. My faithful Frau Grube's still with me, of course."

Herr Reh did himself well. Over the brandy and cigars he grew expansive.

"So when do you expect to see some action?"

"Not until well into the New Year, father."

"Better hurry, Dieter. It may all be over by then."

"What makes you think so, father?"

"My dear boy, I don't have to ask you to treat all I say in the strictest confidence." Herr Reh glanced towards the glass door beyond which sat his two secretaries. "As you know, my work here brings me in contact with people in very high places. Why do you think the Führer has personally ordered there shall be no bombing raids on British towns? Why do you imagine the RAF is confining itself to scattered raids on our fleet? When it ventures overland, all it drops on us are foolish propaganda leaflets."

"Perhaps neither side is ready."

Herr Reh waved his cigar impatiently. "No, it's not that at all. Britain doesn't want to fight Germany. The Führer could wipe out London tomorrow if he wished, but he still expects the British will be willing to make peace, so he does nothing to provoke the situation."

"And France?"

"It may be necessary to subdue France first. But once Britain is isolated, she'll have no choice but to make peace on terms favourable to the Reich."

His father looked at him narrowly. "By then, Dieter, we shall all be part of a prosperous new and greater Germany and you will be able to take up life where you left off—if you so wish. You understand me?"

Dieter tried to picture the British as he knew them—the Bristow family taking up where the Third Reich had decided to leave off. He found it impossible; how could the gap ever be bridged? But as his father had said, it was something that, at least, they were not bombing each other's civilians.

"For the present, father, all I shall dare to contemplate is serving the Reich."

"Good boy. Exactly. Ah, Liese, I haven't yet introduced you to my son."

They shook hands, smiling. She was neat and quiet but her dark eyes were lively.

"An attractive girl," his father said when she had left the office.

Inwardly Dieter groaned. Why didn't they all shut up?

Discipline, drill, the sheer hard slog of intensive military training did not let up for a second. The only compensation was that there was more and more flying. Dieter now found it impossible to imagine that he had suffered a blockage about powered flight. He flew more and more types, obsolete interceptors and reconnaissance machines like the Arado 65 and 68 and the Heinkel 45 and 46. He and a few selected cadets even had a few hours on an operational type. A businesslike biplane, the Henschel 123, had been flown in a ground support role during the Polish campaign by no less an ace than Adolf Galland, the former Condor Legion fighter commander who had been succeeded in Spain by Werner Mölders. Though the He 123 was plainly on the verge of obsolescence itself, it was a mettlesome thoroughbred compared with the rest of the school crates. In it, Dieter experienced his first air-to-ground firing on the gunnery range. His instructor was surprised at his instant proficiency. Apart from his opening burst, all his fire had been accurately within the target area. Even Stecke had only scored fifty per cent hits. Both men were now clearly highly favoured officer candidates. In December, both were made corporal and passed out as pilots. It was now only a question of waiting for the verdict that would decide each cadet's fate, his posting to a branch of the service most suited to him—to a *Kampfgeschwader*, bomber wing; a *Stukagesschwader*, a dive bomber formation; a *Jagdgeschwader*, a fighter wing; or a *Zerstörergeschwader*, the elite "destroyer" formations equipped with the twin-engined Messerschmitt Bf 110 in which Goering himself placed so much faith.

December 1939 was a month which, looking back a year or two later, was the high point of Dieter's war. It seemed that nothing could go wrong. German arms were triumphant.

Peace with England on honourable terms still seemed possible
—he forced himself to believe that. He held his coveted pilot's
certificate. Now, to cap all this, he, Gerhard Stecke and ten
more officer candidates had been selected for the supreme
honour of being addressed by their Führer.

Dieter never forgot the surge of emotion that filled him as he
took his place in the Berlin *Sportspalast* with three thousand
other future officers from all branches of the services.

First, Reichsmarschall Goering and his staff arrived to take
their seats on the stage. The fat, jolly-looking man, in his sky-
blue uniform covered with decorations, strode past within a
few feet of where Dieter stood rigidly to attention. Impossible
to imagine how he had fitted into the tiny cockpit of a World
War One Fokker D VII fighter to become a Western Front
ace with twenty-two victories. But one could see in the twink-
ling eyes something of the magnetism that had made him such
a great *Jagdstaffel* leader, selected to take over the Richthofen
Circus after the death in battle of the Red Baron himself.

Six young pilots who had distinguished themselves in Poland were presented to the *Reichsmarschall* and then the word
at last flew round: "The Führer's coming." At an order, three
thousand young men sprang to attention. Not a sound except
the steady military footfall of the party marching down the
centre aisle. There was the Führer himself in front, with Field
Marshal Keitel and Grand Admiral Raeder on either side, a
pace behind.

Hitler took his place in the centre of the stage. Those mag-
netic eyes looked slowly round the great audience, searching
out the very soul—or so it felt—of every young warrior present. Then, after a perfectly-timed pause, the Führer began to
speak. From the rasping opening sentence Dieter and everyone around him were spellbound by the words. Such power,
such energy, such an appeal to patriotism and love of Fatherland, such an overwhelming sense of the justice of their cause,
a cause that would enable Germans to live in Europe as free
Germans. The Führer spoke of the need of loyalty even to
the giving of life itself. His words did not seem like a warning
of the need to accept death in battle, but a glorious personal
invitation to Valhalla. Dieter stole a look at the faces of his
comrades. They wore the same expression as his own—one of
rapture.

The Führer had finished. With one voice, the young warriors swore the oath, reading it from the card handed to them
as they had entered the *Sportspalast*. "I swear by God, this
holy oath, to obey unquestionably Adolf Hitler, the highest

military leader, Führer of the German Reich and its people, and to serve as a brave soldier even unto death."

When it was over, Dieter felt drained, anxious to fill the vacuum in his soul with wonderful, valorous action. It had been one of the greatest emotional experiences of his young life. He could only compare it to how he had felt after taking his first communion.

The return next day to the hard routine life of the *Kriegsschule* was a chilling anti-climax; but Dieter had prepared himself for this. This was the reality, part of the road to sacrifice of which the Führer had spoken. Anyway, he would shortly get his posting, and the hard graft would then be behind.

Meantime there was cheerful news. On 18 December the German fighters won their first resounding victory over the Royal Air Force in the Heligoland Bight. Apparently the RAF had incredibly sent close formations of Wellington bombers on an armed reconnaissance over units of the German fleet without bomb loads. If ever there was evidence of the desire not to provoke, surely this was it? The British had paid dearly for their indulgence. Twenty-four bombers had set out. Two turned back with engine trouble. As for the rest: JG 1 at Jever in East Friedland received plenty of warning—from Freya the early German mobile radar. More than eighty Bf 109s and 110s, the latter specially attached after numerous British pinprick attacks on the fleet, accounted for over half the RAF force. Three more Wellingtons crash-landed on return to England and were written off.

On this reckoning it seemed as though there would be no need to call Reichsmarschall Goering "Herr Meier", at least in the foreseeable future. It also disposed of the widely held view that "the bomber would always get through".

In the mood of general excitement, the tactical instructors at the *Kriegsschule* emphasised the fighters' success. They hardly touched upon other lessons that might have been learned from the greatest air battle since World War One. They could have surmised that unescorted bombers seemed to have a good chance only at night. Or, conversely, that if bombers were to operate in daytime, they would need a strong fighter escort that could go all the way to the target with them.

One week later even the battle of Heligoland Bight was put out of Dieter Reh's mind, for a splendid thing happened: he was told to report on 1 January to No 1 Fighter School at Werneuchen, close to Berlin. Until then he could go on leave.

Christmas in Hamelin was cold and just as Christmas should be—with snow. Christmas was cold in Britain too. Axeham Vale had been nearly cut off by a heavy fall only a week before. By the time the Bristow family assembled on Christmas Eve, the snow had gone, though a hard frost had returned and persisted.

Christmas offered little joy for Kate. She had spent a miserable autumn and winter, assisting her mother who had become an area organiser for the WVS. She had helped stick miles of brown paper on to cottage windows to protect them from the blast of bombs that never fell. She had shown innumerable country housewives how to seal the bottoms of their doors with newspapers or folded blankets against poison gas which she for one never expected to see unleashed. She had helped mothers fit gasmasks on babies, conducted God knows how many bus-loads of Cockney evacuee children from Exeter station to their foster homes in the Vale. Not once had she succeeded in putting her lover out of her thoughts. Her mother had tried to reason with her. Her reply was always the same: "No matter what happens, we're engaged to be married."

"You can't be, darling. He's an enemy. Besides it may be years until you could see him again."

"Then I'll wait."

"He might be killed."

"So might you or I."

"He might change his mind."

"He won't. He can't."

"Strange things happen when people are separated in wartime, even when they're on the same side."

"I'm going for a ride, mother."

This was always her escape. Her mother watched her tack up Gayboy and disappear up the track leading to the ridge of the valley.

Kate dreaded the Christmas family reunion because she would have her brother to deal with as well as her mother. And if the hard frost lasted there would not be much chance of escaping on Gayboy. Nevertheless she was glad to see Peter when the train drew in at Exeter station. The Lagonda was long ago laid up in the barn, and petrol coupons for the more economical family saloon had to be saved up for errands such as this.

He stepped on to the platform, handsome in his Air Force service dress, the single thin ring of the pilot officer on his cuff and the letters RAFVR—Volunteer Reserve—on his tunic.

"Hullo, Kate." He kissed her. "Where's mother?"

"At home, organising the carol service for the refugee kids."

"Poor little devils, first Christmas away from home. It's nice to be home. You've lost weight."

"Yes," she said shortly. "Perhaps it's rationing."

She sat silent while Peter drove them back through the frosty lanes, with a growing feeling that it was Christmas after all and for a while even she must try to forget the war. When they came to the bend in the road overlooking Axeham village, Peter slowed, as he often did, to savour the view below with an almost possessive love. It was nearly dark, but they could make out the outline of houses and the church spire. A single light chinked from a cottage.

Kate said automatically: "I must tell Mrs Squires to get her black-out fixed properly."

"Go on," her brother scoffed. "The Jerries will never bomb Axeham. It's not worth wasting a stick of bombs on—thank God. So far they don't show much inclination to bomb anything. I almost wish they would. I've been posted to a Spitfire squadron in the New Year."

They all attended midnight mass in the village church. Kate pushed aside the heavy black-out curtain in the porch and caught the familiar furniture-polishy, incensy smell. Christmas service, as snug, safe and warm as two oil-heaters could make it, felt as it had always done inside the church. There were some differences, though: a sprinkling of uniforms, most of them naval, two RAF and a handful of khaki. New faces, too: two elderly, well-to-do ladies who had moved away from London in case the bombing started and were now thinking of moving back again. The vicar had a word for all the servicemen, welcoming them by their Christian names from the altar steps. He moved forward to meet a middle-aged woman in black who sat at the side, in the darkest part of the church. The vicar took her hand in both of his and held it while he talked to her. Her son had been the navigator in a Hampden bomber that had disappeared over the North Sea the week before. The vicar said quietly that she mustn't give up hope: perhaps the crew had been picked up and were now prisoners of war.

Kate knelt and prayed for Dieter, wondering if he was at

mass, too. She had never known him well enough to find out what his views on religion were. Since she grew up church, for her, had been only for Easter, Whitsun, Harvest Festival and, of course, Christmas. But she prayed now with all her heart.

Christmas Day was more of a success than she had dared to hope. She had been dreading the inevitable family talk that must sooner or later come round to what her brother had once scathingly referred to as her "engagement with the enemy". But Mrs Bristow had invited three evacuee children from London's East End to share their Christmas lunch. The boys had never tasted farm-reared turkey before or eaten brandy butter with Christmas pudding. And as for a pudding that lit up with blue flames! "Cor," said one, "it's just like my mum's gas cooker!" Everyone played games afterwards and the children stayed until evening. They had taken to Kate and kept her busy. There was no time for any family talk.

On Boxing Day the frost relented. There was no hunting, of course, but those who were at home and still had their horses met by custom at the big house half a mile up the valley. The Master, on leave from a famous armoured car regiment in France, was there on his big bay. After a stirrup-cup, they hacked up on to the moor, chattering together in groups, those who had been away in the forces exchanging experiences, all speculating what they would be doing by this time next year.

"Could all be over," said a farmer called Marston.

"Nonsense, Charles," the Master told him. "It hasn't begun yet. They call it the phoney war with good reason, but mark my words: the real one is to come. The trouble is to make people realise it. That's what I'm always telling my chaps over in France."

"Seen any Jerries yet, Master?"

"The odd recce plane or two. They seem as reluctant to start it as we are. I wish to heavens we could get in first for once. But the French with their damn Maginot Line—they think all we have to do is just sit there. What do you think, Miss Bristow?"

Kate blushed. "Oh, I just wish it was over . . ."

The Master realised he had made a gaffe—wasn't there something he'd heard about her and some German fellow? He repeated, "Of course, don't we all? Then we could get back to hunting again." He cantered off.

Peter was due to return to his new squadron up north next day. Late that night they sat drinking cocoa in front of the fire. Mrs Bristow had gone to bed; she was not going to let anyone see how she dreaded Peter's departure next morning and, therefore, treated this like any ordinary evening. Brother and sister were quiet and friendly together in the light of the log-fire. So far Peter had made no reference to Dieter, as he had so often done before, and now Kate suddenly said, "Peter, the Master said that real fighting's bound to start soon. Do you think there's any chance of a peace without that happening?"

He said at once: "None at all. The only thing we can be thankful for, especially in the air force, is that the phoney war's given us a bit of time. There's going to be one hell of a scrap before the year's out."

"How long could it go on for?"

"Search me. The last one lasted four years."

"Four years," she repeated. He could see tears in her eyes.

"Kate," he said gently. "Why don't you give it up? The whole thing's utterly impossible. Even if we all survive, we shan't be in any mood to forgive our enemies for a long, long time."

"I shall. I've nothing to forgive."

"Just wait," he said. "You will have."

She was silent for a moment, then smiled sadly: "At least you've always openly disapproved. Mother just says nothing, but you know what she's thinking. It's unbearable. I've got to get away from here."

"Why don't you volunteer for one of the women's services?"

"I've thought about it. If it wasn't for Gayboy I'd go now."

He laughed. "Aren't your priorities a bit mixed?"

"No," she said determinedly. "I can't keep him in wartime anyway. Today I made up my mind to sell him to Charles Marston down the valley. He'll look after him. He'll even sell him back to me later on if I want him. Then I'll be free to go."

"Go where? The ATS? The WRNS? You'd look smashing in navy blue."

Her face set stubbornly, "I don't want to join the services."

"Oh, come on, Kate. You mean you'd feel conflicting loyalties? That's terrifying."

"I'd do just as good a job on the land. I'm a country girl, aren't I, and they'll need lots of land workers."

"I suppose so, Kate"—he leaned forward and laid his hand on hers. "You do realise that in the next few months your German boyfriend and I could be trying to blast each other out of the sky? Personally, the way I feel at the moment, I'd take pleasure in doing so. Let me tell you some day what his precious Luftwaffe did in Poland . . ."

"I don't care," she said.

1940

The snow still lay thick at Werneuchen when Dieter Reh reported to No 1 Fighter School early in the New Year. Despite this, operational flying training started at once on obsolete Arado 68s. The instructor for Dieter's flight was a tough little flight sergeant called Pohle who had flown with the Condor Legion in Spain and with a ground attack squadron in the Polish campaign. What he did with his new pupils in the air was much the same as the drill sergeant did with them on the barrack square. The only difference was that the worst that could happen to you if you made a mistake on the square was an award of extra drills or guard duty. Make a mistake with Flight Sergeant Pohle and you were likely to end up in a wooden box. From the first day he demanded perfection in formation flying and cross country navigation and all this in far from ideal flying weather.

Every time Dieter came in to land after flying as *Kaezmarek*, wingman, to Pohle, he found himself bathed in sweat from the sheer effort of keeping close to his instructor through every evolution in the book. One day Pohle noticed the sweat beads on Dieter's forehead as he climbed out of the cockpit. The temperature on the airfield was below zero at the time and it was snowing.

"Hot?"

"*Ja, Feldwebel.*"

"Just wait till you try flying a 109. That'll make you sweat all right. You weren't bad today. Sometimes you were too close to me. The wingman's job is to guard his leader's tail, not to knock it off. The enemy will try to do that soon enough."

It was the same with all the other instructors at the school. They were first-class professionals all of whom had operational experience. The CO had actually flown under Goering in the Richthofen circus in World War One. Only the highest standards were looked for. Good conduct in flying was tolerated, but excellence was expected as a norm. Such a policy was bound to have its price. If it created keenness, it also created over-anxiety. Possibly it was intended to, so that the unsuitable would be winnowed out like chaff. Some of the chaff was scattered over the field one morning just as Dieter was waiting to take off for aerial gunnery practice. Two Arados collided in a snow flurry directly over the main runway. The fuselage of one, minus wings, fell like a rocket stick fifty yards away. From its number he recognised it as the one in which a room-mate had taken off ten minutes previously. The pupil in the second machine bailed out, too low for his parachute to open.

A few minutes later, Dieter heard the controller ordering him to take off. Training did not stop for mere accidents. As he gained flying speed, he had a glimpse of the ambulance orderlies lifting a body, still wrapped in parachute shrouds. It had a curiously foreshortened appearance: the impact of the dead student's fall had virtually driven his lower limbs up into his stomach.

Flight Sergeant Pohle had afterwards been critical of Dieter's take-off.

"That crash upset you? If you're hoping to go on operations, you'll have to be tougher than that."

While the bad weather persisted, the Messerschmitt Bf 109s stayed in their hangars. They were reputedly tricky enough on the ground, especially with slush on the runways. Rumour had it that in the air they were not very sympathetic to beginners either.

Meantime, theoretical conversion to the 109 continued at great pace. Some students seemed intimidated by the lean, spare little fighter. Dieter felt a *rapport* with it from the first moment he was allowed to sit in the cockpit with Pohle leaning over the canopy making him touch, blindfold, each control and instrument until he knew them as intimately as the position of his own eyes and nose.

When the weather improved around the third week of the New Year, Dieter was considered sufficiently advanced to fly dual in a plane that approximated to the 109 in many respects, except that it was more forgiving of mistakes. This was the Messerschmitt *Taifun*, the 108, one of the sweetest four-seater light aircraft ever built. Designed for sport, it had been one of the steps by which Dr Willy Messerschmitt had arrived, almost by accident, at the 109 fighter, winning the bitter scrap to build the *Luftwaffe*'s standard fighter against the best of the German aviation industry. He had even beaten Heinkel whose elegant He 100 had proved faster in trials. But, whereas the Bf 109 proclaimed in every line, from its slender fuselage adapted perfectly to its big Daimler-Benz engine, to the square tips of its wings and fins, that it was a shark, a killer, its civilian ancestor, the *Taifun*, was every inch a lady, a charmer. So Dieter instinctively treated her like one and, ladylike, the 108 responded. Even Pohle was pleased.

"You handled her as if she was a pretty girl."

Dieter smiled, "Perhaps that's how she felt."

"You got a girl, Reh?"

The first sharp pang for some days. Kate! Dieter nodded.

"Well then, you know a bit about women. But just you wait until you lay your hands on the 108's big sister. She can be a bitch if you don't show her what's what. A proper tigress. She can bite the end off it. Know what I mean? But if you show the 109 who's boss, she'll give you a ride you'll never forget."

Pohle laughed earthily.

The snow finally cleared away in February. The 109s were ready to go. So were some of the pupils. Dieter's class was second on the training schedule. They therefore had a week to wait while the senior class made its debut. The result was far from encouraging. Ground loops were frequent. Because of its narrow undercarriage and powerful engine torque, in unskilled hands the 109 tried to veer right-handed on take-off. If the pilots didn't allow for this and correct it, the little fighter was likely to swerve off the concrete runway on to the grass. By then, the machine usually hadn't gathered enough speed to lift its tail, so forward vision was still largely obscured by the length of engine in front. In this situation, the novice pilot was inclined to panic, opening the throttle even wider, so that the right-hand arc increased. The result was often a broken undercarriage strut. A ground loop did neither machine nor pupil much good.

On the day before Dieter was due to solo came the first fatality. A student called Kleinwort, who had been one of the most promising pilots on the course, found trouble in making his first landing. Three times he came in too fast and was told to open up and go round again. At the fourth attempt he lost flying speed just as he made the turn into his final approach, stalled and simply fell out of the sky.

Dieter's class were assembled at the edge of the field, standing to attention, and waiting to be marched off to a maintenance lecture. Dieter watched Kleinwort's crash happen in what appeared to be extreme slow motion. The fighter did not even have sufficient height to point its nose downward. From a hundred feet, it fell like a dropped plate, hitting the end of the runway in a cloud of dust. For several seconds nothing happened: even the ambulance crews were too surprised to start their engines. Then the class broke ranks, the instructor leading the way. Dieter overtook his NCO within a few yards and was first to reach the crash. Apart from some buckling along its underside and a twisted propeller, the fighter looked undamaged. Surely Kleinwort must be all right? The hinged cockpit canopy was jammed. Inside, Kleinwort sat held upright by his straps. His face, and his lips especially, were a ghastly purple. There was blood at his nostrils and more trickling from the earpiece of his helmet. The ambulance and fire-fighting truck came screaming up. There was a strong smell of leaking fuel.

"Get clear," the sergeant in charge of the first truck shouted. "She may explode."

Dieter's NCO obediently doubled the class some yards away and fell them in again. As they were marched off, Dieter heard one of the ambulance men say: "No hurry. He's dead."

Dieter's turn came two days later. Now he was glad of Pohle's steady bullying. Pohle was no longer with him. There was just the mechanic perched on the starboard wing. But he heard the *Feldwebel's* voice just the same. "Move the grey wheel behind you to one-third flaps. Now the other wheel alongside to take-off trim." Automatically he opened the radiator shutters and checked his fuel. "Pump yellow primer handle on left side of cockpit floor and partly open throttle." Okay. All done. He nodded to the mechanic out on the wing and saw him begin to crank the inertia starter. The whine of the starter fly-wheel built up. That was enough. Dieter waved his mechanic away and heard him shout *"Frei." "Frei,"* Dieter replied and pulled the small black handle just below the magneto switch on the instrument panel. The 1100 horse-power Daimler-Benz coughed twice and a belch of blue smoke came back past the right side of the cockpit from the six exhaust stubs. Almost at once the last of the smoke was wisped away as the propeller caught and transmuted its three black blades into a silver disc.

He saw his mechanic mouthing good luck signs but was now both too calm and too excited to feel that he would need it. For half a minute he ran his engine up, watching temperature and oil pressure gauges. He shut the canopy and locked it just as the controller ordered him to taxi out for take-off. Brakes off and the fighter began to roll immediately. He hadn't realised he had so much power on. Taxiing a bit too fast, it was bumpy on the grass. Ah, there was the concrete apron; smoother now. Turn into wind and wait for clearance.

How the hell were you supposed to see forward out of this thing?

There was the tower telling him to take-off when he was ready. What was Pohle thinking at this moment? Or the ambulance orderlies and fire truck driver? It was just his luck to have to be first of the new class.

He held her against the brakes, the whole airframe shuddering with power. Brakes off, yellow throttle knob all the way forward. He felt himself being slammed back against the armoured seat. There was that yearning to take a stroll to the right they had all been warned about. But now the tail was up and the controls alive. "Touch her up as if she's a pretty girl," Pohle had said. The gentlest of pressures on the left rudder pedal kept the fighter pointing straight down the runway. He was airborne almost before he knew it. Back on the stick and he rose with unbelievable speed, the airfield boundary flashing away beneath him.

Pohle's voice again: "Undercarriage up. Flaps retracted. Airscrew in correct pitch and, for the love of God, close your radiator shutters." Drill and discipline were the things. They worked.

The tower was talking to him again. "You're already too far out. You've overshot the turning point. Turn into normal circuit." The speed was so tremendous after those old training planes, he hadn't realised he'd gone so far. He leaned the 109 into an easy left-hand turn. Now he had to make his approach and get her down again. Mustn't think of what had happened to Kleinwort. Pohle was saying: "It's better to come in a bit too fast than too slow." Speed falling off as he lined up the runway, but still too high at 180. Undercarriage down, flaps down, airscrew nearly idling. One-fifty mph now and his shadow racing up to meet his tyres. Pretty girl, eh? He could hear Pohle saying, "Not exactly a kiss, that landing. You did it so hard you made her squeal." But that squeal was the welcome squeal of rubber on concrete. He was down, braking gradually. Ahead he saw only the engine and beyond it the sky with the propeller turning so slowly he could even pick out the blades. Thank God, he'd made it.

The voice of Pohle from the control tower. "Well done, Reh. Landing a bit rough but you know what they say . . . 'Any landing you can walk away from . . .' Now taxi back to dispersal area and hand over to the next amateur."

That Pohle! He didn't let you get away with anything.

In the next concrete dispersal bay, Stecke was about to close his canopy. Dieter gave him the thumbs up sign and yelled *"Hals- und Beinbruch."* He watched Stecke take off easily, tucking his wheels up almost before he was over the boundary fence. No problem there.

Air gunnery practice began in mid-March. By then there were only eight of the original twelve left in the class. One cadet had been redrafted to a bomber school. Werneuchen judged that this pupil did not have the necessary temperament to fly fighters—too little *élan*. The commandant made no secret of the fact that he considered Luftwaffe fighter pilots to belong to an elite. A second cadet had broken both legs in a landing made with undercarriage, forgetfully, retracted. One classmate was dead. He had hit a petrol trailer on take-off and been incinerated so thoroughly there was nothing left over which the guard of honour could fire a volley. Nevertheless they did so. Gerhard Stecke had been selected for special training on a newly arrived flight of Messerschmitt Bf 110s. Stecke regarded this as a great honour. Was not the 110 the Zerstörer, the destroyer, the tactical fighter in which Reichsmarschall Goering fervently believed? Dieter congratulated him, because he knew this was what Stecke expected. Privately, he thought of flying a 110 as riding a carthorse compared with a steeplechaser.

Air gunnery came naturally to Dieter. The target was a drogue towed at a suitably cautious distance behind a Dornier 17z. The orders were to make one ninety-degree pass at the target, opening fire at will. For this practice, only the 109's two centrally mounted, 12 millimetre machine guns were to be used. The 20 mm cannon firing through the propeller boss was not loaded. Dieter picked up the Dornier easily. He had been told by Pohle to wait until the white target filled half the reflector sight on his windscreen. Then to press the silver button on the control column with his forefinger until the moment came to break. The closer the better for a certain kill, Pohle had said. Dieter made his pass from a cloud layer in a shallow dive. At four hundred yards the slender tube of the drogue came nowhere near filling half the sighting rings. But the white cigar looked so slow and easy, ambling along at just over 200 mph, far easier than a roebuck leaping between the pine trunks or a rabbit bounding among the tussocks. He pressed on his right rudder pedal aiming the fighter and allowing for the deflection as he would when swinging his Männlicher ahead of a buck. He held the nose slightly high to compensate for the drop in trajectory. It was all instinctive. The yellow winking fire of the tracers disappeared into the white sausage. More right rudder to allow for maximum crossing angle and the towing cable parted at the nose of the drogue, releasing it to flutter down into the sea below the air-firing range. Dieter pulled out in a steep left-hand turn. Not much opposition maybe, but his first victory. If he had impressed the gunnery instructor, he, later, made even more impact on the armament NCOs. In off-duty hours, he learned to strip and adjust the 109's guns to suit an individual pilot's needs. They were usually zeroed in to give maximum concentration of fire at 100 yards. Dieter privately felt that it should be possible, with good marksmanship, to make a certain kill at 150 yards. He also studied the effect, both on a ground target and on the guns, of different combinations of ammunition. All this was outside the normal curriculum. The gunnery flight sergeant was glad to give extra tuition to such a talented and appreciative pupil.

The class was a good one. Each in his different way had the qualities No 1 Fighter School was looking for. Dieter liked his classmates. Already there was a flyer's camaraderie strong between them: Weiss, the six-foot Austrian giant with huge red hands, who only just fitted the cockpit of the 109 but flew it more sensitively than any of them. Dölling, the Berlin industrialist's son, a natural playboy, a fiend with the girls of his nearby home town, who had repeatedly been in trouble for breaches of discipline, the latest being that of flying a Jungmeister inverted at fifty feet under a neighbouring bridge. Trückel, the shy Bavarian, who flew like an angel but had nearly flunked on navigation. Then there was the fat cadet, Kolbe, perhaps the most likeable of all. Sergeant Pohle had presented him with a shoehorn to help him get into the cockpit as an award for his first solo in a 109. Fatty Kolbe could always take a joke against himself. He thanked Pohle gravely and assured him that when he was an ace the shoehorn would become his personal insignia. "You'll never become an ace, cadet Kolbe. You're too big a target." Kolbe had laughed at this goodnaturedly. "Then I shall treasure your shoehorn, Flight Sergeant, when I have to get out of the cockpit in a hurry." Lastly, the twin Prussian brothers, Heinz and Fritz Hoffman, always faultlessly turned out, the smartest on parade, a little too serious and close to each other for deep friendship to develop with the others. Nevertheless, everyone, even Pohle, respected their dedication. They were easily the best *Rottenflieger* of the class. But if identical twins can't fly well together, who can? It was even rumoured they knew each other's thoughts so well that they didn't need to speak on the RT.

With companions such as these, Dieter remarked to Gerhard Stecke, how was it possible to feel anything but confidence about the war? How could Germany fail to triumph? He thought of Kate less frequently now. The once intense pain of her loss was cushioned by, and buried in, the almost narcotic excitement of serving Reich and Führer in the most knightly of all service roles, as a fighter pilot. He knew that if he had been able to meet Kate tomorrow, and take up where they had left off that day at Hamelin station, he would have felt as strongly about her as he had then. But circumstances did not permit. He told himself that it was an act of weakness to hope that there could still be peace between Britain and Germany. But he could not, even now, entirely suppress the hope.

The wind was late blowing spring into Axeham Vale that March of 1940. Spring had sent out scouts with white flags of truce beneath the beech hedges but even the snowdrops looked huddled and furtive. Kate saw them with a pang as she walked Gayboy down to Charlie Marston's farm for the last time. She had sold him for £150 with the option of buying him back at the current market price after the war, a date so lost in the future that to envisage it was like trying to picture what lay beyond the edge of the universe. The only yardstick by which anyone seemed prepared to measure "the duration", as it was called, was the length of the other "Great War", and to Kate four years might as well have been a life sentence. Her mother, in full glory as an organiser and placater of evacuees and their often unwilling foster parents, had turned her back on her former liberalism. Once "it" had started she had become exceedingly militant. Hitler was that "silly little man with that stupid moustache who needs to be given a good hiding—*and* he'll get it". Goering was simply "a fat bully", Goebbels "a snivelling little liar". Mrs Bristow rolled out a whole brewery full of barrels and hung her washing daily on the Siegfried Line. She had increasingly lost patience with her daughter who still openly hoped, and half believed, that Neville Chamberlain and Hitler would find a way of settling things. Why didn't the girl wake up and stop mooning after that German boy, nice as he had been? Mrs Bristow thought of Dieter only in the past tense.

So she was glad when Kate announced that she would like

to go away and do some farmwork somewhere else. It might shake her up to leave the sheltered atmosphere of the Vale, with all its associations. The Bristows had an old farming friend, Tom Roland, near Selsey in Sussex, who would be glad to have Kate's help. It was agreed that she would join him at Rife Farm in early April.

It was freezing cold that March in the East Riding of Yorkshire where Peter had now converted to Spitfires. The Spitfire Mark One was even more delightful to fly than the Hurricane. It was some thirty miles per hour faster, better above 20,000 feet but slightly less manoeuvrable. As far as Peter and his squadron mates were concerned, it was the dream plane. They even found time to feel sorry for the Hurricane squadrons who had been posted to France with the BEF. From what they heard, the Me 109 had all the advantages over the Hurricane, except in tightness of turn. Their compassion for the Hurricane boys was in some measure conditioned by envy that the Hurricane squadrons at least had a chance of seeing action. From the censored intelligence reports that reached them, however, it was obvious that engagements between Luftwaffe and RAF in France were as harmless and ritualistic as the aggressive displays of many large animals. They were designed to impress and deter without actual violence. Occasionally the rule was broken by some error of bad taste on either side. A recce plane patrolling the Franco-German border was shot at, or even shot down, shattering the phoniness of the phoney war.

Peter's squadron flew protective patrols over shipping entering the Humber. Once his section leader caught sight of and pursued a Blohm and Voss seaplane laying mines off Spurn Head but lost it in cloud. It was the nearest Peter had come to an act of war.

The Spit was a kind aeroplane to the inexperienced, far more so than its German counterpart. Nevertheless, there were training accidents including one fatal one in which the pilot, a youngster called Derek Parker who had followed an identical path with Peter from the same university squadron, had hit an oil drum on the runway on take-off, damaging the oil-cooler under his starboard wing. Several minutes later, while making his final approach for an emergency landing, his engine had seized and he had dropped to earth like a brick. It had seemed such a gentle crash that it could not possibly kill anyone. Yet, when Peter reached the scene on the fire truck, there was Derek dead in his cockpit.

The crash had been followed by an hour of foot drill on the square for junior commissioned flying personnel under the squadron warrant officer. As they shuffled around half-heartedly, in a reluctant imitation of foot soldiers, Peter asked himself bitterly what this charade had to do with his friend's death and the shooting down of German aircraft?

The crash had been caused by the carelessness of a civilian worker who had left the five-gallon drum on the runway. Even so, it resulted in a temporary curtailment of individual flying. Squadron orders made it clear that Spitfires were even less expendable than trainee pilots.

A fortnight later, on 9 April, the war suddenly lost its phoniness. Hitler attacked the Scandinavian countries and the Luftwaffe was once again in full cry. This time the fighters on either side had little effect on the issue. A squadron of obsolete Gladiators was flown in from the carrier *Glorious* to operate from the surface of frozen Lake Lesjeskog. The Luftwaffe smashed the ice with bombs. The Me 110s of *Zerstörergeschwader* 76 captured Fornebu airfield. Otherwise, for the Luftwaffe it was a massive troop transport operation brilliantly carried through by over 400 Ju 52s.

Helmuth and Greta Reh held a small dinner party to celebrate. A colonel on Udet's staff at the *Reichsluftfahrtministerium* had that day visited the plant to tell the *Herr Direktor* that the Air Ministry approved the opening of a second Reh factory in the centre of Hamburg. A government loan would be forthcoming at once, and the factory was to be in production in six months' time. Herr Reh had wanted to know where labour was coming from, now that all the young men were being mobilised for the forces. Even his younger son, Jacob, had been told to stand by for ground duties with the Luftwaffe, pending his call-up for flying training. He was only seventeen. The colonel had smiled. There was no problem there. A great deal of labour was already coming from Poland. There were many undesirable elements inside the Reich itself who would be made to do their share for the war effort.

Herr Reh had asked the young colonel whether the war wouldn't be over before his factory was in production? The colonel had laughed at this. There was little need to worry. France would shortly be subdued; England would sue for peace; but that would not be the end of it. Greater Germany would need to be doubly strong. There was even talk that, once the war in the west had been won, Germany would look eastwards.

"But we have a non-aggression pact with the Communists, *Herr Oberst*."

"Do you think they would scruple to attack us if it suited them? I give no secrets away if I tell you that it's common knowledge at the ministry that they're developing aircraft to do so now."

Air, strategy was one of Herr Reh's favourite subjects. "Have you heard any more about development of a long-range, four-engined strategic bomber? We should certainly need one if we ever did find ourselves up against the Russians. Their war industries are certain to be buried deep inside their vast country."

The colonel smiled. "That was General Wever's theory— I served on his staff when I was lieutenant. A very far-seeing man. If he hadn't been killed flying his own plane in 1936, we'd be building four-engined bombers now. The top brass nowadays has other ideas. Take Russia. Our armies will advance so rapidly that fast medium bombers like the Do 17, the He 111 and the Ju 88—for which your new Hamburg plant will be making the dive-brakes—would certainly be able to get at the Russkies' factories."

"These bombers are fast, but they're also lightly armed."

"True," agreed the colonel, who was on his third schnapps. "But we've got the finest single-seater fighter in the world to protect them."

"Forgive me, *Herr Oberst*, but seeing that my factory makes the fuel pumps for the Bf 109, I trust you won't mind if I raise a point . . . As a layman, I've always been rather concerned about the 109's lack of range. Three hundred miles isn't much, especially on a there-and-back mission."

"Aren't you forgetting the great new two-seater Messerschmitt, *Herr Direktor*? An overwhelming success in Norway."

"But it had no modern fighter opposition, *Herr Oberst*."

"I think you can take it, *Herr Direktor*, that the ministry and the general staff knows its business." The colonel had put on his cap, perhaps as a sign that Herr Reh had theorised enough. A staff car was waiting outside.

When Herr Reh had seen him to it, the colonel took an envelope from his briefcase. The envelope was marked "personal" and was from the office of General Ernst Udet himself, which no doubt accounted for the freedom with which he had discussed air force matters with a mere civilian.

Helmuth Reh waited until the staff car had gone before opening the letter. Written in Ernst Udet's extrovert hand, it

warmly congratulated him on the new contract, then—nearer
to Herr Reh's heart—added that, as promised, the general had
directed a staff officer to inquire after Dieter's progress at Werneuchen. He had received an excellent report. The young man
was turning out to be exactly the sort of officer the Luftwaffe most needed. When the time came for him to go on
operations, the general would try to see that he was posted to
a good unit and that, if progress merited it, he came to the notice of his superiors.

So Helmuth and Greta Reh had a candlelit celebration dinner that night, with champagne and yellow roses on the table.
Frau Reh recalled that the last time she had seen her husband
present anyone with yellow roses had been when he cut his
prize blooms for the English lady, Frau Bristow. Strange to
think that they were enemies now. Her husband was raising
his glass: "My dear, a toast. To further glorious victories of
the Reich! To the part our new factory will play in them! To
our sons' part in those victories! And to you, my dear."

"To our sons," she answered.

All surviving eight of Dieter's class at Werneuchen had
passed. Dieter and Gerhard Stecke had been promoted to
the rank of *Oberfähnrich*, Senior Flight Cadet. The remaining six candidates were made *Fähnrich*—Flight Cadet. All
that remained now was for them to receive their postings.
Stecke's came through first. As expected it was to a *Zerstörergeschwader*, the reserve wing of ZG 7. Stecke obviously
thought he had the plum job but he managed to be enthusiastic and polite about Dieter's posting, to the reserve wing of
Jagdgeschwader 51. On 1 May they were both sent on a
week's posting leave.

Flight Sergeant Pohle paraded them for the last time, informed them they were the worst class he had ever had, assured them that if he received any paternity orders from any
irate fathers in Berlin as a result of their late night passes, he
would personally see that they were court-martialled. Finally
he said: "If any of you manage to stay alive and actually become officers, remember that I shall be looking for an operational job soon. So Lord help you if I find you in my squadron. Dismiss and good luck."

Hamelin had changed even less than Berlin. Dieter would
hardly have known there was a war on, except that two
friends from his *HJ* days had been killed in Norway. They
had been aboard one of the destroyers sunk by British naval

74

action in Narvik Fjord, almost the only British success of the entire Scandinavian campaign. He called to see the parents, who bore their loss bravely. They were, they said, overwhelmingly proud that their sons had given their lives in gaining such a victory. Dieter was more moved by this attitude than if they had broken down and wept. He could see from the strained look of the fathers and the near-tears of the mothers that their private feelings were very different. Death in a flying accident was one thing; it had to be accepted and got used to. But to see the effects of such a death in the familiar, homely setting of an old friend's house was quite another. It brought the war home to him more than anything had done so far. Well, there would be more to come. They would all have to get used to it as the price that must be paid for victory.

There were changes at home. His father seemed to be working all the hours God gave. For the first three days of Dieter's leave, he was away in Hamburg, supervising plans for the new plant. The biggest surprise was that his mother had been made a director of the company. He knew that she had helped his father, in fact been his secretary, when he had first started the factory, but he had been too young to remember that. Now when he saw her taking the car to the office one morning, he recognised what he had always known about her: that she was unobtrusively efficient. Nevertheless, he was still young enough not to approve entirely.

"Don't be silly, *Liebchen*," she told him kindly. "I'm only part-time, to help your father out. It's my war effort. Believe me, we German women are going to do far more than this before long."

He had long since come to terms with the Kate Bristow situation—or so he had thought until he came upon her photograph in his bedroom chest of drawers. The calm beauty of her face caught him unexpectedly, knocking the breath out of him. Sternly he turned the picture face down beneath his hunting jacket. Then he thought better of it, opened the drawer again, carried the picture downstairs and, without looking at it again, dropped it into the living-room stove. Better to expunge anything that might weaken him in the struggle ahead.

When he called at the factory to drive his mother home late that afternoon, she was still in a meeting. Liese, the new secretary to whom his father had introduced him on his Christmas leave, made him a cup of *ersatz* coffee. He was impressed by the fact that she didn't chatter as many girls did, didn't ask him questions about his flying career, didn't pay him special

75

deference as the boss's son, but merely made him feel at home and at ease by her acceptance of his presence. He watched her as she typed, surprising himself by discovering that he had several times tried to conjure up her features while he was at Werneuchen. He had never quite succeeded because the features of another girl . . . oh, damn it, Kate . . . had always superimposed themselves. Now that he met Liese again he saw that she was quite different, dark like himself for one thing, with naturally wavy hair cut boyishly short and free. She had wide-set eyes, clear grey, that looked at you without coquettishness or calculation. She was, he decided, a girl of character and judgement. She saw him looking and smiled in nothing more than friendliness.

"How long are you on leave?"

"Three more days."

"You must have much to do in such a short time."

He said on impulse, "I was wondering whether you'd do me the honour of dining with me one evening."

"I should like to very much," she said.

"I don't even know your second name." He was embarrassed.

"Schumacher. Liese Schumacher. Ah, here's your mother now."

On the way home Frau Reh talked about the joint production committee she had just attended. "They're all so enthusiastic, so much behind Germany's need for total effort. Everyone at the factory is so helpful, especially to me. Your father's secretaries, for example. They could resent me very much, secretaries can be very possessive about their bosses. But neither old Gertrud, whom, of course, I've known for years, nor the new girl, Fräulein Schumacher . . . So nice."

"I've just asked Fräulein Schumacher to have dinner with me."

His mother was delighted. "Excellent, Dieter. You couldn't find a finer German girl."

Kate Bristow liked Tom Roland immediately, but she found it harder to adjust to the flat countryside that lay behind the sea-wall between Bognor and Chichester, missing the folded secretiveness of the Somerset coombes and valleys and Axeham Vale in particular. Tom Roland grew wheat and barley, four hundred acres of it, on the rich, light alluvial silt that must at some not too far distant time have belonged to the sea that threw itself in splinters of spray against the sea wall. From a tractor seat you could see the masts and smoke plumes of ships moving up-Channel—the English Channel, the moat which no enemy had crossed since the Normans. Along the wall soldiers were building pillboxes at four-hundred-yard intervals and laying barbed wire. At the farm they had all been warned to keep off the beach—mines.

Tom was scornful of these preparations. "The Jerries will never set foot on my land. If they try it, they'll get this." "This" had been a raised pitchfork. Kate was amused by Tom; he was almost too good to be true. To Tom, Sussex was not a county on the south coast, it was the heart and centre of England. Rife Farm stood at the exact centre of that centre and Tom stood in the centre of Rife Farm. Anyone, and that included Hitler, Goering and the whole Nazi crew, was welcome to try shifting him. In his mid-fifties, Tom had taken on the farm from his father who had had it from his father, and so on back for many generations. The Roland connections with the district went back at least three hundred years. His wife died when his second son, Michael, was born and, though he had a part-time housekeeper, he was delighted to see Kate about the place. He worked her hard. The ministry had told him to rear pigs. He had said gruffly to Kate: "You know a bit about livestock. You've kept horses, I hear. You can look after these damned pigs."

"I don't know much about pigs, Mr Roland."

"Tom, girl."

"Tom, then."

"Nor do I, or at least I've forgotten all I once knew. But we'll manage. Mind the smell?"

She laughed.

"Good. As long as it doesn't get into the food. You a good cook, Kate?"

"I can fry an egg."

"Fine, you can do a bit of that, as well. And when you've a spare moment you can exercise the horses."

"Horses? I didn't know you had any."

"They belong to Bill and Michael, my two boys. They're both with the BEF in France."

"Don't you ride, Tom?"

"Haven't got time. Any odd moments I got I used to go sailing. Got a ten-tonner with auxiliary motor, *Golden Plover*, on moorings at Chichester. Have to pull her out for the duration, I suppose, unless the Navy commandeers her."

After she had worked at Rife Farm for a fortnight, Kate decided that she liked Tom Roland very much indeed. He could be brutally blunt but she liked even this directness. Kate could barely remember her own father; she had always felt the lack keenly and so was not surprised to discover that Tom filled part of that need. For his part he found it natural to take a fatherly attitude towards her. For one thing she was his responsibility and Tom Roland was a man to take his responsibilities very seriously indeed. She also touched some special chord in him. It was nice to have a woman about the farm after all these years, but that was not entirely it. He was not a man who could analyse his thoughts clearly, but he knew that he felt a special sympathy for her. Like his two boys, she had lost a parent early in life. Also he could not help thinking what a wonderful wife she would make for one of his sons. He always thought of them in the plural, but he knew when he did so that he really meant his younger son, Michael. Bill would always be all right, but Michael . . . His wife had died giving birth to Michael. Another man might have felt resentment against the child for this. Tom Roland did not. It made him closer still to the boy. Boy? He was twenty. Bill had had two years of his mother's care, but Michael had never even known her. He was more vulnerable. It was Michael Tom was thinking about when he looked at Kate.

Mrs Bristow had, of course, told Tom Roland something of Kate's "trouble", as she now called it. Tom had been sympathetic, but had said: "Well, let's hope she gets this German fellow out of her head soon, the sooner the better. It's hard on her, poor lass, but she'll get over it. She'll have to. She'll meet someone else."

One evening in the farm kitchen, Tom said to her. "You ought to get out and about a bit, Kate. Meet some people."

"People?"

"Young people. Young men. My neighbour's boy's at the RAF station nearby. He's home most weekends. Like to meet him? We could give a bit of a party."

"It's kind of you Tom, but I honestly don't need to meet anyone. I'm quite happy as I am."

"Are you? *Are* you, Kate? Look, your mother told me about your . . . about your bad luck with that young German . . ." he floundered on. "Honestly, it's no good, Kate. Forget him. Start again. I know it's none of my business, but I feel responsible for you here."

She clenched her fists on the scrubbed deal table and said quietly, "Please leave me alone, Tom. My mother was bad enough and I came away from Axeham to escape her. Leave

78

me alone. I shan't change my mind about Dieter, whatever any of you say."

The night before his leave was up, Dieter Reh asked Liese Schumacher out for the second time. Their first meeting had been awkward and impersonal. He had taken her to a popular restaurant and they had danced politely together. He was attracted to her but there was none of the wild ringing of bells he had experienced with Kate. Nevertheless, he had asked her to dine with him again and she had agreed. He named a very expensive restaurant.

"On a *Fähnrich*'s pay?" she smiled.

"I can afford it."

"Nonsense, I'll cook you dinner. You can bring a bottle of wine if you like."

"Where?"

"At my flat, of course."

She said it in such a matter-of-fact way that he was taken aback. He spent the next day in doubt. Contact with fellow cadets at Werneuchen had left him in no doubt what was indicated when girls asked you to their apartment. If that was what she meant, he could certainly not refuse, but at the same time he was disappointed that things should turn out that way. She was such a self-contained girl that it was impossible to judge her intentions.

She cooked him an excellent meal on the small stove in her bed-sitting-room. The bed troubled Dieter but to her it seemed to be simply a place to put trays, plates, bread on. They ate by the open window with the scent of the lime trees from the street.

This time she talked about herself. She had studied economics at Heidelberg, and when she had obtained her degree had decided that she must get to know industry at first-hand, so had trained as a secretary. She liked her present job but had intended to move on after six months to work on a production line somewhere, in order to understand both workers and management.

"But now I don't suppose the war will let me."

"At least you're helping in the war effort. Who knows, you may even save my life one day," he joked. "After all, the machine I'll fly . . ."

"Let's hope the war will be over before you have to risk your life."

"You believe that?"

"I hope that, though I doubt it in my heart. Not as we are being led . . . or should I say misled?"

"*Liese.*"

"You think that heresy?"

"You question even the Führer?"

"My training is to question everything. Economics leads one to believe that wars are inevitable, but that doesn't mean they're excusable. But I can see I've shocked you."

They drank the last of the wine and washed up the dishes. It was the closest he had come to her all evening.

"You're wondering whether you should try to kiss me," she said calmly. "I can understand your uncertainty. Later you may do so when we say good night but please don't think I asked you up here to sleep with me. It would spoil the evening if you thought that."

Dieter roared with laughter. "What a girl you are, Liese."

She smiled. "I wouldn't want you to think that I'm a virgin either. Economics teaches one many things. It teaches one values. Just now, I value your friendship, because I like you very much."

When he did kiss her good night there was nothing calculated or withheld about her response.

"Fly well and carefully," she said. "I want to see you again."

The next day he left for Krefeld, where the Reserve Wing of JG 51 had its HQ. The date was 8 May 1940.

"Flight-Cadet Reh reporting to No 51 Fighter Wing from No 1 Fighter School, Werneuchen, sir."

The adjutant barely looked up. Dieter did not know what he had been hoping for, but he knew that he had been expecting a warmer welcome than this.

"You're assigned to No 2 Flight under Oberleutnant Baer."

A few orderly-room formalities and Dieter found himself in charge of a *Gefreiter*—a leading aircraftsman—being driven round the perimeter track of the airfield to a long, low concrete hut. Even the hut was depressing. The only thing that lifted his spirits was the sight of three rather weary-looking 109s parked in sandbagged dispersal bays. Oberleutnant Baer, a thin-faced, grey young man, did little to relieve his gloom. He did, however, shake hands.

"You're here to learn, Reh. I assume you can at least fly, but probably not very well. Our job is to get you to a pitch where you have some chance of staying alive when we send you to an operational squadron. You can consider yourself still at school here. Relax. There's going to be no urgent need for your services at the front yet. The Luftwaffe seems to be enjoying a breathing space which means no COs calling for fire-eaters like you to fill the casualty gaps. So you can resign yourself to more training. Nothing's going to happen for a bit."

In the pale dawn light of the following morning, 10 May, the good people of Rotterdam and The Hague woke to the drone of many aero engines directly overhead. The bombers of Albert Kesselring's *Luftflotte* 2 were on their way to obliterate the three main airfields of The Hague in one *blitz* blow. An hour later, before the defenders had time to recover from the plastering by He 111s and Do 17s, nearly 500 Ju 52s were dropping and landing paratroops. It was *Blitzkrieg* all over again. Not that the Luftwaffe escaped unharmed. At Ypenburg and Valkenburg airfields, the paratroops ran into fierce opposition and suffered heavy casualties. The lumbering Ju 52s floundered into point-blank anti-aircraft fire. About twenty Dutch twin-boomed Fokker GIA fighters made a fearful killing of what the gunners had left. The Fokkers survived until hordes of Bf 109s appeared and shot the Dutch out of the skies.

At Krefeld that day Dieter practised circuits and landings under a *Feldwebel* who possessed none of Pohle's ribald charm, simply a compulsion to find fault even in landings that were nearly perfect.

By 13 May, a day on which Dieter attended refresher lectures on the basics of aerial gunnery, the war in Holland was practically over. At Krefeld, aircraft identification and boredom filled 14 May in about equal proportions. It was the day the Heinkels of *Kampfgeschwader* 54 obliterated the heart of Rotterdam and the Dutch capitulated. All this time, Belgium and Luxembourg were being over-run and France eaten away. Three thousand five hundred aircraft of the Luftwaffe covered this precision assault. Against this the French put up 800 of their own fighters, backed by a British force of two Gladiator squadrons and ten squadrons of Hurricanes. By 14 May, only thirty of the RAF's serviceable bomber force of Fairey Battles and Bristol Blenheims remained.

The news of victory after victory reached the reserve squadron at Krefeld. Meantime, while Von Kleist's armour pushed almost unopposed through the Ardennes and Von Rundstedt tore through France, the cadets practised formation flying, low-flying attacks, map reading, navigation and parade ground drill.

Surely, Dieter thought, there must be casualties in the air battles in France? Soon they must be called forward as replacements. But the news reports said nothing about Luftwaffe casualties and bulletins issued to the squadron described them as light. News bulletins made much of the new aces that the war was creating. Adolf Galland had shot down three Hurricanes in one day. Wilhelm Balthasar of JG 2, the *Richthofen Geschwader*, was destroying enemy aircraft at the rate of one a day, and kept it up for twenty-one days. But the name that captivated all Germany was that of Werner Mölders. His score quickly rose to twenty-five victories. He had in some mysterious way become a legend. The heart of the legend was his qualities as a leader. Dieter remembered the conversation he had had with Mölders at the *Kriegsschule* and was doubly proud.

What the bulletins did not mention was the ferocity with which the out-classed *Armée de l'Air* had fought. By the time the Allied armies were penned up in Calais and Dunkirk, the Allied fighters, mainly French Dewoitines, Morane Saulniers and American-built Curtis Hawks, had damaged or destroyed 2,000 German aircraft.

The Luftwaffe had won a notable victory. It had cooperated with ground forces in a text-book fashion, but for the moment it was over-extended, over-exhausted and some of its squadrons, especially the Stukas, and transport formations, were down to half strength. Casualties had been high in men as well as machines and the brilliant little Bf 109 had shown its first weakness. It was not an easy aircraft to keep serviceable in the rough and tumble of battle conditions. By the time Reichsmarschall Goering had assured his Führer: "My Luftwaffe will not only take Dunkirk but Calais, too, if necessary," his Luftwaffe, and especially Albert Kesselring's Luftflotte 2, which was to bear the brunt of the battle, were badly in need of a rest.

On 25 May, Peter Bristow's squadron was ordered south. As usual rumours were numerous. The most common was that they were to fly to France to support the Allied armies in a last ditch stand. Long before then Churchill, who had taken over the Government on 6 May, had given the French his verdict: no more British fighters would be sent to France to be over-run by German Panzers or obliterated on the ground by Stukas. Bristow's Spitfire squadron landed at Manston in

Kent. Almost at once they learned what the job was. The BEF was going to be pulled out. They were to provide additional air cover.

For many people 27 May was a summer's day to remember and from many points of view. As usual Kate was up at six but she had heard Tom Roland moving about long before that. When she hurried down to the kitchen he had already eaten breakfast and was piling a strange assortment of gear on to the table. "Get me as many blankets and sheets as you can, love, and bring them down quickly. I'll get the car."

She didn't ask any questions but did as she was told, piling the blankets alongside a crate of tinned food, two bottles of whisky, a first-aid box, a shotgun and three boxes of cartridges. The car drew up outside.

"Help me load this lot."

She laboured out under a pile of folded blankets and came back for the sheets. At last it was all stowed in the back of the old Austin family saloon.

"Now," he said. "Think you can run the place for a few days?"

She nodded.

"Good. Then you can drive me in to Chichester and help me load up *Golden Plover*."

"*Golden Plover?*"

"My ten-tonner. The Admiralty has just called on anyone with a seaworthy boat to make for Dunkirk and bring back as many of the lads as they can. My two boys are over there. If I can't get them, I'll get someone else's sons."

"Have we lost, Tom?"

"Lost," he said, not understanding her at first. Then: "Of course we've not lost, girl. They've got to get *here* before we can lose, and they won't do that."

Many small boats were loading at Chichester. A young naval lieutenant was trying to dissuade a fisherman from crossing the Channel in an open dinghy with a rickety outboard. Outside the harbour hung a heavy sea mist. A siren sounded and beyond that a noise that had become more and more the background to that blazing May week—gunfire. Three Hurricanes, climbing steeply to get above the sea mist, made speech impossible just as Tom got ready to cast off.

"Can't I come, Tom?"

"No," he said. "You stay and run the farm. I'll be back in a few days. It'll take me thirty-six hours to reach Dover. I'll phone you when I'm in." He pointed towards the fading Hurricanes. "No time for faint hearts now."

She watched *Golden Plover* chug out of harbour in company with a minesweeper, an inshore trawler and two cabin cruisers.

"No time for faint hearts now." The words had stung. A squadron of Spitfires roared over, heading for the French coast. Peter, thank God, was still up north. He'd be out of it. Dieter? He could hardly be in it yet. She was deeply troubled by a secret hope that if Britain were forced out of France there might yet be peace.

In Kent, the mist was thick. Peter Bristow lounged in the dispersal hut, trying to look casual. The resident squadron of Hurricanes had flown two sorties the previous day, meeting six Stukas bombing a road junction ten miles inland from Dunkirk. They had knocked down three of them—sitting ducks, a sergeant pilot had said. Then they had been jumped by a dozen 109s. Only the Hurricanes' ability to turn inside the Germans had enabled them to get away with it. They had lost two machines. The pilot of one had bailed out and been seen to fall inside the British lines.

Just then, the operations telephone rang. The waiting was over.

A drill's a drill, thank God, even though your heart's trying to knock its way through your life-jacket. Prop to fine pitch. Mixture fully rich. Open throttle an inch. Unscrew primer and prime engine. Check silver fuel lever raised. Both mag switches on. Contact! Press two black buttons on the panel and the Merlin fires. Now tighten primer. Check radiator flaps open. Oil pressure at 45 before take-off. Red leader already moving. Push yellow throttle knob forward. Bumping over the grass behind him and gathering speed down the runway. Airborne. Undercarriage lever up and forward. Close canopy and flip switch on left of panel to raise flaps. Ted Woodward to port, closing up. The three Vics tightening into squadron formation. Ahead and above, the Hurricane squadron climbing fast as the green countryside swings away beneath. The slower Hurricanes are to attack any bombers they can find. The Spitfires' job is to take on the German fighters.

Peter Bristow is aware that a trial of strength is about to take place. It's the first time home-based fighters, and Spits especially, have met the Luftwaffe head-on. Dungeness ahead. Something he'd forgotten to do in his excitement. He flips on the gunsight switch. The yellow circle lights up in the windshield, two yellow lines on each side. The circle indicates 100 mph allowance in deflection shots. The lines represent the wingspan of enemy aircraft. He adjusts the lines until they measure out what the thirteen foot span of a 109 will look like at killing range.

Ahead now and to starboard there's an enormous pillar of smoke. Finding Dunkirk presents no navigational problems. They're in tight, perfect squadron formation at 15,000 feet. Level with the smoke cloud and still out over the sea, the voice in the ear says, "Turning left, 180 degrees. Go." The starboard wings tilt and nine Spits turn as if on a parade ground. Bloody perfect, Peter thinks, too bloody perfect. Suddenly there are shouts, warnings. Fighters above, behind, coming down fast. The Spit on Peter's left streams flame. Woodward. He only joined them yesterday. Peter breaks right, climbing instinctively. A 109 has gone right through the formation, maybe the one that got Woodward. The little fighter is travelling fast, using the momentum of its dive to get clear away. There's just a chance he can catch it. He pushes the throttle all the way and presses the control column forward. A glance over his shoulder. No one behind. No time to weave anyway. He's at maximum range to the 109 but he keeps his finger off the button. The German fighter starts to ease out, climbing away in a tight right-hand turn towards the coast. The Spit can turn inside him, cutting off his turning circle. Too excited now to know or care about his own tail, Peter sees the wingtips of the 109 creeping out to fill the yellow lines. Right rudder to bring the yellow ring ahead of the German's spinner. Now! A sensation only known on the air-firing range. The Spit shaking and slowing to the recoil of the eight Brownings. Tracers going in. The left aileron shearing away from the 109. Closing the range still, until, finally, the Brownings saw the port wing clear off at the root. Fuselage and one wing spiralling down, detached wing fluttering after slowly. No one bails out. Christ. Where am I? Peter checks his tail. He's inland and a light flak gun is lobbing tracers at him. Got to get out of here fast. He turns for the coast, hedge-hopping, seeing burning lorries, a tank, dead men at a crossroads, then the dunes, long lines of men reaching out into the water and beyond them the boats, all manner of boats. He streaks home across the wavetops, only climbing cautiously when he's in mid-Channel. The English coast ahead and a single fighter low over the sea up front. It's a Spitfire, one of his own squadron. He closes it and waves. Twenty minutes later they are both down. Both have a certain kill but Woodward is gone and one other pilot had to bail out over the Channel. Both went when the Messerschmitts hit them first while they were still in tight squadron formation.

They fly another patrol that afternoon. This time they see bombers, Ju 88s, plastering the beaches, great gushers of sand flying. This time the German fighters come out of the sun. They're something new, twin-engined Me 110s. Peter finds himself closing, head-on at a combined speed of 600 mph. Flash of guns on the 110's leading edge, tracer passing overhead. *Whumpf*. A hit somewhere. He's firing, too. A tiny target, just wings and two engines. Neither pilot wants to break, offering a belly shot as he climbs away. Peter isn't even aware who dodged whom in the end. The 110 has gone. Must get after him. He'll be far slower. The blood drains away from his brain in the turn. When vision clears, the 110 is a mile ahead with nose down for home. Full throttle and gaining on him. Hell. There's a rear-gunner, of course. The gun swings and aims, tracer squirting back far too accurately. *Whumpf* again. Something hits his windshield. Several hits. Got to stop that gunner. The German's gun is slewing sideways and there's no face behind it any longer. Bits flying off the 110. It bursts into flame and falls away towards the beach. Alone again. There are holes in his starboard wing and a smell of glycol. A hit in the cooling system. Peter just makes the English coast as the temperature readings go off the clock. The engine dies as he comes in over the field.

They all agreed that, on first encounter at least, the 110s were nothing compared with the 109s. Three 110s destroyed and a probable, with no one missing this time.

The squadron flew three sorties next day. The scene on the beaches whenever they got a glimpse of it through smoke and low cloud was an indescribable shambles, yet boats were still getting away, though they could see the Ju 88s and the He 111s pounding the dock area to rubble. Peter's squadron never got to the bombers. Each time they found themselves tangling with the fighters, gaggles of them. Most of the battles took place between ten and fifteen thousand and well out of sight of the dying army on the beaches. Peter Bristow wondered what the soldiers thought as the Stukas and Heinkels ploughed in, apparently unchallenged. That day, Peter failed to add to his personal score, but he was hit only once. He had got over the first intoxication of combat and was learning to take care of himself. One of the replacement pilots never had time to learn. A yellow-nosed 109 set him on fire on the last sortie of the day. Peter saw him struggling to free the canopy but he never made it. The boats took off 17,800 men.

On 29 May, the third day of the evacuation, in conditions

of appalling visibility, Peter spotted three Dorniers and led his section down in line ahead. His tracers went in to the crew compartment almost at once and the long, thin graceful Flying Pencil dropped a wing in a wild spin. No one got out and the bomber hit the water four hundred yards off the beach. That at least must have done something for morale down there. His Number Two set a second Dornier on fire. The third bomber dumped its bomb load in the sea and limped away, smoking. Then the 109s jumped them. Peter saw a Spit explode right ahead of him and only just pulled up in time to miss the debris.

They flew the next day and the next and the day after that until all days became one day and the only realities were fatigue and fear and awful certainty that if they lost this they would lose something far greater. Peter knew that, when the operations telephone rang in the dispersal hut, his watery belly would be forgotten in the inescapable routine of action, that when his Spit's wheels lifted off the runway his brain would be clear again of fatigue. He'd plug in the oxygen and switch on before he needed it, just to get a boost.

Back at the squadron faces came and went. The CO returned with his cockpit full of sticky blood and with two fingers of his left hand unaccounted for. The squadron flew in looser formation now, ranging wider, with a tail-end Charlie weaving to watch their rear. It was better, but it didn't always work. They lost a tail-end Charlie in the process of finding out. But now the 109s didn't jump them, so often or so easily.

Incredibly the evacuation went on far below the air battles. On the few occasions they actually saw the beaches, there was a dramatic change. Still the lines of waiting men, but now more and more little white boats. On 29 May 47,300 men got off. Nearly 60,000 on the thirtieth. The highest yet, 68,000, on the last day of the month. Nearly as many on 1 June and on that day the RAF fighters were fought to a standstill. Thirty aircraft from each side went down. So did ten ships, including three destroyers. Next day, Kesselring's *Luftflotte* 2 tried again but it took such a drubbing that this was virtually the end of the Luftwaffe's effort to torpedo Operation Dynamo.

By 3 June it was all over. The squadron had only six machines left serviceable. On 4 June they were rested and Peter slept for eighteen hours. In just six days he'd survived to become a veteran with three kills to his credit and a deep conviction that, good as it was, the German air force was by no means invincible.

The phone rang at Rife Farm on the evening of 4 June. Kate answered it with fear. Every time the telephone had rung for the last three days she'd been scared to pick it up. After each call she reassured herself with the thought that if Tom wasn't back from Dunkirk there could be no one to tell her, so any call must be good news; but she had never quite convinced herself.

The voice said: "I'm back. Can you bring the car to fetch me?"

She burst into tears. "Oh, thank God, Tom. Where are you? Are you all right?

"Bloody tired," he said. And then, "Folkestone harbour. Use all the petrol coupons if necessary."

"I'll come at once."

"No, girl. Come early in the morning. I can do with some sleep first, anyway. *Golden Plover*'s full of holes but she'll float for a bit yet."

"Are you hurt?"

"Not a scratch. Don't worry. You get a good night's sleep, too."

She rattled out of the farmyard in the old Austin saloon as soon as it was light. Two hours later the naval picket on the dockyard gate let her through when she explained what she had come for. *Golden Plover*? There were so many little boats. The lieutenant pointed to the inner harbour. Tired men hardly recognisable as soldiers were still sleeping on the mattresses along the boat train platforms. Piles of abandoned webbing equipment lay on the quay. Arms, too, a few Lee Enfields, some Bren guns, an anti-tank rifle or two. An Ordnance corporal was sorting out what little the BEF had brought back. Canteen vans manned by WVS were dispensing tin mugs of tea. She stopped to ask a sailor the way to the small boats. A flight sergeant wearing at RTO's armband came out of the station. An artillery bombardier spat. "RAF," he said. "That's what they should be doing—playing trains. Where the bloody hell were they when we needed them over the other side?"

Then she saw Tom. He looked older, more tired and dirtier than she could have imagined.

"She's right against the quay. Got to get a few things off her and then let's go home."

If Tom looked worn, *Golden Plover* seemed to have lived a sea age. The top of her cabin was torn with jagged holes. Her mast had gone. There was a dark stain across the once immaculate planking of her foredeck. Her paintwork was chipped and scraped by innumerable boots. A few items of webbing still filled her cockpit.

"What a mess," Tom said. "If she sinks, who cares? If she doesn't, I'll come back and fetch her as soon as I can stand the sight of her again. Never thought I'd say that, but four days like the last four days . . ."

To the lieutenant on the quay, he said: "Ask the Navy to keep an eye on her for me. I'll come back in a few days, maybe."

"Don't worry. We'll look after her. She's done her stuff. And so, incidentally, have you."

As they left the outskirts of the town, he said: "I didn't find them, of course. Couldn't even find their unit. Last time anyone heard of it, it was being over-run north of Calais."

He dozed until they were nearly into Bognor. Then he awoke, like a dozing dog who sniffs the air and knows he is almost home.

"We made four trips," he told her. "Each time we brought about twenty chaps. We were bombed once or twice, but nothing really close, though each bomb opened her seams a bit. The last trip was the worst. We knew it was the last, so we were loaded to the gunwales. Thirty-five dead beat men, three of 'em wounded. Ten miles off Dover, a fighter found us, just when we all thought we'd made it. The bastard made two runs. The first time he killed five and then three more. He'd have finished us but he ran out of ammunition . . . That's the kind of swine the Jerries are . . ."

Rife Farm was in view when Tom Roland spoke again. "There were times in the last few days, girl, when I thought I'd never see this place again. I don't suppose Bill and Michael ever will. Kate, you've got to learn to hate *all* Germans. All of them."

At the reserve wing at Krefeld, the events in France were watched with excitement and envy. Dieter and his fellow cadets in other flights daily expected to be sent to join an operational squadron.

His flight commander, the grey-faced Lieutenant Baer, said drily, "Don't be in a hurry to get killed. The Luftwaffe has more than enough *Experten* to finish off the French, now that we've sent the English back to their kennels."

And so it seemed. Even as Dunkirk was finally occupied, the Luftwaffe launched its last big offensive against the French *Armée de l'Air. Operation Paula* sent in a series of heavy bombing attacks on airfields and aircraft factories around Paris. The two days' offensive cost the Germans twenty-five aircraft, but the French lost one hundred. French resistance in the air had ceased to exist.

Seventeen days later, on 21 June, in a railway carriage in the Forest of Compiègne, Adolf Hitler demanded and received the surrender of France. It was a great day for Germany and an equally great one for Dieter Reh.

The colonel commanding the Reserve Wing sent for him, complimented him on his progress in all branches of his final training. Then he handed him an inscribed document which read:

In the Name of the Führer, I appoint Senior Flight Cadet Dieter Reh to the rank of lieutenant, effective 1 June 1940.

I confirm this appointment in full expectation that through conscientious performance of his duty as an officer in accordance with his oath of service and loyalty, confidence shown by the award of this commission to the aforenamed will be justified. He on his part may call upon the special protection of the Führer. Dated at Berlin, this 18th Day of June, 1940.

(signed) Goering, Reich Minister for Aviation
and Commander-in-Chief of the Air Force

When Dieter had read it, the commandant gave him his officer's dagger. It was magnificent that the highest point of his life coincided with the ultimate triumph of his country.

"Have you any questions to ask before you are sent on operations, Reh?"

"Yes, sir. In your view, is the war over? Will I still have a chance to serve?"

The commandant, a World War One veteran, smiled: "The English are beaten. But I have fought them before, and I think they probably don't know it, yet. I believe you may count on seeing a little action yet. You're posted to 3 *Gruppe, Geschwader* 51."

This time there was no home leave before his posting. Dieter, like Weiss, the gentle Austrian giant from his class at Werneuchen who had been posted with him, eagerly read into this an urgent need for replacements at the front. There could no longer be any doubt who the enemy would be. There was only one enemy left—England. Months of intensive military training had successfully dulled the nerve which used to throb so painfully when he thought of England. Kate, when he allowed himself to recall her, was a romantic memory from a different age. If any regret marred his excitement on being posted to operations, it was that he wouldn't have a chance to see Liese Schumacher before he went into battle for Reich and Führer.

His arrival at his squadron two days later was an anticlimax. Its HQ was still well back from the Channel coast. There was not yet an aircraft for him to fly, though replacements were coming in from the Messerschmitt works at Augsburg "any day now". The chief maintenance engineer told him that when they did he would be assigned one of the existing 109s. "Maybe it'll be a little tired, but at least its nostrils will have smelt powder." Dieter's flight commander, Lieutenant Feuchter, the boyish owner of a large Alsatian bitch called Elsa, introduced Weiss and Dieter to the other pilots. Two, like Feuchter, were lieutenants and wore the Iron Cross at the neck of their flying jackets. They had all scored several victories. Feuchter had fought since the first day of the Polish campaign, his dog following him everywhere. The two sergeant pilots seemed tolerant rather than respectful of their officers and of Lieutenant Reh in particular. After they had watched him make a few circuits and landings in one of the battle-scarred 109s, the sergeants' attitude seemed even less respectful. But then they were not the best landings he had ever made. The talk round the flight dispersal hut surprised Dieter even more. It was not what he expected from a band of glorious and triumphant airmen. They were clearly exhausted men who needed leave. They had flown too many missions, seen too many comrades disappear, and now, worst of all, they were being kept hanging around. Commissioned and non-commissioned pilots alike wanted to know why they weren't being allowed to finish the job they had so successfully begun.

Lieutenant Feuchter had a text-book answer to these questions, which he dutifully trotted out whenever he heard his pilots complain. It was that there was a great deal of reorganisation to be done. Lines of communication had been stretched by the success of the *Blitzkreig* against France. The captured French air bases had to be made serviceable as bomber and fighter fields against England.

The squadron radio increasingly played a new patriotic song, *"Bomben auf England"*. It was blaring out one morning when Dieter came in with his flight commander after a training flight in which he had acted as Feuchter's Number Two, earning his praise for sticking close in some hair-raising evolutions in low cloud. Feuchter switched the radio off, snarling: "That damned tune! It's so much eye-wash. You know what I think? The Führer still hopes the English will make peace with us."

"Do you really think so?"

"I can't imagine what else is holding him back."

On the last day of June, Goering issued his "General Directions for the Operation of the Luftwaffe against England". They stated: "Acting in concert the *Luftflotten* are to operate all out. Their formations, once lined up, are to be launched against defined groups of targets." So far he hadn't defined the targets precisely. The RAF and its installations must obviously be the main ones. On the other hand squadron gossip had it that Admiral Raeder had insisted that ports and shipping should be thoroughly attacked first. The *Reichsmarschall* was known to have assured his chiefs of staff that his Luftwaffe could accomplish both tasks with ease.

Goering's first move was to appoint Colonel Johannes Fink as "Channel Zone Bomber Commander". The colonel liked an office overlooking his work so he moved into a converted omnibus on the cliffs at Cap Gris Nez, just behind the memorial to the British landing in 1914.

The effect of these high-level moves quickly made itself felt on JG 51. New aircraft had arrived and were waiting for them at St. Omer, an airfield near the coast. They were to move there immediately. Instantly, morale shot up. Pilots stopped complaining. The leader of the *Staffel* and his flight commanders took off at once as advance party. Those without mounts, like Reh and Weiss, found themselves drearily handing over stores to an incoming *Stukageschwader*. Dieter looked at the ugly, gull-winged Ju 87s and recalled Ernst Udet's words . . . "Perhaps you will make a fine dive-bomber pilot one day . . ." The general had obviously considered the Stuka squadrons not only to be the cream of the Luftwaffe but also its main war-winning weapon. But then it had been Udet who had sold the entire high command, Hans Jeschonnek, chief of general staff, Erhard Milch, state secretary for air, and particularly Goering himself on the miraculous powers of the dive-bomber. Dieter watched a 109 taking off for St Omer and thanked his stars that one of these neat, lethally beautiful aircraft was to be his instead of a Stuka.

On 3 July, Dieter and Willy Weiss arrived at their new base in the back of a stores lorry. It was raining like hell. The mud around squadron HQ sucked at their flying boots. A 109 with a smashed undercarriage was being lifted by a crane. A replacement pilot had ground-looped it off the concrete runway on to the grass. The rain-sodden ground had done the rest. Despite the rain and the cold it was hard not to feel elated. Things were happening, though no one knew quite what. Dieter reported to the orderly room and received a roasting from the adjutant for not completing his hand-over a day earlier. It had been raining for several days. With weather like this every hour of training they could put in was vital, for the squadron might find itself in action sooner than it imagined. He was to report to the chief maintenance engineer at once and take over a Bf 109.

The chief was one of those professionals who safeguard themselves by understating every case. He indicated a grey-green 109e. "There's your Emil. You're lucky. She's been tarted up a bit. She'll fly—just. But don't expect to break any speed records. She'll be at least five mph slower than the new ones." To Dieter, however, the 109e—E for Emil—was a thing of beauty. Feuchter interrupted his contemplation of the beloved with: "As soon as this weather eases up we'll put in some operational practice. You're to fly as wingman to Sergeant Brandis." Brandis was the sergeant pilot who had so far greeted Dieter with least enthusiasm.

The news had taken a long time to reach Rife Farm. It wasn't until the end of June that a War Office telegram arrived for Tom. Kate was getting his lunch ready to take out to him at Marsh Barn where he was clearing boundary ditches. Telegrams scared her. She immediately thought of Peter, but when she saw it was addressed to Tom she feared for him even more, for a telegram could only contain official notification of his sons' loss in France. She thought for a moment of leaving it for him to see when he came in at tea-time, but instinct told her that bad news of that sort was something Tom could deal with better in the open fields.

Tom was backing the digger with a load of dripping black silt when she drove up. The rife—the Sussex name for these tidal dykes—was already cleared for two hundred yards of its length. Apart from the pile of newly deposited silt, all was neat and clean with the water in the bottom of the ditch flowing freely. Kate liked the rife better where the digger had not yet touched it, with its tangle of sedges, green film of duck-weed and the swaying feathered heads of the phragmites

93

reeds. Tom said: "Looks a hell of a lot better, don't she?" He saw the telegram and his face went blank. Then he held out his hand. "Better look, hadn't I?"

She handed it over. He tore it open with a finger as blunt as the tines on the digger and held it out at arms' length. Outdoors, Tom never carried his reading glasses, A moment later he was down off the digger and dragging her out of the car, hugging and kissing her.

"It's Michael! He's in hospital at Tilbury. Kate love, drive me back to the house just as fast as you can. Oh Kate, I dare hardly believe it!"

He was crying, his thick shoulders shaking.

"What wonderful news, Tom."

"Kate, you don't think it can be a mistake?"

"Of course not. What does the telegram say?"

He read it out. "Contact Tilbury General Hospital believe patient here your son Corporal Michael Roland."

"It must be Michael, Tom."

"Get a move on, girl, get a move on."

They shot off down the rutted track, the old Austin protesting in every spring. "Why do they say 'believe', Kate? Can't Michael talk for himself? Kate, you don't think he's so badly wounded that he's . . . he's dying? Can't you drive this damn car faster? Here, let me take over."

He tried to push her hand off the wheel. Deliberately, she slowed down and stopped the car. She was surprised at the firmness with which she spoke.

"We'll get to the telephone a lot quicker, Tom Roland, if you'll show some of the calmness you showed when you took *Golden Plover* to Dunkirk. Michael won't thank you if you end up in that nice deep ditch you've just cleared out."

After that he sat quiet all the way back to the farm. There, Kate got him a large whisky and the number of Tilbury Hospital.

"I'll speak," she said.

Tom nodded.

After a while they put her through to a ward sister.

"I'm speaking for Mr Tom Roland. He's just had a telegram about his son, Michael. I'm sure you understand he's a bit shaken by the news so could you please tell me the situation before I put him on the line?"

The ward sister said: "I quite understand. You can reassure Mr Roland. His son has a scalp wound from a shell splinter and has only just regained consciousness. He had no identity tags or regimental identification when he came in."

Watching Kate's face, Tom saw that her reaction was one of relief. He snatched the phone from her.

"Is he going to be all right? When can I come and see him?"

"It's early days yet, Mr Roland, but we're very optimistic. Yes, we shall want you to identify him. He may not recognise you yet, of course."

"His sight's okay?"

"His sight will be perfectly all right. But it's going to take time before he's on his feet again."

"Bless you, sister, I'll come at once."

"Tomorrow would be time enough, Mr Roland."

Soon after Dieter's arrival at St Omer, they received a visit and a pep talk from their wing-commander. Colonel Theo Osterkamp was every inch a professional from the peak of his squarely worn forage cap to his riding breeches and polished flying boots. He took off his dark glasses and turned on his officers a face as spare and lean as the 109 he had just stepped out of.

He told them that the JG 51 had been selected for a singular honour. At present it was the only operational fighter wing to face Britain across the Channel. They may all have wondered why there had been a delay. Germany had hoped—still hoped—that Britain would come to her senses. If she did not, then the RAF fighter squadrons would have to be smashed. No one need think that this was going to be easy. The Hurricane and the Spitfire, especially, had shown themselves to be excellent machines. The British pilots would be even more determined enemies when defending their homeland. At present JG 51's activities were still limited. From henceforward they would make operational fighter patrols over the Channel and the English coast to try to tempt the RAF fighters to give battle. Such sweeps would give new pilots valuable experience but no one should expect this period of calm to last too long.

The weather eased at eleven next morning. Dieter's flight was on stand-by. The telephone rang in the duty hut. All morning Dieter had tried to tell himself to keep calm, to read a book or sleep like the sergeant pilots did. Maybe in ten patrols' time he'd be like them. Lieutenant Feuchter put down the phone and shouted: "Cloud base is opening up. Take off in five minutes to patrol the coast off Dungeness."

Outside in the truck, Sergeant Brandis said to Dieter: "Stick close to me, sir. If anything happens I'll try to keep an

95

eye on you. Now mind—don't lose me or you may get a Spit-fire drilling a hole in your arse—sir."

They took off and headed out to sea in a loose formation of *Rotten*. Dieter was amazed at the amount of radio chatter that went on. He was soon to discover that this was a Luft-waffe fighter pilot's failing. Suddenly Feuchter's voice said: "Shut up. Four Spitfires inland, ten o'clock high." Dieter strained but saw nothing. Feuchter said: "I'm going in below them to draw them down. Watch in case they dive." The flight commander and his wingman flipped to starboard and were gone. But the Spitfires continued on their course, refus-ing the bait. Twenty minutes later the flight was back at St Omer without having fired a shot. It continued like that for several days of that cold wet early July. Then, on the tenth, things changed.

At 1420 hours on that drizzly day not only the squadron but the whole of *Gruppe* 3 of JG 51 unexpectedly got orders to scramble. Dieter clung closely to Brandis's tail as they climbed through the broken cloud at 6,000 feet. Just over Calais a *Gruppe* of Dornier 17s swung into view. There was the voice of Dieter's squadron commander giving orders for close escort of the bombers. Target: a large British coastal convoy off Folkestone, making for Dover. As they closed with the Flying Pencils, Dieter saw the other two fighter squadrons of the *Gruppe* climbing to a stepped-up position below. He heard the voice of Hauptmann Trautloft, *Gruppe* commander, tell-ing his men to watch for enemy fighters trying to reach the Dorniers. A few seconds later, Trautloft's wingman reported thirty Me 110s of ZG 26 converging from the south-west. Seventy German aircraft all told. Would the British at last be tempted to fight?

Dieter tried to look every way at once. Below and ahead now were the white V-shaped wakes of the convoy. The ships were the bombers' business. Enemy fighters would come from above. That was where they must concentrate. Trautloft's voice on the R/T again: "Six Hurricanes above the convoy. Leave them alone unless they attack." Dieter was sweating. He switched on his reflector sight, felt for the cannon and ma-chine-gun buttons. Feuchter was saying: "Go for them at once if they dive." But the Hurricanes stayed up top, perhaps hoping to lure the fighter escort from the Dorniers. The thud-ding concussion of flak shook Dieter's Emil. It was well ahead, aimed at the bombers. Dirty brown smoke puffs blew back as the fighters bored on. A stolen look at the convoy in time to see water-spouts from the first bombs and the orange flash of a hit on a freighter. In half a minute the Dorniers were unloaded, streaking for the wave-tops and for home. Suddenly the radio was alive with cries and warnings. British fighters everywhere. Brandis broke right, climbing steeply. Dieter followed him into ragged cloud. When he emerged, Brandis wasn't there any more. A Hurricane crossed his path in a headlong dive. The 109 could outdive anything. He glanced behind—nothing there—and dived after it. Was the Hurricane already out of control? He lined up, closing fast. As he did so, the British fighter dived straight into a twin-engined plane. Dornier? Messerschmitt 110? Impossible to tell. He banked violently to starboard, barely clearing the debris. The R/T again. A voice calling: "I am hit. Going to try to make the coast." He recognised Flight Sergeant Dau of No 2 Flight. Trautloft answering from the centre of the dogfight, detailing an escort to cover Dau back to the French coast—if he could make it. Where the hell was everyone? As he climbed, looking for a target, or even a friend, Dieter saw the 110s of ZG 26 forming a defensive circle to protect themselves, like a lot of bloody circus horses. Fat lot of good that was. Tracer streaked past his port wing. Hell, concentrate or you'll be dead. A Spitfire, coming from nowhere, had overshot, turning left as tightly as only a Spitfire could. Travelling more slowly, Dieter gave his Emil full left rudder to cut across the Spitfire's turning circle. For just a brief instant at maximum range he would have a deflection shot. The graceful elliptical wings of the Spitfire touched the ring of his reflector sight, a shade more rudder, fore-finger on the silver button, firing the two nose machine-guns, thumb on the 20 mm cannon trigger. His Emil shuddering and the tracers entering the Spitfire's engine. As easy as shooting a roebuck crossing a forest-clearing. Cloud of white glycol coolant followed by a blossom of flame and black smoke. The British fighter falling on its back, the canopy flying off and then a white puff of parachute silk. Alone. Alone in the whole sky. Even the convoy had disappeared. He saw the Spitfire hit the sea and dived gratefully into some cloud, turning for home. Ten miles off Calais he joined up with two 109s of 6 Flight. He was soaked through with sweat but elated with his first victory. Mölders' words at the *Kreigsschule* once again: "The great thing is to score your first kill without shock. Then you will quickly grow in confidence." He was glad the English pilot had bailed out. The word "kill" applied to the aircraft destroyed rather than the man in it. Mölders had said that, too. Back at St Omer, Feuchter congratulated him, Sergeant Brandis also, though he wanted to know how Dieter had come to lose him so easily. Dau had belly-landed on the beach at Calais. So had another sergeant-pilot. Two machines lost, all pilots safe. The *Gruppe* claimed six enemy fighters.

This was the day and the action with which the Battle of Britain was later said to have begun.

The weather continued vile but 3 *Gruppe Jagdgeschwader* 51 flew every day. Always JG 51. Even keen veteran pilots like Leo Feuchter asked why the hell their wing, with a full strength of only seventy aircraft, was fighting the war single-handed. What was the other nine-tenths of the Luftwaffe doing? Not that the *Geschwader* would have seventy serviceable Emils for long. Foul ground conditions, accidents and daily contact with the British was rapidly whittling down the number of 109s that could be mustered for the high level sweeps in which Theo Osterkamp paraded his entire wing over Southern England in the hope that the British would come up and fight. But the British never did. They scrambled their fighter squadrons on receipt of early warning by their remarkable Decimeter Telegraphy system—DeeTee for short—and then, when they found the "bandits" were only fighters, returned to base. Dieter regarded these ceremonial parades almost as relaxation. Not every mission was a joyride though.

From his omnibus HQ at Cap Gris Nez, Colonel Fink hurled his meagre forces at the British convoys. His orders were to stop British shipping using the Channel. To do this he could draw on KG 2—a *Kampfgeschwader* of Do 17s—and two Stuka *Gruppen*. It was the latter, mostly Ju 87s, which everyone, including Fink, expected to do the job as brilliantly as they had done it so far against pinpoint targets on the ground.

Orders for Dieter's squadron that morning were explicit. Stick close to the *Stukas*. The British might be unwilling to engage German formations consisting entirely of fighters, but they showed every sign of determination to defend their convoys. After briefing, Feuchter said: "The target is a single large merchant ship making for Dover. Our bombers crippled her off Portsmouth yesterday and she's limping along accompanied by a destroyer, some tugs and a couple of flak ships. Our job is to get the *Stukas* to the target, so stick to them like glue. Until they've dropped their bombs, they'll be vulnerable."

Escort was at squadron strength, or rather what unserviceability had left of squadron strength—two *Schwärme*. Dieter's consisted of Feuchter and Weiss, Brandis and himself.

It was their first experience of escorting Ju 87s. They met

the gull-winged monstrosities—Dieter thought of them as birds of ill-omen—at 8,000 feet, just off the French coast. There were twelve, each with a 500 lb bomb slung externally beneath its fuselage. From the start, close escort was impossible. The labouring *Stukas* were so slow the fighters couldn't throttle back sufficiently to stay with them. Feuchter gave the *Schwarm* orders to weave by *Rotten*, one pair of fighters timing its circuit to keep close to the *Stukas* as the others turned away. It was not easy, especially as, climbing to the attack height of 10,000 feet, the 87s were even slower.

As they approached the target, the *Stukas* split into two formations of six. Dieter's *Schwarm* had been detailed to protect the first group in their dive, keeping as close as possible. The remainder of the squadron would look after the second formation. Coral necklaces of tracer were climbing slowly up from the ships, starting oh, so lazily, and then accelerating suddenly to fantastic speed. The destroyer had opened up with her four-inch guns. In his ear, Dieter heard the *Stuka* leader say: *"Wir greifen an."* We attack. Seconds later the first *Stuka* peeled off, the propeller of its dive siren spinning. It was heading in an eighty-degree dive for the biggest of the ships. One after the other, its five companions followed. Dieter saw Brandis out to starboard ease the nose of his Emil down and dived behind him. Within a few seconds, the two fighters were past the *Stukas* and streaking out ahead of them. It was impossible to keep with them in a dive, no matter how much you throttled back. Without dive-brakes it just couldn't be done. A fighter wasn't designed for such duties. The damn *Stukas* dived at only 150 mph. A flak ship was throwing muck up at the two fighters now. No point in making oneself a target for nothing. Brandis pulled out of his dive, and turned away from the convoy, Dieter following. As they came round full circle they got the whole picture. A dozen Hurricanes had jumped the *Stukas*. It was like shooting clay pigeons. Three 87s fell apart or exploded immediately. A fourth dropped its bomb wide, turned and was picked off by a Spitfire. The fifth *Stuka* went away smoking, low over the water. Of the last there was no sign.

Brandis was after the Hurricanes but the damage had been done. They'd be over the English coast before they could catch them. On the way home they met a solitary Hurricane slowly circling at 5,000 feet. Since the pilot took no evasive action, they both made one firing pass. Dieter saw their bursts strike home, knocking chunks off fuselage and tailplane. The Hurricane continued its lazy arc. As they turned in for a second attack, Brandis shouted: "Don't waste ammunition. He's dead." It was true; as Dieter flew alongside he could see the British pilot dead in his shattered cockpit, yet the plane still flew on indestructibly. The pilot's helmet had fallen off. He had fair hair. Dieter's immediate thought was that it could have been Peter Bristow. They left the Hurricane to find its own burial place in the sea.

The facts were appalling. Of the twelve *Stukas*, seven had been lost and two more severely damaged. All the fighter pilots had the same story for the squadron intelligence officer. You just couldn't fly slow enough to escort the bloody things. Once they went into their dive, they were a sitting target. What was the escort supposed to do? If they couldn't keep with them, which level of the *Stukas'* long, slow dive should they try to protect? Afterwards, Dieter and Leo Feuchter argued heatedly. The orders were to fly close escort, so that's what they'd do, Feuchter said.

"It's nonsense. The only hope is for the escort to be allowed to hunt freely. Hit the RAF fighters before they can get near the *Stukas*. It's the only hope."

"And suppose the Spitfires slip through us and we never make contact?"

"Then we're no worse off than we are at the moment."

"You talk like a damn staff officer, Reh."

"I was up there too, remember? I didn't like what happened to those dive-bomber boys any more than you did. Come on, I'll buy you a drink."

In the mess Dieter ordered *schnapps*. Normally he drank only light beer. The mission had shaken him badly. That close look at the dead British pilot who could have been Bristow had troubled him almost as much as the failure to protect the *Stukas*. No good thinking like that, though.

It went on like that all that week. They lost few pilots, but Emil after Emil became unserviceable, often from accidents to undercarriages caused by the boggy ground, less frequently from battle damage. The English fighters continued to hammer the *Stukas* whenever they appeared over a convoy. By 16 July, Dieter's *Gruppe* had only fifteen 109s flying out of a total strength of forty. But three days later, Dieter scored his second victory and the whole *Gruppe* got a shot in the arm.

On one of Trautloft's ceremonial parades over Dover, what was left of 111/JG 51 met a British squadron of twelve planes climbing in tight formation. The *Gruppe* was in a perfect sun-up position. A warning from Trautloft on the R/T: "Don't attack from astern. They're Defiants." Over Dunkirk a German fighter squadron had made precisely this mistake, believing the British to be Hurricanes. Then the new Boulton and Paul Defiants had scored a sensational success. The two-seater, modelled on World War One principles, had no forward armament but instead a power-operated turret of four Brownings, manned by the observer. Dieter's ears vibrated as Brandis yelled: "Attack from below." They piled on down in a steep dive, pulling out in a curve that drained the blood from the brain. When vision cleared, Dieter saw three of the Defiants a thousand feet above him. The left-hand machine centred in his windscreen. It was like shooting a standing roe. The Defiant exploded at once. As he rejoined Brandis above what was left of the British formation he counted five of the two-seaters falling towards the sea.

Everyone got back safely, though several Emils whose pilots had made beam attacks were badly shot up. When he had assessed the excited pilots' claims the intelligence officer estimated that all but one of the Defiants had been destroyed. The RAF squadron, which was believed to be No 141, could therefore be said to no longer exist. This was near the truth. This Defiant squadron took no further part in the battle in daylight.

Lying on his bed that evening, Dieter listened to the recorded voice of the Führer. That morning victory in the West had been celebrated at the Kroll Opera House, Berlin. Practically everyone had been promoted and decorated. Twelve generals had been made field marshals, including Luftwaffe chiefs Milch, Sperrle and Kesselring. Five new *General-obersts:* Udet was among these. And the highest honour of all, an entirely new rank specially created for him—*Reichsmarschall des Grossdeutschen Reiches,* Hermann Goering. The announcer described the *Reichsmarschall*'s special white uniform, his gigantic marshal's baton, the Grand Cross of the Iron Cross, the only example of this order ever to be awarded. Dieter tried to imagine how the founder of the Luftwaffe must have felt at that instant.

The Führer was speaking: "I make yet another appeal to English good sense. I can see no compelling reason for continuing the struggle. I am sorry for the sacrifices that it will demand . . . If we do pursue the struggle, it will end with the complete destruction of one of the two combatants. Churchill may believe that it will be Germany. I *know* that it will be England."

They argued about England in the mess that night. Leo Feuchter said: "You've seen the way the Tommies fight to defend their convoys. Does it look as if they'll give in easily?"

Dieter was surprised to find himself clinging so strongly to what he had imagined was a forgotten hope. "Surely the Führer wouldn't have made his appeal in such an important speech if he hadn't . . ."

Feuchter laughed. "Even the Führer can't know what the English are thinking. What do you say, Weiss?"

The big blond young man uncurled himself from an armchair. Willy Weiss seldom gave an opinion unless pressed for it. "I believe the moment we start attacking English soil, there'll be no turning back for either of us. We'll have to smash the RAF, their Navy, and then, somehow, we shall have to get across the Channel."

"Invade?"

"How else?"

Until this moment, Dieter had not yet come to terms with the idea that Germany might have to attack England by land. From what he had seen of the British he believed that they would fight for every inch, town by town, village by village, even in Axeham Vale. But perhaps they would heed the Führer's warning.

Three days later he got his answer. In a radio broadcast, the British foreign minister, Lord Halifax, stated there was nothing in Hitler's speech to suggest that peace would be based on justice. All the Führer could offer was threats. Britain was inexorably resolved to fight on.

During the last week of July, the tired pilots of JG 51 received encouraging news. Elements of JG 52, of which Adolf Galland commanded a *Gruppe,* also JG 26, were moving in to help them in the Channel battle. Feuchter was not so happy. Flight commanders had been summoned to attend a conference at which criticism from Luftwaffe High Command had been freely passed on.

Reichsmarschall Goering made no secret of the fact that he blamed the failure of the *Stukas* so far on the fighter pilots. They weren't aggressive enough. They didn't defend their charges closely enough. Feuchter was bitter. Nevertheless, as he explained to the flight, it was his duty to pass on the criticism.

Afterwards Sergeant Brandis complained: "I didn't see the *Reichsmarschall* up there with us when the Hurricanes hit us that first time over the convoy."

Feuchter said loyally: "The commander in chief of the Luftwaffe has done his share of operational flying."

"Yes, on the Western Front in World War One. Doesn't he realise that fighters now have got to range freely?"

"If you were flying a *Stuka* maybe you'd be happy to see some fighters close at hand."

"Not if I was going to be shot down because the fighters couldn't do their job properly."

Weiss asked: "What did our *Gruppe* commander say?"

"He spoke much as I have done. He felt obliged to pass on the criticism, but for his part he knew we'd given of our best and would continue to do so."

Sergeant Brandis said: "It makes you want to spit." Only he didn't say "spit".

In Kent, the morning of 12 August was overcast. Peter sat outside the dispersal hut simply because he found the atmosphere inside claustrophobic when he was on stand-by. The Spitfires of his flight waited thirty yards away in sand-bagged bays. There was an uncomfortable feeling of suspense in the humid air. The day before yesterday there had been an almighty clash against *Stukas* attacking coastal targets with a heavy escort of 109s. The Germans had lost thirty-one aircraft, the RAF nineteen. Peter's No 2 had been among them. Now he watched his replacement, a twenty-one-year-old Canadian, playing with his pet bull-terrier, Heinz. Heinz had RAF roundels marked in red and blue ink on each side of his fuselage and a large black swastika on his rudder. The Canadian, Pat Hay, threw the ball for the bull-terrier and, when the dog returned galloping with it, hurled himself on the animal in a rugger tackle. After a great deal of token growling by both parties the dog stood triumphantly on his master's chest, affectionately drooling saliva on to him. From this point of disadvantage, the Canadian looked up into Peter's face. "He jumped me out of the sun," he said apologetically.

"Don't let it ever happen again."

"Think they're saving up for something?"

"Could be. Maybe they're just waiting for the weather to clear."

At St Omer Dieter lolled on the ground writing to Liese Schumacher. Elsa, Leo Feuchter's Alsatian, came tearing across the grass after a ball thrown by Willy Weiss. The dog's paws caught the edge of the notepaper.

"Can't you children play games somewhere else?"

"All right, all right! Why don't you go inside?"

Dieter looked at Willy sharply; it was unusual for the big Austrian to get rattled. Come to that, he had been fairly short-tempered himself.

"Okay, Willy. No harm done."

Weiss smiled, glad that the tension was broken. He nodded at the low cloud. "Think the balloon will go up once this lot clears?"

"*Adlertag*? The *Reichsmarschall*'s Day of Eagles. I suppose so. Give this weather a chance to clear and, according to Trautloft, that will be it. An all-out attack on English fighter bases."

The operation phone rang. Feuchter called: "Squadron take-off immediately. There's a break in the weather. We're escorting Do 17s in a low-level attack on Manston."

Radar plots were developing steadily along the south coast. Perhaps Eagle Day was here at last. The RAF's radar system was not working quite as effectively as usual. What the Germans knew as the "DeeTee" station at Ventnor, Isle of Wight, had been put out of action earlier that morning by a determined squadron of Ju 88s.

Because of the low altitude at which they crossed the coast, the Do 17s that Dieter's squadron escorted sneaked in before much warning could be given.

Peter Bristow saw Pat Hay knock Heinz the bull-terrier off his chest and start to run for his Spit. When Peter's engine started up, the other flights were already taxiing out, the pilots opening up at once and taking off wherever they could find space. As he began to roll, the first fountain of earth rose from the airfield. A hangar went up in a gush of flame. The concussion of the bombs slewed his aircraft sideways. He sensed rather than saw the first formation of Dorniers overhead. Tracer laced down, the bullets striking sparks, to add to their own phosphorescent fireworks, from the runway. Ahead of him, Pat Hay became airborne in time for a bomb blast to slam him down into the ground again. His right wing torn off, he slithered at one hundred and twenty miles an hour across the grass. More bombs falling from the second squadron of Dorniers. But Peter was off now and climbing. The shock wave from a stick of 100 pounders threw his Spit on to its back. He held her there, climbing inverted, until his nerve returned seconds later. When he rolled out, she answered perfectly and there was a 109 dead ahead, climbing away after a low-flying pass at the airfield. He opened fire at once. Leo

104

Feuchter never saw or heard his attacker. Peter's first burst killed him.

Now Dieter Reh had two new responsibilities. He had adopted Feuchter's dog. He had become flight commander in Feuchter's place. Saddened as he was, he was delighted at the replacement who arrived to fly as his *Kaezmarek*, his wingman. It was Fatty Kolbe, the shoehorn "ace" from the class at Werneuchen. Kolbe had spent the last few months fretting in a squadron based in Germany for the defence of Berlin. The fat boy had not lost any weight, nor had he lost his sense of self-ridicule. At his neck, where he said the Iron Cross would shortly be worn, dangled the miniature shoehorn that Feldwebel Hans Pohle, class instructor, had given him at Werneuchen Fighter School.

Because of the cloudy weather, 13 August, the day Goering had officially decided to open his *Adlerangriff*, misfired, or rather went off in spurts rather than in one rending explosion of simultaneous air attack. Dieter's squadron wasn't in the action until late afternoon and by then he had met another graduate from Werneuchen.

Shortly after 1530 hours, a single Me 110 appeared over the field. One engine was dead, the other smoking. It came in at once, making a wheels-up landing which dumped it on its nose not one hundred yards from Dieter's flight HQ. He was the first to reach it, tearing at the hinged canopy to free the crew. The gunner had no face left: a whole burst of Browning bullets had hit him at close range. His head was red pulp held together by what looked like broken coconut shell. The pilot was undamaged though badly shocked. When they had helped him out, Dieter saw that the blood-covered figure was Gerhard Stecke from Hamelin.

Stecke was bitter. His *Gruppe*, he said, had been murdered. They had been ordered to cross the British coast at Portland. Their mission had been to entice and engage RAF fighters in order to exhaust them of fuel and ammunition so that bombers, following at a carefully timed interval, would find the British fighters refuelling and helpless on the ground. Instead they had been picked up by British "Dee Tee", and probably mistaken for bombers, since the Tommies did not engage fighter to fighter if they could help it. They had been jumped by at least fifty Hurricanes and Spitfires. What made Stecke so bitter was that the Zerstörer, the vaunted "Destroyer", was helpless against the single-engined fighters. All they had been able to do was to form a defensive circle while

105

the British dived through their formation at will. Five 110s had been lost and many, like Stecke's own, had crawled home to die. "Dieter," he said, "you don't know how lucky you are to be flying a 109. The 110 is a dead loss unless you chaps are there to protect us. If I live long enough, I shall apply for a transfer to single-seaters."

"You are shocked, Gerhard. The loss of your gunner . . . I, too, have just lost my flight commander, a fine comrade. *Adlerangriff* has only just begun. There are bound to be reverses. You belong to an elite unit. When you've recovered from to-day's experiences, you'll feel differently. Where is your unit based?"

"Caen."

"You're a long way from home."

"My compass was shot up and without a navigator . . ."

"Our orderly room will report you safe. We'll ask your people to send transport. You must stay the night and rest."

"My *Gruppe* will need me."

"They can wait until tomorrow."

The next four days would have been days to remember if only they hadn't been too exhausted to recall the detail. They were now flying up to three missions a day and they were very tired men. There were moments of triumph, as when the twenty-five Dorniers the *Staffel* was escorting reached the aircraft works at Rochester and bombed it flat without interference from the RAF. There were, for most of the pilots, moments of sheer terror. For Dieter it was the terror of fire. One morning over Dungeness, a Hurricane had caught him flatfooted. The first burst had shorted some electric wiring and damaged his emergency canopy release. For some seconds he had thought that he was on fire and knew he was trapped. The cockpit had filled with smoke. But the smoke had cleared and Kolbe had shot the Hurricane off his tail so that, later, he felt like gold-plating the fat boy's shoehorn for him. It was Kolbe's first victory. There were also moments of sheer pride, like that on 15 August when the cloud unexpectedly cleared in early afternoon and suddenly the whole German air force seemed to be on parade over the Channel and headed for En-gland . . . *Bomben auf England* . . . "Hear the engine singing . . ." For once the words and music of that idiotic song sound-ed like a patriotic anthem. These were mainly the good things, but they were far outweighed by the bad. The nightly gaps in the mess. Shoot a Tommy down and, if he wasn't dead, he had a good chance of bailing out to fight again. As Sergeant

Brandis put it: "It's all right for them. Ever tried rowing home in a leaking Messerschmitt?"

The Channel is twenty miles wide and the water is cold and rough. Go down in the middle and there wasn't much chance that a rescue launch would find you. But the worst thing was the continual note of criticism that filtered down from on high. *Luftflotte* commanders had been summoned to Goering's residence, Karinhall on the Schorfheide, twenty-five miles north of Berlin. They had been told in no uncertain terms that the *Reichsmarschall* wasn't pleased. What's more, as usual he blamed the fighters for letting the bombers down. So air fleet commanders told air corps commanders who told *Geschwader* commanders who refused to accept the criticism but felt duty-bound to pass it on to their *Gruppe* commanders who told their squadron leaders who, with much bitterness, told the men who did the job what was being said about their courage and fighting spirit. And things came to a head on 18 August, the day the *Stukas* were decimated.

It was the Spitfires of 152 Squadron and the Hurricanes of 43 Squadron who finally slew the *Stukas*. Peter Bristow was not in that engagement. His sister, however, was caught on the fringe of the battle. The fields of Rife Farm were an orchestra stall for the battle that daily raged directly overhead. No one in England had any doubt that RAF Fighter Command held Britain's life in its hands. Kate knew this and felt is as deeply as anyone else. She prayed for Peter and his comrades with all her heart. She also prayed for Dieter Reh. When the bombers came over she could feel a loathing for them almost as strong as that expressed by Tom Roland. He took his shotgun with him wherever he went about the farm. "If one of those buggers comes on my land," he said, "I'll treat him like any other vermin." She looked upward at the condensation trails left by the fighters and found it impossible to hate as Tom and everyone else hated. "Let them both be safe, please God," she thought.

She was driving the tractor that afternoon, inspecting on Tom's orders the corn that had been laid by the foul July weather. It wouldn't be ready to cut for a few weeks yet. The first thing she noticed were the dark puffs of ack-ack in the sky towards the Isle of Wight. Almost at once a column of smoke rose to meet them from the ground. The concussion of bombs reached her as a second cloud, much nearer, bloomed over the corn. They must be hitting Thorney Island and probably Ford as well. The RAF were into them. A red flash high in the air as a plane exploded. Dark plumes now towards the ground. Impossible to think that men, young men, were burning and dying in agony up there. From the cornfields of Rife Farm it was all so impersonal.

It did not remain so for long. A death rattle of machine-gun fire somewhere in the blue bowl of the summer sky warned her that the battle was coming her way. The raiders were turning for home with the RAF at their heels. The dark dot trailing a haze of smoke came low over the oak wood from the Sidlesham direction. The engine had a wounded sound. At first she thought it was a British fighter in trouble and then she saw the cranked wings and knew it was the ugliest of all enemy bombers—a *Stuka*. No Spitfire pursued it and none needed to. The German plane was simply looking for somewhere to die. The plane passed her so low she could see the pilot sitting upright and the observer fallen across his gun. The *Stuka* might have been trying to crash-land. Perhaps the pilot had some desperate hope of creeping home undetected above the wave tops. Halfway across the flood meadows towards the sea wall the engine stopped and the plane suddenly nose-dived into the ground. When the brown earth cloud had settled, Kate saw that the *Stuka* had not burned. It lay strewn about the field, so much disjointed aerial scrap, wings, tailplane, wheels scattered, only fuselage minus canopy intact.

She started up the tractor and bounced across the rutted tracks. At the farmhouse, half a mile away, she saw Tom's car start out. She beat him to the wreckage by a short head. The first thing she met was the body of the pilot. He had been thrown well clear by the crash, and the impact had smashed all his limbs so that they lay bent strangely, like a swastika, about his body. His face was undamaged. He was dark like Dieter and about the same age. She didn't know what she had expected to see, something villainous perhaps, with close-cropped hair and duelling scar: not this good-looking youngster who might have been Dieter's brother.

Tom came running up with his 12-bore.

"Good God," he said, "He's only a kid." Then gruffly: "Come on, girl, no good staring at him or the other chap either. They got him good and proper. I'd better phone the military. Only way to look at it is to say: it's them or us and I'd far rather it was them. At least they had the good manners not to crash in my corn."

He covered the dead pilot with an old fertiliser sack from the boot of his car.

The plane that had crashed on Rife Farm was one of twelve that failed to return from the raid on the Isle of Wight and Sussex air bases that afternoon. Six more from a force of thirty Ju 87s of I/STG77 were only good for salvage when they reached the French coast with dead or wounded aboard. All told, thirty *Stukas* of the four *Gruppen* sent out were lost or severely damaged. The shock wave from this disaster reverberated round the German fighter squadrons. Fighter commanders were once more summoned to Karinhall and this time not only *Geschwader* leaders, but officers commanding *Gruppen* as well, including Werner Mölders and Adolf Galland. Rumour had it there was a big shake-up on the way.

The shake-up wasn't long in coming. Rumours travelled in advance like tremors before an earthquake. Goering, the mess talk said, had once again blamed the fighter leaders for the slaughter of the *Stukas*.

Shoehorn Kolbe said: "The trouble is that the fat one"—he had the grace to laugh as he said it—"is still fighting World War One in an open cockpit. He's no conception of the speed things happen up there these days. He sees fighters as the poor relation of the bombers. Besides, he's put all his money on the bloody *Stuka* and he can't believe its number won't come up."

"Its number *is* up," Dieter said. "The talk is that they're withdrawing all the 87s from the battle. The adjutant of a *Stuka Gruppe* landed here this morning. He said they were all going back for a rest on airfields near Paris."

Willy Weiss stirred. "I wish to God you two would shut up and let me have a nap."

The *Gefechtsalarm* rang for the third scramble of the day.

As they ran for their aircraft, Sergeant Brandis shouted at Dieter. "You haven't heard the best rumour of all. It's all round the sergeants' mess. We're supposed to be getting 'Vati' Mölders as *Kommodore*." *Kommodore* was the term given to the commander of a *Geschwader*, irrespective of his personal rank. Mölders was then only a captain.

They took off. Mission: to escort KG 2 to clobber the RAF fighter field at Eastchurch once again. This trip the Spitfires hit them hard as they turned for home. The squadron lost an experienced sergeant pilot. Another Emil had to ditch in the Channel.

For once rumour was right about everything. The *Stukas* *had* been taken out of the battle. Their squadron leader confirmed it in his briefing next day. Those dive-bombers wouldn't be used again until RAF Fighter Command had been beaten from the sky. They'd come into their own again for pinpoint bombing once the invasion of England had begun. But first the RAF had to be beaten. There was good news here. Fighter *Geschwader* from the Cherbourg area were being moved up to reinforce the Channel front. Bombers would henceforward be escorted in greater and greater strength. The faces of several pilots fell. They had fought non-stop for too long. With the unexpected arrival of practically fresh fighter wings they immediately saw the chance of a rest, possibly even of some leave.

The squadron leader heard the muttering.

"Someone has a question?"

"How about a few days off, *Herr Oberleutnant?*"

"You know as well as I do that the job's got to be done first. Besides, high command's criticising the fighters, as usual. We don't want to give them a chance to get back at us, do we?"

Apparently no one did. Every fighter pilot on the Channel coast was extremely sensitive to the fact that he was being held to account for others' mistakes.

The squadron leader said: "I can end with some excellent news. From now on *Jagdgeschwader* are to be led by the most brilliantly successful of our operational pilots. Colonel Osterkamp is to be promoted to major general. Instead to lead us in the air we are to be honoured by having Werner Mölders as our new *Kommodore*. Adolf Galland is taking over JG 26 at Abbeville."

Mölders! Dieter was elated by the news. It was a magic name. During the next few days there was at least a partial lull while the new fighter *Geschwader* moved into the Pas de Calais. There was no lull as far as the new *Kommodore* was concerned. He landed with his wingman and adjutant at St Omer the day after his appointment to command. The Condor head in a circle on a shield—the insignia of JG 51—was already painted on the nose of the *Kommodore's* 109. Their new leader meant to meet as many of his pilots as possible before he led them against the RAF. Dieter was even more impressed than the last time he had seen Mölders at Werneuchen. The fighter leader had somehow grown in authority. Though quite a slight figure, and though he never raised his voice or laughed, he seemed to fill the flight dispersal hut with sheer personality. No wonder his pilots nicknamed him "Vati", the German diminutive for father. As usual, even in the short time available to him, he had done some homework.

"How have things been going since I saw you at Werneuchen? Quite well, by the sound of it. I hear you have four victories, Reh. Introduce me to the rest of your flight, please. I've heard good things about them, too."

When Dieter had made the introductions, adding after each pilot's name his total confirmed kills, Mölders said: "Now let's have your opinions freely, Reh. How could we fighters do better?"

"By free-hunting, *Herr Kommodore*."

"The classic recipe!"

"Exactly."

"But if we are ordered to stick closely to the bombers?"

"Then orders are at least partly incorrect. They are not based on what we experience up there."

"And supposing in the future we are ordered to escort the bombers on longer missions, say to London?"

"Then, *Herr Kommodore,* free-hunting will become almost impossible. We will not have the range."

Möolders nodded. "I can see that this flight not only fights well but uses its head. Now let me tell you what this wing is going to do. Long before it becomes necessary to fly escort duties to the limits of the 109s' endurance, we are going to smash the RAF fighters both in the air and on the ground, smash them to a point at which the need for long-range escort hardly becomes a consideration. As for London, I hope it will never become necessary to bomb a civilian population. Our task is a military one."

"So to achieve that, *Herr Kommodore,* the fighters will be released on free-hunt?"

"Some of them, perhaps. But from now on we shall take the air at *Geschwader* strength and I'll be up there with you."

They snapped to attention as Mölders left the hut.

"What was that new decoration he was wearing?" Kolbe asked.

"Gold pilot medal with jewels The *Reichsmarschall* has just presented it to both him and Galland."

"I bet he was just jealous of my shoehorn, Reh."

Dieter tapped the fat pilot in the stomach. "Watch your weight or the new *Kommodore* will post you to bombers."

They got their baptism under their new leaders three days later. It turned out to be a *feu de joie*. Three fighter *Geschwader* stormed in on the balloon barrage at Dover and set fire to fifty balloons. The smoke of their dying could be seen halfway to London and clean across the Channel. It made them all feel that they were on top again. But in the last week of

August, the pace hotted up. Manston, Warmwell, Debden, Eastchurch, Biggin Hill, Hornchurch. The bombers hammered the fighter bases and hammered them again. Two and three hundred strong, the 109s clustered round the bombers. Whenever they could, the RAF ignored the fighter escort and dived straight for the Heinkels and Dorniers. Dieter chalked up a Spitfire and a Hurricane, Kolbe and Weiss a Hurricane apiece and Brandis a stray Blenheim encountered unexpectedly on the way home from Biggin. It was nerve-racking work being so fettered to the bombers. Close escort made it very hard to score. On 24 August, Dieter got a break. Mölders had decreed that one *Schwarm* per squadron be allowed free-hunting. Dieter's flight had been nominated. He now flew with Kolbe as his wingman. The other *Rotte* consisted of Brandis and Weiss. Hunting just within sight of the bombers heading for Biggin once again, they hit a large formation of Spitfires climbing to intercept. Sergeant Brandis and Dieter got one each. Kolbe damaged a third. They were through the British squadron and safely away in a dive before the Tommies could retaliate. Free-hunting was the thing. If only OKL, *Oberkommando der Luftwaffe,* could be made to see it.

Peter Bristow saw the Spitfire Kolbe had damaged falling away spewing a white cloud of glycol. There was no time to notice if the pilot bailed out, nor was there time to pursue the 109s which had done the job. The Spitfires' task was to get at the bombers. The pilot of the damaged Spit was a Coastal Command type who had joined them as a volunteer two days previously. The other two lads with him had done ten and twelve hours on Spits respectively. What chance did they have? Not much, but then with a quarter of Fighter Command's pilots dead or wounded in the battle, things had reached the stage where anyone who could fly a Spit or a Hurricane was welcome. Peter could barely remember the faces who had passed through the squadron he now led.

He was a thousand feet above the sixteen Dorniers heading for Biggin when he gave the order to attack. At a closing speed of over 600 mph the five remaining Spitfires met them head-on. He opened fire at 150 yards and saw his tracers entering the glass-house in the nose of the leading bomber. It fell away at once. He could imagine the shambles in there and for the first time since the battle had begun hoped that no one got out.

Rife Farm received its share of what, in a later age, would have been called the fall-out of the Luftwaffe's attempt to obliterate Fighter Command. A hard-hit Ju 88 jettisoned a stick of bombs in a stubble from which Tom had just cut the wheat, setting fire to the straw. Tom's curses were as lurid as the flames. The burnt-out husk of a Messerschmitt 109 crashed into a neighbour's Dutch barn. Fortunately for the pilot—one of Adolf Galland's "Abbeville Boys", as the RAF came to know the yellow-nosed 109s of JG 26—he bailed out in the yard of the local police station. Had he landed anywhere near the owner of the ruined barn, he might well have been run through with a pitchfork.

Throughout these terrible days, Kate's state of mind was schizoid. It was impossible not to hate the enemy but equally it was still impossible to hate Dieter. He was merely doing what he had to. She could not believe that he would machine-gun trains as German fighters were said to have done in Kent. She even indulged a fantasy in which he parachuted down on the farm and was harmlessly taken prisoner. What a solution to her personal dilemma that would have been. With Dieter safely behind British barbed wire she would be able to do what she knew her blood demanded—to loathe every German to the point of his ultimate destruction, just as Tom did.

At the start of that last week in August, she received an unexpected phone call from her mother. Mrs Bristow insisted on going to London to ensure that "things" were in order with her solicitor. She did not actually say so, but her daughter knew that what she really meant was that if the Germans *were* coming then she wanted her will to be in order before they arrived. Mrs Bristow had no doubt in her own mind that she would fail to survive an invasion. Posted on the windscreen of her car, below the WVS badge, was Churchill's reminder: "You can always take one with you." To this end she carried Peter's .22 rifle on the back seat, with a box of cartridges kept permanently in the glove pocket under the dashboard. Mrs Bristow also harboured a faint hope that she might snatch a few hours with her son. She was under no illusion about his chance of surviving the present air battles. On top of all this, there was the feeling that by being tucked away safely in the West Country she was allowing the greatest drama since the Armada, a drama in which both her children were sharing, to pass her by. The evacuee problems of Axeham Vale could take care of themselves for a week.

Mrs Bristow decided to stay in a quiet residential hotel near Croydon, and the first thing that greeted her as she stepped

113

out of the train at Paddington was the wail of an alert. The porter said: "We get these non-stop, ma'am, but Jerry ain't coming 'ere yet. 'E's left London alone so far." He pointed ruefully at the glass roof. "But I don't much fancy being under this lot if 'e changes 'is mind."

She took a taxi to Victoria.

As she travelled south she saw twisting vapour trails high in the blue sky and several times heard fast, short bursts of machine-gun fire. An old lady who shared the compartment with her said: "Kent's catching it again. They say it's the airfields mostly. Still, they won't get through to London with our lads up there."

To the south a thin, indistinct trail of brown smoke fell earthwards. It was impossible to know if it was left by friend or foe.

"My boy's up here," Mrs Bristow said. Her voice was choked with pride but also with fear that even at that instant the trail of smoke might mark his grave.

"God bless him, dear, and you too," the old lady said, and leaned forward to pat Mrs Bristow's hand. "They'll never get here," she said comfortingly.

So far they had not bombed London because the Führer had expressly forbidden it. His motives were not of mercy but of expediency. So long as the capital was not attacked there might still be a chance that the British would see reason or at least do a deal. But on the first night of Mrs Bristow's stay in the suburbs the situation changed. She awoke to the thudding concussion of the first blast. The air shook as if it was something solid and a bedroom window-pane shattered. There were four more explosions, uncomfortably close. She got out of bed calmly, remembering to put her slippers on as there would be broken glass about. Half a mile away she saw the glow of a fire, heard shouts and air raid wardens' hand-bells ringing in the street below. She was in the front line at last! In her excitement she forgot that she had raised the black-out.

"Put that bloody light out," a man bawled.

Horrified at failing to observe the discipline she had so often demanded of others in so many WVS air raid precaution lectures, she dropped the blind and hurried to switch off the bedroom light. There was a knock at the door. The night porter stood outside.

"You all right, ma'am? The manager's sent me round to check up."

"Yes, thank you. What *was* that? A German bomber crashing?"

"We don't know for sure yet, ma'am, but the warden says it was bombs. If so it's the first time they've deliberately attacked us civilians." There was a suggestion of satisfaction in the porter's voice.

By now the guests were gathering in the corridors. The manager, a large, organising ex-army gentleman, was reassuring.

The guests talked excitedly, feeling at last they were under fire. Was this the start of a German blitz on London? The sound of ack-ack fire diminished and within ten minutes that same warden who had clanged his hand-bell and shouted at Mrs Bristow came bustling through the black-out curtain in the hall.

"All clear," he said. "You're safe to go back to bed now." He was a small man but somehow he managed to give the impression that it was he personally who had driven off the raiders.

"What was it all about?" the manager asked. "Did the ack-ack shoot down one of their bombers with a full load on board?"

The warden's hand-bell shook with excitement. "No," he said, "you can take it from me those were bombs. Four of 'em. Three on the cricket field but the last one got a semi-detached in Crescent Road. They say there're two dead and a third one missing. Mark my words, once they start bombing innocent civilians they've had it. Churchill will see to that, all right."

Those four bombs and a few other scattered sticks that fell on London that night had a profound effect on both sides of the Channel. It may not even be too much to suggest that they indirectly saved England. Early next morning at the HQ of Air Corps I outside Compiègne, the operations staff officer of KG 1, Major Josef Knobel, was handed a teleprinter signal from the *Reichsmarschall* himself. Scarcely believing it, he read: "It is to be reported forthwith which crews dropped bombs in the prohibited London zone. The supreme commander reserves to himself the personal punishment of the commanders concerned by remustering them to the infantry."

In Whitehall the reaction was equally violent. Here too the supreme commander reserved to himself the right of punishment, only this time it was the whole German nation that was going to catch it, or rather their capital city. The air-raid warden had been right about one thing: Churchill wasn't going to take the bombing of innocent civilians lying down. Hardly had the reports of the night's work reached him than he was demanding of his bomber chiefs that they mount immediate retaliation raids on Berlin. Bomber Command was most reluctant to do so. They saw no military advantage in reprisals. Nevertheless, on the following night, while Mrs Bristow was sleeping soundly after a satisfactory meeting with her solicitor, eighty-one twin-engined bombers, mostly Hampdens, were on their way to Berlin. Due to thick cloud less than a quarter of them dropped their bombs, at random, on the city. It was the first of four night raids on Berlin, spread over the next ten days, and this, at last, was too much for the Führer's self-restraint.

"Since they attack our cities," he cried, "we shall wipe out theirs."

Towards the end of her visit what Mrs Bristow had so much longed for actually came to pass—a chance for a family reunion, perhaps in the present circumstances, the last chance. Kate phoned from Sussex. Tom's boy, Michael, was being discharged from hospital. He was on indefinite sick-leave, and was to go home for his convalescence. Tom couldn't leave the farm itself at that moment; they were too busy with the harvest and were very short-handed. But he had squandered the farm's petrol coupons on sending Kate to fetch Michael home from Tilbury. Kate had heard from Peter. His squadron was at Hornchurch, very much at the sharp end of things. Yes, he was all right, though exhausted. She had spoken to him last night. Now listen: what she proposed to do was to make a small diversion—the petrol would just stretch to it—pick up her mother and drive down to Essex. Peter had told her the name of a local pub where they could all meet and where Kate and she could get rooms overnight. Next day they'd collect Michael Roland from hospital and she would take her mother back to her hotel. The date was 31 August.

The Bristows picked a bad day for a visit to the Tilbury area. Just as Kate saw the dockland cranes appearing in the distance, the sirens went. A few moments later the first bombs began to fall in the docks. Kate pulled off on to the side of the road, and the two women got out and looked skywards. Eighteen Heinkels in perfect formation were showing their pale blue underbellies as they turned away from their attack. Stacked up above and all around were layers upon layers of fighters, three whole *Geschwader* of fighters, among them JG 51. On the fringes of this armada, about 200 planes all told, small parties of single-seater fighters were weaving—Mölders' free-hunting *Schwärme*. One of these was led by Dieter Reh. Dense oily smoke rose from the docks. A brief burst of machine-gun fire as Spitfires and Hurricanes engaged one of the free-hunting groups of Messerschmitts. Two planes fell away while they watched. Above one, a Hurricane, a parachute blossomed. The other, square wing-tipped, fell in flames.

"Our man's all right," Kate shouted. "That other one's a Messerschmitt"—always that unworthy fear that it was Dieter. What she could not know was that the burning fighter belonged to Dieter's *Schwarm* and that inside it Sergeant Brandis was already dead.

Brandis' death hit Dieter as hard as the fragment of 3.7 flak shell that had penetrated his starboard wing over Dover on the way home. Both were a reminder of what they all knew only too well, that the odds were strongly against any of them escaping death or wounding for very long.

Another hazard was increasingly plaguing the 109 pilots. As bombing missions reached out further into southern England, their planes' powers of endurance were stretched to the limit. The Bf 109 had two hours' flying time at the most. Several times lately, Dieter had come home across the Channel with the red light on his instrument panel flickering to warn him that he was down to his last drop of fuel. The Luftwaffe had used drop-tanks on other types in Spain to give extra range. They had been successful there. It was incredible that no one had thought of developing them for the 109. Several pilots from the *Gruppe* had been forced to ditch in the Channel with stationary airscrews. Those who had bailed out had not always been picked up by air-sea rescue boats. It seemed that you had a better chance if you stayed with the aircraft and made a belly-landing on the water. The 109 stayed afloat for up to a minute—with luck—giving the pilot time to clamber out with dry clothes into his dinghy. This very day two pilots had just made the beach at Calais, crash-landing on the sand.

Weiss was more affected by Brandis' death than anyone else. His job as wingman had been to protect him. The Spitfire that had nailed him had been a real hot one appearing from below and opening fire in a climbing roll. Dieter tried to console him. Such fancy tactics usually didn't succeed. There wasn't much that Weiss could have done about it. The big Austrian refused to be comforted.

The squadron commander took a broader view of the Tilbury raid. Intelligence reports showed, he said, that British fighter resistance had dramatically declined lately. It looked as though the RAF had at last been smashed. Even the Zerstörer squadrons would soon feel safe, unescorted, in British skies. As usual he ended his talk by asking for suggestions or questions.

"If we've beaten the Tommies, why don't they give us a rest and withdraw the Channel *Geschwader* to a quieter sector for a bit?"

The speaker was a Bavarian *Leutnant* from No 3 Flight. With seven confirmed victories, he was in no danger of being accused of cold feet. Several pilots nodded in agreement.

"I know you're tired, but you wouldn't want to pull out now, just when one last effort . . ."

"Try me," the Bavarian said.

Peter didn't get to the hotel bar where they had arranged to meet until nearly eight that evening. His mother hardly recognised him. He looked dead tired, indefinably older; his fair hair was long and draped the neck of his blue battle-dress blouse in an unmilitary fashion that suited the polka-dot scarf at his neck. He hugged his mother, then his sister, then his mother again.

"Wonderful," was all he would say. "Bloody wonderful."

Silence fell. After a few moments Mrs Bristow said: "It's lovely to see you, Peter."

"Yes," he said.

Another silence.

"Were you in that air battle we saw today over the docks?"

"Look," he said, "do you mind if I get myself a bloody great drink? What will you have?"

Two other pilots, an Australian and a tall Canadian, had come in. Peter waved to them, "What are you chaps having? The usual? Mother? A gin and tonic?"

"Mother?" said the Canadian flight lieutenant. "Don't say this beautiful girl's your sister, Skipper."

He introduced them, "Mother . . . Kate—two of my squadron. The ill-spoken Australian is Kelly, Ned for short."

"Flies in tin armour," the Canadian explained, "with a sort of coal-bucket on his head. And I'm Pat Hay."

"He's a specialist at landing . . ."

"And taking-off . . ."

"Without wings . . ."

They all laughed uproariously. Evidently the joke was an established one.

Several times throughout the evening Mrs Bristow tried to discover from her son what the battle was like, how it was going. Each time she discovered that the gap between the pilots and herself was as wide and deep as the sky that divided a Spitfire's vapour trail from the ground.

Towards closing time the three pilots were obviously fairly well away. This was too much for Mrs Bristow's motherly solicitude.

"Dear," she said. "Won't you be flying tomorrow?"

The Australian, who was trying to persuade Kate to come outside to look at his Spitfire, interrupted his wooing to say: "Don't worry about our hangovers, Mrs B. A long gulp of oxygen and you're as good as new."

Outside in the car park as they said goodbye, Peter took Kate aside. "Get Mother out of London as soon as possible. Now that the bastards have started on the docks, I've got a feeling they'll take the gloves off completely."

That first week of September two notable personalities arrived in the Pas de Calais. The first required two armoured trains to transport him and his accoutrements. One train was like a luxury hotel on wheels, its sole object being to keep the principal occupant in a style to which he insisted on being accustomed. The second train contained the business end of the deal, the *Reischsmarschall*'s operations HQ. Goering had come, as he had announced in a broadcast, "to take over personal command of the Luftwaffe in its war against England."

The chain reaction that had begun with those accidental bombs on South London was about to culminate in a spectacular explosion. Churchill had retaliated. Now Hitler demanded massive retribution in return. At a conference at The Hague with his two *Luftflotten* chiefs, Field Marshals Kesselring and Sperrle, Goering had proposed that the piecemeal attacks on fighter airfields be abandoned in favour of a mass assault on the most important target of all—London. Sperrle was all for keeping up the pressure on the fighter fields. Kesselring came down on Goering's side. Even if Biggin Hill, Hornchurch and the others were totally obliterated, he argued, the British fighters would simply fall back to bases beyond London. "We have no chance, *Herr Reichsmarschall*," he said, "of destroying the remains of the English fighters on the ground. The only way we can tempt their last reserves into the air is to attack London. They'll throw in everything they've got left to defend their capital." The only question was: who would see that the bombers got safely there? Goering's opinion of the German fighter force was widely known and bitterly resented among the pilots themselves. The story of Adolf Galland's defiance of the *Reichsmarschall* was a classic piece of squadron folklore by now: on a previous visit to the Channel coast when Goering had criticised fighter morale and spirit, both Mölders and Galland had stoutly defended their pilots. Asked if there was anything they needed to help them Mölders had asked for a faster version of the 109 and had been promised one. Galland had replied curtly: "Give me a squadron of Spitfires, *Herr Reichsmarschall*." Now the chief had come to lead his men himself—from the ground.

In his own way, the second visitor that week was almost as flamboyant, but a good deal more welcome. To Dieter's delight, Feldwebel Hans Pohle, their old instructor from Werneuchen, had been posted to Dieter's flight. Little Pohle gave Dieter his smartest salute. "I see you're all still alive. I must have taught you something after all." He turned smiling towards Kolbe. "Don't say I'm *Rottenflieger* to the shoehorn ace. You don't decrease in stature ... er ... sir."

Dieter said: "You'll fly as No 1 to Willy Weiss. He'll keep you out of trouble."

"Talking of trouble," Pohle began.

"You'll be too tired for girls, *Feldwebel*. Besides, there aren't any locally. You can hardly blame the French if they're a bit stand-offish."

Peter Bristow had been right in his premonition about the coming onslaught on London. But Mrs Bristow had not lingered there. Nor had she returned to Axeham Vale. Her motherly instincts had been aroused by the sight of Michael Roland whom she had last seen when he was ten. Michael's head was still bandaged. Though his memory had returned, his sight still varied between half vision and nearly total blindness. The army doctors believed that, given rest and fresh air, recovery would be complete. Mrs Bristow clucked round him like a broody hen and announced she would return to Selsey for at least a week to help look after him. Kate had quite enough to do around the farm, so she was not at all sorry that her mother had volunteered for some of the nursing. She knew her mother well enough to guess that a reluctance to retire completely from the scene of action had at least something to do with her decision to stay in Sussex. Beneath all the mothering and bandages, Michael Roland was scarcely more to Kate than an animated bundle of hospital blue.

They brought Michael home to Rife Farm late on 2 September. The stubble was gold in the evening light but by then he was too tired to appreciate it and his sight had faded as his fatigue had grown.

Five days later, in a specially designed white uniform, an impressive figure stood on the cliff top at Cap Gris Nez, flanked by Field Marshal Kesselring and General Loerzer, commander of Air Corps II. Overhead thundered the first formations of the 625 bombers and 648 fighters who, that afternoon, and throughout the coming night, were to open the battle of London. Goering was there to send them off in person. He referred to these huge formations as his "Valhallas". He swelled even more than usual with pride, and when the reports came in next day of London's dockland in flames, it seemed to the *Reichsmarschall* that all that his Luftwaffe had been waiting for was his masterly touch to bring them victory. For once the RAF had failed to bar the bombers' way.

Exactly a week later, the *Reichsmarschall's* white uniform was crumpled and marked with sweat as he read the battle reports for Sunday, 15 September.

It was going to be the great knock-out blow. By 1300 hours that burning blue Sunday afternoon, 400 bombers were airborne and heading for England. On the British side there had been mistakes during the previous weeks, mistakes, chiefly, in interception. Today there was going to be no mistake. The controllers had plenty of time. The radar plots built up unmistakably to show something massive developing across the Channel. The German formations must be headed for London once again. If this was correct, then they had very little choice but to come in on flight paths almost as predictable as those of a commercial airline. Surprise approach was out of the question. The bombers alone had the necessary range to attack the target from a different direction, but the 109s did not and, without the single-engined fighters, the bombers were dead ducks. As it was, the Messerschmitts had only about ten minutes to spare over the target area. Under combat conditions, this was a mighty small margin. Thus the bombers were tied to the fighters and the fighters were tied, both by lack of range and by orders, to the bombers. Under the right conditions it was an ideal situation for the defence. Today, conditions were ideal. The trouble with the Germans was that they didn't really believe there was much defence left. By 1330, when the battle with the first wave of bombers was at its height, 300 Hurricanes and Spitfires were in the air simultaneously. In his underground operations room at Uxbridge Air Vice-Marshal Park was at that moment telling Churchill that there were no fighter reserves left.

Peter's squadron met the first wave of Dorniers just west of Canterbury. People sometimes say that the fighter pilot's war is a gentlemanly affair of chivalrous cut and thrust. On that sunny afternoon of 15 September it was more like a medieval hand-to-hand mêlée with mace and axe. Peter was part of a two-squadron attack that went straight through the Dornier formation at point-blank range. At least one fighter collided with a bomber. Men who bailed out were lucky if they fell clear. Bombers turned for home with crew compartments streaming with blood. A 109 of Dieter Reh's squadron over-heated. On landing at St Omer its wing was found to be streaked with blood and its air-intake partly blocked with a chunk of human flesh.

One hundred and fifty bombers got through to London but their bombing was scattered and ineffective. If only a second wave could have followed immediately, then the Spitfires and Hurricanes would have been caught, out of fuel and ammunition, on the ground. But the German fighters were at full stretch also and they had farther to go for replenishment. The bombers did not return until two hours later and by that time the RAF were ready to meet them again. By the end of that summer's day, for ever after to be celebrated as Battle of Britain Day, 58—not 185 as the British later claimed—German planes were down on British soil or in the Channel, and up to one-quarter of the entire attacking force had been destroyed or damaged. No wonder the *Reichsmarschall*'s special uniform was crumpled and sweaty. The following day he sent for his commanders, including Theo Osterkamp, in charge of the fighters, and told them that once again the German fighter pilots had, through their lack of devotion to duty, turned what should have been triumph to disaster and let victory leak away into defeat. Henceforward, he decreed, if the fighters couldn't protect the bombers, they would have to deliver the bombs themselves.

By the end of the month this was to have serious repercussions on the German fighter force. On Dieter Reh's flight the effect was felt almost immediately. Despite the heavy losses inflicted on both bombers and fighters during the onslaught on London, Dieter's *Schwarm* had come out of the vicious air fighting remarkably well. Pohle had been a great acquisition. His complete professionalism had been just what they needed in the free-hunting role to which they were still assigned.

Though there was little enough free time or energy left between sorties for anything save sleep, they had managed to talk and evolve tactics which served them well against the RAF. The flight, and especially the two *Rotten* consisting of Pohle and Weiss, Reh and Kolbe, fought as a group, covering each other, making openings for each other, and working out ploys which served best in given situations. By common acknowledgement, Dieter's marksmanship was exceptional but then this was something born in him, a coordination of hand and eye learned and perfected with a deer rifle. In the few leisure moments when they weren't lying exhausted outside the dispersal hut, he tried to impart to Weiss and Kolbe, mechanically, what he knew instinctively about deflection shooting. Even Pohle, his ex-teacher, listened. Eventually, at Dieter's suggestion, each member of the flight had his armourer zero his guns to converge with maximum concentration of firepower at what he took to be his own ideal killing range. The armourers had quite sufficient to do to keep the 109s serviced let alone to play around with fancy adjustments to suit individual pilots' whims. But they did it gladly enough. The natural bond of loyalty between ground crew and pilots was particularly strong in Dieter's flight. This was because the fliers themselves, and the flight commander in particular, commanded special loyalty. Dieter never let anyone get away with anything. At the same time, he never asked anyone to do anything he wasn't willing to do himself. He considered every detail that would make them more effective in combat, even down to the types and proportions of ammunition loaded into the belts for the 13 mm machine-guns. They had all found that you could knock large chunks off a Hurricane and that it would still keep flying.

After one unsuccessful hammering Willy Weiss had declared: "The damn things seem to be made of a number of inessential spare parts. Blast half of the fuselage away and they still keep flying." Dieter's answer was to vary the machine-gun loadings with a higher proportion of *Panzerminen*, explosive bullets.

The *Schwarm*'s score mounted. Dieter now had nine kills, Pohle three, Weiss six and Kolbe five, all achieved without serious damage or wounds.

Despite the fact that he flew nearly as many missions as the rest of JG 51, Mölders still found time to visit individual squadrons and whenever possible to fly with them in turn at the head of his HQ flight. He knew all about Dieter's flight and its successes and, though he was careful not to hold them up as something special, he tactfully conveyed their techniques which were, after all, very much his own, to other flights and squadrons. Mölders had marked down Reh and his men as a small unit sufficiently flexible to be used experimentally. On the morning of 18 September, Dieter received the order to report to *Geschwader* HQ: the *Kommodore* wished to see him.

As usual Mölders was immaculate when even his adjutant looked as though he had slept in his uniform. His dark hair was neatly brushed back, moustache carefully trimmed, Knight's Cross worn as formally at the neck of his black leather flying jacket as if he was about to attend an ambassadorial function. He had in fact already flown one mission over England that morning.

Dieter saluted smartly and received an equally smart return of the courtesy.

"How goes it, Reh?"

"Well, *Herr Kommodore*."

"I hear great things of your flight. Is Feldwebel Pohle a help to you? I thought so. That's why I sent him. Sit down, lieutenant. Now, have you heard of Experimental *Gruppe* 210?"

"Fighters that carry bombs?"

"Yes. As you know, they have been very successful. But the 110s have shown themselves too vulnerable."

Dieter nodded. He had heard of the disastrous raid on Croydon a month before in which the leader of the *Gruppe*, Hauptmann Walter Rubensdörfer, had been lost with his entire staff flight of bomb-carrying 110s.

Mölders went on: "OKL believes that we fighter pilots must deliver more of the bombs ourselves . . ."

"But, *Herr Kommodore* . . ."

"The case against using fighters to deliver bomb loads has already been put, I assure you. Forcibly put. Nevertheless it looks as though some of us are going to have to do it."

"But the fighters are having a hard enough time without having to carry a dead weight."

"Agreed."

"A 109 with a bomb-load ceases to be a fighter."

"Dieter," Mölders said quietly. "We know all this. You must leave the protesting to such as myself . . ." The use of the Christian name coupled with the rebuke was a friendly touch.

"Meantime accept that we must obey orders. OKL will probably demand that our fighter-bombers fly as part of the

124

bomber formations. I personally do not accept that this is the best way. I am detaching your flight as experimental *Schwarm* with my HQ squadron. Your 109s will be immediately modified to carry bomb-loads. We're going to have to produce some answers very quickly for Field Marshal Kesselring. There are very few of the original pilots of *Gruppe* 210 left to do any instructing. Anyway, they're going to be busy themselves. Fighter-bomber operations will start very shortly at ordinary squadron level. And Reh . . ."

"Yes, *Herr Kommodore.*"

"What I have told you is confidential. Your flight is simply being detached for special duties here. There's going to be enough bitching in the squadron when the news gets out that we're being turned into bombers."

Weiss and Kolbe received the news of their transfer with mixed feelings. It was undoubtedly a great honour to have been selected for experimental work by "Vati" Mölders himself, but it was a wrench to leave the surviving comrades—and there weren't too many of those with whom they had fought the bitter battle of the last three months. Pohle took it much more resignedly. He had not yet formed close squadron attachments. He was a professional who fought where he was told and Mölders was the greatest professional in the business.

In the event, they weren't to move for three days. The partially stream-lined racks that would hold the single 500 lb bombs they were to carry had not yet arrived from the supply depot of *Gruppe* 210.

At the end of those three days, even Weiss, the most conservative of the four, was quite ready to move on. The vicious and costly battle of 15 September, and the inquest at Goering's HQ the following day, had left deep marks on everyone. It was no secret that Goering had lashed out once again at the fighter pilots, blaming them for the slaughter of the bombers, openly accusing them of cowardice, threatening even to scrap the fighter arm if it couldn't defend the bombers better. "Uncle" Theo Osterkamp, JG 51's old *Kommodore,* now general in charge of fighter operations, had jumped up and lashed back. But the slur remained. None of the details of the row ought to have escaped beyond the walls of the conference carriage on Goering's special train. But the Luftwaffe was so bitter that it was too much to expect that all the staff officers summoned to hear the *Reichsmarschall*'s tirade would keep their mouths shut. The story that Goering had declared that since they couldn't protect the bombers, the fighters would have to deliver the bombs themselves had also leaked out. In the squadron, the news that Dieter's flight was being pulled out to conduct special experiments caused more speculation. Dieter swore his men to silence but this didn't stop the other pilots guessing, and the favourite guess was that the flight was to form a cadre for future bomb-dropping operations. When the bomb racks arrived and the mechanics began to fit them, Dieter could no longer deny that this was to be part of their task.

The tall Bavarian who had beefed at OKL's refusal to rest some of the Battle of Britain squadrons now demanded to know which squadrons in the *Gruppe* were to be converted. "Bad enough for the bastards to blame us for everything," he snarled. "But to turn our fighter planes from race-horses into pack-mules . . . What the hell can they expect of them?"

"We don't know that they're going to convert us."

"You bet the bloody fools are! And the fact that you chaps are going to act as guinea-pigs means that we're going to get the job."

"Mölders didn't say anything like that. Besides, you can bet *your* life that he, above all people, will fight to maintain our proper role."

"You think so? Just tell me, Dieter, what chance you think he or anyone else has against a raving lunatic like old barrel-guts."

On 20 September, the day before the *Schwarm*, complete with its bomb racks, was due to move to HQ squadron, the Luftwaffe's new weapons scored a success. Kesselring sent 22 109s carrying bombs against London. Thinking they were just fighters, the British didn't bother to intercept. Each plane unloaded its bombs into the city from 12,000 feet and then, lightened for flight, became a fighter once again and dived flat-out for home. Encouraged by this, Kesselring immediately sent in a second wave which still left the British wondering where the bombs were coming from. Already the fighter-bombers were being talked about as "Light Kesselrings".

Mölders told his new experimental staff flight about the success as soon as they reported for duty. "Good as the results are they won't last, once the British have tumbled to the trick. Such fighter-bombers can only have limited nuisance value. Soon they're bound to start suffering heavy casualties. The way I see the fighter-bomber being most useful is in a hit-and-run low-level role against specific targets. If we have to take on the task, that's the way I intend to play it. Your job is to get in some intensive practise with the 109. Practise bombs are available, and a bombing range is being set up behind the sand dunes. Flight Sergeant Pohle has flown ground support in Poland. He'll have useful suggestions about aiming and developments of simple bomb sights. Reh, within two days I want your ideas on *Rotte* and *Schwarm* tactics that will get our heavily laden 109s to the target and safely back again."

The *Schwarm* started flying soon after breakfast next morning. With a 500 lb concrete practice bomb slung underneath them, their slender Emils felt like women in labour. They made a dozen runs each during the morning, varying the angle of approach from hedge-hopping in level flight to a screaming *Stuka*-like dive from two thousand feet. By lunchtime, they were all getting reasonably close to the target. Hedge-hopping, the hardest approach of all, was seemingly the most effective. But placing the bomb accurately in a flat-out low-level attack took some doing. Dieter already had ideas about an elementary aiming device using a combination of known air speed and appearance of the ground target in the reflector sight.

The vapour trails still wove in the clear summer sky above Rife Farm. But, as September ended, the occupants no longer looked up towards the fighter battle with such apprehension. In the flat fields, the harvest was long in. The RAF had reaped its harvest, too, reaped where the Luftwaffe had sown. Everyone knew that a respite, if not a victory, had been won. The German air force lurched in to the attack with large bomber formations twice more before the end of the month but now it was like an out-pointed heavyweight, leaden on his feet, who launches blows by reflex but without skill, without fighting heart or cunning. Though the British weren't to know it, the Luftwaffe had lost fighting heart and no one felt more bruised than the fighter squadrons who had been unjustly blamed for the disaster.

Tom Roland was exultant. "The little man with a moustache won't come now autumn's on the way," he said, almost with regret that the shotgun on the back seat of his car was unlikely to be used this season in defence of his Sussex acres. "He's lost his chance to invade us. Your brother and his pals have seen to that." He couldn't resist adding: "Those Jerry fighter pilots may be all right at shooting up defenceless small boats . . ."

Kate turned away. She didn't intend to let Tom get a rise

127

out of her. Even more, she did not want him to discover that a subtle change was taking place in her feelings towards Dieter Reh. The air battle had played its part in this change, of course. In the last few weeks it had been impossible not to share the general hatred that England felt for the Luftwaffe. But there was more to it than that. The chasm between England and Germany was no longer bridgeable. It was as wide as death itself. It was only possible to think of her German lover as if he was cut off by death. Perhaps this was even the literal truth. By thinking that way she could at least preserve her memory of him. Yet, though she could change thus far, she was unable to move one step towards the hatred, contempt even, which her countrymen, and Tom in particular, felt for the enemy both collectively and individually.

Tom had another powerful reason to feel joy as September closed and the air battle settled down to its final grim phase—the night bombing of the capital—for Michael was fast regaining strength, his sight returning to normal. Michael owed Kate a great deal for his recovery after Mrs Bristow had gone back to Axeham. When she wasn't busy about the farm, and often when she was, Kate nursed him, moved his chair into the still hot September sun, helped him to walk and, when petrol allowed, took him to the sea front. Kate liked Michael, his quiet humour and his courage. She was aware that Tom watched her, hoping that something would spring up between them. For her part, Kate was aware of no current flowing other than friendship. Dieter might be dead in thought, or, terribly, in fact, but either way, that part of her seemed to have died with him.

The last big pitched battle of the month, that of 30 September, brought dreadful news: Peter had been shot down over Kent. Caught by two yellow-nosed 109s, his Spitfire had fallen five thousand feet before he had managed to break free. The thing a pilot most feared had happened: he had burned. Even so, he had been lucky, for the flames had contented themselves with only one side of his body. Left leg, hand and left side of face had all suffered. Returning from a trip with Michael to Bognor she had rushed into the farm kitchen to tell Tom that Michael had at last managed to walk the length of the front without sticks. She had anticipated Tom's reaction of joy. Instead, she saw sorrow on his face. The squadron had just telephoned: Peter was conscious and had been moved to a hospital at East Grinstead where they treated the most serious burns.

The golden September weather tailed away. October came in with increasingly bad flying conditions for the Luftwaffe. Few of the bomber crews had the blind-flying experience to cope with the banks of cloud that often blocked their way to London. Now the Luftwaffe was paying dearly for all those Ju 52 transports squandered in the lightning campaigns against Holland and Norway. Some of the crews of those transports had been drawn from blind-flying schools and this even included the instructors. Many of these key men had not returned. Without the essential navigational training, bomber formations became broken up by cloud, emerging as a straggling string impossible for the German fighters to protect. When they flew round the cloud banks, then they often missed joining up with their fighter escort altogether and became even easier meat. The Luftwaffe's bomber force turned almost exclusively to night bombing and this shifted the load, as the tall Bavarian lieutenant had gloomily predicted, on to the fighter *Geschwader*. Not even Mölders and Galland were able to block the *Reichsmarschall*'s edict. One-third of the fighters on the Channel coast were henceforward to carry and deliver bombs. Nothing could have hit the German fighter pilots harder. It was to them the ultimate degradation.

Within four days of reporting to HQ squadron Dieter found himself once more in the *Kommodore*'s office. After Dieter had saluted, Mölders waved him to a chair.

"I hear your chaps are getting pretty close to the target now. But what I really want to know is what ideas you're developing for protection of the fighter actually carrying the bomb."

Dieter said: "You must know the answers already, *Herr Kommodore*, for you yourself invented the *Rotte*."

"Don't tell me that's your only recommendation, that we fly in pairs?"

"Not quite. We believe that in bad visibility it's quite possible for a single fighter-bomber to come in low over the wavetops, attack a target just inland before it is detected and then escape easily when it becomes a fully effective fighter once more without its bomb load. Carrying a bomb externally has appalling effects on an Emil's flying ability. Even a Hurricane can easily outclass us when we're what we call pregnant."

"And supposing we have to fly twenty or thirty miles inland to get rid of the bomb?"

"Then we have only a few alternatives. The first depends on bad weather once again. Approach the target above cloud and dive through it, though finding the target will require some very accurate flying which may be beyond most pilots' abilities. The second is simply to escort on the *Rotte* principle. The second fighter will not, of course, carry a bomb. It will operate in its proper role. Should the *Rotte* be intercepted, then we strongly suggest that the bomb is dropped immediately."

"Anywhere?"

"Exactly, *Herr Kommodore*. The only value these pinprick attacks can possibly have is to annoy the enemy and keep him on his toes, so what does it matter where the bomb falls? The main thing is to conserve our fighter force for the day when it's needed."

"And when do you think that will be, Reh?"

"When the British find time to hit back at us."

Mölders' usually serious face relaxed into a smile. "Well done. I think your answers are very much to the point. Now is the time to tell you that I have orders that one-third of all our 109s are to be equipped for bomb-carrying immediately. When I have had time to talk over your suggestions, we'll have a conference for flight and squadron commanders and I may want you to give your views then. Meantime, forget those concrete bombs. Get the armourers to fit you with some real ones. When the weather's right we'll let you try out some of your theories over the water."

The surgeon was hopeful about Peter. The face, he said, would be repaired; though he couldn't guarantee it would be as handsome as formerly, he could predict that the girls wouldn't actually run from it. To Kate it seemed a callous way of putting things, especially as it was said in her brother's presence. But it seemed that the great man knew what he was doing. Though she could not see much of Peter's face beneath the bandages, she knew that the eyes were trying to smile. When they were left alone he wrote on a pad with his undamaged right hand: "Ask him when I'll be able to fly again." She nodded, noting that he hadn't used the word "whether".

The visit was a short one, for Peter had to nurse his strength, and he was unable to talk because of the bandages round his face. She smiled, squeezed his hand and promised that she would let their mother know that he was safe. As she left the room Peter waved the paper with the message at her.

The surgeon was waiting in his office. "You're going to ask how he's going to be," he began. "And he's already told you to ask me when he'll be able to fly again . . . They all do," he added almost sadly. "As if they hadn't had enough. Well, young lady, you're far too sensible to be tactful with. Your brother's taken a pasting. I'll reassure you about one thing. By a miracle, his left eye has escaped damage. With luck we can do quite a good restoration job on him. But as to flying, I'm not sure. How can I be? Plastic surgery's a tricky job. It's a question of how well his controls will answer when we've done the needle-and-thread work. All I can tell you at the moment is that we've patched up far worse wrecks than him and got them back into the air. Though, if it were me," he added, "and I'd done what these young men have done, I'd never want to leave the ground again. By the way, it may cheer you up to know he's been put forward for a DFC . . ."

That night, Kate telephoned her mother and broke the news, making it sound as reassuring as possible. Mrs Bristow's reactions were predictable. "Thank God he's out of it. I'll come up by the first train in the morning."

Kate said gently: "The surgeon doesn't want us to see him again, until after his first operation."

"But I want to be near, dear. I'm so far away in Axeham."

"Then you'd better come to Rife Farm, mother. Tom won't mind a bit. Then we can go over to visit Peter together when the time comes."

By mid-October the role of the special *Stabs-schwarm* had become established. Its tasks began to expand beyond *Geschwader* experiments with "Jabo"—fighter-bomber—technique. A crack aerial marksman himself, the *Kommodore* recognised the same talents in Dieter Reh. He saw, too, that Dieter had managed to communicate some of his own skills to his flying companions. Within the *Schwarm* itself, his adjustments in zeroing guns to each pilot's optimum range, his experiments with different loadings of ammunition, had borne fruit. During the last fighter battles of September and the weary slogging matches with the RAF that accompanied the start of the fighter-bomber offensive, Reh and Kolbe, Pohle and Weiss had between them added ten more victories, without serious damage to their own aircraft. The benefit of the techniques they developed had begun to have a useful effect within the squadrons themselves. During mid-October, Mölders directed them to tour the squadrons, instructing on fighter-bomber tactics and showing by example that it was possible to put the beloved Emil to *Jabo* use without completely compromising oneself as a fighter pilot. The *Kommodore* had chosen his men well. All four were popular pilots. Dieter, especially, had the diplomatist's touch. He never tried to teach more experienced officers or NCOs to suck eggs. The *Stabs-schwarm* was there on the *Kommodore*'s instructions to be helpful rather than to play the part of headquarters' men who had come to show how it should be done. The hardest part was selling the hated use of the 109 as a light bomber. JG 51 was an elite unit, nevertheless it was impossible not to notice how morale had suffered during the battle against Britain. Strain and losses had played their part, but this was something that the squadrons could have coped with. The thing that had really shaken the individual pilots was that they had given of their very best against an implacable enemy only to be blamed for their High Command's failures. Talk everywhere was surprisingly open about the extent of these failures. Though the pilots had complete faith in the Emil, they had little good to say about the rest of the Luftwaffe's equipment. Everyone knew that the *Stuka* had proved a wash-out and that the twin-engined Zerstörer, the 110, was useless against the single-engined fighter opposition. Though they had a great admiration for the bomber crews they were said to have let down, most of the 109 pilots had no time for the bombers themselves. Too lightly armed and armoured, too slow, these were the verdicts on the Dorniers and Heinkels. Only the Ju 88 emerged in the fighter boys' estimation as earning anything like full marks. And though no one would say a bad word against the beloved Emil, it was widely believed that the new marks of Spitfire would shortly put their mounts at a disadvantage if a better, faster Messerschmitt 109 didn't come off the assembly lines at Augsburg soon.

It was, of course, the right of the pilots to bitch. They were no different in this respect from their opposite numbers across the Channel, except that at Biggin and Kenley, Hornchurch and Eastchurch, no one felt that he had been let down by his leaders.

Dieter and his group joined in these arguments heatedly. Coming from HQ their word was likely to be taken for the *Kommodore*'s official view. Dieter was always careful to make it clear that as far as strategy was concerned they had no official view or official information on which to base a view. They were simply there to help get on with the war. All the same, he was repeatedly asked: "But what does Mölders think the RAF will do now?" To which he replied: "The *Kommodore* hasn't let me into the secret yet but I'll tell you what *I* think. As soon as they get their breath back, they'll be coming over to see us and, when they do, the flying-boot will be on the other foot. The Tommies will discover what it's like to fight over unfriendly territory and to have a Channel between you and home when you've got the worst of a dogfight. Mark my words, they're not going to find it any easier than we did."

Meanwhile there was the bombing to get on with. With one in three planes modified to carry a bomb there was plenty of room to employ Dieter's now approved technique of *Rotte* escort, using days of bad visibility for low level, hit-and-run attacks on coastal targets. The *Stabs-schwarm* made a point of flying with squadron pilots under instruction, sometimes carrying the bomb themselves, sometimes flying the fighter escort.

In mid-October, the word came from East Grinstead that Peter was through the first operation on his hand and face—the leg would be tackled later—and that he could have visitors. The day was one of low cloud and intermittent, scudding rain. Despite this Kate had allowed her mother to talk her into taking the coast road; they would drive along to Littlehampton and then on to Brighton because, as Mrs Bristow said, "The sea air will do us so much good, dear." Some spare petrol coupons had come their way via a farmer friend, and Kate agreed. After Brighton, they would cut inland to Lewes and then north to East Grinstead. The day might clear yet, and it would be a nice run.

They left Rife Farm at 10 a.m., allowing themselves an hour to Brighton where they planned to have coffee at a shop on the front that Mrs Bristow remembered.

At about the time they were entering Hove, the engines of eight 109s were being run up at St Omer. The fighters were grouped in four separate *Rotten*. One plane in each, the one flown by a pilot of the resident squadron, carried a 500 lb bomb. The escorting aircraft wore the insignia of the HQ squadron. Today Dieter had decided that he and his three colleagues would fly in the escort role. The broken weather was perfect for *Jabo* operations. Orders were elastic. Recently, since fighter-bomber raids had begun in earnest, the Tommies had moved additional light flak guns, mostly Bofors, on to the coast. Once in the air, the four groups would split up, Dieter and the lieutenant he escorted heading for Hastings, Pohle and a flight sergeant for Eastbourne, Weiss and a first lieutenant for Littlehampton and "Shoehorn" Kolbe, paired with a second flight sergeant, for Seaford.

The eight planes hammered across the Channel at sea level. Five miles off the coast Kolbe ordered his companion, a quarter of a mile ahead, to pull up into the low cloud at eight hundred feet. The cloud was far more continuous than either of them had expected. From time to time they glimpsed grey waves beneath and once, by a miracle, they spotted each other. Kolbe, whose job it was to navigate the *Rotte,* had been concentrating so hard on keeping in touch with his companion that he had wandered off course. Now the coast was coming up fast. A decision was essential. Seaford must be to port. "Turn left down the coast. Right down on the wavetops now. Hit the first gun position you see." Five hundred yards ahead, the grey-green 109 banked to comply. They were whipping the white crests with their slipstream. Almost at once a large town to starboard. Seaford! They'd made it. Now to find a target, unload and away. Tracer coming up from port, out to sea. *Jesu!* A pier. Flak guns on the end of a pier. The place had two piers! This wasn't Seaford.

Mrs Bristow had just ordered scones when the two planes blasted in from the sea. She heard the popping of light ack-ack and looked inquisitively out of the window. Kate, who had gone out to park the car, noticed men running to the sand-bagged gun position on the esplanade. She saw the bomb leave the plane and come hurtling in almost horizontal flight over the heads of the running gunners. It was incredible how slowly it all happened. Fascinated, she followed the parabola of the bomb. It hit the tarmac behind her, bounced, literally bounced like a stone playing ducks-and-drakes. It carried on in mid-air, minus its fins, turning over and over now like a skittle. The bus coming round the corner caught the bomb full in the upper deck and disappeared in a sheet of flame.

The 109 that had released the bomb was screaming away out to sea in a climbing turn, reaching the grey, torn veil of cloud before tracers from the end of the pier could reach it.

Closing fast from behind, Kolbe saw with horror what the bomb had done. He had just time to depress his nose and fire a quick burst of cannon and machine-gun at the Bofors emplacement. Most of the burst hit the sandbags. One 20 mm cannon shell struck the No 4 of the gun, the loader, squarely in the chest, taking the lower half of his head away. The last shell of the entire burst, fired high as Kolbe pulled out over the shambles of the bus, struck the windscreen of Kate's car. A two-inch sliver of glass from the driving mirror passed straight through one cheek and out of the other just below the right eye. Such was the shambles around the remains of the bus that it was some time before her mother found her, by the car, unconscious in a puddle of blood.

Christmas was cold on the Channel coast of France. Dieter, along with all the other fighter pilots at St Omer, had hoped for leave. It was well-known that both Galland and Mölders had requested that their *Geschwader* be withdrawn from the front on which they had fought so long and exhaustingly for rest and recuperation both of men and machines. So far, nothing had happened. On Christmas Eve, they received compensation. The Führer himself unexpectedly arrived at Abbeville and made a speech to selected officers from the various squadrons. It was a great honour to have been picked to attend. Listening to him, Dieter felt again the magic that he had first experienced in the Berlin Sportspalast. The Führer had no doubts about victory. In fact, the war was as good as won. Germany had beaten one enemy after another. The danger of a Soviet attack had been nullified by the non-aggression pact. There was no need to worry about England against whom the Luftwaffe had fought so heroically. U-boat production was being steadily increased. Thousands of new aircraft would shortly pour off the production lines. It was only a question of time before England's knees sagged beneath her.

When the Führer had finished speaking Dieter felt that incandescent patriotic glow that he had constantly experienced in his basic training days, a flame which he imagined had been stamped out by the weeks of nerve-straining fighting whose only reward had been recrimination, accusation even, from High Command. Now he saw that it was Goering who was the author of the distrust and bitterness within the fighter squadrons. The Führer's personal armour was as bright and untarnished as ever. With such a leader Germany must triumph.

When they had fervently returned the Führer's salute, they walked out into the frosty air towards the officers' mess. Dieter thought: "It's Christmas and it's going to snow tomorrow." Everything seemed glowing and wonderful again after the Führer's words. Only one thing could have made it more so—to be going home to Hamelin to see Liese Schumacher. He had thought a great deal about her lately. Throughout the past months they had corresponded more and more regularly. That other once painful tug at the heart over there in the starry darkness towards England had become dulled, as impersonal now as the green, hedge-rowed landscape he had fought

135

over all those weeks. Gone, something wonderful but something light-years away and now as far and cold as the frosty stars.

The door of the former French Officer's mess laid a rectangle of light briefly across the night and a mess servant snapped it shut as an NCO barked a command. The Tommies had taken up regular scattered night raiding. It never did much damage but tonight a few stray bombs from a Wellington on Abbeville would be most unwelcome. But no alert had gone and the sky was innocent of the bombers' drone. Perhaps the RAF would rather celebrate Christmas Eve quietly in its own way, too. Dieter thought of Peter Bristow for the first time for weeks and wondered whether he was still alive and if so what he was doing. He was aware that he was doing this in order to probe his reactions: he barely felt a twinge.

There was a further surprise in store: the officers who attended the speech had been told to report to the mess afterwards to drink the Führer's health. Inside the anteroom, mess servants hovered over a table laden with glasses of champagne but the drinks were not immediately offered. The reason was quickly apparent. Within a few seconds, Galland, followed by Mölders, came in to the mess and ordered quietly: "At attention, gentlemen." Almost at once, the Führer entered, followed by his entourage. Dieter felt his heart knocking more than it had ever done in air combat. The Führer passed rapidly among the pilots, Galland or Mölders introducing them by name and describing briefly their roles and their totals of aerial victories. When Dieter's turn came Mölders mentioned that Leutnant Reh and his *Schwarm* were assigned to tactical and weapons development and to fighter-bombing in particular.

The Führer's hypnotic eyes seemed to burn into Dieter's brain. Hitler turned to Mölders and said: "It is of vital importance to harass the enemy by these means. The fighter-bomber has a crucial part to play."

The champagne was at last handed round. Galland and Mölders jointly proposed the Führer's health coupled with the victory of the Greater German Reich. Hitler did not take a drink himself but bowed stiffly and marched out to the waiting cortege of Mercedes, followed by his staff officers.

For the RAF there was no question of a Christmas truce, not while Churchill was in charge. Duty flights of the Headquarters *Staffel* at St Omer were twice scrambled to intercept Spitfire sweeps. On the second occasion Dieter and Willy Weiss tried to catch a photo-reconnaissance Spitfire that came down the coast at 25,000 feet and, despite the fact that the 109 was a better aircraft at high altitudes, were left standing. Willy Weiss blamed the empty bomb racks on their Emils. How could they be expected to make interceptions with exposed ironmongery dangling beneath their bellies, causing the most hideous drag?

Dieter, remembering the Führer's words about the vital need for fighter-bombers, said: "We'd have had our work cut out to catch him anyway. Those PRU Spitfires are stripped of almost everything except engines."

"It's not the proper way to use an Emil."

For the mild-mannered Willy to be so critical was symptomatic of the general feeling. Perhaps if he had heard the Führer speak last night . . . The truth was that they were all over-extended. To have to fly on a fruitless mission on Christmas Day had been just too much. They needed leave badly.

Leave was coming at last. As usual, rumour preceded the event and for once rumour did not measure up to reality. The Channel coast squadrons were to be withdrawn to home bases in western Germany. Once there, the *Reichsmarschall* had personally decided the pilots were to be sent on a free ski-ing leave to the Arlberg in Austria. They drew lots. Dieter was in the first batch to go. A week at home in Hamelin and then a week in the Austrian Alps.

1941

He was once again surprised how little Hamelin had been changed by the war. People still seemed to be living as though the life and death struggle over Britain had never taken place. But this did not apply to the Reh household. When he arrived, Dieter found his father away in Hamburg supervising the completion of the new factory. His mother was out, too, putting in a full-time day at the Hamelin factory. He felt a sense of depression and anti-climax at discovering the house empty and then, unexpectedly, there was a sound from his brother's bedroom. He bounded up the gleaming wooden stairs, calling Emma, believing it was their old servant. Instead he ran full tilt into his young brother Jacob—Jacob in a *Fähnrich's* uniform.

"They didn't tell me you were home."

"They didn't tell *me* about you, Dieter."

They wrapped their arms around each other.

Dieter held his young brother away from him. "The future ace. What are you flying?"

"Taifuns, 108s, our class is just about to graduate to the real thing. And you? How many victories do you have now?"

"Nine, and I don't see how I'm going to get any more. Mölders has put our flight on to experimental work."

Jacob was duly impressed. "Mölders! You mean you fly with him? Do you think you'll be able to find me a place in your squadron?"

"Learn to fly and to stay *alive* first. The RAF doesn't give second chances. Take your training seriously. The war will last long enough for fire-eaters like you." Dieter was amused to hear himself talking like one of the instructors at Werneuchen.

He hoped to hear Liese Schumacher's voice when he phoned his mother at the Hamelin factory. Instead he got a motherly welcome from Gertrud, his father's old secretary. Frau Reh, she said, was in a production meeting. He wanted to ask about Liese but was afraid of appearing too obvious. Gertrud had no such inhibitions. "Fraulein Schumacher has gone to the Hamburg plant with your father." He wanted to ask when she would be back, but instead asked whether they had started the building work there yet. Gertrud laughed. "You boys at the front haven't been doing all the work, you know. We get on with things at home in the Reich these days. Started? The factory is nearly finished." He heard his mother's voice in the background and then she was at the phone.

"Dieter. How wonderful to have you home, *Liebling*."

He was glad that only old Gertrud was in the office. *"Liebling"* was a little embarrassing for a fighter pilot. Just the same, as always, he glowed in response to his mother's warmth. He had always had respect for his father, but his mother he adored. Beneath her veneer of brisk efficiency were deep stores of affection. She rushed on in an unaccustomed flow of words. Had he seen Jacob? How lovely it was to have both her airmen sons home at once. They would have a special celebration dinner together that night. What a pity father could not be there!

"When is he due back from Hamburg, mother?"

"In three days' time."

"Perhaps I should go and see him there tomorrow."

Then one of those quick intuitions for which he loved his mother: "That would be very nice, Dieter, but Fraulein Schumacher is coming back tomorrow with some documents. I'm sure your father will understand if you stay in Hamelin till his return."

Meanwhile Hamelin had several welcome surprises for Dieter. Gerhard Stecke had been sent on leave while his Zerstörer squadron was being re-equipped for special duties. Even better, Heine Müller was at a basic training centre for bomber pilots nearby. The four young men met in the *Bier Keller* they had patronised in their gliding days with the *HJ*.

The proprietor greeted them expansively and declared that the first two rounds should be on the house. He introduced them proudly to his other customers. "Four young eagles with not a feather out of place. They say that loud-mouth Churchill says the RAF will mount a nonstop offensive. 'Nonsense offensive' is what the radio calls it, and for once the radio is absolutely right."

Dieter looked at Gerhard Stecke, remembering the shocked state in which he had last seen that good-looking face after the crash-landing at St Omer. Stecke was giving nothing of his feelings away. He said smilingly: "Nonsense offensive? Yes, I should think that's about it."

"You Luftwaffe boys certainly showed those Britishers something. Of course, I'm not saying they can't fight."

"Well, that's something," Dieter muttered to his brother.

Stecke heard him. When the proprietor had gone back for more *Steins* of beer, he said with a hint of reproach: "Dieter, forgive my saying so, but I feel the civilian public must be given every ground for confidence. Radio propaganda is skilfully designed to get the very best results from those at home."

Dieter laughed. "At least you and I know, Gerhard, that when the British do hit back we shan't dismiss the front end of a Spitfire as sheer nonsense. You, more than any of the rest of us, have cause to know that! Come on, let's drink up and forget the civilians. If the 'nonsense offensive' really does get going, they'll be able to judge for themselves whether Dr Goebbels has the right slant on it. RAF night bombing is building up quite a bit already."

The tension eased slowly as the evening wore on. Without Stecke, the two Rehs and Heine Müller would soon have relaxed. The quiet-spoken Müller was full of self-deprecating stories about his training as a bomber pilot. He was, he claimed, the only pilot on the course to have bombed his own airfield—with a dummy practice bomb that had stuck in the release gear and fallen out into the commandant's vegetable garden as he came in to land. As a result the commandant had sent for him to ask whether he would rather be posted to Wellingtons or Hampdens. He did not expect to be operational for another three months at least and then Berlin had better look out. Slightly overawed by his brother and Stecke, Jacob did not talk much but what he did say made it clear that he was far advanced in fighter pilot training and as keen as mustard. Dieter was reassured to discover that the training course was skimping nothing. It was still aimed at producing the most accomplished *Jagdflieger* in the world.

After Müller had caught the last bus back to camp, Stecke, now considerably mellowed, returned to the Reh house where the three young men sat drinking schnapps into the early hours. They hadn't been able to talk freely in the Keller but now Dieter asked: "What's this special job you're being trained for?"

"Night-fighters, but night-fighters with a difference. You've heard of Major-General Jozef Kammhuber?"

"Of course, even we day birds know about the Kammhuber line." Dieter turned to Jacob. "It's a belt of searchlights right

140

across Germany's front doorstep with a night-fighter assigned to a set zone all along the line."

Stecke said: "Yes, the *Himmelbett* system. 'Heavenly beds,' each bed occupied by a night-fighter. But that's only part of it. Kammhuber has far more adventurous ideas than that. Ever heard of intruder operations? That's what we're being trained for." He looked round. "I suppose I'm free to tell you? I mean security . . ."

"Oh, for God's sake, Gerhard," Dieter said impatiently. "We're all in the same air force."

"Very well then. We're being trained on specially modified Ju 88s and Do 17s. The Ju 88 C6 I'm flying has a solid nose in place of a bomb-aimer's perspex panel. Instead of bombs we carry forward armament of three 20 mm cannon and three MG 17 machine-guns. We have a crew of three, not four. Our sort of night-fighting is to be offensive. We operate over English bomber bases, joining their returning bomber streams as they circle to land and then shooting them down on their own airfields."

The Rehs were duly impressed with General Kammhuber's imaginative stroke.

"And that isn't all," Stecke continued. "Soon the home-based fighters in their *Himmelbett* defence zones won't have to rely on searchlights to find their targets for them. Each *Himmelbett* will have its own DeeTee system, similar to the British radar but more highly developed, for guiding night-fighters on to their targets."

He looked round triumphantly, almost as if he had invented the whole thing himself. "Of course, I tell you all this in confidence."

"Of course."

When at last Stecke left Dieter yawned and said, "I never realised what a pompous ass Gerhard had become."

"But those night-fighters have a great future ahead of them just the same."

"You stick to day-fighting. There's quite enough to cope with without having to learn to shoot in the dark."

He telephoned next day as soon as he judged Liese had had time to get off the Hamburg train and settle down in her office. His excuse was that he wished to speak to his mother, and the chance was, of course, that old Gertrud would answer him. If so he would have to think of some other excuse to telephone again later. He could simply have asked for Fräulein Schumacher, but this seemed to look too eager.

Liese answered. "Hello, Dieter. I'd been hoping you'd call. How long are you home for?"

She was so open and straightforward compared with his own devious shyness. Strange that he had never felt shy with Kate, but that had been one of those blinding, love-at-first-sight affairs, so spontaneous and inevitable that neither had time nor inclination to think or hold back. Why was it different with Liese? He had to admit to himself that he was slightly intimidated by her. She was so cool, so matter-of-fact, so very much in control of her own life.

"I shall be in Hamelin for four or five days and then we've all been given a free week's ski-ing leave."

"Marvellous! You certainly deserve it. You've had an awful time." She was the first civilian he had met who seemed to appreciate that fact.

There was silence.

"How's the factory?" he asked.

"Going up fast, very fast." Was there a note in her voice that suggested criticism or perhaps something stronger? Disapproval?

"Liese, I was wondering if you'd have dinner with me?"

"Of course I will. But nowhere expensive."

"Why not? I've got plenty of pay saved up. We haven't exactly been living a wild life down there on the Channel coast."

"I certainly shouldn't blame you if you had."

"Let's go to Gustav's."

"It'll cost you a fortune."

"Tonight, Liese, only vintage champagne. We'll really celebrate."

She kept him waiting half an hour in the bar at Gustav's so that he had plenty of time to survey the scene. Apart from the sprinkling of uniforms there might not have been a war in progress. The women were smart and excellently dressed, especially those with serving officers, for wives and families of service men received generous special allowances. Some of the women looked almost too prosperous. Liese, he saw at once, struck just the right note. She wore a simple black dress with a gold chain at the waist and gold clasp at the throat. Several heads turned to acknowledge her entrance but she didn't appear to notice. She was sure of herself, or perhaps genuinely unselfconscious. She came up to him smiling. He clicked his heels correctly, bowed and kissed her hand.

"You're very *gallant, Leutnant,*" she said, "but very formal." She kissed him lightly on the cheek. "Come, let's eat. I'm starving. Never mind the usual ritual of cocktails. They're so expensive, they ought to be banned in wartime."

"We can drink at our table," he said. "I promised you vintage champagne."

"Nothing of the sort. We'll have a reasonable bottle of hock."

"Really, Liese, you're so practical."

The evening at Gustav's was a success. Dieter soon lost his shyness. He had a good sense of rhythm, a fighter pilot's feeling for curves and turns you could practically see as solid shapes. At first when they danced, he felt rather as he had during the early days at Werneuchen, frozen at the controls. But with Liese it was impossible to be inhibited for long. She moved as naturally as she breathed, body to body, all the way down. Yet he could swear there was nothing deliberately provocative or teasing about this. She liked dancing and this was the way to move as one person, to get maximum enjoyment from the rhythm. Dancing with Liese, he found himself making steps and turns he never believed himself capable of. It was like flying a 109—with added benefits. She used little perfume, yet her crisp black hair smelt as sweet as flowers. He had been a long time on the Channel coast! The occasional thrust of her pelvis as they turned together, the soft pressure of her little-apple breasts . . . It would have been unreasonable if he had not had hopes that they would end the evening in even closer contact back at her flat. Much as he wished to, he was afraid even to hint at this proposition. For her part she gave no indication that such an ending was part of her plan for the evening.

Just after midnight he took her home in a taxi. They kissed good night outside. He arranged to call her next day and that was that.

Instead, she rang him next morning. His father had sent back a whole pile of work that she would have to tackle when her normal working day was over. It would take her at least two hours and by then she would be too tired to be much company. She hoped he would understand.

Dieter said: "Let me take you out to dinner afterwards."

"Please, no. All I shall want is to make myself a simple meal at home."

He couldn't bear the thought of not seeing her when time was so short. In a few more days, he'd be off to the mountains ski-ing, and then back to flying duties. Desperately he said: "I have an idea. I'll cook you supper at your flat so that it's ready when you come home."

"You? Cook?"

"Of course. I'm very good at it. Then we can talk while you eat and afterwards you can throw me out when you're tired."

He heard her laugh. "Very well, *Leutnant*."

She came home about nine, looking worn out, kicked her shoes off and threw herself down on the bed. From the tiny pantry Dieter tried not to look too obviously at her long, fine legs over one of which the skirt had risen, showing her stocking top. She could not see him looking, but, after a moment, she noticed that her skirt had ridden up and pulled it down. Once again, he was sure that the gesture was not deliberately provocative.

"Your cooking smells delicious."

"Cheese soufflé. It's all I know how to do. And a bottle of *Liebfraumilch*."

"Lovely. I'm starving."

They sat on the bed and ate.

"Dieter."

"Yes."

"What do you think of the war?"

"It's going very well."

"But do you think it is *right?*"

"I suppose no wars are right, but we were forced into taking action against the Polish massacres. After that, everything else followed. Once a war starts, there's no good being half-hearted. If one is, one loses. War has to be total."

"Even against civilians?"

"The British were the first to bomb a city deliberately, so presumably they think so. Now, like everything else, the process can't be stopped."

"Surely there must be limits, Dieter? Don't you set yourself personal standards as a fighter pilot, for instance?"

"Yes, we all do. They say that Goering asked Adolf Galland what he'd think of an order to kill enemy airmen parachuting to safety over England, and Galland told him he'd refuse to obey an order to commit murder."

"Yet the English pilot could easily get into another machine next day and kill *you*. Isn't that illogical?"

"Yes, I suppose so. Perhaps we fighter pilots are a little old-fashioned in some ways."

"Supposing you received an order to attack civilian targets?"

"We wouldn't receive such an order. Our job is to destroy the enemy air force. We're hunters."

"But you now carry bombs. I know because our factory has received a sub-contract to make bomb racks for the 109. Your bombs can't always be aimed at military targets, surely."

"Liese, why do you concern yourself with such matters?"

"Because it's important for me to know how *you* think about them."

"All we fighter pilots have time to think about is how to stay alive. But I'll tell you this: Mölders has strong views about such things. Early in the battle against Britain one of our best pilots, Leutnant Joppien, shot up a train with cannon fire. Mölders nearly had him court-martialed. In my own experimental flight, one of the pilots under fighter-bomber instruction unintentionally dropped a bomb meant for an English flak gun on to a double-decker bus. Mölders had him grounded until he was satisfied that it was an accident. As far as possible we try to fight a clean war. Now, Liese, I'm on leave so can we please talk of something else?"

"I'm sorry, Dieter. Forgive me. Make me a cup of coffee, and then I must get some sleep."

"May I kiss you, Liese, please?"

She smiled at him. "When you go you may. I make it a point of never promising what I'm not prepared to give."

"May I see you tomorrow night?"

"I'd like that very much. I know a good cheap restaurant with Austrian food."

*

When Herr Reh returned from Hamburg next day, Dieter immediately saw several changes in his father. He wore a party member's badge, for one thing. He had always been inclined to pomposity, but now he had developed a curt, almost military manner as well. Perhaps, thought Dieter, this was simply the result of business pressures. He greeted his son with a Nazi salute which may have been done largely for the benefit of the foreman and works' manager who were in the outer office at the time. In reply, Dieter put his arms round his father's shoulders and embraced him.

Herr Reh turned to his work people proudly. "Here's the reason why we must all work harder, make greater sacrifices if necessary to give the young men who are fighting for us the finest aircraft our skill and labour can provide." Dieter almost expected his father to end this speech with *"Heil Hitler."* It was, in fact, a fair imitation of the Führer's style!

145

His father was speaking again, addressing the roomful of colleagues almost more than Dieter.

"How many aerial victories do you have, my son?"

"Nine, father."

"And do you not find our aircraft superior to the RAF's?"

"The Spitfire is a fine aeroplane, too."

"Ah, but our pilots are better trained."

Dieter had the front-line man's inherent dislike of propaganda. Cautiously he said: "The British were running short of fighter pilots by the end of *Adlerangriff* but now they will train and build up again. We mustn't expect anything to be too easy."

Dieter sensed that this was not what his father wanted to hear. Herr Reh dismissed his foreman with a wave of the hand, a gesture uncharacteristic of the man-to-man relationships his father had always enjoyed with his workmen. He signalled Dieter to follow him into his private office, and when the door had shut, said coldly, "You must realise, Dieter, it is absolutely essential always to give the most positive picture to our civilian workers."

"I only spoke the literal truth. The Spitfire is a remarkable aircraft and it's flown by pilots who really know their job."

"In war, the literal truth is not always the best medicine for the people."

"I wasn't aware, father, that the German people were ill."

"Ill! Of course, they're not ill. How could they be, when they've been fed on victory after victory? But this doesn't mean that doubts should be put in their minds."

"But you, father, do you believe the Luftwaffe hasn't put a foot wrong? In its choice of machines, for instance? You must be very close to things through your friendship with Ernst Udet. What does he say about the way we fighter pilots have been blamed for everything, when it's really the design of the bombers and the battle tactics that have been at fault? Tell me that, father?"

"You're naturally tired and overstrained, Dieter. The week's ski-ing leave given by the *Reichsmarschall* himself will soon set you up. And when you return I should like you to do something for me, or rather, not for me but for Germany."

"What's that, father?"

"I should like you to tell all my workers about our victories in the air, with especial reference to the Bf 109 we help to make here in Hamelin and the Ju 88 we shall shortly be working on in Hamburg. You should see the way that Hamburg factory has gone up . . ."

146

"If you'd like me to, father. I can't say I'm very keen on lecturing . . ."

"It would work wonders for production. And it would be good for Reh Fabrik. A new idea to get the men who fly the planes to talk to the men who build them."

Dieter laughed. "You'll find that most of us would rather face a *Geschwader* of Spitfires."

"I'm sure you'll say all the correct things."

"Be sure, father, I won't say the wrong ones—but you mustn't expect me to monkey with the truth. No one should think that it's a bed of roses up there."

Liese was an hour late at the restaurant that evening.

"Dieter, I'm so sorry, but you really mustn't blame me. It's all your father's fault."

"Does he need to keep you so late?"

"Oh yes. He's becoming quite an important man in the aircraft industry."

"So I've noticed." He was surprised how resentful he felt at twice having been deprived of her company.

"You mustn't be angry about it. After all, there's a war on."

"So I've heard. Do you know I'm not even allowed to enjoy my leave in peace? I've been told that I must lecture to my father's employees."

"Well, please don't blame me." She put out her hand on his for an instant, reassuringly. The gesture disconcerted him. When he was with her he felt so much younger, though there were barely a few months between their ages.

"I daresay father means well but it's a bit much, sticking me up on a platform."

"You'll do it awfully well. Besides, doesn't it fit in with the doctrine you were expounding last night . . . that once you start war, there's no use being half-hearted?"

He laughed. "I'm shot down in flames."

"Don't say that, even as a joke."

He was embarrassed and delighted that her cool practicality could be touched by superstitious fear for him.

"Okay, I'll be a good boy and do what father asks. But it's just that I have so little leave, so little time to see you. I wish I didn't have to go on this damn ski-ing leave, but it's more or less an order."

"I shouldn't have let you be too hard on your father for over-working me. I've got a week's holiday coming, and he's agreed to my taking it now."

"When I shall have to be away in the Austrian Alps?"

She paused for a moment regarding him quizzically. "Do you really want to see me?"

"You know I do."

"Then I shall tell you that I have friends who keep a small hotel in the Arlberg. I could stay there and we could ski together. Or is there something in Luftwaffe regulations that forbids that?" She was smiling now.

He caught her hand. "Liese! Of course not. Can you fix it so that we both stay at your hotel . . . ?"

"Hey, not so fast!"

"I was about to say, in separate rooms."

"You go too fast again. Don't go dashing down the ski slopes like that without looking to see what's at the bottom, or you'll come an awful cropper."

"Shall I come a cropper with you, Liese?"

"Let's start on the nursery slopes and see how we progress."

Conditions were perfect in the mountains. Plenty of light, dry snow. Dieter had never lost his childhood love of snow. When snow came it brought with it a wonderfully secure feeling. Even the way in which it deadened sound provided a barrier against the world. Here snow was present all the time, a guaranteed insurance policy against reality. The *Reichsmarschall* had for once guessed right: this mountain leave was exactly what his battered aircrews needed. The endless white slopes where the most sinister trails were only those made by a comrade's skis were the perfect antidote to an endless blue sky where a curving trail too often meant an enemy's approach or a friend's death. The little town of Lech was filled with airmen, many of them from JG 51. Some had brought wives and girlfriends. Just the same, Dieter was relieved that there was no one from his own *Geschwader* staying at the small five-bedroomed guest-house belonging to Liese's friends.

Liese skied far more skilfully than he did. They spent the first two days on the nursery slopes, toning up and getting fit. Instructors had been detailed to make sure no one tried anything beyond his capabilities. Practice was supervised by a major from staff HQ. When they reported to the instructors on the first morning it was like being back in officer training.

"Gentlemen," the major said, "you are here on leave, to get fit both in mind and body. About the first we can only hope. About the second, OKL will take it very badly if the snow manages to inflict more casualties on you than the enemy did. You will therefore attend basic instruction until you are passed out as able to fly solo. Carry on and please enjoy yourselves."

On the third day Dieter was told that he had regained his ski-legs sufficiently to take-off on his own. He took off with Liese. As they left the ski-lift on the Kriegerhorn to launch themselves down an intermediate slope he put his arm around her, saying: "You lead. I'll be your wingman to prevent anyone else getting at you."

They sailed down through the pines at a pace that made him feel as though he were once again following Flight Sergeant Pohle on his first aerobatic flight; but Flight Sergeant Pohle had never looked as his present *Rottenflieger*. At the end, as he kicked off his skis, he tried to fix the picture of her in his mind, sure that this was the best moment he would know for a long time.

It had been a day as perfect as a snow crystal. The evening was flawless, too. They sat in front of an open log fire, dipping into the fondue and drinking cold, dry, white wine, too physically tired and relaxed to feel the need to talk. They touched hands occasionally. The war was as far away as the Crusades. They were both sleepy yet neither wanted the evening to end. They made a pact to stay until the big central log in the fire collapsed. Just after midnight the log fell, sending a firework shower of sparks up the chimney.

"Time to go to bed," Dieter said. "More ski-ing tomorrow, remember."

They walked up the stairs hand in hand. Where the corridors to their respective rooms separated, Dieter kissed her lightly as he had done on the previous two nights. This night she clung to him. He eased her away and looked down, almost startled at the warmth of her response. She was smiling up at him.

"Time to leave the nursery slopes, Dieter. Be careful of the board outside my bedroom door. It creaks very loudly."

The bed was a large, old-fashioned double one, so large that at first, in the darkness, he couldn't see where she lay in it, she was so quiet and still. He was as nervous as a virgin. She whispered laughingly, "You missed that creaking board." He nearly turned back. The fact that she could joke at such a moment frightened him, for it emphasised her experience even more than his timidity. He supposed he had expected everything to be glorious music or pure romance, like the opening passages of the Siegfried Idyll. He wanted her so much, yet he wasn't sure he would be able to do anything about it.

"Dieter," she said, "you'll catch your death of cold out there."

He slid carefully beneath the covers on the opposite side of the bed and lay still as though any part of her he touched might give him an electric shock. Electric shock was certainly the wrong term; there was no current flowing in his body at all. She put out a hand to hold his and they lay thus, a foot apart, just making contact through their finger tips. His mouth was dry and he didn't know what to say. With Kate it had been quite different. There had been neither time nor inclination to think.

Liese said: "Thank you for a wonderful day."

"I'm ski-ing better, aren't I?"

"Yes. It's lovely just being together on the mountain. To-morrow you'll be ready to go higher."

They lay listening to the utter silence of the weight of snow above them on the roof. The old wooden house creaked in its bones.

"It's got rheumatism," she said.

It was ridiculous. After all, back in the squadron the pilots did nothing but talk about the girls they'd had or were going to have.

She said: "It's a very big bed but that's no reason for using all of it." But she made no move towards him and he knew that she wanted him to make the first possessive gesture.

Clumsily he put an arm over her waist and half-heartedly tried to pull her towards him. "My God," he thought, "what a fool I'm making of myself, when it all should be so wonderful and easy." But the gesture, fumbling as it was, had been enough. She moved in against him. They lay there quietly. After a while, when nothing more had happened, she felt him trembling. He was ashamed that she would know from their closeness that he had not stirred and was not able to make love to her.

She put her face against his shoulder, saying, "I feel so drowsy after all that fresh air and then the fire and the wine. It's heavenly, just to fall asleep feeling so at peace with every-thing."

And so they fell asleep. But in the early hours of the morning, with the frost creaking and cracking outside the window, he dreamt that the ski-lift had taken him to the very top of the mountain and awoke to find that it had. He stirred against Liese and almost without waking she put her mouth to his and reached for him with her hands and it was all as easy as their up-soaring, on-rushing, down-swooping ski-run had been.

150

This time, too, they were at the bottom of the mountain far too soon. As they clung to each other the picture of her he had held in his mind, as he had kicked off his skis, came back to him and he knew that he'd been wrong about one thing. There *had* been a better moment already, and better ones yet to come.

They skied again next morning, more confidently, taking the three-star route, negotiating seven miles of deep snow that was sometimes treacherous, knowing that if they struck trouble no one would automatically come looking for them. But all went well, ending in a breath-snatching run down between the trees that required as much concentration as flying an Emil in a dogfight. They returned to the hotel about tea-time but tea was not uppermost in their minds. They went straight to bed and made love and slept and then made love again.

It was like that for the remaining three days, except that towards the end they were more moderate, though only fractionally so.

The last night of all they lay in Liese's bed spent and happy. Liese had persuaded her friends, who must have known pretty much what was happening, to let her have a fire in her bedroom, so they had made love by firelight and then lain and looked at each other in that softest and kindest of all lights.

She touched him where he was, at the moment, weakest, teasing him gently. "So I've exhausted you at last."

He laughed. She was such a wonderfully natural lover that he marvelled that he had ever felt frightened, even shocked, by her candour. "It's all very well for you. You've nothing to prepare, not even your mind."

"How little you understand women then, *Liebling*. If you only knew how long it took me to prepare my mind for you."

"Was I so awful, so naïve or something? Perhaps it was because I was the boss's son."

"That least of all. It was because with you I wanted to be sure."

"Liese, I love you."

"I know. And I love you. Perhaps you think because I've had some previous experience, I take men to my bed lightly."

"How can you even suggest I would think that? Liese, I love you, I want you to marry me."

She withdrew her hand in mock horror. "But lieutenant, I've only just met you."

"Liese, don't fool around, please. I mean it."

She kissed him. "I know you mean it, but there's a war on.

Funny things happen to men and women in wartime. Let's not rush things."

"You're *not* sure?"

"I've told you. I love you, Dieter. Isn't that enough?"

"No, it's not."

"Then for the moment it will have to be. Are you afraid I'll run away? Don't you trust me?"

"Of course, Liese, more than anyone."

They made love for the last time shortly after dawn. This time it was with desperate tenderness. Afterwards they lay together, dreading to draw apart. When they eventually did so, each could feel the fear in the other at the coming parting.

"There are still forty-eight hours left," she said.

"But today we'll be travelling and tomorrow you'll be back at work and I shall have to give my talk at the factory. Then it's on with the war again."

"The war," she said, "how I hate it!"

"Many women don't feel that way."

"Then they're fools. Any woman must hate war. War takes away husbands and sons and . . ." she added quietly . . . "lovers."

"Don't worry about me, Liese."

"What makes you think you're invulnerable, though God send that you are?"

"God? I didn't think he fitted in with your notions."

"It was a slip. You can't entirely suppress the reflexes of childhood. One misses God in situations like this. But now, of course, we have the Führer."

"Liese!" Dieter was scandalised. "Surely you can't fail to believe in him? If you'd met him face to face as I have . . ."

"Yes," she said coldly. "I might have been hypnotised, too."

"Liese, how can you criticise the man who has achieved so much for Germany?"

"Perhaps because I hate the methods by which so much has been achieved. But much more than that, I fear so much what lies ahead for Germany . . ."

He sat naked on the edge of the bed, shivering. The air in the room was warm but not nearly as warm as her body had been. He was shivering because it seemed that they would end in a quarrel. If they were going to quarrel he would feel more dignified with some clothes on. As he pulled on his uniform trousers, he said: "Liese, you must believe in victory for Germany."

"I wasn't talking about victory—at least not just a military victory. I fear because of the things I have seen, at the factory in Hamburg for example."

"Good God, what about the factory? It's gone up like lightning, hasn't it?"

She, too, was dressing, but on the opposite side of the bed.

"Dieter, I'll never try to hide my feelings from you so I must tell you that I've seen things at our new factory which have made me ashamed."

"What things?"

"Do you know why it's been built in record time? Because Poles and Jews have been made to work like slaves and treated worse than pigs. I've seen some horrible things."

"There'll always be injustices, especially in wartime."

"These are worse than mere injustices. I saw an SS guard knock a young Pole unconscious with an iron bar just because he was a bit slow in getting to his feet."

"Liese, you can't hold Germany responsible for the excesses of a few bullies."

"I hope I don't have to. But I can't help being doubtful of any system that encourages them."

"I respect you for your doubts and you're right to tell me, but I just hope you don't go around telling anyone else."

"So you've sensed it's dangerous to be critical in public? Well, that's something."

He faced her across the bed.

"Liese, you must appreciate that I'm a serving officer, engaged in daily combat with the enemy. That's all I can afford to think about."

"My love," she said, "I realise all that. But it's equally important that you and I are always honest with each other. Already I can see you're concerned about my loyalty and whether I support your struggle. Don't worry. I'm a German woman and so I stick with my country whatever happens. But it's a poor country if it can't afford criticism when criticism is needed."

The argument left them subdued until they were aboard the train, then, slowly, the warmth between them came back once more.

Towards the end of February, Kate went home to Axeham. She was a strikingly different Kate in appearance; but what everyone who met her in the village recognised at once was that she was also a different Kate in attitude.

The sliver of glass had done more damage than had at first

appeared. It had cut several facial muscles. This was bad enough but a fragment of metal that had travelled with the glass had shattered the upper jaw. For some time it had been touch and go whether she would lose the sight of her right eye. The surgeons, however, had done an excellent job. Gone was the perfect, ripe-peach beauty that had captivated Dieter Reh eighteen months before. She was still handsome but the cutting and stitching, bone-grafting and plastic repairs had given her face a drawn, tight look, as if the available skin was being stretched to its limit. There was a hollow high up on the right cheek for which no plastic surgery could fully compensate. She looked, inevitably, older and there were those, including her family and Tom Roland, who privately held that she was a good deal wiser.

Because of the surgery involved, her convalescence had taken much longer than she had expected. She had used this time not only to recover from the ordeal but to get her thoughts clear. This had been almost the most painful part of the whole experience. The injuries the fighter-bomber's attack had inflicted on herself were something she might have accepted as a hazard of war. It was what that same bomb had done to the bus that had really brought her, as Tom would have said, to her senses at last.

Between the time her mother found her lying in her own blood that day on Brighton front and her eventual removal by ambulance, she had regained consciousness. She had had a fair amount of time in which to do so for the good reason that the havoc caused by the bomb had been so appalling that the ambulance men had neither eyes nor time for anyone with what appeared to be minor injuries. The bus had been full of school children. Many of the children had been reduced to shreds and tatters of flesh. Even in her shocked state, Kate could recognise the sodden red thing that lay in the gutter alongside her as the buttocks and leg stumps of a little girl, possibly not more than ten years old. The front section of the bus had simply disappeared. The blast had peeled back the upper deck so that what was left of it pointed skywards at an angle of forty-five degrees. The few children still living had been hurled to the rear of the lower deck, and it was the living and barely living that the ambulance men and medical orderlies were trying to extricate. This portion of the bus was where the screaming was coming from. Through a mist of her own blood, Kate saw a soldier carry out a boy of about five, whose right arm was reduced to a dangling red skein of sinew and splintered white bone. She had had no conception what high explosive could do to the human body. Shock took over and she had passed out again.

The doctors had been worried that she did not appear to have the resilience and powers of recovery her obviously healthy physique promised. Only her mother and Tom Roland, who visited her every week, had any idea of what might be going on in her mind and, rightly or wrongly, they did not consider it their business to pass on the information. For the first month she had lain in a darkened ward. Barely able to talk, unable to read, she had inevitably been thrown back upon herself. It was only towards the end of this dark period that she had begun to recover and the reason was that she at last knew where she stood. Split loyalties no longer existed.

She had argued with herself that the effect of a British bomb on German civilians would have been precisely the same; that the pilot certainly hadn't known what the bus contained and probably wasn't aiming for it anyway; that had her brother Peter been ordered to carry a bomb he might have caused exactly the same awful slaughter. None of this weighed with her. It was the terrible contact with the reeking, shrieking shambles that had been the bus that had convinced her of the totality of war that Britain was fighting. It was possible to be detached as long as a falling bomb was a smudge of smoke half a mile distant, or a falling plane a smear against the sky. A disembowelled child was something that not only cancelled out reason, it released hate.

Once Kate Bristow had recognised this she began to recover fast. After six weeks she was allowed to look at her reorganised face in the mirror. She found it not as unfamiliar as she had feared. Surgery had made her look stern and implacable, which was rather the way she felt. The surgeon's knife had excised Dieter Reh from her life and she found this strangely easy to accept.

She wasn't the only member of the Bristow family to have, as she said with bitter humour, to put a new face on things. Peter had been discharged from East Grinstead while his repaired body came to terms with itself. He arrived at Axeham a week after Kate. The doctors had ordered him a month's sick leave, at the end of which time they would see him again and consider his request to return to flying duties. On the face of it, Peter said—both Kate and he caught themselves deliberately making jokes of this kind—he had a good chance of finding himself back in the cockpit of a Spitfire before summer came round. Thank God, his eyesight had escaped damage; his oxygen mask had saved him there. His blond good looks had suffered far more than his sister's. The left side of his face, from chin to cheek, looked as though some kind of red rubber solution had been poured on to it and allowed to solidify. The skin used to repair the burn damage had been taken by the surgeons from his right buttock. "It's really rather a question of cheek to cheek," he told friends who asked after his progress. It had been part of the healing process at East Grinstead to learn to accept and joke about the shifting round of tissue that made once handsome young men at least presentable again. The left leg had healed well apart from a little stiffness. Peter's main concern was for the fingers of his left hand, two of which looked rather like scaly crab's legs. On the advice of the doctors, he carried a rubber ball which he continually squeezed to exercise the joints. "Hell," he said to Kate, "if they let Douglas Bader fly with tin legs, they surely can't refuse me with just a bit of skin missing."

Mrs Bristow had survived the bomb blast at Brighton with nothing worse than a slightly damaged ear-drum which made her shout more than ever. She was proud of her own minor injury and overwhelmingly proud of the DFC awarded to Peter on the very day he was shot down. What delighted her almost as much was that Kate had so clearly emerged from her state of patriotic schizophrenia. She was now barely recognisable as the same girl, outdoing even her mother in her militancy.

One evening Mrs Bristow asked: "What are you going to do once you're fit again, darling?"

"I shan't go back to Rife Farm."

"No, dear? Well, I suppose you might find farm work a bit heavy."

"It's not that. I want to get into the WAAF—not just as a cook or bottle-washer. I want to be operational."

"But you can't fly, Kate, and these women ferry-pilots they're talking about have had years of experience."

"I don't have to fly. Peter says most of the operations room staff are girls. I'd have a good chance of being put forward for a commission. WAAF officers do quite responsible jobs on the operations side. I'd feel I was doing something to help people like Peter and not just looking after Tom's pigs."

"That's winning the war, too," her mother said dutifully and predictably. "Tom will be very disappointed but I'm sure he'll understand. When will you break the news to him?"

"Don't worry, mum. I adore old Tom. I'll go down very soon and tell him personally."

That a full recovery was going to take a little longer than she had hoped, Kate realised when she visited Charlie Marston's farm down the valley to see Gayboy.

The bay was in fine shape though she was disappointed her horse didn't seem to recognise her and just went on tearing away at his haynet.

Marston laughed. "He'll soon remember you when you get on his back. Go on. Tack him up and take him out for an hour or two. You know you're welcome whenever you're at home."

She put his bridle on and slid the saddle into position along that familiar ridge of the back. He felt different somehow but then she realised that Charlie had only trace-clipped him to leave him a good coat for winter. She'd always had Gayboy fully clipped out because she hunted him, often twice a week. No hunting these days.

She was looking forward keenly to the moment when she rode him. Gayboy was understandably fresh. As soon as she was in the saddle, he skittered sideways and did a little buck. She steadied him, but he began to prance and misbehave. She felt herself sweating and hit him with the crop to show she wasn't in the mood for tomfoolery of that sort. At once he did a half-buck and kicked out. It was nothing more than a display of minor irritation, the sort of thing she would have laughed at in the past. Today, however, Gayboy's antics worried her. Temporarily, her nerve had gone. She dismounted and led Gayboy back to his stable. When she had put the tack away, she walked home slowly up the valley reflecting that her convalescence was by no means fully complete.

She told her brother about it.

"I shouldn't worry, Kate. To tell the truth, I've been wondering myself how I'll feel the first time I climb into a Spit. All you did, Kate, was try to get back in the saddle just a shade too early."

"Maybe there's a lesson there for both of us."

He laughed. "Don't worry about me. The quacks won't let me fly again until they're absolutely certain I shan't prang the bloody thing."

"Are we still that short of aircraft?"

"No. Beaverbrook must be pushing them off the assembly lines pretty fast now. What we need are the experienced pilots to fly them. That's my best hope of getting back into the air fairly soon. Do you realise that towards the end of the battle we had chaps with us who'd only had ten hours on Spits? The

157

Jerry pilots were largely pros who'd flown over 100 hours before they went on ops. I'm living for the day when we can reverse that situation."

A week later, Kate went to Sussex to thank Tom for his many kindnesses and to tell him of her decision. She was afraid that he would be bluff and hearty and say something like: "Time you learned to hate Jerries, lass, *all* bloody Jerries."

She had underestimated him. He put his arm round her and said: "I'll certainly miss you, we all will, even the old pigs, but if that's what you've made your mind up to do . . . "

"I have, Tom."

"Good for you then." He gave her a long and appraising inspection. This, too, was typical of him. So many people had felt awkward and looked at her scars furtively. "You're just as beautiful, girl," he said, "but in a more mature kind of way. There's someone who will confirm that, I'm sure . . . Michael, Kate's here."

She heard Michael hurrying downstairs. Tom saw her surprise and smiled. "You're not the only casualty who's been recovering. Michael's nearly one hundred per cent now. He's getting his medical next week and he's almost certain to be passed fit for duty."

When partially crippled by his wound, Michael had always struck her as squat and rather ungainly. Now that he moved under his own steam, she saw that his lack of height was more than compensated for by his wide shoulders and narrow waist. He was well-proportioned, and, like Tom, as strong as an ox.

He put his arms round her and kissed her heartily. "Kate," he said, "I *love* your new face." He so obviously meant it, that she laughed with pleasure.

Dieter's talk to his father's employees was a success. The occasion was a little more formal than he had expected. Seats for three hundred had been arranged on the main machine-shop floor and a platform, draped with swastikas, built for him out of packing cases. When he had asked what he should say, his father had taken him into his office and closed the door.

"This could be very important to both of us, to all of us, my boy."

"I can see a pep talk might do the workmen a bit of good but I don't see how it can help *me*. I'm a fighter pilot. We tend to be fairly reticent . . . "

"All credit to you, my son, but when I tell you that staff officers from Chief of General Staff Hans Jeschonnek's department will be in the audience . . ."

"Jeschonnek! He's as big a shot as Udet."

"Bigger these days. Jeschonnek has the Führer's ear. You could easily say he's the main architect of the Luftwaffe from now on."

"Not Udet?"

"Poor Ernst, he's had a trying time. He's not really cut out for the rough and tumble of politics."

"But he's a real airman. He understands our problems."

"Real airmen aren't necessarily the best people to solve them."

"He's still head of the Technical Office?"

"Of course. That's his line. But he'd much rather be flying than seeing others do it. Anyway, as I was saying, there'll be a colonel and a major from OKL in the audience. If your talk is a success, as I'm sure it will be, the idea may be widely adopted."

"What idea?"

"My idea of getting our air aces to tour aircraft factories and fill the workers with a sense of dedication." Herr Reh's eyes shone. "It's a question of letting a little of the glory rub off on them."

"It's not all glory, father, seeing your friends disappear or burn up in mid-air."

"Then in your talk today you must stick to what *is* glorious. Talk with enthusiasm about your own experiences, the efficiency of your beloved Emil."

"I can do that all right."

Dieter was a good ambassador, as the *Hitlerjugend* had rightly judged when they had sent him to England in 1938. He found his lecture surprisingly easy. He glossed over the fiasco of the *Stukas*. He talked about the advantages the 109 had over the Hurricanes and how it out-classed even the Spitfire Mark One in many aspects of performance. He modestly described some of his own successes.

At the end he got a standing ovation and warm personal congratulations from the two staff officers.

Later he was able to slip away and, for the last time, spend the night with Liese. Last time! He had to be realistic. It might actually be just that.

There was a surprise waiting for him back at the Headquarters *Staffel*. The squadron had been issued with a handful of the new type of Messerschmitt, the Bf 109f. Two of these had been allocated to the experimental *Stabs-schwarm*. As flight leader, Dieter naturally got one and, since his wingman had to be able to keep up with him, Flight Sergeant Hans Pohle had another. Dieter found Willy Weiss and Shoehorn Kolbe dejectedly examining the new mounts in the dispersal area. Their own battle-worn Emils stood a little apart from the two new aircraft. Kolbe saw Dieter approaching and said in a scornful tone. "Of course, they're all very nice if you like something flashy, but you have to admit they don't have the character of the Emil."

To some extent this was true. Gone were the uncompromising square wing and tail tips of the classic Battle of Britain 109. Gone too, the bracing struts beneath the tailplane. The result was a much cleaner-looking fighter with rounded wingtips, a huge spinner faired cleanly into the engine. The wing was not only slightly longer but its section was a good deal thinner. In fact the fuselage and landing gear were the only elements that had not undergone basic redesigning.

"Where the hell do they put the guns?" Willy Weiss asked. His and Kolbe's Emils had been fitted with 20 mm cannons in each wing. "There isn't room for more than a pea-shooter."

Superficially the criticism seemed justified. A 20 mm cannon muzzle poked through the centre of the spinner. Two grooves on either side of the engine cowling suggested that two machine-guns were the 109f's only other armament.

Dieter came up behind and slapped them both on the back. Both sprang instantly to attention as if they had been totally unaware of his presence.

"At ease, gentlemen."

Kolbe remained ramrod straight. *"Jawohl, Herr Oberleutnant."*

"Cut it out, Shoehorn."

Willy Weiss couldn't keep up the joke any longer. His open nature demanded that he share his pleasure with Dieter.

"Haven't you been to the orderly room? You've been promoted, Dieter. Congratulations."

"And they've given you one of the new toys into the bargain," Kolbe said. "There just isn't any justice." They noticed Dieter's sun-bronzed face. "That tan will soon wear off here," Weiss said.

"Traces of lines beneath the eyes, dark shadows, a pouch or two. Obviously a successful leave. Ours comes up pretty soon," Kolbe said. "Perhaps *we'll* be promoted by the time we get back."

There was a great deal of squadron argument about the new "toys". Werner Mölders already had a good few hours on the 109f, and was all in favour of it. It was nearly 20 mph faster at 20,000 feet, had a better service ceiling and was even more manoeuvrable than the Emil. What worried most of the pilots —including those who had actually flown the few new machines available—was the reduction in armament.

The 109 they had been flying had two machine-guns firing through the propellor and one 20 mm cannon mounted in each wing. The new fighter had therefore reduced its over-all firepower by one 20 mm cannon. It had returned to an idea tried out without success by the Condor Legion in Spain—a cannon mounted between the cylinder blocks of the engine and firing out of the propeller boss. In Spain, this arrangement had produced too much vibration and the gun had usually jammed after a few shots. Though the engineers had long ago got over these problems, many of the leading fighter pilots, including Adolf Galland, were bitter about what they called an armament regression. Rumours got around the squadron that Battle of Britain ace Walter Oesau had declared that he would refuse to fly the 109f so long as his ground staff could get enough spares to keep his Emil in the air. Werner Mölders' reaction was predictably calm and objective. In a brief talk to the pilots of his HQ squadron he told them that they would have to learn to shoot straighter, but added that the additional speed and manoeuvrability of the 109f would give them the advantage of getting in close enough to be able to do so.

Dieter and Pohle flew the new 109 and were delighted with its responsiveness and speed of climb. As expert marksmen, they were detailed to evaluate the effectiveness of the armament. The result of three days' practice on the air-firing range convinced them both that the 20 mm cannon had a poor trajectory, the result of its comparatively low muzzle velocity. They put in a report accordingly. There was no doubt in either of their minds, however, that, in the 109f, the Luftwaffe had a very fast machine indeed that should be able to cope with any improvements the British might introduce into the already formidable Spitfire. When they voiced this opinion in their respective messes, they usually found themselves in a heated verbal dogfight with the Emil conservatives. The traditionalists soon received a tragic boost to their argument. An HQ flight lieutenant with fifteen victories to his credit had taken a 109f up on a routine training flight. While diving the aircraft at high speed, he made a frantic radio call that the airframe was vibrating violently. A few seconds later, the whole tail unit broke away, fuselage, wings and pilot plunging vertically into a pine forest.

By the time Weiss and Kolbe returned from their leave, all 109fs had been grounded as a result of this and three earlier fatal accidents. When JG 51 returned to face the RAF on the Channel coast in April, 1941, it was still equipped with Emils. Meantime the Augsburg works was said to have discovered the cause of the failures in the f-type and was speedily correcting it.

JG 51 was back at St Omer to find that an almost incredible change had taken place. With the onset of better spring weather, the RAF had swung wholeheartedly over to the offensive. At least twice a day there were scrambles to intercept formations of Blenheims escorted by Spitfires. The bombing, largely ineffectual, was aimed at airfields, including Audembert, St Omer and Abbeville. If it caused no particular material damage, it did keep up a continual pressure on the German fighter squadrons. But the thing that really struck Dieter was that the roles had been completely reversed. Now it was the Messerschmitt pilots who endured the nerve-wracking wait for the alarm bell. In addition, there were still the unpopular fighter-bomber raids to be flown. By May the 109f was slowly filtering back into service. The Messerschmitt technicians claimed that they had beaten the bugs out of the tail failure. It had been due, they said, to excessive vibration set up between engine and the new strutless, cantilever tail.

Among other duties, JG 51 had been instructed to train and recruit new pilots. Inevitably the *Stabs-schwarm* found itself heavily involved in training, which meant, to Dieter's chagrin, less opportunity for operational flying. So it was early May before he scored his tenth kill and first bomber, a Blenheim. Meantime squadron pilots were consistently piling up victories.

As a leading participant in the training programme Dieter became increasingly drawn into staff matters at *Geschwader* level. On 10 May he attended a wing training conference presided over by Mölders himself. As they left the headquarters hut, he found himself walking alone beside the *Kommodore*.

"How are things going, Reh? Glad to hear you got your tenth. A Blenheim, wasn't it?"

"*Ja, Herr Kommodore.* I wish I could get more combat flying. If the *Stabs-schwarm* isn't allowed to shoot down a few Tommies occasionally, we shall not only have lost our touch but we shan't have anything to teach the new boys."

Mölders laughed. "Don't worry. There's plenty of time. The Führer hasn't given up the idea of invading Britain. Maybe, before this year's out . . . Meanwhile we've got to have as many trained pilots as we can teach."

The spring evening was closing in. On the far side of the field some 110s were warming up in preparation for night-fighting exercises. Alongside them, mechanics worked on a night-fighter version of a Ju 88 that had come in during the early hours of that morning with some flak damage in the tail. Dieter remembered that Gerhard Stecke was now on intruder operations over English air bases and made a mental note to try to contact the crew. Perhaps they were from the same squadron and had news of him.

Mölders gestured Dieter into his living hut. An orderly on duty in the hallway sat by two telephones, one red, one black. "All quiet? No messages?"

"Nothing, *Herr Kommodore*."

"Thank God we're not night-fighters. Those lads are going to be increasingly busy from now on."

In confirmation, the tin roof of the hut shook as one of the 110s lifted off the end of the runway. Mölders led the way in to the inner room. They had hardly sat down when they heard the telephone ring.

"Damn. That's the Command phone."

The orderly burst into the room. *"Herr Kommodore."*

Mölders said quietly. "I like you to knock, whoever it is on the phone. You know that, corporal."

"But it's the *Reichsmarschall* himself."

Mölders hurried out, leaving the door open so that Dieter could hear every word of the conversation.

"Scramble the whole *Geschwader, Herr Reichsmarschall?* What for? There are no enemy aircraft of any sort flying in . . . Flying *out?"* There was a longish pause. Then, "I see. Does the 110 carry any distinguishing markings? Taken straight from the aircraft park at the factory? You realise there's only about fifteen minutes to full darkness?"

Reichsmarschall or not, Mölders' voice had taken on an edge of polite but unmistakable opposition. "With respect I would suggest that the air will be full of 110s at this time. There will be grave dangers both to them and to our 109s. Besides, surely if the Deputy Führer manages to get to England the British defences will . . ."

Dieter could hear a furious outburst from the Berlin end of the line.

At last Mölders said quietly: *"Jawohl, Herr Reichsmarschall,* at once . . ."* And the phone clicked down.

"Reh, come here, please. You heard that conversation, of course. I know I can rely on your complete discretion."

"Of course, *Herr Kommodore.*"

"Apparently Kommodore Galland has received the same mad order to scramble his entire wing. Well, it's an order. We shall have to send at least one plane up. Is your Emil at readiness?"

"Yes, at dispersal."

"I'll call dispersal and tell them to have it run up. Borrow my staff car."

A second 110 roared low across the roof.

"My orders, *Herr Kommodore?*"

"Officially you're to search for the Deputy Führer, Rudolf Hess, who has taken off on a private peace mission to Britain. But my personal orders to you are to patrol as far as the coast and land again while there's still plenty of light left. Even if you could identify his plane, it's inconceivable he'd take a route to England this far south."

Dieter's mechanic, Korporal Streib, was standing on the wing of his 109. "What now? Are they turning us into night-fighters?"

Dieter laughed. "I just thought I'd like some evening air."

"Don't go sniffing it for too long, sir. It gets chilly up there at night."

"Thanks!" He buckled on his parachute harness and called, "All clear?"

A few seconds later he was climbing away into the disc of the setting sun. By the time the coast was beneath him, it was dark enough for the blue flames from his exhaust ports to be disconcertingly dazzling. Time to head for home. He called the controller and was told to join the landing pattern at 2,000 feet, for the 110s were still taking off. If necessary, the tower said, they'd put the flarepath on for him.

Dieter throttled back, idling comfortably round the circuit at the height given him. The landscape below was beautifully mellowed in the red light, its features exaggerated by long shadows one never saw in daylight. The Deputy Führer might have gone mad, but he at least had to thank him for the joy of flying in this peaceful twilight.

He made a wide turn to port, heading back towards the field again. If they didn't hurry up getting the rest of those 110s airborne, he'd certainly need that flarepath. He wasn't particularly worried at the thought.

Suddenly, something hit the armoured plate behind his seat. Instruments disintegrated. There was a searing pain in his scalp and blood pouring into his eyes. He kicked right rudder hard, the plane answering sluggishly. Petrol and flames. This was how death came. Air rushing in momentarily, keeping the fire from him though feeding it elsewhere. Why so much air? He groped over his head and found the canopy had gone. Only seconds to get out. Unconsciousness and ground both rushing towards him. He kicked out like a swimmer, drowning in air. The aircraft was on its back. He was out and falling. He did not remember pulling the release handle of his parachute.

It had taken only seconds, and the Havoc that had slid quietly in behind him was already bombing the airfield. The Luftwaffe were not the only ones to discover the effectiveness of twilight operations.

When Dieter hit a wheat field alongside the main road to St Omer he was already unconscious. He might have died of shock there in the May darkness, had not a passing dispatch-rider seen him fall.

It was typical of "Vati" Mölders that he found time three days later to call in at the hospital. "You can only stay a short time, *Herr Kommodore*," the ward sister said. "The *Oberleutnant* has a good deal of metal in his right side and his head wound is going to take some time to heal. Cannon shell splinters, a great many of them. The damage is mainly superficial but there's enough to cause severe shock to the whole system."

"Will he fly again?"

"Always the same question! It's for the doctors to answer, but I daresay he'll be out of here in a month. He's tough and determined, *Herr Kommodore*. Yes, he will fly."

Dieter was propped up, his head hidden in bandages, his whole chest encased in heavy white wrappings. Mölders surveyed him kindly, hands clasped behind his back. "Well, now it's happened to both of us, eh? But don't worry, I was soon flying again. So will you be."

Dieter reached for his notepad and pencil. "What shot me down?" he wrote.

"A British intruder. Pity it didn't catch the Deputy Führer instead. I have the official communiqué here to show you."

Dieter read: "Party Member Rudolf Hess recently managed to obtain an aircraft against the Führer's strictest orders forbidding him to fly on account of an illness which had been growing worse for years. On May 10 at about 6 p.m. Hess took off from Augsburg on a flight from which so far he has not returned. It seems that Party Member Hess lived in a state of hallucination, as a result of which he felt he could bring about an understanding between England and Germany. This, however, will have no effect on the continuance of the war."

"We now know he reached Scotland and then bailed out. Quite a feat, really."

Mölders saw the question in the eyes peering through the visor of bandages.

"It will probably be about a month before you are fit again. Don't try to rush it. I've picked you for an interesting and important job, Reh. You're a bright young man whose talents are by no means confined to flying."

Dieter's eyes showed alarm.

Mölders patted his leg beneath the blankets reassuringly. "It's a job that will give you more than enough front-line flying. We need a special test and training unit, one which can try out new ideas in combat conditions and at the same time keep in touch with the thinking at OKL. There's always the danger of Luftwaffe High Command and the front-line fighter pilots drifting apart. Perhaps you've noticed it." His eyes twinkled. "No, don't try to talk. You're the man I want for the job. And before you ask me, yes, you can take the rest of your *Stabs-schwarm* with you. I'd like to see several units like yours set up, but for the moment OKL has agreed to start with the Channel front. That's where you've had your experience. Soon, there will be others . . . Enough said. Now, you're to think of nothing except getting well. By the way, your recommendations about replacing the 20 mm nose cannon on the 109f with something with a higher muzzle velocity look like being accepted. Other experts agree. It seems they're going to try the MG 151, a 15 mm job but with a much greater accuracy and striking power."

Dieter was writing on the pad again: "Will I still be under your command?"

Mölders nodded. "You will be responsible to the office of the Inspector of Fighter Aircraft, and I believe that in due course I may have quite a lot to do with that."

Kate Bristow did not enjoy her basic training as a WAAF. She liked most of the girls but she was too fastidious by nature to take to the enforced gregariousness of barrack-room life. She found that the standards of personal hygiene of her

166

female companions in arms left a lot to be desired. For many of them the "in arms" part of it had only one interpretation. The frankness with which they discussed their amorous encounters with the airmen and local soldiery frankly shocked her. Because she kept aloof from such conversations, she knew that she was thought a bit of a prig. Her only close companion throughout basic training was a fat East End cockney called Rosie Lee whose entire family had been wiped out in Goering's last fire raid on London on the night of 30 December 1940. Their bond was that both girls really wanted to do something active against the enemy. Most of the others, although patriotic in a general sort of way, were in the WAAF because they had to be in something.

Rosie said repeatedly: "Katie, I *hate* the bloody Jerries. I'd like to see the whole sodding lot of them burn like my dad and mum did. Anything I can do to help wipe the bastards out . . . You feel the same, don't you?"

"I used not to, Rosie, but now I want to crush them so that they can never do this again to anyone."

"Good for you, Katie. When you're an officer . . ."

"Who says I shall be?"

"Well, you will be, won't you? You've got a bit of class."

"It isn't a question of class, Rose. It's where I can be most use. I want to get on the ops side."

"Well, when you've got your commission, don't forget me. I don't want to spend the war peeling spuds and cleaning up after those other dirty bitches. I want to help send our bombers on their way. Your brother's a pilot, isn't he?"

"Yes, fighters. He got shot down in the Battle of Britain. He's doing a spell as a controller on the south coast at the moment but he hopes to be back flying before long."

"He'll be able to put in a good word for you, I expect," Rosie said with confidence. "You'll be a section officer in no time."

For Dieter in St Omer hospital it was a particularly galling month. The Luftwaffe had thrown itself on Crete in an incredibly costly yet triumphant invasion. Apparently, Chief of Staff Hans Jeschonnek had saved the day at the most critical moment by ordering the airborne landing of an entire mountain infantry division on Maleme airfield while it was still in the hands of the New Zealanders. German losses had been frightful, both in men and transport aircraft. But by early June Hitler was able to boast that there were no more unconquerable islands. The newspapers declared that Crete had been merely a dress rehearsal for the coming invasion of Britain.

One of Dieter's *Stabs-schwarm* came to see him every few days and tell him the news: It seemed that the Tommies had been steadily increasing their pressure. Squadrons of Blenheims escorted by up to fifty Spitfires were daily visitors. JG 51 had suffered many casualties. Even Pohle had had a narrow escape when caught by two Spitfire Mark Vs, the new and vastly improved version of the versatile British fighter. His 109f had been badly shot up, and he had escaped only by firing all his guns in a dive, the smoke fooling the Tommies for a crucial instant into believing that he was on fire. In that instant he'd found some overcast and escaped, but his fighter had become a complete write-off after a wheels-up landing at Audembert.

In the second week of June, Dieter was allowed up to walk in the grounds. On one of his weekly visits Willy Weiss found Dieter moodily contemplating vapour trails left by a departing Spitfire sweep.

"Try to find out from the quacks when they'll let me loose, Willy. They won't tell me. It looks like you boys need reinforcements up there."

"Reinforcements are just what we're not likely to get. There are some very odd rumours going about."

"What?"

"Whole wings are packing up as if they're going to move out. Do you suppose it could be North Africa now that Crete's ours?"

Dieter was immediately anxious. "Who's moving out? Are we?"

"Not so far, but they say we're likely to do so at any moment."

"Has the *Kommodore* said anything?"

"Not him. But whenever I see him he seems pleased and excited about life, and you know how cautious Vati usually is."

"I'd better get out of this damned hospital quickly. Something's up and I want to be with you all when it happens."

But the doctors were adamant: Oberleutnant Reh would not be fit for flying for some weeks yet. On 14 June they agreed to discharge him for non-flying duties and advised him to report back to his squadron for sick leave. He arrived at St Omer to find the airfield in a state of chaos. A long line of Ju 52 transports was being boarded by ground staff with their personal baggage. Very few 109s with JG 51 markings remained in evidence. Instead, there were fighters from JG 2, Richthofen *Geschwader,* and JG 26, *Schlageter*. A 109f with a Mickey Mouse insignia taxied in and a short vital man with a large dark moustache and smoking a black cheroot popped out. Dieter saluted as he recognized Adolf Galland, ebullient leader of the *Schlageter* wing. *Schlageter* was a medieval German hero but the man who flew with the Mickey Mouse on his engine cowling was a modern hero, like Mölders. People said that Galland was the Richthofen of the Luftwaffe, the extrovert aerial hunter, while Mölders corresponded to Oswald Boelcke, the first-war ace who had been a master air tactician and planner before an accident robbed Germany of his talents. Galland waved his cheroot cheerfully at Dieter just as Mölders and his adjutant came out to meet him. They were friends and rivals, these two. Both now had something approaching seventy aerial victories.

Dieter walked over towards the *Stabs-schwarm*'s dispersal area. There were no fighters in the sandbagged bays. He found a disgruntled group of pilots playing with Elsa, the Alsatian bitch, who came bounding forward to meet him.

Shoehorn Kolbe said: "Welcome home, but you're a bit too late. They've just taken our 109s away from us. The war's over."

Willy Weiss said: "There's a rumour they're going to give us a new fighter to try out. In fact, there are all kinds of rumours. The only solid fact seems to be that JG 51 is moving out and leaving us behind."

An orderly came out of the hut and saluted.

"The *Kommodore*'s compliments, *Herr Oberleutnant*. Will you please report to him at his office immediately."

Mölders was at his desk when Dieter marched in and saluted. The second officer in the room lounged almost full-length in an easy chair, peaked hat tilted well forward over his eyes so that the face was obscured. A black cigar was clenched between teeth. Even without the cigar, the reclining figure needed no identification. Only two men in the German armed forces wore the Oak Leaves to the Knight's Cross which decorated this officer's tunic, the highest award for valour: Werner Mölders held one, Adolf Galland the other.

Mölders returned Oberleutnant Reh's salute and gestured him to stand at ease. Galland sat up a shade straighter and adjusted his cap to a jaunty angle.

Mölders said: "Welcome back, *Oberleutnant*. I hope you're nearly recovered. I say 'nearly' because I'll tell you straight away you're not going back on flying duties immediately. I promised you an exciting job. Oberst Galland is taking over from us here with the *Schlageter* wing. They've over 500 kills to their credit—not quite as many as JG 51, but it's a start."

Though not without a sense of humour, Mölders seldom laughed; this was the nearest he ever got to a joke.

Galland waved his cigar good-naturedly. "We haven't had so long on the Channel coast as your lot. But don't worry. Now we're holding the fort practically single-handed, we'll soon overtake you."

"Maybe, but don't forget we'll have tremendous opportunities for high scoring, also."

Galland said: "Okay. We'll see about that but why don't we put this young chap out of his misery."

"What I tell you now, Reh, is in complete confidence, though you may, of course, pass on the broad outlines to the three other pilots of your flight. Your flight is to become a special *Lehr- und Erprobungs-schwarm*, an instructional and experimental unit on call to the *Richthofen* and *Schlageter* wings on the Channel front. You will take your general orders from the inspector of day fighters department in Berlin. When you are flying on operations you will come under the direct command of Kommodore Galland, who will use your collective talents as he thinks best. From time to time he may post other experienced or promising pilots to you, but for the moment I see no need to alter the personnel. Yourself and Feldwebel Pohle have natural fighter pilot skill and are excellent marksmen with the ability to evaluate weapons. Kolbe and Weiss have been piling up their kills while you've been away. Kolbe has eight and Weiss fifteen, mostly Spitfires. You should make an excellent team. Any questions?"

"Yes, *Herr Kommodore*. I understand we have no aircraft to fly."

"That will be taken care of. Weiss, Kolbe and Pohle are to report to the Fighter Training School at Schleissheim. There they will undergo a conversion course on the new Focke Wulf 190 before returning here to fly the 190 in combat later in the year. Back at St Omer they will gain combat experience in it and help convert some of the squadrons of JGs 2 and 26."

"And myself, *Herr Kommodore*?"

"You will report first to the Technical Office, General Udet's department, at Luftwaffe HQ, Goldap. While you are forbidden to fly you will, among other duties, be familiarising yourself with new fighter developments."

"Am I permitted to ask where JG 51 is going?"

"You are not, *Oberleutnant,* though you will discover before very long, no doubt."

Galland said: "It's a pity you're not allowed to fly yet, otherwise I might ask you to accompany me as my wing man on a jaunt across the Channel before tea."

Dieter looked beseechingly at Mölders. But without looking up, the *Kommodore* said: "Forbidden," and was already deep in his papers.

Dieter approached his interview at "Robinson," the surprisingly English codeword denoting Luftwaffe HQ at Goldap, with some trepidation and a good deal of distrust. This showed in the fact that, although he put on his smartest uniform, he had abandoned his No 1 peaked cap in favour òf his front-line model with its carefully tweaked-up wire front and bent sides. It was the fighter pilot's trademark and stated clearly that he was no desk-borne warrior. A few seconds after he had shown his pass, been checked out by a security officer and passed on to a junior staff officer in the department of General Ernst Udet, he had begun to feel that the hat was an indulgence he should have resisted. Superbly turned-out figures passed in the corridors, more like courtiers than serving officers. Once he caught the flash of scarlet lining on a greatcoat, a general, Milch perhaps or Jeschonnek. In his rakish cap he felt, in this company, as though he had forgotten to shave.

The young staff officer was friendly. Had he fully recovered from his wounds? Had he yet had a chance to fly the new FW 190? What did he think of the improved Spitfire?

Dieter was guarded, monosyllabic, almost sulky in his replies. He felt resentful of this dapper young chap chatting in such a matter-of-fact way about what were to him and all front-line pilots matters of life and death. He was angry with himself for being surly but then he recalled the insults the fighter squadrons had had to suffer from OKL. The young *Leutnant* smiled and said: "I know just how you feel. I shall be pretty thankful to get back to flying myself. I got shot down by a Blenheim, of all things. Over Ostende, just after Christmas . . . Ah, the General will see you now."

"General!" Dieter was staggered.

"Yes. You seem to have friends in the right places."

Dieter marched in and gave his best salute.

Udet waved and held out his hand. "Never mind all that. How are you, my boy? I've been hearing all about you from your father. Great fellow, your father, we could do with a few more like him. He's likely to end up very highly placed in the aircraft production industry of the Reich. He gets on with things, which is more than I can say for some people around here, eh, Horst?"

The young staff lieutenant said tactfully, "The general would rather fly an aircraft than sit at a desk."

"Exactly," Udet said. "But someone has to sit at the desks and shoot down the paperwork. So let's get on with it."

The staff lieutenant clicked his heels and withdrew.

"Sit down. Sit down, lad. You notice we don't go in for a great deal of formality in this office. Just so long as the work gets done."

The phone rang and Udet began a long conversation from which Dieter gathered that some new engine, or rather pair of engines, on a new-type bomber had once again repeated their tendency to overheat and catch fire. He guessed it was the new long-range strategic weapon, the Heinkel 177. As Udet talked, Dieter thought how the great man had altered since he had seen him last at his father's factory. Never a heavy man, he had lost over a stone in weight. The jolly Udet personality which made him internationally popular vanished as he discussed this latest crisis. Udet's voice became querulous, his manner increasingly irritable. In the end he slammed down the phone and strode over to the window, turning his back on Dieter. When at last he moved, it was towards a cupboard whose door opened to reveal glasses and brandy bottles, one almost empty. The general poured himself three fingers of cognac and snapped it back. When he at last turned his attention on Dieter again he was smiling and composed.

"We have our problems here, you understand. But these bloody politicians and some of our military colleagues too, for that matter . . . It makes you wonder who they're fighting, the British or us fellows who are trying to turn the planes out for them. But, now, why I sent for you." He sat down behind his desk. "Mölders' idea for a *Lehr- und Erprobungs-schwarm* as a link between Luftwaffe Command and the men who have to fly our products in action is sound, very sound. If I have my way, we'll expand the link to cover bombers and dive-bombers, too. But your lot are the guinea-pigs. Your being forbidden to fly is a blessing, though I know you don't see it that way. For one thing it will help to keep you alive. Going back up there against the Spitfires when you're only half fit certainly isn't the way to reach old age. You agree?"

Udet was back on form, asking questions but never waiting for an answer.

"Your father hit on a fine idea when he got you to talk to his workers. Over the next month production went up more than ten per cent. It's settled down a bit now, but that's human nature. Since then we've tried it out with bomber pilots as well, and it works. A pep talk from you lads does wonders on the factory floor."

Udet saw the apprehension on Dieter's face.

"Now don't get ready to give me a burst. Talking isn't all I'm going to ask you to do. Your *Erprobungs* flight is going to have to evaluate quite a few new types on operations before we finally win the war. The factories you will be ordered to address . . ."—Udet put a slight accent on the word "ordered" —"will be those working mainly on new fighter types. You'll be shown some of them in the strictest possible confidence. You'll be on oath to pass on no single detail, not even to your own flight. The idea is that you, at least, will be familiar with future developments. Even then, we shan't show you everything, not by any means, merely the planes that are likely to come into front-line squadrons' hands very shortly. You'll find that the German aircraft industry teems with new ideas. Far too many new ideas."

Udet rose and poured himself another large brandy. He went on. "So many new ideas . . . It's my luck to have to squash some of the wilder ones. It makes one unpopular, I can tell you. All the same, we've got to rationalise, cut down to a few basic excellent types we can produce easily and in quantity. You'll hear a good deal about ELK. ELK is the codeword for my scheme to streamline our aircraft production. As far as new bombers go, we're going nap on the He 177. Four engines but coupled in pairs. Though she's a twenty-ton aircraft, she's being fitted with dive-brakes so that she'll be able to make pinpoint attacks on shipping, for example. There's been a great deal of criticism of the dive-bomber but we're not deserting the principle. However, the 177s' main role will be hitting the enemy's industry at long range, where it hurts most. As for the Me 210 . . . That's going to be some baby, I can tell you! It will have everything the *Reichsmarschall*'s famous Zerstörers lacked . . ."

Dieter felt both embarrassed and flattered that Udet should talk to him so frankly. Perhaps it was the brandy? The general sensed his doubts and said jovially: "I assure you the *Reichsmarschall* wouldn't be offended by my saying things like that to you. After all, we're all flying men, and flying men, especially fighter pilots, can't help talking shop whenever they meet."

Dieter asked: "What are my actual orders, *Herr General?* You'll understand, I'm sure, that I'd like to get my lecture tour over as quickly as possible and return to flying."

"Quite so, quite so. Young Horst will give you a detailed itinerary of the aircraft plants you're to visit and the dates you're expected there, also a list of the men you contact in each case. You'll find the red carpet will be put down for you. They're very keen on the whole scheme, these manufacturers. You're to start with the new Reh factory in Hamburg, in which case you'd better report to . . . let me see . . . to a Herr Helmuth Reh in Hamelin." Udet winked. "No doubt you'll need a few days at home to get the feel of things before you start."

Dieter phoned Willy Weiss at Schleissheim and told him the news: "Don't go and get yourselves killed before I get back."

"Don't worry, Dieter. They haven't even got any new types for us to fly yet. We're likely to be stuck here back at school for at least a month."

"Good. Then you can't start piling up kills ahead of me. Try to protect the local virgins from Pohle."

"What virgins?"

"Don't be surprised if I return to the fold a married man."

"Now I know your head wound isn't better."

As soon as he got off the train at Hamelin he telephoned Liese.

"Liese, darling. I bet you never expected to hear me."

"I've been expecting you to call for the past hour," she said calmly.

"How could you?"

She laughed. "We have our methods, lieutenant."

"Liese, I've got a wonderful surprise for you. I'm going on a tour at home here in Germany."

"I have your itinerary here, lieutenant."

"Liese, don't be so bloody official. Is there someone in the office with you?"

"Yes."

"Liese, I love you."

"I quite understand, lieutenant. If you care to come round directly, we can discuss all the details."

She was alone in her office when he arrived. When he saw her his heart felt as though it had just half-rolled off the top of a loop. He made a move to take her in his arms. She took evasive action, slipping away easily, behind the shelter of her desk.

"Not here, lieutenant, please."

He felt ridiculously piqued. "Who was that with you in the office? You didn't have to be so stuffy."

"The works manager, *Liebling*. You surely can't expect me to flirt with the boss's son in office hours."

"After what I've been through, I've a right to expect a warmer reception."

She saw that he was genuinely upset and put a hand gently to the place where he still wore plaster on his head. "Wait," she said. "There's a time and place."

He caught her hand and kissed it. "Six weeks, Liese, and I'm bound to be able to get back to Hamelin quite often."

"You may not find that necessary."

"What do you mean?"

The buzzer on the internal phone went. "Your father's ready to see you now."

"Where's my mother?"

"She's at the Hamburg plant. Now that your father is more and more concerned with Air Ministry affairs, she does several days each week at each factory. She's magnificent."

Herr Reh had had a partition knocked down to make a more imposing office. A new picture of the Führer hung behind his desk, and he wore a party member's button. Turned so that those approaching the desk could see whose picture it was, stood a signed photograph of Ernst Udet.

"My son," his father said, "and a hero, too. How is the head? Was it a great air battle in which you were shot down? Did you get your man first? Not even my friend Udet seemed to know."

"It was a secret mission," Dieter said dryly.

"Ah, then I mustn't ask questions."

"I'll tell you if you like, father."

Dieter had no wish to be discourteous to his father. He had a good German's respect for his parents, but lately he had found his father's starry-eyed optimism, as expressed in his letters to hospital, too much at variance with what the frontline pilots felt and expected.

"No, no! Even in my trusted position, I mustn't hear information regarded as secret."

"But it isn't a secret any more, father. I was sent up to look for the Deputy Führer and shoot him down before he could get to England; but a British night-fighter moved in on me."

175

His father lowered his voice as though he himself had spoken these embarrassing words. "My boy, that certainly *is* secret information. Poor Hess. He had been mentally unwell for some time, of course. Whatever you do, you mustn't hint at this when you speak to my workers. A night-fighter—that part is all right. You'll be visiting plants where they're working on night-fighter devices. You were flying a 109 at the time, of course, not at all suitable for night flying. That will do splendidly as a peg on which to hang the need for speedy production of the finest night-fighting equipment. That way neither the 109 nor yourself need come badly out of the account."

"I've no wish to excuse myself, father, I was caught with my pants down, that's all."

"Very modest and generous of you, my boy, but generosity is something we can't afford to offer the enemy."

"I promise I'll say nothing about Hess—although, if you ask *me*, he wasn't the only one to have gone crazy that night. To order day fighters up at night to look for a black needle in a pitch-dark haystack . . ."

"Dieter, I am sorry to find that you've got very critical."

"Getting shot down makes you inclined to question things, father."

"Quite so, quite so. And naturally you're still a bit shaken up. Well, here's some really excellent news for you. In the confidence that you will say *all* the right things, I've made . . . er . . . certain arrangements of which I think you will approve. Your tour will be quite an arduous one. There will be many arrangements to make, hotel reservations, train times to be studied, letters to write. In short, you'll need a secretary to look after you . . ."

His father grinned slyly.

"I've told Fräulein Schumacher she is seconded for special duty for a few weeks. I gather you won't disapprove of the idea? In wartime, young men . . ."

Dieter cut his father short. "Please, father, it's not like that at all. I love her."

"Excellent. She's a highly competent young lady. I don't think you'll find that any personal feelings she has for you will make her any the less efficient in making your tour a smooth-running success. As to your personal relationship, I know that as a serving officer you will behave with perfect discretion. The heroes of the Reich must be above reproach."

"Liese, you didn't tell me."

"I didn't know whether you'd approve."

"Approve! You must be crazy, darling."

"I shall be very correct, the perfect secretary—at all times."

"Not at all times," he teased.

"Dieter, we must behave ourselves. This is an official trip and I'm responsible that it goes without a hitch."

"Are you working for me as from this instant?"

"Though you may not know it, I've been making bookings for you and fixing up rail warrants for the past week."

"Good. Then here are my first instructions. You will dine with me this evening and bring with you all the details of our tour. I wish particularly to check on the hotel accommodation, Fräulein Schumacher."

"I've already told you that we must behave and this means that I've reserved single rooms. We shall have a staff officer from the Inspector of Fighters' office along with us most of the time."

"Give him one of the single rooms and we'll share the other."

She laughed despite her determination to be serious.

"Where is your discipline, *Oberleutnant?*"

That night Dieter did not go home and when he walked in at breakfast time his father didn't ask where he'd been.

Hauptmann Manfred (Mano) Rumpler was a tall, thin sallow officer in his early thirties. He had been a barrister in civilian life. He had a needle-sharp mind, a biting tongue and a disinclination to do a stroke more work than was absolutely necessary. He was, in fact, the perfect staff officer as described by Field Marshal Kesselring, whose famous dictum Dieter had learned as an officer cadet. "There are four types of officer: the merely stupid I make platoon commanders. God protect me from the stupid and industrious. They are worth a battalion to the enemy. The brilliant and industrious I appoint my corps commanders. The brilliant and idle I reserve for my staff. They will find a short cut round everything."

Had Mano Rumpler been known to the Field Marshal he would, no doubt, have received instant employment. As it was, his talents for fixing things had found a ready home in the Inspector of Fighters' office in Berlin. It was to Rumpler in Berlin that Oberleutnant Dieter Reh and his personal assistant Fräulein Liese Schumacher reported on 20 June 1941.

Though they were temperamental opposites, Dieter took to Rumpler straight away. As they drove north to Hamburg for their first engagement, Rumpler talked freely. His briefing was amusing, laconic. He took for granted the fact that, as an operational pilot, Dieter would hate the whole thing. On the other hand, he asked Dieter not to underrate the value of what he was about to do. "Our gallant works," he said, "haven't yet felt the war very personally. Perhaps the RAF will change that, but at present, they can do with a pep talk. As for some of the bosses—well, they're coining money, no doubt, but with a few exceptions, your father for instance, they're not always teutonically efficient. Mind you, they've been messed about.

"Far too much stop-go," Rumpler went on, "and on the whole too much go. Too many individual plants being allowed to produce too many specifications for new types. And, of course, the dive-bomber fiasco. Thank God, our office isn't responsible for the bombers. Dear old Udet has made the most tremendous mess of the whole thing. He talked Goering and all the rest into putting their money on the *Stuka*. Well, I don't have to tell you what a mistake that was. And now all his old chums are gunning for the poor chap. I doubt very much whether he'll be able to stand up to them much longer. Milch, Jeschonnek and the *Reichsmarschall*, especially. They're all blaming him . . . You saw Udet at Robinson? Then you must have noticed a change in the poor fellow."

Dieter said: "You're painting a pretty gloomy picture."

Rumpler's tone became less flippant. "The point is, Reh, it could be gloomy, damned gloomy. You've noticed a tendency not only to blame the fighters for everything but to look on them as poor relations of the bombers? I thought you might have done . . . Our task is to persuade our lords and masters that stepping up fighter production is absolutely essential both for offensive work and for defence. Though it may seem incredible now, we're going to need thousands of fighters for defence here in the Reich before we're through."

They were approaching the outskirts of Hamburg. "Ah well," Rumpler said, "we can at least relax tonight in the excellent hotel that Fräulein Schumacher has booked for us. Tomorrow, you start work. The first one will be easy. It's your father's own factory."

Liese and Dieter managed a drink alone in the bar before dinner.

"What do you think of Rumpler?" Dieter asked.

"He's very intelligent—and critical. I like that. But he's a shade too acid for my palate." She squeezed his hand. "Wouldn't it be nice if there were just the two of us?"

"Later . . . ?"

"I'm not sure. I don't feel at ease. It's as if we're on parade."

Liese and Mano Rumpler got on better at dinner. They found they were both music-lovers, of opera especially. They shared an unpatriotic distaste for Wagner. Mozart was their ideal. After dinner, Rumpler excused himself. The lovers strolled through the darkened streets together. Once they heard the drone of engines across the sky.

"Wellington?" asked Liese.

"No. Ju 88. Hear the pulsing throb? The engines are unsynchronised. You can always tell one of ours."

Liese shuddered. "Let's hope we never hear too many of theirs."

They felt close to each other walking in the darkness, sharing the thought of danger in the dome of the night far above. When it came to bedtime, Liese said: "I can't. I don't know why it is. If only we weren't on official business."

"Good God," he said. "What's got into you, Liese? All those months stuck there down on the coast and now . . ."

"Are you forgetting last night?"

"What's different now?"

"I don't know. I suppose I'm more of a German than I suspected. Being on duty like this makes me feel that I must conform. Perhaps tomorrow night. Perhaps I'm just tired."

It was the first time Dieter had seen the Hamburg factory. It was much larger than he had expected. He was proud to find his mother so ably in charge of such an undertaking. She was not at all self-conscious of Hauptmann Rumpler, Liese or the several factory executives who were in conference with her when Dieter burst in. She simply hugged and kissed him as if he were still a little boy.

"Dieter, how lovely of you to come to talk to us! We'll have a glass of Kirsch and some almond cakes and then we'll go down to the dining-hall. By then they'll all be ready for you."

Dieter eased himself away fondly just long enough to introduce Mano Rumpler.

Mano bowed, and said: "I've told your bright boy he'd better talk to some purpose since everyone will be downing tools to listen to him."

Frau Reh found time to squeeze Liese's arm. "You'll be a big help to him, I'm sure."

179

Dieter was a little shaken to find so many assembled to hear him. After a moment's nervousness, the kind of qualm he felt just before take-off, he soon got into his stride. He was an easy, natural speaker, and his audience was ready to be impressed.

He didn't pull any punches. He told them that the enemy was tough and determined and had excellent aircraft. To beat him, you had to be equally tough and determined and have better aircraft made with better components ...

Afterwards Rumpler said: "Unless you're careful, you'll never see a cockpit again. You were good, very good."

When the works manager took them round the factory, Dieter discovered that Reh Fabrik was making much more than dive-brakes. A whole department was devoted to electronics. One hush-hush workshop was assembling prototype radar units that would home night-fighters on to their targets from two and a half miles' range. The sets were something quite new. They were called Lichtenstein BC.

That afternoon they moved on—to the Messerschmitt works at Augsburg. They arrived dead-beat at their hotel just before dinner, but their spirits picked up over the food and wine. There seemed to be no shortage of either.

Mano Rumpler was strangely restless and excited. "Let's have a night-cap in my room," he suggested. When he had poured them each a brandy, he locked the door, rather sheepishly checked the first-floor window, then said in a conspiratorial manner, "Children, I have some amazing news for you. It's so Top Secret I can hardly bring myself to tell even you." He looked at his watch. "Within six hours everyone will know." He paused. "By dawn the Reich will have marched on Russia."

Dieter was stunned. So that was where all the fighter wings from the Channel front had gone, including his own beloved JG 51. His first reaction was one of envy. The Russians were so backward. Piling up victories against the Russian air force would be so easy. His second feeling was of shock.

"But the *Reichsmarschall* made it quite clear that Britain was the main enemy and Crete merely a dress rehearsal for her conquest."

"Bluff!" said Rumpler.

"You mean that Germany doesn't intend to invade Britain?" Somewhere in his subconscious flashed a faint signal of relief.

"I didn't say that. The Führer apparently intends to conquer the enemy in the east first and mop up Britain afterwards." There was a hint of sarcasm in Rumpler's voice, a tone which he might have used on an unreliable witness in court.

"And you don't think it can be done?"

"I didn't say that, either."

The two men had almost forgotten Liese. It was, after all, their war. Now they were taken by surprise by her vehemence.

"Of course it can't be done," she cried. "It's the most criminally irresponsible thing those lunatics have done yet. Doesn't our beloved Führer know what happened to Napoleon? Has he no idea how far it is to Moscow or how cold the Russian winter can be? Germany will either bleed or freeze to death. Oh, it's crazy, crazy, apart from any ethical obligations of a so-called pact of friendship."

Dieter put his hand over her mouth. "Liese, you're overwrought. Even if you think these things, you're most unwise . . ." He turned to Rumpler: "Mano, you're a staff officer, what do you think?"

Rumpler smiled. "Calm down, you two. We're all friends here, there are no Gestapo about. I suppose, Liese, you aren't a Communist by any chance? Not that I mind."

"I'm a German," she said.

Dieter insisted: "What do you think of it, Mano?"

"It's a colossal gamble. If it comes off—fine. Our leader's been a lucky gambler, so far."

"He's a military genius."

"It's the popular belief, but all Europe believed that about Bonaparte, and he got stuck in the Russian snows."

Dieter said: "He had to rely on horses and cannons. His troops had no proper warm clothing. We've got Panzers and *Stukas* . . . even the *Stuka* will come more into its own against the Ivans."

"Maybe. But the gamble is that we must win in one tremendous knock-out blow . . . If we're still at it when winter comes . . ."

Liese was still furious. "You soldiers treat me as if my opinion isn't worth hearing. But what do you make of a supreme commander who goes against his own theories? Have you read *Mein Kampf*? Never make war on two fronts, the good book says. How many fronts is Germany fighting on now? We're fighting Britain, holding down France, Scandinavia, the Balkans, Greece and Crete. We're committed in North Africa and now the Soviet Union. How can we ever find enough men or machines?"

Mano said admiringly: "Would you like a job as my junior after the war? Of course, I agree with you. But let's be good practical Germans. How does the latest master-stroke affect our own particular aims and objects, namely to build the most efficient fighter force possible? I'll tell you the way I see it.

"No matter how desperately bad the Russians are at air combat to begin with, they're bound to get better—if they last long enough. Whatever happens, their country is too vast for a lightning victory. One: conditions on forward airfields are bound to be primitive so we can expect a lot of fighter write-offs through accidents and damage as well as in combat. Two: OKL will insist on using fighters as close support weapons for which they were never intended. The all-round drain, on 109s especially, will be enormous. Three: the British are already aware that they're faced by only two wings across the Channel. They're getting more and more aggressive. Their night-bombers are probing deeper and deeper into the Reich. If the Americans ever come in—and it may be a temptation now we've started on Russia—we'll have high altitude day bombing to contend with as well. You've no doubt heard their claims to be able to drop a bomb into a pickle-barrel from 20,000 feet? Of course, that's a bit of Yankee ballyhoo, but the Flying Fortress they've developed is a remarkable machine. So is its bomb sight. Even if the Yanks don't join Britain, our attack on Russia is going to give the RAF a useful breathing space . . ."

"You're looking on the black side of everything," Dieter insisted.

"My professional legal training teaches me to face the worst that can happen before I build up my own structure of defence."

"You mean of attack, don't you?"

Rumpler looked suddenly serious: "No, I don't. For attack purposes our leaders will give the Luftwaffe whatever they think it needs. But for defence? I very much doubt if they even see the need for it. And yet to build up a strong fighter force to protect our own country is our No 1 duty. And don't forget that fact when you stand up tomorrow morning to exhort the workers, drunk with the promise of new victories. The Reich is going to need an awful lot of fighters, whatever *Reichsmarschall* and Führer may think."

When they parted, Dieter did not even try to persuade Liese to let him share her bed. They were all too disturbed by the implications and dangers of the coming attack on Russia. When they awoke next morning, the radio in the hotel lobby was already blaring out the news. It was Poland all over again. German tanks and motorised infantry, backed by the invincible Luftwaffe, were already deep into Russian territory. Resistance was crumbling all along the invasion front.

"Isn't it wonderful?" the beaming hall-porter asked. "We'll soon show those Russkies what's what."

Mano Rumpler's sallow, ascetic face wore its most sardonic expression as he politely agreed. "Yes, at this rate we'll be in Moscow in a month."

"It won't take that long, *Herr Hauptmann*," the porter said. "The Führer knows what he's doing."

A Ju 52 took them all the way south to Augsburg. Dieter's talk went down well at the Messerschmitt plant. He was honoured by the fact that Dr Willy Messerschmitt introduced him personally. There were so many workers at Augsburg that, in order not to stop production, he had to repeat his lecture three times. Twice he was interrupted by the factory public address system putting out news from Russia. Each time, the news of fresh mileage gained in the first few hours of the attack brought cheers from his audience. Could it be that Mano Rumpler's pessimism and Liese's outright disgust were totally unjustified? Whatever happened, his duty was to inspire the men who produced the thoroughbred fighter he loved.

The Messerschmitt foremen—no doubt they had been primed to do so—asked intelligent questions. How could the 109 be improved from a pilot's point of view?

Dieter said: "Make it turn tighter than a Spitfire. Make it faster yet and above all make more and more of them."

The Messerschmitt men stamped their feet to show their approval. It was a heady atmosphere that morning of 22 June 1941.

Afterwards Dieter and Rumpler were once more escorted round the plant, this time by a chief development engineer. Once again he was surprised how freely their guide talked. They were shown several 110 night-fighters fitted with Lichtenstein and Wurzburg radar systems. They inspected the 210, the 110's much vaunted successor. "Hell of a lot of teething troubles," the Messerschmitt man explained. "We're being pressed by Udet's department to get it into service, but we're a long way off that yet." Dieter was amazed at the variations to

183

which the 109 was being submitted experimentally. "We'll get a lot out of the old war horse yet. The only limitation is the tiny size of her airframe. In two or three years' time we'll have taken the 109 about as far as it is capable of going, but I don't see her out-living her usefulness before then."

"And then?" Dieter asked.

"By then," said the chief development engineer, "we'll have given you boys something so fast it will make the 109 look as though it's going backwards."

"Any clue what it is?"

"Absolutely top secret, but if you come up to my office I'll let you see a model mock-up of the kind of machine we have in mind. It's only a toy, mind you."

There were many models locked away in a large office safe. The one he took out and placed on his desk was a twin-engined job with long pointed nose and well-streamlined cockpit canopy set high on the fuselage. Dieter tried to visualise how much forward vision the long nose would give on take-off. Even less than a 109, he decided. The model didn't tell him much. The engines were strangely blunt-nosed, perhaps because the model had no spinners. For something to say, and because he knew he wasn't supposed to ask pertinent questions, he observed politely: "The engines don't look very streamlined for an ultra high-speed job."

The engineer laughed. "I'm afraid you're right. That's because we haven't put any propellers on the model. They break too easily."

"I see. What's she called?"

"Oh," the engineer said, "she may not even see the light of day, but we give each new design a type number. This one is the 262."

The tour got under way at an almost bewildering pace. It would have been completely bewildering had not Liese been there to smooth out the day-to-day details of travel and accommodation. She also acted as secretary to them both, and to Rumpler in particular. Dieter soon discovered that Mano was no passenger on the trip. He was shrewdly assessing production blockages, supply shortages, manufacturing short cuts and managerial snags, all of which were taken down in shorthand by Liese and neatly typed in daily reports.

The schedule was a tight one. They seemed to be covering almost as much ground daily as the victorious German armies in Russia.

Dieter was amazed how widely spread was Germany's fighter production, how many small factories in small towns seemed to be making vital components or sometimes the same components. He remarked on this to Rumpler one evening.

"That's one of poor Udet's troubles. For a totalitarian state, our vital industries are remarkably go-as-you-please. You'd think every factory in the Reich would have been completely regimented and told exactly what to produce, but not a bit of it! Udet's ELK scheme is a beginning, but it will take a long time to rationalise production. Never forget that the Luftwaffe is only six years old. Its roots are the private enterprise firms who, three years ago, were still designing aircraft for sport and civil transport and cutting each other's throats to get orders. Your pet 109 was virtually 'an accident. We wouldn't have it but for Willy Messerschmitt's talent for building light sports planes. Now we need an industrial genius to make sense of it all. Meantime, what do we have? A trio of opposed personalities. Milch, our secretary of state, schemes to get Udet, the head of the Technical Office, fired. Chief of Staff Hans Jeschonnek just touches his peaked hat to everything Hitler and Goering tell him, and you know what they tell him—'the fighters have let us down. Give us as many bombers as you can.' "

Dieter soon began to find that giving what was basically the same lecture day after day became extremely wearing. His relationship with Liese suffered. She insisted on remaining the essence of propriety as far as their love-life went. Sometimes they would get away together to a cinema or a restaurant in the evening, and then they would both feel the current flowing between them as strongly as ever, but when they returned to their hotel Liese went firmly to her own room and Dieter less firmly to his. Once when they had a spare afternoon and Mano had gone off to visit some Leipzig relations, he persuaded her to let him come to her bedroom. They made love because Liese was in the end no more able to hold back than he was. Yet it was far from the miracle they had known together in the Austrian Alps. She clung to him afterwards saying she was sorry that she had been no good but she felt ill at ease. She couldn't explain why. Maybe it was because Mano might come back at any moment.

"Good God, Liese, I thought you were emancipated."

"I thought so, too, but somehow I feel furtive. Perhaps I'm more old-fashioned than I thought."

"Perhaps," he said sulkily.

"I do love you, Dieter."

"I know. That's why it seems so strange that you can't be as you were at Lech. In the Alps . . ."

She began to cry. "Oh, don't start that again!"

Mano Rumpler increasingly sensed the strain between them. One night towards the end of the fourth week he said: "Children, I hate playing gooseberry. I'm quite prepared to stay in a separate hotel if it helps. Or, better still, why don't you get married? Then you can fight together and sleep together quite legally."

To Dieter's surprise, Liese began to laugh. He asked, "Will you, Liese?"

"Yes," she said, her laughter dying down. "It's an extraordinary sort of proposal. Mano, you don't look like Cupid."

"I agree. But I am a staff officer and that's probably even more use. On Saturday we have a free half-day in my home city, Dresden. I'll arrange a special licence. How would that do? It's the most beautiful city to get married in, the loveliest in Germany."

"Mano, you're a miracle! You shall be best man."

"Naturally, my dear fellow. Let's have a bottle of champagne on you to celebrate."

In late July, the Bristows had a rare family reunion in London. They arranged to meet in a favourite haunt of Peter's, the small downstairs bar of Scott's Restaurant just off Piccadilly Circus. Peter arrived first. London that summer of 1941 wore a temporarily relaxed air. The Luftwaffe bomber force, heavily engaged in Russia, had left the capital alone for the moment. No one expected that this could last for long and the total defeats in Greece and Crete, as well as the early German successes in Russia, prevented undue optimism. Still it was enjoyable to be able to sit in the cool, oak-panelled bar without interruption by siren, bomb or gunfire. The bar was shared by three RAF officers and their girlfriends, not all of them yet in uniform, also a noisy group of Royal Artillery NCOs and gunners from a heavy anti-aircraft battery stationed in the Thames Estuary. In those days, Scott's was a rendezvous for a certain kind of British "other ranks" which was already fast disappearing. These were the young men for whom Scott's had been an habitual West End meeting place in peacetime. They had joined as Territorials and were still proud of their lowly staus as gunners or junior NCOs. It seemed to confer on them the cherished badge of amateurism for which they had learned a reverence at public school and in Rugby clubs. Their days as amateurs were numbered and they knew it. One, who wore the white tabs of an Officer Cadet Training Unit, was obviously the butt of his friends who had so far escaped this awful fate.

Peter rose as his mother and sister entered. There was someone with them, and he recognised Tom Roland's son, Michael.

He kissed his mother and shook hands with Michael. "Nice to see you, Mike."

"And you, Peter. You look great."

"And my interestingly different sister." They had learned to tease each other gently about their scars.

"She looks just beautiful to me," Michael said. "And I think the uniform suits her, don't you?" Peter stood back to admire his sister's WAAF uniform, and pick an imaginary hair off her tunic.

They were all very aware of the posters which said: "Careless talk costs lives" and "Be like dad, keep mum." So in the crowded bar they talked only generalities. Upstairs in the restaurant, secure at a corner table, they felt freer to discuss their current activities, although none of them was exactly secret.

Mrs Bristow had become a WVS area organiser for North Devon with HQ in Exeter. Kate, now past her basic instruction, had got her wish: she had applied for, and been granted, the first vacancy on a course to train operations room staff. Michael, passed fit for duty, found himself guarding a bomber base in East Anglia against possible German parachute attack; a task, he said, which had made him one of the best cookhouse whitewashers and dustbin burnishers in Eastern Command. It was Peter who had the most surprising news: a medical board had passed him fit for operations again. He was to undergo a refresher course on Spits, but first he had an appalling chore to perform. Some bright spark at the Ministry of Aircraft Production had hit on the idea that if a few flying types toured aircraft factories, it would encourage the men on the factory floor to work a bit harder.

"You know the sort of thing—the man from the ministry asks lathe operator how many planes he's turned out that week.

" 'Fifteen,' says the workman.

" 'Spitfires?' asks the ministry man.

" 'Oh, fighters!' says the workman. 'I thought you said lighters.' "

187

They all laughed, uncomfortably, aware that there might be a grain of truth in the story.

Peter said: "That's the sort of thing I'm supposed to discourage. I don't suppose many of these stories are true but I bet there aren't any of the same kind circulating in Nazi Germany. They'll be absolutely organised there, even if they have to shoot a few shop stewards in the process."

Dieter and Liese were married in a brief civil ceremony in Dresden, a city whose baroque beauty the war seemed never likely to touch. Mano Rumpler was their best man. Afterwards Mano treated them to an expensive lunch with two bottles of vintage champagne.

"Strictly speaking," he said, "the bride's father should pick up the bill for the wedding breakfast, but seeing that you two never thought to let either of your parents know, I suppose I'll have to do the honours."

Dieter was overcome with remorse that in the hustle of their tour he hadn't found time to tell even his mother.

Mano said soothingly: "Both your parents know your feelings for each other, otherwise your father wouldn't have let his best secretary go to look after you. When we've drunk the rest of the champagne, we'll compose a lovely telegram, and after the shock has worn off, you'll find that they'll be delighted . . . Oh, by the way, children. Although it is still early in the day, you might care to know that the accommodation reserved for you at the hotel is, in fact, the bridal suite."

There were ten days of solid travelling and lecturing still ahead. The tour was no less arduous but now there was Liese, warm and loving again, waiting at the end of every day. By the start of the final week they were far out towards the Polish frontier. There, the always patriotic Dieter received two shocks, one of them horrible. Perhaps he should have been prepared for them, for that last morning at Lech in the Arlberg Liese had warned him of the first of these and they had quarrelled about it. Now he saw with his own eyes that what she had said then was indeed true.

At the railway station where they disembarked Liese and Mano had gone ahead to check on accommodation, leaving him to await their return. A train composed of cattle trucks stood at an adjoining platform and there were SS troops standing along the permanent way beside it. Suddenly a shouting and stamping arose from one of the trucks. The door slid back revealing a mass of humanity in striped, pyjama-like suits. One figure leapt or perhaps fell on to the track. Instantly an SS man cocked his machine-pistol and fired a burst into the prostrate man's body. It was then that Dieter saw that the "man" was a woman with a shaven head. Two more guards came running up and forced the press of prisoners—for such they must be—back into the truck, clubbing them with their rifle butts. Dieter stared in shock at the body of the woman now being pushed into the truck from which it had a moment before fallen. The cattle-truck door slammed on living and dead. He turned to an SS captain who came hurrying along the platform.

"What happened? Who are they?"

"Polish criminals. Shot while trying to escape. They're like wild animals. All this consignment are guilty of murderous attacks on German soldiers. They don't deserve to live."

Dieter went into the men's lavatory and threw up. As he retched, he heard the train puffing and clanking out of the station. When he emerged a few minutes later there was nothing to show that the incident had ever taken place except a red stain on the track ballast and the brassy gleam of a few spent cartridge cases. Surely the brutality of their treatment must far outweigh whatever crimes those people had committed? He remembered Liese's story of the Polish worker struck down with an iron bar at his father's new factory. Surely such horrible things must be isolated incidents? He would talk to Mano about it—but not to Liese. He must come to terms with himself first.

He told Mano that evening.

"I believe you. The SS are bastards."

"But they're supposed to be an elite arm of our armed forces."

"Elite, my arse. They're born bully-boys. You must realise, Dieter, that every nation, like every individual, has a dark side to its character. It's something we Germans especially have to be constantly aware of. There's a hairy ape in our cupboard armed with a damned great club."

"But don't the authorities . . . even the Führer . . .?"

"Don't be so naïve, dear boy. In wartime especially it's handy to have some well-trained bully-boys around. So long as you keep them chained up. The danger is when the chain becomes too long or individual links too weak."

"Even if those Poles, and I suppose they were Poles . . ."

"Poles or Jews or, worse still, Polish Jews."

"Even if they had committed crimes against our army, surely justice demands some form of court martial? What I saw was murder."

"My dear boy, get this into your young head. You and those who fight your sort of battle are the only elite at this time and place and we will be happier if we concentrate on that."

The second shock was mild by comparison. It was something that had been growing slowly throughout the last month, coming to a head at the last three plants they visited. These were all small factories specialising in experimental cockpit pressurisation, for the latest and future marks of the 109. Dieter had had some experience already of fighting at high altitudes in unpressurised cockpits and was consequently fascinated at what these three entirely different and independent plants had to tell them. The staggering fact was that all were pursuing quite separate lines. No one had thought of directing or guiding their activities or pooling their resources and brains. Each was proceeding as though the competitive free market of peacetime still existed. When he ranted, Mano said: "I warned you that our aircraft industry wasn't quite as coordinated as you pilots have every right to expect. Well, that's what I came along for—not that I have much hope that our Technical Office is in any shape to do much about it. I don't really think poor Udet's "Operation Elk" has had much chance of growing a set of antlers with which to defend itself, let alone beating some sense into the aircraft industry. What we need is some standardisation and tough ministerial direction."

Eight hundred miles away in the south of England, Peter Bristow had begun his tour of aircraft factories supplying the RAF. He found himself teamed up with a Wellington skipper who had survived the battle of Heligoland Bight in 1940 and an Australian Hurricane pilot with ten victories to his credit. The three pilots stoically accepted the chore they had been given. In the train on the way to visit their first assignment, a plant making aero engines, they talked cynically about their future civilian hosts.

"They'll probably all be on strike," suggested the Australian.

"For better danger money," the Wellington captain suggested.

"What we really need to shake our war industries up," Peter said, "is a touch of Nazi ruthlessness."

A black Ministry of Aircraft Production Humber saloon was waiting to take them to the aero engines plant. They were ushered straight into the office of the managing director, a tough little, grey-haired Yorkshireman.

"Sit down, gentlemen, sit down. You'll have to excuse me if I seem a bit disorganised, but to tell the truth, I've only been here twenty-four hours myself. You chaps aren't the only ones who can get posted whether you like it or not. The ministry's just hauled me out of a Midland factory making landing-gear to try to knock some sense into this lot. Beaverbrook and his minions are in no mood to be buggered about, I can tell you. I've got exactly three months to raise production here, otherwise the whole damn plant'll be taken over by Rolls Royce. How's that for ministerial toughness? So somehow or other it's up to management to get some co-operation from the factory floor. You lads have come along at a very opportune time, I can tell you. Our workers need a shot in the arm."

It was early August when Dieter and Liese Reh returned to Hamelin. Mano had left them a week before. The orders that had sent him hurrying back to the inspector of fighters' office in Berlin made Dieter long to be back in action himself. Werner Mölders, while leading JG 51, now deep in Russian territory, had been appointed inspector of fighter aircraft. Typically, Mölders intended both to direct fighter operations in Russia and to shake up and reorganise the Berlin office in charge of the whole fighter forces of the Reich, and Mano had been sent for because Mölders wanted his personal report on fighter aircraft production. Dieter recalled Mölders' remark at St Omer when he had said that he might soon have some influence in the inspector's department. Well, now he was in charge of it!

Dieter's head wound gave him little pain now; he had no doubt that he would be passed fit for flying duties at once. His only trouble was that since the murder of the Polish woman at the railway station he had suffered spells of sleeplessness—such as he had never known before, even at the height of the Channel battles. He knew that Liese was aware of this, even though he lay still so as not to disturb her from the deep, healthy sleep she enjoyed so effortlessly. It occurred to him that if he told her of the incident it might cease to trouble him so severely, yet for some reason he held back. The truth was

191

that he did not want a discussion with her that might in any way weaken his faith in Reich and Führer. He told himself that once he was flying again such thoughts would disappear.

Dieter had hoped to meet Mölders again at his new HQ in Berlin. The *Kommodore,* however, now a lieutenant general, had left for the Russian front the day before. Mano Rumpler greeted Dieter with the news that he was to report to Room 279 at the *Luftfahrtministerium* at 1800 hours that evening to give a personal account of the factories he had visited. Mano's own written report had been read by Mölders, who had already asked for an interview with the *Reichsmarschall* to discuss certain aspects of fighter production. When Dieter asked to whom he was to report at the Air Ministry, Mano smiled and said that he was not instructed to divulge that but that he rather thought the duty would occupy the whole evening, possibly well into the early hours. Liese, alas, would not be able to attend. However, with the *Oberleutnant*'s permission, Mano would take to himself the honour of entertaining her and would afterwards escort her back to the hotel to await Dieter's return.

Mano had welcome news of the *Erprobungs* flight. They were still at Werneuchen. The new Focke Wulfs had taken longer than expected to come from the factory with the result that conversion to the new machine had only just been completed. There was news, too, of their new *Kommodore.* Adolf Galland had been shot down by a Spitfire over St Omer on the very day Dieter had started his tour. Goering had forbidden him to fly until he was fully recovered but Galland had totally ignored this and had suffered a second narrow escape when a British 20 mm cannon shell had exploded on the armoured plate Galland's mechanic had fitted against orders behind the *Kommodore*'s head. In each case, disobedience of orders had been overlooked. Galland had given his mechanic 100 marks and some extra leave. The Führer had awarded Galland the Oak Leaves to Swords to the Knight's Cross of the Iron Cross, a hitherto unheard-of decoration for bravery. All this only made Dieter keener to rejoin his *Schwarm* and lead them back into the air. But first there was the unknown ordeal of the interview at the Air Ministry to be faced.

The identity of the occupant of Room 279 was indeed a shock. As Dieter entered, prepared to salute some high-ranking staff officer, his father rose from behind the desk to meet him.

"Well, well, my boy, I'm sure you never expected to find me here?"

Herr Reh wore a civilian suit of brown barathea, but cut like a military tunic and with a Party Member's badge on the right lapel. He caught Dieter's look. "Ah, my suit. How do you like it? It has military overtones, wouldn't you say? I had my tailor make it on service dress lines for the days when I am on duty here at the ministry."

"You've not given up running the factories, father?"

"Dear me no, but thanks to the efficiency of your dear mother, and our other executives—and now I hope, too, of your own charming wife—congratulations by the way, I can't say the marriage was totally unexpected—thanks to all these good people, I now have the chance to serve Germany at a higher level. Our good friend, Ernst Udet, asked me to put in at least two days a week at the ministry to help co-ordinate our industrial effort. So how could I refuse?"

"Congratulations, father."

"I can't deny it's a feather in my cap, though that, naturally, is not the prime consideration. There's a great deal of streamlining to be done, as you yourself may have noticed . . . I hear first-class reports of your tour, by the way."

"I'm glad. But now I want nothing more than to get back in action."

A secretary knocked. "The car is ready, *Herr Direktor*."

"Good. Now you'll be able to make your report in person to the man who matters."

"Whom are we to see, father?"

"You'll soon find out. It's a great honour to be asked to his private residence."

The Mercedes whisked them through the fashionable streets of Berlin. There were more uniforms now than Dieter had noticed before. The women were still well-dressed and the shops well filled. There was a lightness in everyone's step in tune with the fine early August evening and a poster which said: *Von Kleist's Panzers approaching Smolensk.* Only when they turned off the Unter Den Linden towards a residential area of expensive apartments was there a jarring note: a single building had been destroyed by a bomb, showing up like a gap in an otherwise perfect set of teeth—a reminder that the RAF could get to Berlin even if it could not yet do much damage.

Since his father was obviously enjoying the drama of the situation, Dieter did not press him as to their destination. He had, however, guessed long before the Mercedes stopped in front of a luxurious house standing in its own walled garden. Typically, their host met them in person as they emerged from the lift. *Generaloberst* Udet held out his hand to Reh senior and slapped Dieter on the shoulder.

Dieter saluted. Udet waved his hand. "Off duty now, my lad." Dieter had last seen the general six weeks ago behind a desk. Now, as he stood under the chandelier in the hall, he seemed to have shrunk in size; some essential quality seemed to have left his ebullient stocky body. He looked shrivelled and ill, with bags under his eyes, and he had clearly taken quite a lot of alcohol on board.

A Luftwaffe *Gefreiter* in dress uniform came forward with a tray of champagne glasses as Udet ushered them into his apartment. The study was a wonderland to Dieter; the walls were covered with photographs: Udet in the cockpit of a World War One fighter, Udet in a group of leather-coated pilots of the famous *Richthofen* Circus; a wooden propeller from a 1917 Fokker D VII inscribed with a total of 72 aerial victories, giving aircraft, type and date; photos of Udet with Charles Lindbergh, with Hanna Reitsch, Germany's greatest airwoman; Udet at international air displays, standing beside the Heinkel 100 in which he had set the world speed record; Udet holding the propeller of one of the Curtis Hawks he had brought back from America and which had been the basis of his and the Luftwaffe's whole disastrous dive-bomber philosophy; a picture of two World War One pilots standing with their arms around each other—one was Udet, the other his old wing-commander of Western Front days. Hermann Goering.

Udet watched the young pilot's eyes ranging over this aviation museum.

"Something to look back on, eh?"

"Yes, *Herr General*, and a great ideal to look forward to."

"H'm. Maybe." Udet examined some of his photographs as if he had never looked at them properly before. "Some good times. Some good friends." His glance lingered on the picture of himself with the *Reichsmarschall*. "Times at least change, eh?" He gestured more champagne towards the Rehs and himself took three fingers of cognac.

"Sit down, Oberleutnant Reh. Tell me your impressions of our aircraft manufacturing potential. No, I'll tell you. It's a bloody mess. But it won't be by the time my operation ELK has stirred those boys up with a good prod or two of his antlers. We could get it all humming along beautifully if it wasn't for the politicians and their bloody intrigues. That's why I've pulled in your father and a few far-seeing industrialists like him to help me sort it all out. Well, lad, what *were* your impressions, eh?"

"Perhaps a little less free enterprise, a little more regimentation, *Herr General.*"

"Precisely. And what did you think of some of the new types you perhaps saw?"

"Where sheer inventive genius is concerned our aircraft designers are second to none."

"Agreed. The problem is to pick the winners."

"Fighting on so many fronts, we shall need great numbers of fighters, *Herr General.*"

Udet smiled: "As a fighter pilot you could hardly be expected to say anything else, but the fact is that Führer insists on bombers. We're already producing 350 new fighters a month. That should be enough for anyone."

"The RAF is getting more and more aggressive, *Herr General.*"

"When our long-range Heinkel 177 starts bombing them . . ." Dieter's father began.

"Ah, *when*. If only we could find a way of stopping its damned engine from going on fire . . ." Udet stared into his replenished brandy *ballon*. He shook his head as if coming out of a troubled dream and said abruptly: "That's enough shop for the moment. I expect you and that smart fellow Rumpler have put it all in a written report, anyway. Let's eat and drink and relax a bit, eh?"

Just before midnight, Udet led the way to his gunroom.

"I seem to remember, my lad, that you're a pretty fair shot. Let's see if you can beat the old warrior, eh?"

Sporting rifles of many calibres gleamed under their protecting film of oil in racks lining one complete wall. A horizontal show-case was filled with revolvers and automatics of various nationalities and periods, from a pair of gold-inlaid Navy Colts, dated 1880, to the latest Olympic target pistols.

"Choose your weapon."

Dieter selected the pistol he was most familiar with, a Lüger automatic.

Udet approved: "The finest service pistol in the world. Now which shall I take? I'll give you a fair chance, my lad— the Navy Colts, black powder, ball and percussion caps, given me by a United States Army Air Corps general. Have a drink, young Reh."

Udet drew back a curtain, revealing target frames and blocks of lead already hammered by the impact of many bullets.

Dieter was aware that his hand was no longer as steady as it should have been, but he outshot the general on the first two targets. Udet continued to fill Dieter's glass as well as his own, and before long Dieter had difficulty in focusing on the target. The competition became a confused pattern of concussions, powder fumes, an occasional glimpse of his father watching them both from an armchair with an amused smile on his face, adding to the general smokiness of the air with the blue clouds from a long Havana cigar.

By the fourth target, Dieter was only just in the lead. Udet refilled his champagne glass, and said: "Once more. You'll see. I'll win. I have the gun here to finish it off. Finish anything off . . . my beautiful Mexican Colt."

Hazily Dieter knew that, just as Udet had intended, he was now far less in a state to compete than was the general. Dieter shot first, missing the outer ring twice, putting two in the magpie ring for a total of six points; the last shot was off the target altogether.

He collapsed in a chair because he could no longer stand. Distantly he heard the general calling his shots. "One for you, Hans. One for you, dear Erhard. And the last three all for my oldest friend, Hermann."

Dieter passed out. When he came to he was in the staff car on the way back to the hotel. His father had vanished but Mano Rumpler was waiting for him in the lobby.

"I thought you might need some help," he said sardonically.

By early September they were back together again, based on Abbeville, with the famous "yellow-nosed boys" of JG 26. The Focke Wulf 190, designed by Kurt Tank in response to a request from the *Luftfahrtministerium* as long ago as 1937 for an alternative fighter to the Bf 109, was a revelation to Dieter and all who flew it. Powered by a BMW 801 radial engine, it had a top speed of 400 mph. It could outdive, climb or zoom the 109f. Its four MG 17 machine-guns, two in the upper fuselage and two in the wing roots, provided at least adequate fire-power. Only at high altitudes did its remarkable performance fall off. Up to 20,000 feet it was likely to be more than a match for the Spitfire Vbs coming into service across the Channel.

The *Erprobungs-schwarm* was now fully equipped with the 190. Their task during the first weeks of September was to visit those squadrons of JG 26 whose new mount it was to be and to demonstrate its abilities and characteristics before conversion. On one of these visits, Dieter had a pleasant surprise. A young blond lieutenant suddenly appeared round the corner of a hangar and gave him an exaggeratedly formal salute, his hand almost covering his face. The effect was somewhat spoilt by the fact that the face hidden by the salute was having some trouble in composing itself.

Dieter said rather pompously: "What is the joke, lieutenant?"

The hand snapped down and revealed the grinning face of Jacob, his brother.

"Jacob! When were you posted here?"

"A week ago. I haven't been in action yet."

"Plenty of time for that."

"Any chance of joining your outfit, Dieter?"

"Hey! You have to prove you can fly first."

"Try me."

"I might do that."

"Couldn't you take me on my first sortie? I'd fly as wingman to you."

"No, thanks, I want to stay alive for a bit."

Jacob's flight commander readily gave permission for an operational training flight over the Channel with Dieter as escort. Dieter watched with approval his brother's tidy take-off in a battle-scarred 109f. He was amazed at the ease with which his Focke Wulf 190 closed with the 109. They climbed towards the coast at 10,000 feet.

"Look out for yourself, young Jacob. You're on your own. When you come out of those clouds ahead, I'll be looking for you."

Dieter had slid away round the cloud bank, climbing for an up-sun position from which to make a mock attack. But when he looked for the 109 emerging from the cloud, the sky was empty. Only one explanation. Jacob had doubled back into cloud. Dieter put down the nose and pushed the throttle all the way forward to the safety stop. He passed through the cloud bank at over 400 mph. As he came out into the clear beyond he expected to see Jacob's 109 ahead. It wasn't. Fighter pilot instinct made him swivel his head like a nervous falcon tethered to a block. His glance showed him a glint up-sun. Precocious little bastard! He was being jumped. Dieter yanked the 190 round in a blood-draining climbing turn to port in time to see the 109 overshoot. Then he half-rolled and executed a split-S relying on superior speed to catch him, but Jacob had found the cloud and vanished.

He called up on the R/T: "I suppose you think that's clever?"

"Not too bad."

"Game's over. I'm closing up on you."

As they re-formed the traditional *Rotte* at 15,000 feet well out over the Channel, Dieter suddenly had a crazy impulse. "You've passed, Jacob. Let's go looking for trouble."

"Horrido!" Jacob gave the fighter pilot's traditional cry of exultation, the equivalent of the RAF's "Tally ho!" St Horridus was the Luftwaffe's patron saint, a product of mess parties rather than of formal canonisation. *"Horrido!"* was also cried after a kill.

"Shut up! We're going to annoy the RAF."

The British coast was ahead, partly hidden by cumulonimbus cloud. They crossed at Folkestone, turning north. Just inland, Dieter saw the two Spitfires five thousand feet below. The Rehs were in a beautiful position with the sun behind. He waggled his wings and pointed, and saw Jacob acknowledge.

"Wir greiffen an."

Immediately the 109's nose went down at an angle of forty-five degrees. The Spits weren't expecting trouble and still hadn't seen them. He recalled Mölders' advice: "Try to get a young pilot his first kill without shock."

"Let him have it. *Now!* Jacob."

He was so busy watching his young brother's tail that he forgot to fire. Jacob's tracers stitched the flank of the Spit about the wing root. It burned at once and fell away out of control. The second Spitfire broke right before he could get more than a two-second burst into it. Remembering his duty as a wingman he scanned the sky for opposition. No one there!

"Home, Jacob."

"Horrido!"

"You can say that now. Well done!"

The surviving British Spitfire pilot landed to tell his intelligence officer that he'd been attacked by an entirely new type of German radial-engined fighter. But no one believed him.

"Could only have been a captured Curtis Hawk," said the IO. "They've got a few over from Dunkirk days, but I can't imagine they'd risk coming over here in them. Too bloody dangerous. The other chap was a yellow-nosed 109, you say?

Perhaps they were both 109s. Mistakes have been made before in the heat of battle."

"I tell you it was something new and horribly manoeuvrable. Luckily for me they both seemed in a hurry to get back to France."

The IO put in the pilot's report with his own doubting qualifications. It wasn't until a week later when a Spitfire sweep tangled with a gaggle of these strange fighters over Amiens that the penny began to drop: the Germans had got something entirely new after all.

Despite the excellent early combat reports of the 190, Mano Rumpler was depressed. Fighters were barely coming off the production lines fast enough to replace losses on the still-expanding Russian front, let alone build up the Channel defences against the increasingly aggressive RAF. Udet appeared to realise the need which Mölders, on his rare lightning visits to Berlin from Russia, emphasised again and again. "Give us fighters and yet more fighters." Yet Udet seemed a defeated man, unable to cope with Erhard Milch who had wanted him out of the job from the start. Nor was Chief of Staff Hans Jeschonnek any help to Udet. He listened only to the Führer and had become his yes-man. As for the *Reichsmarschall!* It was true that Goering had approved of Udet's decision to let Kurt Tank build the Reich's first radial-engined fighter as far back as 1940. Goering had even ordered Udet and Tank to "turn them out like Frankfurters." But there was precious little sign of Goering's backing for Udet or his production plans now. Goering still appeared to believe that the defence of the Reich would never become necessary, while all the Führer wanted was bombers for revenge and attack. Alas, on this score, too, it was plain that Udet had backed a wrong horse. The long-range He 177 with its four engines, paired in tandem, was showing itself more and more reluctant to fly without catching fire. Though bomber production was not the concern of Mano's office, the facts of the He 177 disaster inevitably came his way from reliable sources. German Bomber Command was reluctantly having to fall back on so-called improved versions of medium bombers like the He 111 and Ju 88, whose shortcomings were already apparent. Poor Udet!

What depressed Mano on this early October day was that he had just heard that Udet had returned from a more or less enforced leave of absence on the *Reichsmarschall*'s hunting estate on the Rominten Heide to find his office carpet being pulled from under him. The head of Udet's planning staff, General Tschersich, had been dismissed in his absence, and his chief of staff, General Floch, had been posted without warning to the Russian front. Udet had clearly been thrown to the wolves.

Mano Rumpler was sad for Ernst Udet, but his depression was rooted in something deeper: an intuitive feeling that everything was coming apart at the seams.

November was a bad month for fighter activity. For days on end, mist and fog grounded the two wings which Adolf Galland of JG 26 and Walter Oesau of JG2 were busy moulding into a small but shining shield against the only enemy in the air whom they both considered should be taken seriously —Britain. Bad visibility gave occasional opportunity for hit-and-run fighter bomber raids. The *Erprobungs* flight had its work cut out training pilots as well as making trial sorties with the 190 in a *Jabo* role, a task which was to the liking of none of them. There were one or two bright spots in the November murk. Willy Weiss and Shoehorn Kolbe added a Spitfire Mark V apiece to their scoreboard and Dieter accounted for a lone Blenheim that came over in eight-tenths cloud to bomb St Omer airfield. They had also received reinforcements. Two more Werneuchen graduates of Dieter's class, the Prussian Hoffman twins, had been posted to the flight from Jever, the main fighter base on the German Bight to the north. Both Hoffmans had eight kills to their credit and were reckoned to have the right temperament for both experimental work and instruction. The *Erprobungs* flight now carried a chevron which showed its aircraft were attached to the HQ Squadron. In addition, Dieter had obtained permission for his pilots to paint their personal insignia on the cowlings of their aircraft. So Kolbe had his shoehorn and Willy Weiss an edelweiss bloom. Pohle had wished to have a pair of girl's legs in black stockings but had been forced to settle for a hammer and anvil—he had been an apprentice blacksmith before joining the Luftwaffe. Dieter had always known the emblem he would choose if the time ever came—a roebuck's head. He instructed the squadron sign painter to give his buck a real trophy head and to position it with horns tilting forward in a charging attitude. As a final touch he had an RAF roundel impaled on one of the horns. The Hoffman twins solved their problems quite simply. The Zodiac sign of Gemini was embellished with a figure "One" for Fritz and

"Two" for Heinz, for that was the order in which they had been born.

The dripping November gloom was slightly relieved by the arrival of Mano Rumpler in a Ju 52. The Inspector of Day Fighters working under General Mölders, who was once again back in the Crimea directing operations there, had sent Mano on a liaison visit of Channel fighter units to report on their problems and difficulties.

Mano sought Dieter out in his quarters on the evening of his arrival, 15 November.

"You look happier than when I last saw you, my boy."

"I made no pretence about it, did I? Flying for me, every time. Talking I leave to experts like you, Mano. If only we could get some decent flying weather."

"What do you think of the FW 190?"

"It's a hell of a good kite but I suppose I'm really a Messerschmitt man at heart. If we ever have to fight at high altitudes, as we did over Britain, I'm putting in for a 109 again."

"What about armament?"

"Adequate. The centrally mounted machine-guns aren't so subject to G-forces as wing guns. But I'd like to feel there were a few cannon around as well as machine-guns."

"That's much of what your dear *Kommodore* said. By God, that man Galland is a ball of fire. He doesn't seem to mind what he says or whom he says it to. He needs to watch his tail a bit."

"I shouldn't worry about him, Mano. He's already given the *Reichsmarschall* a burst or two, I hear."

"Galland sees clearly that the day's going to come when Germany will need every fighter she can lay her hands on and I'm not talking about a close support role for the army. That's all the top brass seem to think about. Mind you, they've got their hands full in Russia, too bloody full."

"Is it going to be all right there?"

Mano's sallow features became even more parchmentlike. "The winter's here already. At the very best we're bogged down until the spring."

The morning of 17 November was once again overcast and dull. Certainly not favourable flying weather for operations over the Channel. Dieter had just told his duty pilots to stand down until further notice when the orderly room called. He was to report to the adjutant at once.

Mano was in the office when he arrived. The adjutant was

unusually formal, saying, "This officer has been recalled to Berlin immediately, and the *Kommodore* would like you to fly him. The quickest way is to take him in the HQ communications *Taifun*. We've checked with the controller. Apparently the weather's improving over the Reich. You should get off within the hour."

"When do I report back, sir? Today?"

The adjutant said drily, "I daresay you'll find the weather will close in as soon as you reach Berlin. It may even shut down for twenty-four hours."

"Thank you, sir."

Directly they were outside, Dieter said to Mano: "What's this all about? Why are you so important all of a sudden?"

"I can't talk now. I'll tell you once we're airborne."

"Okay. If you insist on being so damn secretive."

"I do."

"I'll just have to be patient then."

Once the beautiful little four-seater Messerschmitt was in the air, Dieter asked, "Well?"

"It's terrible, Dieter. Udet's dead."

"*What!* How?"

"I'm not supposed to know the truth, but my CO leaked it. A gun accident."

"Udet? Never!"

"Quite. All the same that's the way it was passed to me. Whatever the exact truth is there's bound to be a shake-up all round. That's why I'm wanted back. Apparently Mölders is expected to fly home from the Crimea."

They were above cloud now. Dieter called base and got a reassurance about the weather ahead. He checked his course and sat silent for some minutes, shocked by the news. Then Mano said gently, "I know you had a high regard for him. All you young pilots did. He was something of a folk hero even to me."

"A gun accident!"

"My CO stressed the word 'accident.' "

"Then there are only two possible constructions . . . murder or suicide."

"You saw Udet recently. He was breaking up under the strain. He felt he was being blamed for everything."

"Did you learn anything else?"

"Only that the gun in question was his favourite Mexican Colt."

Dieter remembered Udet saying, through the alcoholic haze

of that evening at his apartment, "One for you, Hans. One for you, dear Erhard. And the last three of all for my oldest friend Hermann . . ." Milch, Jeschonnek and Goering. The three stools he had fallen between. And, "My lovely Mexican Colt. The pistol to finish anything."

An hour later, as they turned into circuit for Tempelhof airport, they heard the official announcer intoning the sad news:

"The general in charge of Luftwaffe supplies, General-oberst Ernst Udet, has been killed testing a new weapon. He died of his injuries on the way to hospital. The Führer has ordered a state funeral for this officer who died in so tragic a manner. The Führer has perpetuated Generaloberst Udet's name by bestowing it upon *Jagdgeschwader* No 3."

Before leaving the airfield, Dieter had telephoned Liese to tell her that he was coming to Berlin, and there was a message from her with Mano's orderly sergeant at the Lindenstrasse office: she would be at the hotel where they had stayed that night of the party at Udet's flat. There was a message, too, from HQ Squadron, Abbeville. Dieter was to stand by in Berlin in order to fly the officers attending Udet's state funeral back to their Channel bases.

Udet's body was lying in state at the air ministry. High-ranking Luftwaffe aces had been summoned to act as guard of honour, and Galland and Oesau were coming by special train from France. The General of Fighters, Werner Mölders himself, was rushing back by air from the Crimea.

Mano said: "If you ask me, Mölders is glad of the chance to twist the *Reichsmarschall*'s arm about fighter replacements and spares. He's being pushed to the limit out there. Our general will want to know who Udet's successor is going to be so that he can state his point of view at once."

Berlin dripped in the November mist. The weather at Tempelhof closed in again next day. Even if Dieter had not received orders to stay, it would have been impossible to get off. Liese and he luxuriated in the respite, lying in bed late, loving as though the opportunity might never occur again, a thought constantly unspoken between them. For the same reason that he had withheld his shock and horror at the murder of the Polish woman prisoner, he now kept to himself what he knew of Udet's death. He was troubled by the deception but feared his loyalties would be even more troubled by Liese's bitter comments on the Reich's leadership.

He telephoned Mano's office on the morning of the state funeral. Still no orders to return. Would it be possible to attend the funeral? Mano went away and talked with his CO. Yes, it would be possible to squeeze him in with the party from the general of fighters' office.

Dieter dressed hurriedly in his best uniform and by luck found one of the few taxis prowling the streets like tired jackals. The absence of taxis and private cars had grown noticeably great since the Russian offensive had begun. Equally noticeable was the increase of women in uniform. Girls of the Women's Air Force—the *Luftwaffen Helferinnen,* in- blue open-necked tunic with eagle on the left breast were particularly in evidence.

Mano met him on the steps. The party was ready to leave. As they climbed into the waiting military bus, Mano whispered: "The general has been unable to get here. His Heinkel's been held up by bad weather."

The ceremony was deeply impressive. The guard of honour of Luftwaffe aces—Galland, Oesau, Lützow, Pelz, all in jackboots and steel helmets, huge ceremonial Luftwaffe swords held steadily at the salute. Wagner's Funeral March from *Götterdämmerung* played by the Berlin Philharmonic. Goering in light grey uniform with brown boots and enormous spurs. Rows of *Wehrmacht* generals. Party leaders. Dr Goebbels in a brown leather cloak. Then Goering standing alone before the rows of microphones.

"Now we must take leave of you. The thought that you are no longer with us, dear Udet, is inconceivable. It is not my task to praise your services, for by your deeds you have become immortal . . . You gave our brave young pilots confidence in their weapons, for what you conceived and flew, they took for granted . . ."

Dieter could not repress the memory of Udet saying as he fired the fatal Colt: "And three for you, my dear Hermann."

Somewhere there was something grievously at odds.

The *Reichsmarschall* was winding up grandiloquently: "Your death will strengthen us. And now I can only say, farewell, my best friend! Arise to Valhalla!"

Afterwards the procession wound its way through the sad grey streets to the Invaliden cemetery.

The weather was appalling. There could be no question of any of the high-ranking Luftwaffe officers who had attended the funeral returning to their commands by air. Galland and Oesau, anxious to join their wings and escape the deep melancholy that enveloped Berlin, decided to take a train back to France.

Liese's leave of absence from the factory was officially up. She was torn between a sense of duty which told her that the boss's son should not ask special favours and the agony of having to leave while Dieter was still delayed in Berlin. But here they both had a stroke of luck. A message from Herr Reh had been delivered to the hotel: he was spending the rest of the week at the Air Ministry and was rushing back from a business trip to Austria. He would need Frau Reh's secretarial services at the ministry during his stay.

Liese threw her arms round Dieter in the hotel lobby, kissing him enthusiastically while the hall porter smirked.

"I wish my wife would decorate me like that," he said.

Dieter was embarrassed by Liese's fervour in such a public place. They hurried upstairs, to the openly lecherous amusement of the hall porter. In their bedroom, later, they lay relaxed in each other's arms; but a note of sadness echoed back for Dieter from the day just past.

Liese said drowsily, "Isn't it wonderful that I can stay, Dieter?"

"Wonderful, *Liebchen*. But you'll have to work for father during the day, of course."

"But there'll still be the nights, *Liebchen*."

"You'll fall asleep over your shorthand book if I have any say in the matter. Anyway, why do you suppose my father has cancelled his trip to Austria?"

"I suppose he wants to be around to pick up the pieces after General Udet's death. Or, better still, rearrange them to suit himself."

"I'm surprised he didn't get here for the funeral."

"Your father has a well-ordered sense of priorities."

Her voice was carefully neutral. He knew again that she might become critical in a way that would disturb him. He got out of bed quietly.

"Liese, let's have a marvellous dinner to celebrate your stay. We'll ask Mano. The funeral got him down rather badly. And this damned weather doesn't help."

Mano was over an hour late at the restaurant. He hurried across the floor, slumped down into a chair, burying his face in his hands.

"Get me a cognac, a double cognac."

"Mano, what's wrong?"

Dieter could see that the tight, dry unemotional face was close to tears. Mano seized Dieter's hand. "I've got to tell you. It'll be known soon enough, anyway. Mölders is dead, killed when his Heinkel lost an engine and crashed making a blind approach for an emergency landing at Breslau. He insisted on pushing on, despite previous engine trouble. His pilot saw some cable railway wires too late. Stalled. Went in from 100 feet. They're all dead, except Mölders' aide. Oh God! Why him of all people? We're cursed."

Dieter felt as though he was going to faint. When he was about to speak, he asked: "Who's going to take over?"

Mano looked up from his brandy glass. "I don't know. But they've sent a signal ahead to stop Galland's train. He's to come back to Berlin straight away."

The state funeral hadn't fooled anyone in the squadrons. By the time Dieter landed at Abbeville two days later the rumours were all around. Not only had Udet committed suicide but Mölders also.

When a *Feldwebel* on his ground staff asked if this were true, Dieter stood the man to attention for ten minutes, threatening to put him on a charge of spreading malicious and dangerous rumours. When he finally calmed down he said: "You knew him, sergeant. You served in JG 51. Surely you knew he was a man of deep religious conviction who could never contemplate suicide. His plane crashed in bad weather. It could happen to any of us."

But still Mano's question in the restaurant that fatal evening persisted: why, above all people, had it had to happen to "Vati" Mölders? There were other and more immediate personal questions. With Mölders dead, what would happen to the experimental and training flight which had been so very much his brainchild? One question, at least, was not long in being answered. Eight days after Udet's funeral, Adolf Galland again stood in the guard of honour at an open grave at the Invaliden, and when Mölders' spirit, too, had been bidden to arise to Valhalla, Goering beckoned Galland aside and said to him: "Now it's your turn. I appoint you general of fighters to succeed Mölders."

Galland, it was said, had been horrified by the news, though half expecting it. He had immediately set up his HQ at OKL at Goldap but he had made it very clear that he did not intend permanently to exchange a pilot's seat for an office chair. One of his first acts had been to confirm that he wished formations to operate exactly as he had left them.

The year ended in heavy gloom for the pilots on the Channel coast. On 6 December Von Bock's army had ground to a freezing halt in sight of the suburbs of Moscow. Despite sub-zero temperatures, they had no winter clothing. As compensation, the supplies department sent them red wine for Christmas that was frozen solid in the containers when it arrived. The Japanese attack on Pearl Harbour had awoken the Americans and ranged them against the Axis. The Afrika Korps had fallen back ahead of Auchinleck. The Führer had taken on supreme command of all armed forces, including the Luftwaffe. Bad weather and Spitfires still punched occasional holes in the Abbeville mess. The German fighter pilots needed a shot in the arm and, early in the New Year, they got it.

1942

Kate Bristow woke up in the double bed of a Bayswater hotel still not quite sure how she had got there. The faint glimmer of the February morning thrust a shaft of grey London daylight between the imperfectly closed black-out curtains. The light touched the gold badges on the lapels of her brand new WAAF junior section officer's uniform, fell across the floor to the bed and to her companion's face. She had never before awoken to find herself in bed with a man, and she looked on the tough young face, relaxed in sleep, with tenderness, though not with either love or lust. She no longer had to ask herself why she had agreed to go back with Michael Roland to his hotel room. He was so eager, yet anxious for her, that she had found it impossible to refuse. After all, she had thought wryly, she was giving nothing away that she could not afford. It was time that she obliterated that other sealed-off, long-forgotten love. She, who had herself been so young not long ago, felt sad for Michael as he slept in the extreme vulnerability of his youth. She touched the scar on her cheek. Last night with her fingers clenched in his wiry hair she had felt the ridge of scar tissue in Michael's scalp where the fragment from a German mortar had laid it open. They had both been through the same furnace but Kate felt instinctively that she had emerged the harder steel. She gently touched the place where his scar lay. Michael stirred in his sleep.

It was time to be going. The train that would take her to her first posting as a commissioned officer left in exactly an hour and a half. She eased out of bed, let the slip in which she had slept fall to the floor and washed herself vigorously all over in the tepid water offered by the hotel's fuel-rationed heating system. She was not self-conscious, should Michael be awake and watching, although they had made love in the dark the night before, mainly because Michael had thought she would want it that way. Well, if he was awake he must surely have a good idea what she was like by now, her practicality was part of her new self.

Kate had no inclination to let the Women's Auxiliary Air Force defeminise her. She clipped her precious nylons to her suspenders as carefully as if she was dealing with a time-bomb. Ladders were one of the major horrors of war. As she tiptoed across the room to get her skirt, she saw that Michael was awake and watching her.

"I thought it was the chap who was supposed to sneak out in the early hours."

"It's not early. Anyway, I didn't want to wake you."

"And miss a sight like that!"

She laughed: "You'd have seen more if you'd been awake a few minutes earlier."

"I was."

"Now who's being sneaky?"

"Come over here, Kate."

She smiled. "It's too late for that now. We've both got trains to catch."

"When will I see you again, Kate?"

"With you joining some hush-hush unit and me reporting to a fighter base with my brand new commission, we're hardly likely to get more leave straight away."

"But our postings are only a few miles from each other. You must see me before next leave. I want to marry you, Kate."

She fastened her skirt. "Dear Michael, you mustn't think that just because of last night . . ."

"But, I know you. You wouldn't go to bed with just any-one."

"You're not anyone, Michael. But don't get wild ideas about marriage simply because it's wartime."

Something was up for sure. That first week in February, the overworked squadrons of JG 2 and JG 26 had been made up to strength with thirty extra 109s apiece. Twelve of these had even been posted to St Omer from fighter training school, near Paris. The *Erprobungs* flight had received orders to be-come part of the HQ squadron. Each day they flew practice sweeps out to sea to escort E-boats moving along the coast. If they took off from Abbeville, they landed at Le Havre. Every day they operated between different bases, spending a maxi-mum of thirty-five minutes over the E-boats. When they touched down, they were refuelled by obviously reinforced ground crews at an unbelievable speed. Rumour had it that these intensive exercises were in preparation for a seaborne offensive against Britain in the spring. The general himself, Adolf Galland, was a good deal in evidence, buzzing around, as Pohle said, as though someone had stuck one of his famous black cheroots up his backside.

On the afternoon of 11 February, they finally learned what it was all about. As leader of the *Erprobungs* flight, Dieter was summoned with all other chiefs of flying units down to squadron leaders, to the general's conference at Le Touquet. The orders he took back in a sealed envelope to his pilots were scarcely believable. They were also immensely exciting.

Junior Section Officer Bristow was on watch 0800-1200 hours in the Operations Room at Hawkinge. As yet she only acted as trainee assistant to a section officer who had served as a WAAF at Biggin when the Heinkels flattened it in 1940. Kate was still inexperienced enough to find the atmosphere of the Ops Room totally intoxicating, even when there was not much doing. There was not much on the board this morning. Activity during the past week had been slack apart from German E-boat and fighter movements close to the French coast and some mysterious plots apparently coming their way. Radar indicated that these were made by quite large bomber formations, but the strange thing was that they always petered out before reaching the English coast. Several times the controller scrambled Spitfire squadrons who reached the point of interception only to find empty sky. It seemed that the Germans had invented some new tricks to confuse the British radar and were trying them out. At night, Coastal Command carried out some unusually intense mine-laying along the French and Dutch coasts. Wellingtons had been to Brest to make life noisy for the crews of the two German battlecruisers *Gneisenau* and *Scharnhorst* bottled up there together with the cruiser *Prinz Eugen*. But there was nothing unusual in this. Bomber Command had been trying to damage the three warships for months past. They had made, all told, 299 attacks, with the loss of forty-three aircraft, all without tangible result.

"Two PRU Spits airborne 0815 Baker One Nine." A WAAF with a wooden rake moved a numbered block out on to the large-scale squared map of the Channel rather as if it was a roulette chip, which in a sense it was, though in this instance a losing one. Before long there were two chips on the Table. The Photographic Recce Unit Spits had split up, one heading for Boulogne and the other turning for the Cap Gris Nez–Ostende section of the coast. Nothing would be heard from them until they landed with their photographs. The routine early morning recce was carried out under strict radio silence.

"They're at it again," the controller said. "Newhaven radar reports up to twenty Jerries milling around off Le Havre. Better put them on the board. They seem to be moving up-Channel at about 20 knots. No 11 Group Fighter Command has been informed but are taking no action yet. They think it's more Air-Sea rescue practice."

Shortly after 1015 the resident Spitfire squadron reported it was sending up two planes on an operational training flight. Kate recognised her brother's voice on the R/T calling for clearance for take-off.

"*Some* training flight!" the assistant controller said. "That's Bristow and that Canadian madman. They're out looking for trouble."

At approximately 1030, in mid-Channel, they found it in the form of a couple of 109s practically down on the wave-tops. Delightedly they dived in to attack, but the Germans skidded round on one wing tip and raced for home. Bristows and Hay dived after them. In half a minute they thundered out of low-lying scud to find themselves crossing the bows of three capital ships at full speed. Now it was their turn to stir the wave crests with a wing tip as they got the hell out of it. Peter had time to register that there were twenty or more 109s and 190s up top. A pair of 190s detached themselves in pursuit, but when they found they were unable to close quickly, they soon gave up. Plainly they were under orders not to pursue, since they had every advantage. Equally Peter was under strict Flight Command orders to maintain radio silence. He had no doubt what they had just seen. A flick of the R/T switch and he could have told Hawkinge that the three German battleships were out of Brest and steaming at full speed for home through the narrows. Now, unbelievably, the unbelievable would have to wait twenty minutes until he landed.

Five minutes later a second pair of PRU Spits sighted the battleships with their aerial escort. But the pilots likewise were bound by radio silence. Thus it was that the news didn't get out until nearly 1100, by which time the German squadron had been at sea for nearly fourteen trouble-free hours.

Dieter Reh and his flight had been over the convoy at first light to take.over from the thirty 110 night-fighters who had been patiently circling during the hours of darkness. He had leap-frogged up the coast, landing to be refuelled at the dif-

211

ferent bases laid down in his sealed orders. It had all gone like a parade ground movement. Sixteen fighters, continually over the warships, increased for a ten-minute period to thirty-two when the relief arrived. The orders said: "If engaged, 35 minutes over the flotilla. If not, stay for a further ten minutes when the relieving fighters show up." Dieter led the *Erprobungs* flight out to sea again at 1230, after their third refuelling. Until then there had been no real action, simply the intrusion of the two Spits, but that was already two hours old. Why had there been no British retaliation apart from a few wild rounds from the Dover coastal batteries that fell a quarter of a mile short? Next to the absence of enemy aircraft, the most amazing thing was the total silence in his headphones. The German fighter pilots, usually the least radio-disciplined and most vocal aerial group on earth, had taken their general's dire warnings to heart. The importance and grandeur of the operation had impressed them even more than Galland's threatenings.

The silence was at last shattered by the fighter controller aboard one of the battleships.

"Torpedo bombers ten miles north. Red escort detach and intercept."

Red escort included Dieter's flight. He peeled them off and headed towards the Kent coast. Almost at once he saw the attackers. What he saw staggered him. Six ancient biplanes, Swordfish, limping along at ninety knots. Above them ten Spitfires. The rest of the escort would have to take care of those. His orders were to stop the bombers at any cost, even if it meant ramming.

The eight 190s roared in on a frontal and beam attack. Because of the lumbering approach of the Swordfish, the fighters had time to get off more ammunition than normal. Dieter watched cannon and machine-gun fire striking home. As he flashed over the leading Swordfish, he saw cut bracing wires streaming in the wind, gashes in the fabric wings and a rear-gunner standing up firing in an *open* cockpit. The 190s turned sharply and came in from astern. But now the problem was not to overshoot. Dieter yelled to his flight to lower flaps and undercarriage. With the drag thus imposed, he slowed up enough for one longish burst at the leading Swordfish of the first group of three. The punishment those ancient crates could take! The three biplanes staggered on, manned by dead or dying crews. It was time to pull up and break if the 190s didn't want to be shot down by their own flak. The destroyer escort had opened up with every weapon it could command.

Climbing looking for the Spitfire escort, positioning himself for a pass at a second group of three Swordfish, Dieter watched the leader he had shot up lurch over the destroyers and totter on towards the battleships. It was impossible, magnificent. The *Scharnhorst* had opened up with everything, even main armament, huge shells throwing up fountains of water that crashed down on the biplanes' torn wings. Then it was over. The leading Swordfish lost a wing to a direct hit. It kept going long enough to release its torpedo. The second biplane dropped its torpedo at the *Gneisenau*, flew on directly at the muzzles of her guns, barely cleared the superstructure and hit the waves beyond. The last Swordfish, streaming flame, released its torpedo at the *Prinz Eugen* and then blew up. There was neither time nor need to attack the second V-formation. These three planes and their nine men had simply disappeared into the ring of steel and smoke. Not a man survived. Not a torpedo found its mark. It was heroic beyond the demands of heroism.

They fought throughout that long, grey, cloud-scattered February afternoon. Whirlwinds, Beauforts, Hampdens, Wellingtons. The RAF threw everything in and still it was not enough. The Beaufort torpedo bombers, newly arrived in the south of England, weren't ready for immediate action. The twin-engined Whirlwinds were no match for Galland's hornet escort. The RAF's bombers had been armed with armour-piercing bombs which were useless when dropped from the low altitude dictated by bad visibility and cloud conditions, so bomb loads had to be changed to general-purpose high explosive at cost of precious time. The only successes on the British side were scored by mines on *Scharnhorst,* later on *Gneisenau,* off the Friesian islands, and *Scharnhorst* again when just inside home waters. But still the battleships ploughed on.

Dieter led off his flight from Le Touquet in the darkening phases of later afternoon. The weather was good on take-off but the battleships were now so far to the northeast that return to the Pas de Calais was impossible. Airfields in Holland were the only hope and there the weather was still right down on the deck. All knew everything was at stake and no one hesitated. On this, the fourth sortie of the day, Dieter came out of cloud directly behind a Wellington. The rear-gunner had only begun to swing his power turret before the bomber became a flaming torch that disappeared to light a cloud briefly with a red glow.

Dieter and Pohle landed at an emergency field as darkness

fell. The Channel dash was over. They had hardly been out of their cockpits since dawn that morning. The German fleet had succeeded where the Spanish Armada had failed, and two fighter wings of the Luftwaffe had made it possible. Galland had done it with 250 aircraft of which no more than thirty-two had been over the convoy at any one time. The day had marked a high point in the German fighter pilots' war. They did not know it then but it was not likely to be exceeded again.

Kate came off watch at 2000 hours that night feeling as though she had been up there in the battle. The table was practically clear of plots. The blue space that represented the Channel was an empty chess board at the end of a long game. Its blue paint gleamed under the Ops Room lights, giving no clue to the fact that sixty British and seventeen German planes had disappeared with most of their crews beneath the waters it represented. Kate had returned to duty for the final phase of the running battle, when the Blenheims and Beauforts were making their last desperate bombing runs in the rapidly deteriorating weather. The blackness of mood in the Ops Room was as deep as the depression which was now aiding the battleships in their final run to safety. Only one thing brightened the gloom, the epic of the Swordfish!

The controller coming off duty said wearily: "Well, at least Coastal Command's mines have done some damage. If that chap Eugene Esmond who led the stringbags doesn't get VC it'll be a bloody disgrace. I'm going to get drunk."

Kate went straight to the mess phone and called her brother. Peter was all right. He had got a 190 and damaged a Dornier 217. Yes, he agreed, it had been a perfectly bloody day. A complete cock-up from the word go. He was now going off to get drunk.

Kate didn't drink much. However, there was another palliative available. She could get a late pass, and Michael Roland's Combined Ops Unit was only three miles away. His fifteen-hundredweight truck was not exactly the bridal suite on a February night, but it had served once before. She wondered if she was becoming a tart. The war did funny things to a girl.

That early spring of 1942 brought Dieter good news as well as bad. The best news was that Liese was pregnant as the result of a forty-eight-hour pass in Berlin in January. There was good news about the *Erprobungs* flight, also. They were to return to the work for which they were best suited—testing out

214

new ideas in action. The FW 190 had endeared itself to Dieter but he remained at heart in love with that little shark of an aircraft, the 109. They were given two 109s to try out with "bath-tubs" containing 20 mm cannon beneath each wing and there was a rumour that they would be getting an entirely new mark, the 109g, before the autumn.

But there were aspects of the war that increasingly worried Dieter. His job took him more and more into contact with the office of the Inspector of Fighters, now being rejuvenated by the dynamic Adolf Galland. The staff officers there—with the exception of Mano Rumpler, for whom he had the greatest respect—were not chairborne warriors. They had all felt the G-forces of a fighter's seat pressing against their backsides. What he learned from them filled him with foreboding. The Americans had started to land air force personnel in Britain; and the RAF's night bombing attacks were becoming increasingly troublesome. Not only night attacks: the RAF had even attacked the Renault works outside Paris in broad daylight. Rumour said that the RAF's Bomber Command had got a new fire-eating chief called Harris.

In reply, what were the Luftwaffe Command doing? God only knew the reason for some of their decisions. The Führer himself was said to have stopped Kammhuber's highly successful intruder attacks against British bomber airfields, simply because bombers shot down over England were of little encouragement to the German people at home.

Gerhard Stecke had written Dieter a surprisingly bitter letter on the subject. His crack intruder squadron had been disbanded, and Stecke himself posted to Sicily where the Luftwaffe was apparently expected to fight yet another triumphant campaign in support of an unknown and untried general called Rommel.

He had heard from Heine Müller, too. Müller had spent a diabolical winter frozen-stiff with an He 111 wing on the Russian front. Heine had faint, but only faint, hopes that conditions would improve with the coming of spring.

Dieter had to believe that the Führer knew what he was doing. With the spring, the Russian campaign must, just must, come to a triumphant conclusion. Despite setbacks, perhaps things weren't so bad after all.

But then on the night of 28 March something happened that caused terror as well as fury right through the Reich. Nearly 300 bombers of Air Marshal Arthur Harris's new command came in from the North Sea and unloaded 500 tons of high explosives and incendiaries on the ancient Hanseatic port of Lübeck. It was the first time the RAF had bombed a civilian target in any strength and, though the German public was not told the full extent of the slaughter, over 300 died with 700 wounded or missing.

When Dieter got over his horror at the burning of this largely wooden, medieval city, his spirits soared. Now everything Mano Rumpler had talked about must come true. This was a warning of what the RAF, aided by the Americans, might do to the German homeland. Now the Führer and *Reichsmarschall* must act in the obvious way. They must authorise the accelerated building programme of fighter aircraft which General Galland demanded and which Field Marshal Milch, Udet's successor, was ready to implement.

Instead the Führer did something quite different: he reached for a copy of Baedeker to confirm which were the towns of historic interest most treasured by the British.

A few weeks later Mrs Bristow stayed late at her office in the country town of Exeter to clear up her paperwork and to compose a letter to her commandant asking for a transfer to the Greater London area. She had made up her mind to ask WVS headquarters whether they couldn't find her a job in London. True, the German bombers had spent themselves for the time being. The brutes had too much on their hands elsewhere and serve them right. But she had no doubt that Hitler would sooner or later return to attack the heart of England, and London was where that heart beat. She had, as she constantly expressed it, smelt powder during the Battle of Britain, and she had seen both her children marked for life by the Luftwaffe. Her fighting spirit demanded that she should be where the fighting was going to be when the civilian population was called upon to face the bombs once again.

She was on the point of locking her desk when she heard the first wail of the sirens. Their song had been a familiar one back in 1940, even though few bomber formations had strayed so far west. It was probably just another false alarm. But then she heard the quadruple concussion of a salvo of ack-ack shells far off in the night sky. Perhaps the Jerries really were having a go at last, probably at Exmouth. She switched off the lights and took down the black-out blind. Above the roof-tops on the opposite side of the street, a string of pink pearls, Bofors tracer, rose lazily towards the half-obscured stars. Searchlights had begun their theatrical and seemingly ineffectual striking of the clouds. That familiar rising and falling drone, so well remembered from her brief acquaintance with the London Blitz, was followed by a succession of concussions that shook the foundations of the house. Bombs! How ironic that the Luftwaffe should have come to peaceful Exeter while her letter asking for a transfer lay on the desk, the buff of its utility, already twice-used envelope pale in the light of a fire started somewhere far away in the city.

Mrs Bristow felt fear, as any sensible person feels fear when they realise that high explosive is being aimed in their general direction. She also felt elation. Action was here at last and she was in the right place to deal with it. As soon as the raid was over, canteens would be needed to serve hot drinks to ARP workers, wardens, Fire Service men. Provided the phones weren't damaged, she could mobilise all this from her office. For the moment, better leave the phone untouched; there would be far more urgent calls blocking the switchboard. The noise was by now the most frightening thing about the raid. Probably all noise and little damage, she told herself. A comet tail of flame marked the sky where a raider died. They were right overhead now, pinpricking the ancient city with incendiaries. Plaster fell as a stick of six HE bombs landed not a quarter of a mile away, testing the elderly office building in every one of its mortar joints. She heard another stick fall, even closer, somewhere over towards the cathedral. They wouldn't dare bomb that! But then, look what they had tried to do to St Paul's. The words of an old lady who had survived the worst nights of the London Blitz, until the eventual demolishment of her home forced her to accept evacuation to Axeham, came back to her. "Those Jerry bombers were so low, dear, we could hear them undoing the chains to let the bombs go." At the time she couldn't imagine what the old lady had meant, but the sound of the next stick starting on its way down made it quite clear. It *did* sound like chains being rattled, or perhaps coke being shot on to a corrugated iron roof. "When you hear that," the old lady had said, "you know someone close by is going to cop it."

Mrs Bristow only had time to realise that it was going to be she who would cop it but none even to dive under the table, as she had advised so many others to do in her ARP lectures.

Some bombs suck, other bombs blow. This one sucked. If you could have watched it all happen in slow motion, you would have seen the 500-pounder hurtle into an empty garden square fifty yards away. The invisible pressure waves set up by its otherwise harmless explosion took a giant's deep breath directly in front of the house wall behind which Mrs Bristow sat. It sucked out the entire front of the building between gable and pavement as easily as a human breath accidentally inhales a fly. For a split-second, the interior was revealed like a doll's house in cross-section. Then the floors began to fold inward; attic on third floor, third floor on second. Mrs Bristow, still in her chair, had been thrown to the carpet by the time the accumulated weight of rubble and plaster reached the first floor where she lay.

The ARP rescue party and the National Fire Service men did not unearth her for two hours after the All Clear.

"Poor old girl," said the fireman who found her. "The only bloody house in the street to catch it." Gently he removed the fragment of brick that had lodged in her open mouth.

Helmuth Reh paid one of his increasingly rare visits to his Hamburg factory. Following Udet's suicide, he had been drawn more and more into the central planning of aircraft production. He had felt Udet's passing more as a danger to his personal advancement than as the deep personal loss of a friend. Whenever a change takes place at high executive levels, he knew, there is always a risk that old faces will get swept out of office with the former occupant's furniture. The fiercely ambitious Erhard Milch, however, saw in Helmuth Reh exactly the sort of ambitions that would never be a threat to him but which could give useful impetus to his own personal war aims.

Herr Reh was extremely pleased with what he saw at his Hamburg plant. The radar wing working on the Lichtenstein location set for night-fighters was in full production. The mania for dive-brakes which had possessed the Luftwaffe in Udet's day was cooling a little. The factory was still turning them out for fighter- and medium-bombers but the repeated disasters overtaking the four-engined Heinkel 177 had at least partially persuaded the Air Ministry of the folly of trying to make a 20-ton strategic bomber attack in a power-dive. The section of the plant that had been working on 177 dive-brakes was therefore fast being retooled to turn out pressurised cockpits for yet a further development of the faithful Bf 109, the 109g.

After their management meeting, husband and wife sat down to what, for war time, was a sumptuous lunch in the board-room. Helmuth Reh had brought a hamper of luxuries from Berlin—a lobster, some *pâté de foie*, a cold roast duck with orange sauce, a selection of cheeses that had long vanished from the shops, and a magnum of vintage Moët et Chandon.

"The privileges of office, *Liebchen*. We shall call them a small reward for a success in which you undoubtedly share. You have done a wonderful job here, Greta."

"Thank you. I've tried to carry on as I know you would have wished . . ."

"And Liese, how is she? How is my grandson, or perhaps granddaughter, coming along?"

"Liese is well—very well. She's nearly three months gone now. The baby should be born about mid-October."

"Good, good! By then we shall have finished with Russia. Malta will have fallen to Kesselring's *Luftflotte* 2 . . . nearly three thousand air-raids since our assault on the island began! And when Malta falls, Rommel and his Afrika Korps will have no more problems. The way to the Suez Canal will be open. It's all coming our way, Greta. The only enemy left will be England and, as the *Reichsmarshall* says: 'Once I get my *Geschwader* back from Russia we'll soon settle them.' "

"If only it all works out like that . . ."

"It will, *Liebchen*, you'll see."

"One can't help being worried about our German homeland, though. Lübeck and Rostock deliberately burnt to the ground . . ."

"By the British air pirates!"

"But soon it will be the Americans too. Roosevelt claims America will soon be turning out 5,500 planes a month. Can that be true, Helmuth?"

"All bluff. No one denies the Americans can build cheap, fast motor cars, but aeroplanes are something different. I should know."

"Even if it were half that number!"

"Then we will beat them at their own game."

"Roosevelt speaks of two heavy bombers, the Fortress and the Liberator. We shall need many fighters to stop them."

"That's what Galland keeps insisting, but, of course, he's an interested party."

"So are we, Helmuth. Our sons will be up there facing those great bombers."

"Don't worry, don't worry. We can turn out the fighters if it becomes really necessary. Milch has offered one thousand a month by the end of the year. Know what Jeschonnek replied? 'Where the hell would we put even 500 fighters a month? What we need are bombers to hit back with.' Of course, we all know that Jeschonnek—a capable enough staff officer—is the Führer's yes-man. But if the Führer puts fighters for defence into second place and demands more bombers for attack, then that must be the proper policy."

Frau Reh was still uneasy.

"But the American Flying Fortress?"

Her husband snorted. "Flying Coffin more like! That's what our fighter-pilots call it. You must have faith, Greta."

No one could accuse the general of keeping his arse stuck to a desk. Wherever he could find an excuse for doing so, and quite often when he couldn't, he touched down at one of the Channel bases of JG 2 in his famous 109f with its Mickey Mouse emblem. Frequently he called informal meetings with his pilots. Trying to beat sense into the High Command about the urgent need to build fighters for the defence of the Reich was one part of his job, keeping in touch with the men at the sharp end of the deal was another. The thing that was particularly exercising the general's mind at this moment was an intelligence report that the American general, Spaatz, newly arrived in Britain, intended to build up a force whose main striking power would be twenty-three squadrons of B 17 Flying Fortresses. So he had asked squadron commanders to assemble for him any pilots who had already made contact with the few B 17s the Americans had presented to the RAF.

Only a handful could be mustered. Among them were four members of the *Erprobungs* flight, Reh, Weiss and the Prussian Hoffman twins. The general stubbed out his black cheroot.

"Well, gentlemen, give me your opinions of the Flying Coffin, as our propaganda experts insist on calling it. Do you all agree with that description?"

A captain from JG 2, the *Richthofen Geschwader*, said: "No, *Herr General*. The only time I met them, on their way to Brest, I nearly had my tail shot off and only just got back in one piece."

"If I remember, the combat report on that occasion said they were at 35,000 feet in two flights of three?" The general carried notes but did not need to refer to them.

"Correct, *Herr General*. We made a beam attack by *Rotte* and damaged the rear bomber. But we were lucky. They threw a lot of stuff at us."

"*Oberleutnant* Reh, what do you think of their firepower?"

"Potentially tremendous, *Herr General*. Leutnant Weiss and I bumped into a straggler limping back on three engines after a daylight raid on Rouen. The tail, upper and belly guns gave us a bad time. We made a standard stern attack, and we damaged him slightly. We would have finished him off if a squadron of Spitfires hadn't appeared."

"If I remember the details of that one," the General said, "you were flying the early 109f with the lighter armament?"

"Correct, *Herr General*," Willy said. "If we'd had something with a bit more punch . . ."

"An FW 190, perhaps, with plenty of cannon-power?"

"Perhaps. If we could have got up to him *and* held our performance. He was at 33,000 feet. When first reported with two others, he was even higher—38,000. The 190 isn't too clever upstairs."

"Has anyone here shot a Fortress down?"

Where the other pilots had merely straightened their bearing and spoken respectfully, the two Hoffman twins clicked their heels. Dieter winked at Willy Weiss. Though the Hoffman twins were welcome new members of the experimental flight, their Prussian correctness was something of a joke to the old hands.

"Where was your victory, then?"

"Over Bremerhaven, *Herr General*. We took off from Jever with plenty of warning so we had height on our side. The other two *Rotten* made textbook beam and tail attacks. Fritz and I decided to go in head-on at the leader. He burned and a wing fell off shortly after we broke."

When everyone had given what information he had, the general, a freshly-lit cheroot clamped between his teeth, summed up.

"So far, gentlemen, Flying Fortresses have only been operated by the RAF who are apparently disappointed with their performance . . . The Americans presented them with twenty on a trial basis. Our Intelligence analyses their results as follows: thirty-nine daylight missions flown; eight Fortresses lost; no German fighters shot down although . . ." he looked round smilingly ". . . we seem to have had some luck there. The bombing record is rather bad, too. We estimate that only two of the 1,000-pounders carried by Fortresses scored direct hits on their targets and this despite the boasted Norden bombsight.

"From captured crew interrogation we believe that the RAF favour turning them into night-bombers." He paused. "I can see by your faces that you wouldn't be opposed to such a decision and I can't say I blame you. My views are well-known; properly used. the B 17 Flying Fortress presents a serious threat and one that can be countered only by the correct fighter tactics. That's what we have to work on in the next six months." The general puffed his cheroot.

"Could you explain, *Herr General,* what you mean by 'properly used'?"

"Certainly. The RAF, as you have found, has been flying between 30,000 and 39,000 feet. The Fortress was designed for maximum performance between 24 and 27,000 feet. Above 30,000 not only machines but crews are at a serious technical and practical disadvantage. The next mistake the RAF has made is to operate them in far too small formations. If they had sent all twenty over at once we might have been in serious difficulties. Such a formation would mount some 240 heavy machine-guns." He looked closely at the pilots, perhaps afraid that he had painted too gloomy a picture, but he saw there was nothing to disconcert him there.

Major Egon Mayer, *Kommodore* of JG 2, said: "We shall soon work out tactics to deal with them, *Herr General,* if the Yanks do bring them over in daylight in any numbers. They're a damned big target."

The general smiled his famous smile. "Quite so. Thank you for all your help, gentlemen. Your first-hand information is invaluable to us chairborne warriors."

Two days after the Exeter raid, Kate and Peter Bristow travelled down from Paddington together on compassionate leave, to attend their mother's funeral. Peter had often watched men from his squadron set out on similar leaves and had signed compassionate passes for his own ground staff after their home towns had been bombed. He could not, however, entirely accept that it had happened to his own mother. Exeter had always seemed so much out of things, so little worthwhile as a target, that he had been certain that, so long as his mother remained there, she would be safe.

For most of the journey Kate was silent. At Swindon they pushed their way up the corridor past the piles of kitbags and the often sleeping servicemen who had failed to get a seat. In the open door of a lavatory, four sailors were playing solo, the dealer sitting unconcernedly on the lavatory seat. He looked up and smiled cheekily at Kate: "Hope you don't want to spend a penny, miss?"

They reached the dining car over this assault course of human obstacles, and ate Spam fritters and boiled potatoes followed by rice pudding.

Looking out over the peaceful fields and hedges, Peter said: "It seems so far away from the war, all this . . . I'm glad she was in her office. She'd have wanted that. I bet she was organising air raid precautions right up to the last minute."

"All that brown paper! She and I used to show them down in the Vale how to stick strips of it on to their windows—try ing to keep out bombs with brown paper . . ." Her voice began to shake. She had sometimes clashed with her mother but she had loved her for her great kindness and understanding.

At Newton Abbot, they bought a paper to learn that Norwich and York had been the targets of raids similar to that on Eketer. The press called them "Baedeker Raids" and attributed them to Hitler's spite. The towns seemed to have been selected simply because they were cathedral cities. It was the act of an Attila, the mark of the Hun, the press said.

The ceremony at Axeham village church was almost unbearable. Both the Bristows felt that the tap-root with their birthplace had been torn out for good. The coffin looked tiny, draped with a Union Jack. Afterwards the vicar took Kate's hand, "She died in action, my dear, in the service of others, as she would have wished."

To Peter he said quietly, but not so quietly that the mourners from the village could not hear, "Give them hell, Peter. Next time, and every time you get the chance, give the swine hell."

Neither had any wish to spend the night in the grey stone house their mother had ruled for so long. The vicar drove them to Exeter where they caught the night train. As it pulled out, the sirens had begun to shriek and the first flashes of gunfire to light the sky. The Luftwaffe was making a second Baedeker visit and this time one that would do far more damage to the heart of the old town. Carried out by ninety bombers specially withdrawn from Sicily, it largely burned out the centre of the city, destroyed nine churches and killed or wounded more than three hundred citizens. But it was still nothing comparable with what the RAF had done to Lübeck and Rostock.

Throughout May of 1942 Liese was a compound of joy and despair. Though giving every atom of her energy and intelligence to help and support the increasingly complex professional life of her boss and father-in-law, she remained deeply convinced that the war was not only wrong, but going wrong. The attacks on Lübeck and Rostock were to her an awful portent of what could happen to every city in the Reich. At first she could not appreciate why the civilians she met in her

223

travels from factory to factory were not equally worried. True, they expressed concern, even admitted the raids were "dreadful" or "shocking", but the long-term implications of an air power that could deliver such blows did not appear to trouble them. She soon came to understand the reason: her job gave her access to the true enormity of casualties and damage. The general public simply knew what the radio said, which wasn't much.

The joy in her was the joy in Dieter's child which she carried. She had never hidden from herself the dangers to which Dieter was exposed; but the child was his, an insurance policy against the worst the war could do to her. She cherished it with secret rapture, feeling her smooth stomach although there was nothing to feel yet.

During the last week of May, Helmuth Reh sent for her and told her he wished her to go with him to the Ruhr to visit several makers of alloy components for the new 109. There was nothing unusual in this. She had not left the Hamburg plant for ten days and was quite looking forward to the trip. She made out the itinerary as usual, noting that they were due to stay the night of 30 May in Cologne.

She found that the hotels in the centre of the city were fully booked; not even mention of the Air Ministry could budge the booking clerks. She at last accepted a second-class hotel a mile from the railway terminus. She did so with reluctance since the *Herr Direktor* liked only the best and made no bones about saying so, even to his daughter-in-law. But the obduracy of those booking clerks was to save both their lives.

The baby was playing her up that evening so she made this an excuse to go to bed early, for the truth was that she found her father-in-law in a disgruntled mood—the inferior accommodation had, as she predicted, made him peevish. In such a state he was liable to fall back on the gloomier aspects of his working day, and out of office hours, Liese did not find the inadequacies of a certain factory's inspection system on engine cowlings for the 109g the most fascinating of subjects. So she excused herself around nine, and wrote to Dieter. Having put the envelope down unsealed so that she could add a postscript in the morning, she fell asleep.

She awoke some time later under the impression that she was being suffocated by noise. The dominating sound was a deep drone. Her first reaction was that this was from Luftwaffe bombers setting out on a raid: if so, she had never heard so many aircraft in the sky before. Dazed as she was with her first sleep, she did not realise the truth until the room was lit by a magnesium glare. Almost at once the concussion of the first bombs shook and shook and shook, becoming a thunderous drum roll that rose and fell in intensity without a break, and still the drone overhead grew deeper. The raid—and it must be on the scale of the terror attacks on Lübeck and Rostock—was obviously directed at the heart of Cologne.

Stray bombs were now falling in the streets nearby. Plaster fell on the floor. Her windows flew to splinters. Someone, perhaps cut by flying fragments, was screaming on the floor below. She got to her feet, only to be thrown back on to the bed by a blast wave that tore away the wooden frame of the already shattered bedroom casement. It was three minutes since she had woken and already the heart of the city was becoming a furnace.

She could feel blood on her face but this was nothing. The baby was all that concerned her. The hotel had handed her a printed slip giving directions in the event of an air raid, and she remembered that guests were supposed to make their way to the cellars. Where were the cellars? At that moment her father-in-law flung open the door. "Quick, Liese. Follow me at once."

The corridor was pitch dark despite the fires outside. Ahead she could hear Herr Reh pushing his way among other frightened guests.

"Wait," she called. "Wait! I can't see." She tripped, hitting the banisters of the narrow staircase, and pitched headlong to the bottom, down fifteen steps. She felt an agonising pain in her stomach and lay moaning while strange legs and feet stumbled against her in the dark. When Herr Reh and the hotel manager with a torch found her five minutes later, she was sitting upright against the wall, holding her abdomen and sobbing. Though the drone of bombers overhead was louder than ever and the drumbeat of bombs hurt the ears, she no longer cared for her own survival.

They lifted her and carried her down to the cellars. As she sat on a bench she felt the blood running down her thighs and knew that she would lose the baby.

The all-clear went ninety minutes after the first bomber had reached the city. Cologne did not know it, but it had been picked for Arthur Harris's first thousand-bomber raid.

In the morning there was no question of getting away from Cologne. Two-thirds of the bombs dropped had been incendiaries. Four thousand houses had been gutted, communications had ceased to exist. Liese lay all morning on a hotel bed that was gritty with fallen plaster and stained with smoke. The smell of burning wood filled every crevice of the room. Though she lay very still, she knew it would do no good. Her baby was as much a victim of the raid as the 460 civilians who would eventually be accounted dead or missing.

Even on the outer circles of the general's staff, Mano Rumpler felt the scorching fury of his mood. Rumour had it he had told Milch, told Jeschonnek, told the *Reichsmarschall*, that Cologne was the writing on the wall in letters of fire and blood. If the Reich did not arm itself with fighter aircraft for defence now, and in ever-increasing numbers, then its cities would be obliterated as Cologne had been by the RAF at night and what was left standing would be flattened by the Americans in daylight. The story was that Milch, always a practical man, had agreed with him. The *Reichsmarschall*, it was said, had swayed between panic, agreement, hysteria and abuse. In the event it had not mattered what anyone had said for the Führer had refused to listen. The Führer had repeated that he was not interested in defence, merely in revenge. His only reply to Cologne was to send out an inadequate bomber force against Canterbury.

Faced with what he openly described as idiocy, the general had resorted to his usual antidote. He had returned to JG 26 to shoot down a few Spitfires. It was during this flying and fighting visit that the *Erprobungs* flight received special orders. These orders immediately cancelled any chance Dieter might have had of compassionate leave to visit his wife. He had been shattered by Liese's news, but the letter from his mother saying that she was all right after the miscarriage and was back in Hamelin being looked after by the family went some way towards reassuring him.

He wrote to her daily, telling her lovingly that what they had achieved together once they could soon achieve again, and as far as he was concerned, the sooner the better. But for the moment he had to put leave out of his mind. He had a job to do that would go a long way towards protecting her and his family in future from what had happened at Cologne.

The new experiments were described to the *Erprobungs* flight by the general himself. The general was not only a good fighting man—did he not hold the Reich's highest award for bravery, the Diamonds to Swords of the Knight's Cross of the Iron Cross?—but he was an excellent general as well. Though he burned with disgust at what he considered to be the maniac decisions and indecisions of the *Reichsmarschall* and his staff, he never communicated this distrust to his juniors. So he now pointed out to Dieter that though there was a long way to go to achieve what was needed for fighter defence of the Reich, some promising steps had already been taken. Huge bomb-proof fighter control stations were being built right across Germany. Each would require an operations staff of a thousand men and women. The increasingly effective radar, coupled with the existing spotting and intelligence systems, would be able to direct both day and night fighters on to the enemy's bomber streams. General Josef Kammhuber's night-fighters already had their work cut out against the RAF. Did Oberleutnant Reh realise that on the night of the Cologne raid thirty-one RAF heavy bombers had been shot down? The turn of the day-fighters would come. The key to the successful vectoring of 109s and 190s on to the daylight attackers was a new ultra-short wave radio called the Y-system.

It was this that the pilots of the *Erprobungs* flight were to test on operations. What's more, in order to test its range under combat conditions, they would be free to operate from any base between Jever and Brest.

For the moment combat was likely to be limited to action against Blenheims and medium bombers escorted by Spitfires. "But, don't worry," the general added, "the Americans are coming, and we have to be ready for them."

Michael Roland, propped on one elbow, lay looking at Kate asleep beside him. The Three Pigeons at Yeovil during the balmy month of July was a good deal more conducive to romance than the back of his fifteen-hundredweight truck in winter. One day and night of their forty-eight-hour leave had gone.

Kate lay asleep covered only by a sheet. He lifted this carefully so that he could enjoy the sight of her lying there naked, her back towards him. He experienced that strange fainting feeling, tingling at the back of his neck, which was only partly desire, the rest all melting tenderness for her. He stroked the short blonde curls at the back of her neck and, without actually touching her skin, traced the straight line of her spine until he reached the cleft of her buttocks. The urge to wake her by entering this valley with his finger tips was almost uncontrollable, but there would be other times. For now it was enough just to look. For a girl who rode a lot, she had a fantastic backside, not spread or broad as was supposed to be the fate of women riders, but neat and taut, literally hollow-cheeked. He smiled to himself at this honest lechery, then let the sheet fall gently, studying his own body where it lay exposed outside the bedclothes. He was proud of his body, always had been. Back on Rife Farm he had been able to heave hundred-weight sacks of grain on to his shoulders when he was quite a kid. Now the body was in its prime, toughened and fined by Combined Ops training. He was pleased with his body, pleased that it had had the strength to recover from the beating it had taken at the time of Dunkirk. For such a dark young man he was remarkably lacking in body hair.

His skin was smooth and tanned by days of training, stripped to the waist in the summer sun. He knew that Kate liked his body, liked its owner very much too, even if she did not quite yet love him.

Michael's study of his own physique was not entirely narcissistic. His body had felt steel once and knew what steel could do to flesh. Now he looked at himself, visualising not so much with fear but with a sense of regret what a splinter from an 88 millimetre air-burst or a jagged sliver of mortar bomb would do to the satin wall of that stomach, the taut rib cage of that chest. It seemed such a bloody waste.

This leave, for the first time, he had sensed that Kate might have agreed to marry him; but this leave, for the first time, he had not asked.

Kate stirred and said sleepily: "Michael, you were watching me."

"How did you know?"

"I could feel you."

"I never touched you."

"Touch me, then."

As his finger tips traced her spine again and found the valley where he had hesitated earlier, a voice inside his head seemed to be saying, "Make the most of this, Michael. Even if it's all snatched away, you've had your share of good fortune in this one instant of time."

The ultra-short-wave Y-sets that the *Erprobungs* flight now carried in their 190s were an unqualified success, which was a lot more than could be said for some of the other experimental ironmongery and gadgetry they'd been asked to try out. Feldwebel Pohle, now top scorer with nineteen kills, had not yet recovered from his operational experiences with a special gun-pack designed for use on photo-reconnaissance fighters. Fixed beneath the aircraft's belly, this fired backwards, supposedly to deter any enemy that got on to the otherwise unarmed recce machine's tail. Testing this piece of extravagant rubbish in action meant that Pohle had deliberately to place himself in front of an enemy aircraft and then try to shoot it down when it least expected it. Plainly the experiment had to be made on something fairly tame. Willy Weiss suggested a barrage balloon. In the end Pohle surprised a solitary Anson on a communications flight, loping along like a yellow crow over Romney Marsh. He appeared out of a cloud, slid briefly and cautiously in front of the lumbering, low-winged, twin-engined monoplane and pressed the button. God knows where his shots went. There was no satisfactory way of aiming. The upper gunner of the Anson got over his surprise at these antics with remarkable presence of mind and squirted a burst through Pohle's rudder.

Making his report to the intelligence officer later, Pohle said condescendingly: "That Tommy did very well in my estimation. It isn't everyone who can shoot straight when they've just been farted at."

The backwards firing gun-pack was abandoned soon after Pohle's experience. Shortly afterwards Pohle received the Iron Cross, Second Class, a reward, he said, for what he had just, but only just, lived through.

But even Pohle agreed that the Y-sets were the goods. They enabled the flight to receive vectoring instructions at great range from the new area control rooms being set up at Stade on the Lower Elbe, Deelen near Arnhem, Döberitz close to Berlin and Schleissheim near Munich. The fighters were no longer tied to local operations rooms. If the pursuit of raiders demanded it, they could be handed over from one area to the next. During this testing period, they had occasional dust-ups with Spitfires and Blenheims, but their instructions were to keep clear of trouble when possible and to bring back as much information as they could about operating difficulties and procedure. This state of affairs lasted throughout early August.

On the morning of 17 August, Dieter and Willy Weiss had just taken off from St Omer on a routine flight to test a new set of crystals in the Y-system radio. As far as they were both concerned it was something of a joy-ride. The day was fine and clear with scattered cloud at around 15,000 feet, the height at which they had been instructed to fly. It was always possible that the peace would be shattered by the intrusion of the new Spitfire Vb, but they were not seriously disturbed at the thought. At 15,000 the 190 was more than a match for even the latest model Spit. They had planned to land at Le Touquet for lunch. They were still climbing when the radio began to crackle with instructions. "Broadcaster One. Broadcaster One."

This was Dieter's call sign. He acknowledged, giving his position and height.

"Broadcaster One. Twelve plus heavy babies crossing the coast at 20,000 in Gustav Caesar Five. Intercept and engage. Acknowledge."

Dieter acknowledged and turned inland, starting to climb. This was unusual, a direct order to engage. Now the controller far below in one of the new centres which the pilots had already christened "Battle Opera Houses" was directing all other fighters actually airborne on to the target and scrambling a squadron of 109s at Audembert. Another minute and they should be able to spot the enemy formation. Out on his port beam, Dieter could see Willy Weiss, sitting up tall beneath the streamlined Plexiglas canopy of his 190.

"Look out for the Spits, Willy. They're probably up top."

"Christ," said Willy. "There are the bombers! Eleven o'clock high. Christ, look at them! They're heading for Rouen."

Dieter pressed the radio switch. "Broadcaster One. Have spotted bombers in Anto Quelle Four. Fortresses. Eighteen of them."

The great silver machines, in close formation, were barely 1,500 yards away now. Dieter experienced something very like the infantryman's feeling when first confronted with a tank. They were so bloody *big*. Why had the RAF suddenly taken to using Fortresses again in daylight? Then he spotted the markings. These weren't Tommies, they were Yanks! Already the fingers of tracer were reaching out from the tight box of bombers. The range was still far too great. The untried American airgunners must be nervous. Well, they weren't the only ones. Eighteen Fortresses added up to around 220 fifty calibre machine-guns. The *Rotte* hesitated like two hyenas on the edge of a kill that was still very much in possession of a pride of lions. No good hesitating. Where was the fighter escort? Maybe there wasn't one. These babies could probably look after themselves. He saw the big bombers lift as their bomb loads fell away in long layered strings. As one plane, the Fortresses banked and turned to starboard for home, Dieter kicked right rudder hard, turning away from the Fortresses to get in a position from which to attack them head-on.

"Spitfires ahead and coming down."

"Hold on, Willy. We're going in at the Yanks."

The Fortresses were completing their slow wheeling movement. As they did so, Dieter leaned into a left-hand turn that brought them out in a shallow dive one thousand yards ahead, in the bombers' path. He lined up on the leading plane of three on the right of the formation. At a closing speed of close on 600 mph the glasshouse in the nose of the Fort was filling the illuminated lines of his reflector sight at a horrifying rate. Machine-gun and cannon buttons to "fire". Blast! Their own flak was opening up. An eighty-eight burst slewed his fighter sideways just as he pressed the tit. A split-second to see his tracers making strikes far out on the starboard wing. Then forward with the stick, scraping under the monster's belly by inches, noticing crazily as he dived past that the lead plane of the entire formation carried the name "Yankee Doodle". No time for sight-seeing. Half roll and dive in the classic evasive manoeuvre. A hell of a clang as two bullets hit the armoured plate at his back. Where was Willy? Where the Spits? Willy's voice on the radio. "You okay? Christ, those things throw some shit at you·. . ." Then the usual babble of excited Luftwaffe voices. American voices. British voices. The Spitfire escort was tangling with the 109s from Audembert and the eighteen Fortresses—unscathed except for a few holes—were headed back over the Channel.

In the captain's seat of "Yankee Doodle", General Ira Eaker, commanding the US Eighth Air Force and this particular Fortress formation on the first daylight raid of its kind, said: "Well, boys, that'll do for a start. We sure hit those marshalling yards smack on the nose." The general was elated for he seemed to have proved the British wrong. Fortress formations *could* succeed in precision bombing in broad daylight.

When Dieter landed, his mechanic Korporal Streib said: "That's the last time I give you a nice new radio set to play with. Another inch to the right and those two bullets would have fixed it for good."

"They might have fixed me."

"No such luck."

Dieter grinned, for he saw that Streib had his fingers crossed as he spoke. The ground crews, "blackmen" the aircrews called them, had a special relationship with their pilots. They could get away with murder.

Two days after General Ira Eaker led his eighteen Fortresses to Rouen and back without loss, Michael Roland landed on the French coast. The big show his unit had been preparing for was under way at last, after several false starts. The job of

231

his commando in "Operation Jubilee" was to silence the batteries to the north of the town so that the landing-craft could hit the beaches at first light.

Squadron Leader Peter Bristow took his Spitfire Vbs to Dieppe as soon as there was sufficient light to take off. Since his mother had been killed, he had flown with a new, cold determination to knock Germans out of the sky, bombers especially. This, he realised, was not a particularly logical approach, seeing what the RAF had done to Rostock and Cologne. Logic did not enter into it. Personal revenge did.

In the grey drizzle of that winter morning, the town was not hard to spot. Oily smoke, lit by gunflashes, was visible from halfway across the Channel. It was always hard to tell from the cockpit of a fighter what the state of the game was down on the ground. One was far too busy concentrating on the state of the game up top. Nevertheless there did seem to be a bit of a pile-up on the beaches and not much progress yet into the town itself. It certainly didn't appear that the Canadians had caught the Jerry defences with their pants down. On the other hand, the Luftwaffe was not up and about in strength. Perhaps they could hardly be blamed. The RAF was using sixty squadrons in support of the Dieppe landing. To oppose them, the Germans had only two fighter wings, *Geschwader* 2 and 26.

Jacob Reh of 4 Squadron JG 26 was among the first wave of German fighters to be scrambled. With limited defence resources, the German controller had only launched one squadron from each of the two wings until he had some idea of the enemy's strength and intentions.

Jacob, now a veteran of five kills, had as his wingman that day a young sergeant pilot who had not yet fired his guns in anger. He was destined never to do so. A nearly direct hit from the 4-inch dual-purpose armament of a Hunt class destroyer dissolved his FW 190 in a fireball of burning aviation fuel. Jacob Reh felt the intensity of the heat-burst inside his own cockpit. There could be no question of looking for a parachute. Only a few smoking fragments remained, falling towards the green Channel. Jacob found himself alone in the sky. At that moment Peter Bristow was alone, too. He had led his boys into a mix-up with the 109s of JG 2. One of the Spits had gone in like a bomb, striking the water in a white burst of spray and disappearing immediately. He had sent a Messerschmitt home trailing black smoke and white petrol vapour. It would almost certainly burn. Now with things hotting up, he was returning to refuel and rearm.

The 190 came at him head-on out of a wisp of cloud and opened fire at once, amazingly accurately, from about six hundred yards. The range was too great to squander much of his remaining ammunition so he gave a discouraging two-second burst and then flicked away to port before the 190 could correct his aim. From the moment it started, he knew this pilot was a hot one. He had expected him to overshoot but there he was still tucked in behind. All right then, he'd out-turn him. He leaned the Spitfire to port so hard that she began to tremble in a pre-stall shudder. The bastard was still there, out-turning him. Any second now the tracers would come searching. Peter felt the scalded skin under his face mask prickling with sweat. This could be *it*. The one you eventually met who was better than you were. The only hope now, if he couldn't out-turn the Focke Wulf, was to out-dive him. He pushed the stick sharply forward and right, ramming the throttle open. Jacob Reh was caught by surprise for just two seconds, and two seconds at an air-speed building up rapidly to 500 mph were just the grace Peter Bristow needed. Those right turns had totally disorientated him, but now he saw that his seventy-degree dive was pointing him directly at the back of the town. That bloody 190 was still with him, too far away to shoot accurately but too close for comfort. Another thought: if he wanted his wings to stay with him, he'd better start easing out of this dive. The pull-out drained the blood from his head sufficiently to cause a partial black-out. Where was the Hun? Christ, he was good! Still there. Tracer past his port wing. Kick right rudder, then left. Right down over the roof tops now, jinking to miss a church steeple. If he didn't get away soon he'd run out of fuel, anyway. Hammering out over the harbour. Flak coming up from ships. Whose? Theirs or ours? What the hell did it matter? Both navies shot at anything on principle. That last tracer came from no ship. It was fired horizontally. The bastard was still there. One last hope. The front of the Spitfire's throttle gate was closed by a safety wire. Slam it through the copper wire and you could get a few extra revs. Leave it slammed forward too long and you'd probably seize your engine. Peter rammed the throttle knob through the safety wire and felt the Spit respond. Jacob Reh knew that he, too, had met a good one and that his enemy was about to escape. He even felt almost glad that he would do so. There was still room for some shred of chivalry in the air, if not on the ground. The red warning light on his instrument panel reminded him of fuel shortage. As he climbed over the cliffs of town, Bren gun fire from the commando that had successfully captured the German coastal battery there made an ineffectual attempt to grab at him. Angry he banked round and made one low-flying pass over the commando's position, firing a long burst at where he imagined the Bren to be.

Most of his bullets flattened on the well-built concrete of the Todt organisation's West Wall. One, however, passed through a weapon slit and caught the gunner in the throat, killing him instantly. The gunner's name was Michael Roland.

Kate Bristow had remained on duty in the Ops Room almost all that long day of "Operation Jubilee". The section officer who should have relieved her had gone down with 'flu shortly after mid-day and the controller gave Kate permission to stand an extra watch. Knowing her involvement with her brother, he kept a close eye on her. These personal relationships could play hell with judgement and efficiency. However Kate always seemed to be able to handle the situation and so, because he needed every cool hand he could get, he let her stay.

All Kate knew was that she had an inexplicable dread about what was going on over there. Peter led his squadron on three sweeps in support of the landing that day. Several times she heard his voice pitched up in the heat of a dogfight, but later had heard him report each time that he was back and landed in one piece. But still the dread remained. Was it just fear for the whole force of 3,000 Canadians who appeared to be taking such a beating? Or for the hundred-plus bombers and fighters the RAF lost against estimated Luftwaffe casualties of under forty? When she finally came off duty at 1800 hours she knew how bad it had been over there when the controller said wearily: "Well, lads and lassies, it seems to have been a pretty bloody awful day. The only thing that seems to have gone to plan was the capture of the coastal batteries by the commandos." It was only then that her dread found a point of focus. Michael! She'd been so caught up with Peter all day that it had never really hit her that Michael's unit . . . But wasn't it supposed to be an all-Canadian landing? Though she was almost too tired to stand, she caught Rosie Lee, the WAAF driver going off duty, and asked her to drive her to the nearby village where Michael's commando had been billeted. Rosie saw no reason why RAF petrol shouldn't be put to such a good cause, and she would have done it for Kate, anyhow. When they reached the camp, there was a sentry from a strange unit on the gate.

In the Lindenstrasse office of the Inspector of Fighters, Mano Rumpler read the month-old reports on the Dieppe raid with little satisfaction. There were those on the staff who held "Operation Jubilee" to have been an unqualified success for German arms. With 2,000 of the Canadian invaders killed and 1,000 captured, this was at least an understandable interpretation. There were, however, other angles. One was that it might give the Führer further evidence that he was not only invincible but proof against invasion. More immediately damaging was the loss of nearly forty aircraft, most of them fighters. With fighter production steadily climbing under Erhard Milch, this loss should have been a drop in the bucket. But there was little chance of JGs 2 and 26 on the Channel coast receiving the replacements they so badly needed. The spring offensive that was to have finished off Russia, so that the Luftwaffe could turn its attention to Britain, was already slowing down. The Russian Air Force, at first hopelessly outclassed, was now hitting back hard. Russia swallowed every fighter Milch could offer it. Unfortunately, Russia was not the only front with an appetite for 109s and 190s. Kesselring's *Luftflotte* 2 had hurled itself at Malta with losses that had temporarily exhausted it, while in North Africa, German fighters were spread thin to resist the combined attacks of the RAF and the US Ninth Air Force.

The general had been around creating merry hell again. His theme was always the same, that the Reich was where the fighter force was most needed and must be built up. To these arguments the Führer's answer was always the same: revenge and attack.

There were one or two rays of cheer. One lay on his desk in the shape of a confidential document from Field Marshal Milch's office. The Messerschmitt 262 jet fighter was to be put on the production schedule, though this did not mean it was going into actual production.

Another piece of paper brought more dubious cheer. The *Reichsmarschall* had at last made a more or less realistic statement about Germany's fighter strength. He had written: "The Bf 109, in its various developments, and then the FW 190, have both been caught up, and to some extent overtaken, by the English and American fighters, particularly as regards climbing powers. To my annoyance, these also seem to have greater range and this is very unpleasant. Above all, the Spitfire is ahead, a thing our fighter pilots don't like . . ."

The *Reichsmarschall*'s diagnosis was, for once, correct. But the likelihood of his prescribing the right medicine was remote.

True, there were promises of high-performance fighters to come. The Bf 209 and 309 were intended to replace the overworked 109. Then, a fast tandem-engined job, the Dornier Do 335, was promised. But all these had been on the drawing board in Udet's day. Under Milch's plan to produce as many of the standard types as possible—in fact giving quantity preference over quality—they were likely to remain simply blueprints. As evidence of Milch's policy, the first of the new mark Bf 109, the 109g, was soon to reach front-line squadrons.

Mano sighed deeply. His barrister's mind, trained to evaluate odds on available evidence, was forced to conclude that Germany was on a crest, if not over it. She had committed herself on so many fronts that it was difficult to see how she could win the war. Nowhere was this truer than in the air, and, without command of the air, all else was surely lost.

To hell with it! He had some leave coming. Dieter Reh was on leave also and had invited Mano to spend a few days with the family in Hamelin.

Dieter had seen Liese only once since she had lost the baby, on a forty-eight-hour compassionate pass to Berlin. She had looked drawn and had seemed depressed then. Though this had worried him a good deal, he had put it down not only to her losing their child but also to the horror of the 1,000-bomber raid on Cologne. Now, as the train drew in to Hamelin, he was shocked to see her standing on the platform waiting for him looking almost haggard. She had lost at least half a stone in weight. As she saw him, her face relaxed and became almost happy, the way he remembered her. She clung to him saying over and over again: "Oh, Dieter. Oh, Dieter."

"Yes, it's me. Didn't you think I'd come?"

"I don't know what I thought. These days I just seem to spend the time expecting the worst."

"Cheer up, darling. We can easily make another baby."

He had meant it as a joke but she burst into tears.

Mano Rumpler turned up in Hamelin the next day. Whatever his personal views about Germany's future conduct of the war he was determined to enjoy himself, moreover to see that those with him should share his holiday mood. When Mano was with them Liese relaxed. He insisted on taking them both to dinner at the most expensive restaurant in town, the one to which Dieter had first taken Liese. Mano talked amusingly and danced well. He kept the conversation away from the war except to tell scandalous anecdotes about people in high places, the *Reichsmarschall* especially. There was one sour note to all this: he made no secret of the fact that he did not wish to be overheard by any SS officer or unidentified civilian who might be Gestapo.

When they parted in the early hours, and went to their rooms, Liese grew depressed again. She was obsessed with Mano's fear of being overheard.

"What kind of Germany is this, where one dare not even make a joke without fear of the Gestapo?"

"Mano was exaggerating."

She turned on him sharply: "Did you really think that? Do you think Mano, an intellectual, is the sort to be frightened by shadows? By reality, yes. He knows that he's just the sort the Gestapo hate most. He's clever and in a position of some importance. He's the kind they keep dossiers on. They have concentration camps for people like Mano who don't precisely toe the line."

"Don't be absurd, Liese. Mano's a loyal serving officer. Just because he likes to crack a joke at the expense of that fat buffoon . . ."

"Now *you're* at it! You'd better be careful, Dieter. Serving officers are all right at the moment, but wait until things start going wrong, really wrong. Uniform won't protect you if you speak out of turn then."

"Liese! You're not well, not yourself."

"Oh yes I am. I've seen a good deal more than you, that's all."

"What have you seen?"

Dieter experienced a vivid, horrifying vision of the murder of the Polish woman prisoner, on that railway station months ago. It was by no means the first time that scene had returned to him. Several times, after a bad day in the air, he had dreamed of it. Once the victim had been not the Polish woman but Liese.

Liese cut into his thoughts, saying: "I've already told you some of the things I've seen. That young worker struck down with an iron bar. Old men and women driven through the streets like animals just because they're Jews. If that isn't enough for you I'll tell you something else. You remember the Roths who lived in Kirchenstrasse? You should do. You were at school with their son. He was killed on the Russian front last November. But recently his parents just simply disappeared. They were taken away in the middle of the night and have never been heard of since."

"Perhaps they moved."

"They were Jewish, weren't they?"

"Of course. Everyone knows that, they never made any secret of it. But their son gave his life . . ."

"So now they're just an old Jewish couple with nothing more to contribute."

"Liese darling. You're the one who should watch what you're saying." He had a sudden terrible vision of her talking like this in a public place, being arrested perhaps. She saw the fear in his face and knew it for what it was.

"There," she said triumphantly. "You *know* what I'm saying is true. Don't you? Your fear for me shows that you fully realise such terrible things can happen."

"Whether I know it or not, whether I believe it or not, I can't allow it to influence me. I'm a fighter pilot. That's all I know."

Before Mano left two days later to see his own parents in Dresden, he took Dieter aside.

"I didn't want to tell you earlier but you'll see it in the papers in a couple of days anyway. They always delay depressing announcements until they can counter them with something cheerful."

"Oh God, Mano, not more bad news?"

"Yes. I always seem to bring it with me, don't I? This time it's Marseille, killed when he bailed out over the desert."

"Marseille! Not shot down, surely?"

Hans Joachim Marseille was not only the Luftwaffe's youngest top-scoring fighter ace, but Galland himself had described him as the greatest virtuoso of them all. At twenty-two years of age, he had scored 158 victories, mostly in North Africa. On one day alone, he had shot down fifteen Curtis Tomahawks and two Spitfires. It was inconceivable that an enemy pilot should have defeated him.

Mano said: "It seems that his 109f caught fire. The cockpit filled with smoke. He was on the wrong side of the lines and so his companions urged him to stay with the aircraft. At last, when he could stand the fumes no longer, he jumped. Apparently he struck the tailplane and was knocked unconscious. His parachute never opened."

"At least the enemy didn't defeat him."

Mano's face had lost its gaiety. It was sallow and drawn as

he said: "In one way that's perfectly true but from what I hear of it he was fought out, physically and mentally. You can fly against the odds we're facing in North Africa for just so long before something gives way."

Three weeks later when Montgomery's artillery barrage broke over El Alamein, Dieter recalled Mano's words. How long, he wondered, before the odds were stacked hopelessly high against the few fighter squadrons entrusted with the defence of the Reich?

As soon as she could get leave, Kate Bristow went to Selsey to see Tom Roland. After the news came that Michael had died at Dieppe she felt as she had never felt before, as though her last root had been cut. It was almost a sensation of personal weightlessness, as if she floated in a vacuum. There was still Peter, but if her brother kept flying on ops, as he had every intention of doing, what chance did he have of surviving?

She had never really believed that she would marry Michael. She did not for a second regret that he had been her lover. Now that he was gone, she was intensely glad that she had given herself to him. She felt his loss more than she would have thought possible. Dearest Michael.

At such times there had to be recognisable points of reference to cling to. The corporate tension of the Ops room was one of these, Tom Roland was another.

Tom had had several weeks to recover from Michael's death by the time Kate reached Rife Farm. He hugged her. "Both of them gone, love. No one to leave the place to now. You'd better have it."

She stood in his arms for a moment, silently. Then, "Can I stay for a few days?"

"Good God, girl, stay for ever, if you want, you know that."

She made some tea and unearthed a tin of anchovies from a place in the kitchen cupboard where she'd hidden it, two years previously—anchovy toast was one of Tom's favourite delicacies. That the tin was untouched showed the way Tom had looked after himself since, living off what was easiest to find and cook.

The big metal farmhouse teapot, the huge cups with flying pheasants on them, the cosy luxury of the warm strips of anchovy toast, all rekindled the old closeness between them.

She touched Tom's hand. "You know that Michael and I . . ."

"I always hoped you two would get married one day."

"We talked of it a great deal."

This was the literal truth, but she felt dishonest, knowing that Tom hoped she would say that they had actually been engaged.

"On our last leave—we spent it together in the West Country—we both agreed that wartime wasn't the best time for marriage."

Tom said sadly. "You might have given me a grandson."

She smiled. "We might have done that, anyway, but I doubt it. Wartime's not the time for that either."

"I'm glad he had his happiness with you, Kate."

"We *were* happy, Tom, very happy."

He crossed to the window and stood looking out over the stubbles. "Five hundred acres," he said, "and no Rolands to leave them to."

Kate worked on the farm for the five days of her week's leave. It helped her and it helped Tom too. Only a fragment of the crashed *Stuka* still lay in the marshy meadow. Most had been taken away for salvage, and nettles and ragwort grew through what remained. She drove the tractor, helped stack wheat straw, fed her old enemies the saddleback pigs and set off to spend her last day in London before returning to Hawkinge.

There she immediately noticed one startling change. The West End was populated with a new kind of serviceman. He was tall he was short, he was fair and he was dark, but every single one of him had one thing in common—the most extraordinarily mobile hips. These hips were somehow exaggerated by the cut of his uniform. She noticed this as a fact, in the same way that she would have noticed the shape of a particular kind of tree or bush liberally distributed in a landscape. The fact that these were American air force men did not make a special appeal to her as it plainly did to many service women on leave in Piccadilly that evening. Michael's death had numbed her. The war had cost her two different kinds of lover. German and English. Her feeling was that she never wished to expose herself to that kind of wounding again. So although many of the unattached newcomers looked at her with obvious pleasure and interest, she remained locked away and apparently unaware of their glances.

There was a quiet little bar in Jermyn Street called "A la Broche" where she had sometimes met Peter and his friends. She urgently needed a drink and some privacy. She wished now that she had stayed on the farm until her leave was up. A drink would fill in the hour until it was time to see Bing Crosby and Bob Hope in *The Road to Morocco*.

The little bar was empty except for one American lieutenant wearing the shoulder flashes of the US Eighth Air Force. He stood with his back to her, swirling the ice in a Whisky Sour. Sipping her gin and tonic, she had to admit that the Americans really knew how to design a uniform. Those light trousers set off by that darker jacket—and those hips. She could see what the girls saw in these transatlantic invaders; they certainly had style. She thought of Michael's crumpled battledress and Peter's best RAF uniform, with the beer stains from many a mess party worn like wound stripes, or maybe decorations. She looked away as the American lieutenant turned round. If he ran true to form, he would most certainly appraise her. She did not particularly mind. She was neither flattered, nor offended. She just didn't care. He was crossing the room towards her.

"Excuse me, m'am. You'll have to pardon me if I'm acting like an American in London is supposed to act, that sounds like a standard line, too, I guess. But you're just like a girl I met in England in '38."

Kate looked up, prepared to be polite, kind even, but absolutely not interested in whatever the American had to suggest, even a shared drink. Instead she found herself looking into a face she had indeed seen before.

"Charles. Charles Levitson!"

"That's right," he said. "The very same. And, for Pete's sake, it's Kate Bristow, Peter's little sister! I can see it now. Somehow in this dim light, from the bar . . ."

Kate smiled. "I've changed a bit."

"For the better, ma'am, though as I remember the 1938 model took a lot of beating."

"It did," she said. "It's had one or two head-on crashes."

"Say, it's real nice to see you again. Tell me, I'm almost scared to ask. Is Pete okay?"

"You mean Squadron Leader Peter Bristow, DFC. Yes, he's alive and very much kicking, though he's undergone one or two facial modifications, too."

"You people've had a hell of a time."

"And now you're here to help us pay it back," she said lightly.

"Say, what're you doing tonight?"

"I swore I wouldn't get picked up by an American. As a matter of fact, I was going to the flicks."

"May I join you? I'd like that. Then maybe afterwards we

241

could get a bite to eat. We Americans have a club right here on Piccadilly."

Road to Morocco was just what Kate required, a gorgeous piece of Hope-Crosby-Lamour clowning with one great hit song "Moonlight Becomes You." And afterwards, over unfamiliar American food that was at least more plentiful and varied than the British variety, Charles Levitson filled in details. He had flown his B 17 across the Atlantic in August via Labrador, Greenland, Iceland and Northern Ireland. Now his squadron was in Essex completing operational training as part of General Ira C. Eaker's daylight bombing force. He talked with love of his B 17. The crew hadn't named their Fortress yet. The navigator, Hank Nokovsky, had a girl-friend called Katie back in Ohio. The co-pilot had wanted to name the bomber *Catydid*, which was a kind of grasshopper, but the navigator had complained that this was insulting to his girl-friend on two counts, not least of which was the pun. As captain, Charles had the deciding vote. Meeting Kate tonight had enabled him to settle the whole argument. Their B 17 would henceforward carry the simple legend "Kate".

1943

From the moment Dieter Reh first taxied the 109g, he knew she was a bitch but a pedigree bitch at that. His first reaction on opening her up and feeling the torque of the 1475 HP DB605-A-1 engine was that he wouldn't care to have cut his teeth on her. From the start, this latest development of the Messerschmitt factory was a character, just as the square-tipped Emil had been a character. The few Luftwaffe pilots who had already flown her had given her a name. As the "E" had stood for Emil, so "G" would never be anything other than G for Gustav. The 109f had proved itself a fast, if underarmed, aeroplane. There were those who swore by it, including Gerhard Barkhorn, the Luftwaffe's second highest scorer whose successes were mostly on the Russian front. Nevertheless the 109f always remained just that—a number and a type, never a personality.

Dieter folded his wheels before he was over the end of the runway at Jever. His Gustav G-1 was a powerpack, an aircraft so packed with power that her slender model-girl airframe had had to let out her dress as far as she could go without bursting her seams. There wasn't an unused cubic inch left under her engine cowling. The fact was that, with the Gustav series, the 109 had reached the peak of its life. Before it was all over, more Gustavs would be built than any other fighter in the history of aerial warfare. Before the war was over, the 109g, in its later developments, would have long gone over the hill and far down the slope beyond. The Bf 109 which had evolved as an aircraft to protect German bombers on the offensive was to end up as a defensive weapon whose cutting edge would prove hopelessly blunt.

With Pohle sitting out there to port in a second Gustav, Dieter decided to see what the machine would do. Throttle wide open and control column as far to the rear as it would go, they soared up through the clouds as in a high-speed lift. When they levelled off at 20,000 feet, it was a little under seven minutes since they had left the ground. Flying his first Gustav, Dieter experienced a kick he hadn't felt since the successful conclusion of the "Channel Dash," a feeling that the

German fighter pilot was on top again. The pressurised cabin gave such a sensation of freedom at this altitude. German technology had once more come up with the answer that would keep the fighter arm ahead. Pohle had left his R/T switch at transmit. He heard him singing one of his usual bawdy ballads and told him to shut up and follow him down. He put the Gustav into a dive which would have torn the wings off the old Emil. Life was great again.

When they landed, there were two ferry pilots waiting in the dispersal bay. They smiled apologetically and presented their written orders. Sorry, but the six new Gustavs just delivered were ordered south immediately, probably to Sicily. Others would no doubt be coming from the factory to replace them in due course.

In the end, Charles Levitson compromised with his crew. The navigator, Nokovsky, with the girl-friend called Katie back in Ohio, thought that whereas "Catydid" had been assuming too much about his girl, without the special knowledge of the subject which he alone might or might not have, plain "Kate" was too reserved and severe. Charles, who had read English literature at university, dredged up a quotation which anticipated Broadway and Hollywood by a decade. He suggested "Kiss me Kate". There followed a long wrangle about whether the pin-up who carried this slogan should be a blonde or brunette. The girl in Akron, Ohio, was a brunette. Charles Levitson said that, being the only gentleman aboard, he preferred blondes. They voted, the ballot coming out at five all. Finally the squadron sign-painter settled it. He embellished the B 17's nose with a reclining lady whose legs were closely modelled on the world-famous undercarriage of Miss Betty Grable, while her fuselage, including two magnificent in-line engines, were strongly influenced by the equally celebrated Petty "Esquire" girl. While the crew argued, he gave her auburn hair. The legend "Kiss me Kate" was strategically placed across her torso since the words were all she wore and a squadron order had gone out: "no nudes."

On this pale morning of 27 January 1943, "Kiss me Kate" reclined over the North Sea in a temperature many degrees below freezing at 21,000 feet, headed for Wilhelmshaven. In the captain's seat, Charles Levitson felt a different sort of cold, the unavoidable chill left by the uncertainty and fear of a first mission. He was not alone in this. It was the first experience of combat for nearly all of the 550 Americans who rode beside, around and above him in the total armada of fifty-five

Fortresses. For the Eighth Air Force, too, it was a notable first —its first daylight attack in strength into Germany.

The controller at Jever had got the message early. "Large bomber force building up off East Anglia," the long-range Freya radar had told him. He still could not tell exactly *how* large and, anyway, he only had a few squadrons of FW 190s belonging to JG 1 under Lieutenant-Colonel Dr. Erich Mix available. Of the *Erprobungs* unit, only Willy Weiss and Kolbe still had mounts after the withdrawal of the flight's new Gustavs. They obtained permission to scramble with the last *Staffel* of JG 1 and caught up with the Americans on their final approach to the target.

The skipper of "Kiss me Kate" took comfort from the silver phalanxes of B 17s gently rising and falling in the still, rarefied air around him. "Keep a sharp look out for fighters," he told the crew for the tenth time.

Willy Weiss caught his breath when he saw the size of the Fortress formation. His first thought was: "We can't go in there." But his reflexes had already acted against his sense of self-preservation. The textbooks still said "attack from astern and above" but JG 2 and JG 26 had already proved you must throw the textbook away against these four-motored giants. Height was on his side. Pushing the throttle wide open, he began to overtake the bomber boxes well out to one side.

Charles Levitson heard tail and ventral gunners yelp simultaneously: "Here they come, two bandits overtaking, out of range to starboard."

"Watch 'em, boys. Hold your fire."

The bomb doors were open and the bombardiers leading the formation on to target—Wilhelmshaven's dock installations and harbour.

A mile ahead of the right-hand bomber box, Willy Weiss flicked into a steep turn to port and together they streaked in directly at the nose of the outside Fortress. The bomber came up on them so fast that they had to open fire almost as soon as they had begun their pass. Willy saw his strikes going in, saw the starboard outer start to smoke, saw the tracer from the nose gunner reaching for him. The closing rate was so fast that he only just reacted in time to dive under the belly of his target and felt its wash buffet him.

"Kiss me Kate" was too far from the scene of this particular attack to do much about it. Nevertheless her belly gunner fired a burst in the general direction as Weiss and Kolbe half-rolled and dived, his bullets weaving themselves into the lattice work of tracer that seemed to enclose the two fighters briefly in a cage, but a cage whose bars were too widely spaced to hold them. They were gone but others would be coming.

Charles Levitson stared, fascinated, at the bomber that had been hit. It was losing height and dropping behind. Its bombs fell clear, jettisoned, well before the rest of the bombardiers had released them. It began to turn back for England, alone. In a few seconds it was lost to sight. He wondered who it was and whether they'd make it. Twelve heavy machine-guns! They should have a chance. His own bombardier was exulting about the accuracy of their bombing run.

"All you guys keep on your toes for fighters!"

"A bunch of bandits dead ahead, high. Here they come."

For the second time Charles Levitson felt that strange metallic taste on his tongue. His waist gunners were shouting as they fired. The 190s were gone but a Fortress in front was turning in a slow spiral, like the falling leaf aerobatic they used to practise in two-seater trainers. But a Fortress wasn't a two-seater. It had ten men aboard. He tried not to imagine the chaos in that twisting fuselage. Magazines, machine-gun belts, oxygen bottles, all tumbling about. Dead, dying or wounded men, the latter struggling to get out against the centrifugal forces of that spin. "Kate's" ventral gunner was hammering away again, filling the Fortress with cordite fumes and the tinkle of spent cases. A 190 dived vertically through the bomber box ahead of them without anyone laying a glove on it. Far below, the spinning Fortress had lost a wing and two parachutes flowered above it.

"Two guys got out," the tail-gunner reported as if he had been seeing things like this every day of his young life.

"Captain to tail-gunner. If you don't want to join them, watch the goddam sky."

They were well out over the North Sea now on the way home.

The taste of metal polish on Levitson's tongue had gone. "Jeez," he thought, "we've made it. We've survived." And each of the nine others with him was thinking exactly the same thing.

When they had rolled to a stop at their base in Essex they found a jagged hole in Kate's left nipple. No one had heard the bullet come or go.

"Paint a swastika over the patch," the navigator suggested. They were champagne-light with the effervescence of survival. They'd been, they bombed and they'd come back again.

And though the fighters had been unbelievably fast, there hadn't been too many of them. It hadn't been so bad after all. No one claimed to have shot a Focke Wulf down and only three Fortresses had been lost. The squadron commander said three out of five-fifty was a small price to pay and that they'd proved daylight bombing in strength really worked. But each crew member of "Kiss me Kate" remembered the Fortress turning back alone and the one with the wing falling off, and that was what stayed with you after the champagne bubbles had burst in your brain.

In March, Dieter was once again sent on leave waiting the delivery of the latest Gustavs. February was a dour and dripping month and the news was dismal to match it. On 2 February, Stalingrad fell. General Paulus' Sixth Army had disappeared to a man and with it much of the strength of the Luftwaffe on the Russian front. In North Africa, Rommel was fighting for his life.

Dieter found Liese tight-lipped and depressed. Her mood contrasted strongly with that of her employer. His father had received several promotions in the hierarchy of Erhard Milch. It was plain that he regarded any setback to German arms as only temporary. He hinted at wonderful new weapons that would soon leap off the drawing-board and with which the Führer and the Reich would sweep all before them once more. Dieter listened politely to his father, merely remarking that he hoped the aircraft industry had something up its sleeve to counter the growing and combined threat of Lancaster and Stirling by night and Fortress and Liberator by day. His father tapped the side of his nose confidingly and told him not to worry about that.

His father's complacency did not unduly disturb Dieter for he had expected it. His mother's attitude of mind troubled him much more. She had lost none of her determination to tackle the task before her. She even spoke enthusiastically of what the Hamburg plant was doing. But he sensed in her a sadness of spirit, a mother's despair for all the young lives poured away in Russia. She clung to him with desperate affection such as he had not felt from her since he was a little boy. It made him want to cry for her and it drove a deep chill into him. He sensed that she feared she was about to lose him. He kissed her and broke away from the embrace, shaking himself as a swimmer who has been nearly drowned by an overpowering wave shakes the water from his head. A combat pilot couldn't affort to indulge such depressing fantasies.

In the midst of the gloom occasioned by the news from Stalingrad there shone an unexpected ray of cheer.

Dieter had often feared for the good-natured Heine Müller. Surely such an aerial innocent simply could not survive on the Russian front. But now here Heine was, knocking on the front door, complete with bomber pilot's clasp and Iron Cross.

"Heine! I feared you were dead at Stalingrad."

"So did I. But you know I have the luck of the devil. I got nicked in the leg by the Ivans—nothing serious—and was sent home just before the final collapse, otherwise I'd probably be six feet under the snow by now."

"Come to dinner with Liese and me."

"I heard you were married. You'd have been a fool if you hadn't shot this one down."

"Actually she jumped me. Out of the sun, too."

Heine gave Liese a hug. "My dears, I'm delighted for you both. If only it wasn't for this damned war."

Liese said sharply: "You feel that too, Heine."

"Of course, most wars are futile and some are damned disgusting."

"Which is this one, Heine?"

Müller's reply was a shock, even though he laughed as he said: "Both futile *and* disgusting but there's nothing left for us except to try our hardest to win it, I suppose. If you'd been on the Eastern front as I have, you might wonder whether that's going to be possible any more."

The genial Heine was more his old self when they went out to dinner at a restaurant that no longer pretended not to be feeling the wartime pinch. His stories still had the self-mocking tone they all knew, but now there was a bitter tang to many of them. In one operation the Russians had dropped guerillas behind the German lines. Being short of parachutes, they had packed their partisans into wooden crates full of wood shavings and dumped them out of slow-flying transport aircraft from low altitude into deep snow drifts. Amazingly, many of the raiders had survived. After this, Heine said, the rumour had got around that the Luftwaffe was equipping its aircrews with wooden dual-purpose parachutes, approximately six feet long and two feet wide. If they didn't work, at least they would do away with the need for burial. Heine had his own payoff to the story: like most other High Command ideas for the Russian front, the plan hadn't worked in practice. The designers hadn't allowed for the fact that the ground was frozen so hard that the coffins splintered on impact.

The way Heine told it, you couldn't help laughing—or noticing the underlying sense of the hopelessness he felt at trying to beat Russia, even if you could beat the Russians.

Liese wanted to know what the Russians were like.

"We only see them through a bomb-sight which, as you may judge, is a great leveller. Our military propaganda tells us that they're little better than savages but savagery has a knack of reducing men to a common denominator. If they *are* savages, then my fear is that we'll have to out-match them in savagery as well as everything else. The Russian winter is the cruellest thing imaginable. Its temperature makes acts of cold-blood the normal rather than the exception. But get me off this subject. I'm on leave."

Later, after Liese had gone to bed, they sat talking in the living-room of the Reh house as they had a little over a year before, when Stecke and Jacob had also been on leave.

Dieter said proudly, "Young Jacob could become another Marseille. . . . He's already got twelve kills, only ten behind me. He's a natural. All this testing and experimental flying my flight gets stuck with gives my brother an unfair advantage over me."

"Have you heard from Gerhard Stecke recently?"

"I saw his father yesterday. Reading between the lines, he's had a hell of a time in Sicily. These incessant raids on Malta have been no picnic. He got wounded slightly on one trip. Another time he had to ditch in shallow water off Augusta when he couldn't make his base at Catania. But he's survived so far."

"I wonder if he's still such a fanatic or whether he sees the realities of the situation as you and I do, Dieter. Do you realise the kind of people we're fighting for?"

"We're fighting for Germany, Heine."

"Of course, and have no choice about that. But I mean our leadership."

"Goering?"

"You fighter boys surely don't need to be told how he's dropped you in the shit at every opportunity. And it goes far beyond that crazy *Reichsmarschall.*"

"There's still the Führer."

"Surely you don't still believe in Santa Claus?"

Dieter was shocked. "You're entitled to your opinions."

"But I'd best keep them to myself."

"Precisely."

"Dieter, although you're trying to be loyal, your heart tells you what kind of regime we're really being led by."

"Oh God," Dieter said desperately. "How the hell do I know? I'm a professional soldier of the Reich."

"Yes. So it's harder for you to admit the truth."

"What truth?"

"Let me ask you this: have you any Jewish friends?"

"Not really."

"You think you haven't. But what about me? Do you realise that though, for the record, I'm conveniently Aryan, way back somewhere I've got a few Jewish ancestors. If the SS ever wished to get rid of me—not that it'll be necessary, the way we're losing aircrews in Russia—don't you think they could find that out? Doesn't it ever worry *you* that you haven't got blond hair and blue eyes?"

"Don't be damned silly. Millions of Germans are dark."

"Yes, but before all this is over, thousands will have been sent to extermination camps for far less."

"*Extermination* camps! I know there are concentration camps for politically unreliable people . . ."

"*And* racially impure people. Jews and Poles, for instance. Don't tell me you've never heard of that kind of thing. Have you never seen anything that's troubled your racially pure conscience?"

Dieter's face betrayed him.

Heine said: "All right, old friend. Don't tell me. I can see that you have. But you can't have seen anything like the horrors most of us have witnessed in Russia. Once I made a forced landing beside one of those camps. Rows and rows of Russian civilian corpses, many so thin they can't have weighed more than a few stone, some with bullet wounds, men, women and children, frozen stiff as logs and stacked one on top of the other like firewood."

"That's horrible, horrible! If it's true, what are you going to do about it?"

"The same as you. Fight the war because it's become a fight for our own survival. But personally I'm going to pray that the madmen who have led us into this, and lead us now, are replaced by sane men who can lead us out of it."

"You were always a strange one, Heine, but you never used to question things as you question them now. What would it be like if all serving officers thought like you?"

Heine shrugged. "We would perhaps get some leaders we could respect."

"It's different for you, Heine. You're a civilian at heart and always will be. But I'm a professional. I went through the rigorous training of a regular officer. I took a special oath to the Führer."

"And the ideals you were taught were the age-old military ones. You were trained to use aircraft and guns, not gas-chambers for mass extermination and gas ovens for mass cremation."

"All I know, Heine, is that you and I must fight the enemy to the limit of our ability."

Liese was asleep when Dieter went up. Any other night he would have woken her, sure that she would be eager to make love. Tonight he was far too disturbed by his conversation with Heine. He fell asleep at last but tossed and turned so that Liese woke in the early hours. She watched him moving about in his sleep and heard him cry out and knew that he was having one of his nightmares. After a minute or so she put the light on. He woke almost at once and sat up, his pyjama jacket sticking to his back with sweat. He stared at her as though he didn't immediately recognise her.

"It's all right, *Liebchen,* you were having a bad dream."

He shuddered as though he wanted to be sick.

"Was it about flying?" she asked.

"God no. Least of all that."

"But you've had them before. You told me as much once."

"Everyone gets nightmares. Perhaps the food at the restaurant . . ."

"Perhaps," she said. "Is it always the same dream?"

"It seems so real each time."

"Maybe it *is* real. Does it concern me?"

"Sometimes. When it's really horrible, like tonight, it does."

"It's about something that happened to you, isn't it? Tell me. It will be far better if we share it."

She could see that he was almost in tears. She pulled his head against her shoulder as a mother might, and said gently: "Tell me."

So he told her what had happened at the railway station and how, in the dream, the murdered woman was sometimes her.

At the end she said: "You should have told me before. Let me guess why you kept it to yourself. You did so because you were afraid I would say something to undermine your loyalty . . . You should have known me better, *Liebchen.* Has Heine been talking to you? Is that what made you dream like that?"

"Yes," he admitted. "Heine told me about the extermination camps. Is he telling the truth, do you think?"

"Heine is not the one to invent stories of mass murder."

The phrase brought back the newspaper headlines after the attack on Cologne in which Liese had lost her child, their child, and 400 Germans had lost their lives—BRITISH AIR PIRATES COMMIT MASS MURDER.

"Mass murder," he said. "What's so different between what Heine saw and what the RAF did to Cologne and are doing now all over the Ruhr?"

"Perhaps not much. I told you long ago what this war would do to us all."

"Liese, I'm so confused."

"You mustn't be. Your duty is to defend your country, as mine is to help your father produce the planes you need to do so. But you must never be blind to the crimes that are committed in Germany's name . . . If we can help her to survive, then we must hope and pray that she gets the leaders she deserves . . . Come now, my love, you need to sleep. Perhaps I can even help you a little."

Back at Jever, the new Gustavs were waiting. It was the moment for which Dieter told himself he had been waiting, too. The Yanks were, as yet, still probing with their B 17s, but the probes were becoming deeper and more persistent.

The conversations with Heine and Liese had left their mark. Dieter assured himself that combat would drive any doubts from his mind. Yet, twice, when he led the test flight against Fortress formations, he was horrified to discover that he lacked his old split-second timing and decision. Once he had broken off a frontal attack too early and had received a burst from a Yankee nose-gunner that had shot his cooling system to pieces. He had been lucky to land with a seized engine. Another time he had pulled out too late and had sheared a wingtip on the tail fin of a Fortress. That time he had gone into a spin and had had to bail out. The only consolation was that his wingman, now Oberfeldwebel Pohle, had got the Fortress, Pohle's combat report stressing the courage with which his No 1 had pressed home his attack. Dieter knew that it was not so much courage as lack of judgement. If he kept on like this he would not only continue to damage badly needed fighters but he would very soon get himself killed. Of the two he was inclined to think the latter was the lesser disaster. With dread he recognised symptoms of the malaise that had afflicted him at flying school when his loyalties were split over that English girl. It was the first time he had thought of Kate for many months.

Somehow he had to break himself of this state of mind. Even if such things as Heine had described *were* going on, it wasn't his business to think of them. His duty was to shoot down bombers. He longed to talk to his companions about his fears. Did they, too, suffer from the same terrible inner doubts about crimes, yes, crimes, there was no other word for what he himself had witnessed, committed in Germany's name? And, if they did, did they just write them off as things that were bound to happen in wartime? That most of the fighter pilots he fought with were disillusioned by the quality of Germany's military leadership was beyond doubt. How many, though, had any knowledge of the atrocities Heine had described? Possibly very few, since most had been confined to the heartland of the Reich and the occupied territories of the West. Comparatively few had travelled as Dieter had done to the Polish borders and these things seemed to happen principally away from Germany's domestic doorstep. But then, he argued with himself, few could have avoided seeing Jews herded through the streets. To put Jews to street-sweeping was one thing. Even Dieter now realised that *Hitlerjugend* conditioning had made this seem acceptable. But wholesale extermination was something abhorrent to a fighting soldier's code. Could the Führer really know about such things? Wasn't it possible that these acts were the work of extremists directed by unscrupulous elements of the Party without the Führer's approval, let alone consent?

On the whole that did not seem possible either. Whom could he discuss this with? The members of the *Erprobungs* flight were as close as comrades of a select unit can ever be. This still did not make discussion with any of them easy or even desirable. The Hoffman twins were Prussians, dedicated to serving a military ideal. There would be little change to be got from them. To Pohle, his wingman, he was as close as comradeship can bring two men, but Pohle was an NCO, a warrant officer. "Shoehorn" Kolbe characteristically made a joke of any issue he found unpalatable. That left Willy Weiss, the gentle Austrian giant. One evening when they were alone in Willy's quarters, Dieter asked: "Do you believe these stories you hear about atrocities on the Russian front?"

"Theirs or ours?"

"*Theirs,* of course. You think we could be guilty of atrocities?"

"In a war of that sort any army can be guilty."

"But supposing the crimes were against civilians?"

Willy looked at him with amused candour. "Ever heard of bombing cities? Isn't that directed against civilians?"

The conversation settled nothing. It came back to the same stale viewpoint. In total war, anything was acceptable.

In late May, Mano received orders to stand by to accompany the general on an important visit. Mano's chief, the inspector of day fighters, was away on the Russian front. From previous experience the general had a high regard for Hauptmann Rumpler's integrity and discretion. When Mano heard that their destination was the Luftwaffe testing ground at Rechlin, he suspected that he was about to see something on the secrets list. The general would hardly make a personal visit to inspect a new version of the 109 or 190. Mano had a fair inkling of what the new weapon might be. If his suspicions were right, he only hoped the tests would prove satisfactory. German arms could do with some good news, the Luftwaffe especially. All that week the Afrika Korps had been fighting a last-ditch stand as it was herded into the Cape Bon peninsula. Rommel had already left. Such fighter units as remained were taking their aircraft to Sicily, leaving the bulk of their ground staff behind to be swept into the Allied prisoner-of-war cages. A staff officer who had been flown home specially to report had told amazing stories of 190 pilots who had crammed their faithful "blackmen", their mechanics, into the narrow tunnel of the fuselage behind the cockpit rather than leave them to certain capture. Some of these fighters had touched down at Gerbini and Catania with three men on board. When Mano joined the general's small entourage to set out for Rechlin, the death of the Afrika Korps seemed certain within hours.

They were driven across the airfield in two large Mercedes staff cars. Mano's guess had been correct about the aircraft the general had come to fly in person. Two of them stood alone on the concrete apron, grey-green and shark-like, sharp noses pointing, disconcertingly from the pilot's point of view, skyward. They had twin engines, mounted low on each wing. As in the model the Messerschmitt engineer had shown Dieter two years previously, they had no propellers. Before Mano stood the Messerschmitt 262, the world's first jet fighter. Fritz Wendel, Messerschmitt's Chief Test Pilot, had successfully flown it over a year previously. Since then, though he had been told all about its fantastic possibilities, Goering had refused to show enthusiasm for the project. Hitler was simply not interested in fighters unless they were for attack. Jeschonnek merely echoed the Führer's views and Milch was dedicated to turning out as many of the standard production models as possible. Now the general had come to see for himself. The staff car in which Mano sat with one of the Messerschmitt engineers and an official of the Air Ministry remained a respectful hundred yards distant from the two machines. The general's car drove right alongside one of the jets. A slight dark man, Fritz Wendel came forward to shake his hand. Mano could see the general making typically expansive gestures. Wendel remained stern-faced and serious, as he explained flying technique. After all it was his special toy and a very expensive one to bend.

The Messerschmitt man was explaining to Mano, "There's quite a lot to learn in one lesson. It's not like a conventional aircraft at all on take-off. For one thing the tail won't come up and the rudder is dead until you do get it up. So until then you have to steer with your brakes, which would be fine if you could see where you're going. But you can't because the nose is still tilted in the air because the tail won't leave the ground."

"What's the answer then?"

"Wendel worked that out. When you reach 130 kph you apply the brakes sharply. The nose tilts forward if you do it right and from that moment on you have airflow over the tail assembly and no problems. Listen! They're starting up."

It was hardly necessary to listen. Mano's eardrums felt as though they had been punctured with a red-hot knitting needle. The general was now in the cockpit and mechanics were starting the second engine. Almost at once there was a burst of flame. The starboard engine was on fire. The general was used to getting out of fighters in a hurry. He now did so but almost before he had retired to a safe distance the blaze had been put out.

"That's a nice start," Mano said.

"These things happen on test."

"But we don't have many generals like that to spare. He's a good one."

The general was climbing into the second 262. This time both engines started without mishap. The jet shivered with a great shriek of power against her brakes. Then she shot forward, speed building up until half the runway had gone. Still the nose was pointing skyward and the tail wheel remained stuck to the tarmac.

"If he doesn't do something soon, he won't have enough runway left to stop," the Messerschmitt man said gloomily.

At that moment, precisely opposite the marker Wendel had laid out, the pilot dabbed his brakes. In seconds, the 262 had floated easily into the air and was climbing at a rate that had its occupant pinned to his seat with a G-force of pure ecstasy.

"I told you he was a good general," Mano said.

He had not expected this particular pilot to be content with a few circuits and bumps. He was not disappointed. A four-engined Me 323 on test came lumbering over at that moment. The 262 appeared like a peregrine stooping on a crow and was gone, climbing away in a steep turn that whipped it instantly out of range of its victim's possible vengeance. When at last the jet came in to land there were grins on everyone's faces, including those of Wendel and Dr Willy Messerschmitt.

The general climbed out in a state of obvious delight and began to clap everyone on the back. The mechanics had killed those banshee engines now. Mano could hear the general shouting to Wendel: "Flying? I tell you it was exactly as if angels were pushing me."

When they flew back to Berlin that evening they were all wildly enthusiastic. The general's excitement was infectious. If only the 262 could be put into production straight away, it would make mincemeat of those Yankee bombers. It was at least 120 mph faster than anything else that flew.

Next day the news came that the Afrika Korps had surrendered.

Shortly after Mano received this dire news an *aide* placed on his desk a copy of the cable the general had sent to *Reichsmarschall* Goering.

"The aircraft 262 is a great step forward. It will guarantee us an unbelievable advantage while the enemy sticks to the piston engine. The aircraft opens up completely new tactical possibilities."

The general had not been idle in other fields. If OKL would not immediately give him the fighters he needed, then he would have to juggle round his existing forces to deal with the Americans by day, leaving Kammhuber with his ever-expanding *Himmelbett* system of individual night-fighters tethered to the radar-directed zones to oppose the RAF after dark. In the north at Jever, he had formed a new *Geschwader* by splitting JG 1, bringing in new recruits and even by withdrawing nine serviceable aircraft from Africa. Things were that bad. He'd also taken JG 54 from the eastern front and posted it for defence of the Reich at Oldenburg.

There were all sorts of theories about how to tackle the Fortresses. Heinz Knoke of 5 squadron JG 1—at Jever—had created a nine-day wonder by developing a technique for dropping a bomb from his fighter, timed to explode in the middle of the massed American formations. Knoke's squadron had scored some sensational early successes by this method. However, no one, including the inventor, believed that the tactic could succeed for very long, especially when the Yanks started using fighter escorts.

During this phase, Dieter and his flight had two main tasks, to teach the recruits of the new *Geschwader* at Jever some anti-Fortress tactics and to evaluate yet a later mark of the 109g. To cope with the heavily armed Fortresses and Liberators, the Messerschmitt factory had replaced the 30-calibre MG 17 machine-guns with MG 131s which were slightly heavier than the American bombers' 50-calibres. The only snag to this was that the breeches and ammo chutes were too big to be concealed in the top of the fuselage above the engine. The Messerschmitt designers had solved this by giving their elegant but overworked little aircraft two streamlined swellings, one on each side, forward of the cockpit and slightly below canopy level. The pilots already had a name for this desecration of their beloved 109. They called it *Die Beule*, the "Bulge". Shoehorn Kolbe had shown his regard for the arrangement by painting bug-eyes on the bulges.

After their first few sorties in *Die Beule*, Dieter formed the definite opinion that the Bf 109 had now gone over the top. It was no longer the sweet and tractable lady it had once been. The added torque of the more powerful engine made it a handful on take-off. The bulges hadn't helped in terms of visibility or manoeuvrability. From now on, they might make it faster by souping up the engine still further. They might give it more fire-power by hanging cannons under its wings, but it would be like a beautiful woman getting older, fatter and desperately anxious to retain the attractions of her youth.

Dieter, Pohle, Weiss and Kolbe had a vivid demonstration of this over Bremen one day. On this occasion the Yanks had introduced an entirely new element. For the first time they had a fighter escort with them. The German pilots had been briefed to expect this. The first glimpse of the escort was, however, something of a shock. They were twin-fuselaged P38s—Lockheed Lightnings. Dieter decided to ignore the escort and go for the bombers in a frontal attack. Theoretically it should have been easy to outfly the cumbersome

Lightnings. In the event they found themselves in for quite a scrap. Though they shot down a Liberator, the Lightnings accounted for one of the new pilots of JG 11 and severely shot up another 109g. That evening, though, depressed at having lost one of JG 11's new pilots, the old anxieties troubled him again and he slept badly. This time when he dreamed about the murder in the Polish railway siding it was the face of the dead pilot who looked up at him.

On 24 July, Liese received an urgent telegram to report to her boss at the Air Ministry in Berlin. She obeyed reluctantly because she knew Frau Reh was deep in production problems at the Hamburg factory and needed all the secretarial help she could get. Though the telegram was marked *very urgent*, Liese was inclined to take this with a pinch of salt. These days everything for her father-in-law was urgent, even the emptying of the office ash-trays. But Frau Reh was nothing if not loyal to her successful husband and so she insisted that Liese leave that afternoon for Berlin. The RAF's night bomber force had been quiet for several days. As she drove Liese to the station, she said, "Let's hope that things keep nice and quiet for a while. Enjoy yourself in Berlin and give my love to Helmuth."

That evening Frau Reh had a light supper in the office and worked late. Just before midnight she decided that she had done enough. She walked through the radar wing on the way to her car because she liked to say goodnight to the night shift. It was good for morale for them to see that the bosses were putting in a few extra hours, too. The factory was now producing some long-range radar as well as the Lichtensteins carried in General Kammhuber's night-fighters. One of these sets was on test at this moment. As she passed, the foreman called out to her: "Frau Reh, what do you make of this? I've never seen a signal like this before. The set has gone crazy."

She looked in the glowing green screen and saw that it was almost obscured with a rash of white blips like crawling insects.

"It must be faulty."

"It was working all right five minutes ago. We followed our own night-fighters taking off on patrol quite plainly."

"Well, you'd better find the fault before we send it out," she said laughingly. "You'll be getting Reh Fabrik a bad name."

"Not us, Frau Reh. We're too proud of our work. Goodnight."

"Goodnight. Enjoy your breakfast. I'll be getting up about the time you're turning in."

"Sleep well, Frau Reh."

It was a clear night outside. She rather enjoyed the drive through the empty streets to her flat in the suburbs. She had hardly started the engine when she was aware of heavy aircraft overhead. The guns hadn't opened fire so the planes must be friendly. Then a parachute flare lit the factory yard like daylight.

A raid! Should she make a dash for the suburbs or stay in the factory? She sat irrresolute, waiting to see what developed. It might only be a nuisance attack by Mosquitoes, the bane of Hermann Goering's life. "The Fat One," people said, "can't even swat a few mosquitoes." It was true. These wooden-framed twin-engined machines were too fast for the night-fighters to catch. It was a long time since the *Reichsmarschall* had invited the people to call him "Meier" if a single enemy bomber penetrated the Ruhr! While these thoughts passed through her mind, whole sections of the city began to glow with fires. Among the fires the first high explosive bombs were falling.

This was no Mosquito attack. This was a big one. No wonder the RAF had been quiet for the last few days. She ran to her office and pulled down the switch of the alarm bell which made it compulsory for workers to seek the basement shelters. Then she began to put important papers into the fireproof safe. The aircraft noise was by now stupefying. She knew what Liese had experienced that night in Cologne. But even Cologne could not have been subjected to incendiaries on this scale. Within minutes the factory was ringed by fires. In fact the whole city, except the small area surrounding the Reh works, seemed to be ablaze. By day the factory had a well-drilled fire-fighting system but at one in the morning there was only a skeleton crew available. Her first instinct had been to send the night shift to the shelters, but now there seemed to be comparatively little high explosive falling and the white glare of an incendiary burning on the concrete of the yard outside decided her. She picked up the emergency phone connecting the office with the shelters. Slightly out of breath, the foreman answered her.

"Everyone all right?"

"So far, Frau Reh."

"Listen, this seems to be a fire raid. Get volunteers to put incendiaries out. Spread them right through the factory. The roofs are the most important places."

"They'll all go, I'll see to that."

"Good. Make sure they use sand." She put down the phone, picked up a bucket herself and dashed outside to smother a bomb that threatened to incinerate her car.

Two hours later, they had put out thirty bombs and fought a small fire in a store-room, but the factory had survived. The same could hardly be said for much of their surroundings. The heat of the blazing city seared flesh. Smoke tainted with burnt paint, woodwork, and something that smelt dreadfully like burning flesh, set them choking. When daylight came soon after four the sky was obscured by a smoke cloud that rose several thousand feet into the air and had drifted out seventy miles into the North Sea. Whatever else had happened, they had survived. For the moment there was no way of telling who else had done so. All phones had ceased to work and there was no mains water. To remedy the latter, Frau Reh directed that three emergency pumps be rigged to take water from the canals that bordered them on two sides. If the fires spread, they would have means of fighting them.

Hamburg flattered itself that it had the most efficient civil defence system in Germany and so it had. But even this was hard put to cope with what had just taken place.

At eight a.m. a Fire Control Officer got through on a fire engine to them to tell them that all communications with the city had been cut. The worst hit areas were being sealed off. Movement about the city was for the present forbidden. They had emergency rations? Good. Then they were to stay where they were until further notice. The fire control officer departed.

Two hours later, the US Eighth Air Force arrived and stoked up the fires. Miraculously, Reh Fabrik survived this one, also.

With blessed relief, the following night passed peacefully except for the roar of fires and the explosions caused by engineers blowing up buildings to prevent one patch of fire joining up with the next. The Fortresses made a further daylight raid on 26 July. This time a stick of HE bombs demolished a machine-shop at Reh Fabrik and killed three workers, but they had long been expecting it and were almost too exhausted to feel the reality of the blow. At dusk that evening, they received a supply of rations from a civil defence truck and settled down, longing for a second peaceful night.

Just after midnight, 700 aircraft of RAF Bomber Command arrived over the blazing city to finish the job. Finish it they most certainly did. This time Reh Fabrik was in the eye of the storm, the first firestorm in history. So many incendaries fell in such a short time, so many fires fed upon, so many other fires that the heart of Hamburg became like the flame of a blow torch. It was not so much a fire as a meteorological phenomenon. The temperature at the centre of the holocaust was around 1000° C. The air at 2,000 feet above the stricken port was heated to such an extent that the force with which it rushed upwards was sufficient to suck in tornado-force winds from the outskirts several miles away. Trees, people, the melting frameworks of trucks were sucked in and disappeared. What would burn disappeared. That which wouldn't burn, melted. Shortly before the firestorm broke loose, Frau Reh had given a frantic order for her remaining workers to retreat to the deep shelters. When, several weeks later, rescue workers dug their way through the fused wreckage of the factory and reached the cellars where forty people had sheltered that night, they found nothing but a scattering of human ashes. This was as much as remained of most of the 55,000 citizens of Hamburg who died with Greta Reh in the RAF's Operation *Gomorrah*.

Mano Rumpler was certain that the last chance for the Luftwaffe had come and that Hamburg marked the hour of decision. The paths ahead were clear—total disintegration under Allied bombing attacks or defence of the Reich behind a strong fighter force. Events at OKL recently had not led anyone on the staff to believe that rational decisions were likely. A fortnight ago the Allies had invaded Sicily. The tattered German fighter forces there were fighting a heroic last-ditch stand against swarms of Spitfires, Lightnings and Tomahawks escorting Fortresses and Liberators. Their few remaining airfields were pattern-bombed all day by Mitchells and Marauders, so that replacement fighters were often destroyed on the ground before the raw recruit pilots had a chance to get killed flying them in their first few sorties. In the midst of this bloodshed and chaos, the *Reichsmarschall*'s contribution had been to send out an order that one officer per squadron— it didn't matter which one—be court-martialled for cowardice in the face of the enemy. Was there any wonder that German fighter pilots were desperate at the way their commander-in-chief had betrayed them? The miracle was that they fought as they did.

The effect of Hamburg was astonishing. While the city still burned, conference after conference was called at all levels of command, starting with the *Reichsmarschall*'s HQ at Rominten. The death of Hamburg, and the threatened demise of numerous other German cities in the same fashion, had concentrated the collective Luftwaffe mind wonderfully. Mano attended some of these as *aide* to Oberst Lützow, Inspector of Defence Fighters. Directives came thick and fast and, for once, they all made sense. The reason for all those crawling blips that had fogged the radar screens on the first night of the Hamburg terror was now revealed. Tons of silver-paper strips, cut to half the wave-length of the long range radar sets, had been washed up along the North Sea coast. It was *Düppel,* something the German radar experts had been working on themselves for some time. Dropped from high altitude the strips drifted down, reflecting a signal of the defence's radar screens, each strip giving the same reaction as would a single aircraft. No wonder the Wurzburgs and Freya radar scanners had been put out of action. The British name for the device was "Window".

On the second morning of Hamburg, Field Marshal Erhard Milch had sent out an order long overdue. A copy lay on Mano's desk. Full-scale and top priority production was to be given to the Lichtenstein SN2, a radar set that would not be fooled by *Düppel*. This last order stirred guilt in Mano. In the panic of the last few days he had forgotten that Reh Fabrik was nearly in the centre of Hamburg. Reconnaissance photographs taken to assess the damage had just come in. As far as he could make out, the factory lay right beneath the densest part of the smoke cloud.

Helmuth Reh was in Berlin to attend a conference on the future of the Me 262, so his wife would almost certainly have been looking after things in Hamburg. And Liese? She often came to Berlin to help her father-in-law at the Air Ministry. He was terrified to pick up the telephone and call Herr Reh's office at the ministry. He was saved the decision. His own phone rang and Liese spoke to him. Her voice was quiet but controlled. "Mano, we've just heard. It's all gone and everyone with it . . ."

He sensed that she would break down if she had to mention her mother-in-law by name.

"Everyone killed, you understand."

"Yes, Liese dear, I understand. You're with your father-in-law?"

"Yes, he's here, safe . . ."

"Does Dieter know?"

"Not yet."

"Liese, darling, I'll try to get a message to him, personally."

262

She was sobbing now. He put down the phone gently as if not to disturb her grief. Before he could put a call through to Jever, the last known location of Dieter's flight, his chief, Oberst Lützow, came bursting in.

"Rumpler, do you realise our fantastic general is at last getting somewhere. It's scarcely believable, but all the top-brass are agreeing with him. Milch, Jeschonnek, even the *Reichsmarschall*, have come round to his view that defence fighters must have top priority . . . It took Hamburg to do it, but there's time yet to turn the tide. As an immediate step they've released the night-fighters from being tied to *Himmelbett* zones and put them on free chase now their radar sets are useless. Goering is supporting Major Hajo Hermann's Wild Boar scheme. He's to get an increase in machines. I tell you, things are moving at last. You'll have to hold the fort here for a bit. There's to be a final conference at the Führer's HQ. I'm to go along to back up the general. That won't be hard."

When Mano at last got through to the adjutant at Jever, the *Erprobungs* flight had moved out. Fighter units were being shoved around like draughtsmen in an effort to make life hard for the Americans. At that precise moment, the Gustav with the roebuck emblem was patrolling at 20,000 feet above the smoke cloud that had been Hamburg. Looking down on the obliterated centre Dieter had little doubt that his mother, at the least, had perished. The certainty made the central issue of his life perfectly clear. Whatever terrible doubts he had had about the motives or methods of the Third Reich were irrelevant from now on. Even seen from 20,000 feet, the aftermath of *Gomorrah* told him that fighting for the survival of German cities and citizens was all he could afford to consider from this moment on.

The controller's voice said: "Heavy babies in Antoquell-zero. Direction south-east. All fighters in the area converge." Out of the corner of his eye he saw Pohle's con-trail as he, too, turned to intercept.

Mano was still at his desk when Oberst Lützow got back from the *Wolfsschanze*, the Führer's so-called "Wolf's Lair" HQ. The inspector of day fighter's face was grey. He threw himself down in a chair and didn't speak for three or four minutes. Mano waited respectfully.

"Mano," he said at last. "It was bloody incredible. I wasn't there, of course, not at the crucial interview, but I saw the *Reichsmarschall* when he spoke to the general afterwards and I was present as *aide* to the completely constructive confer-

263

ence that took place beforehand . . . For God's sake get me a drink."

Mano went to the first-aid cupboard intended for air raid precautions and other emergencies and poured his chief a large brandy.

He gulped it down. "Thanks. We had complete agreement about what had to be done. Oberst Peltz, chief of the close support and fighter bombers, was with us, though he stood to lose most by diverting the whole fighter strength to the defence of the Reich. Even Goering was willing to change course completely. It was marvellous and unbelievable. Everything the general had risked his neck for was coming true. Finally, the *Reichsmarschall* left us to get final approval from the Führer for our unanimously agreed policy. It just needed his rubber stamp.

"I suspect he stamped all right. All over the bloody floor, in a rage. He certainly stamped on Goering. After a bit, Goering and his *aide* came out. We all looked up expectantly. Goering walked straight past us without looking at anyone. His face had fallen in and his jowls wobbled like those of a sick bloodhound. I've seldom seen a man so shattered. God knows what Hitler actually said to him in there, though we got the general gist of it afterwards. After about ten minutes, when presumably our supreme commander was fighting to regain his self-control, Goering sent for the general and Dieter Peltz. The Führer, he told them, wouldn't hear of defence. Terror must be met by terror. The Luftwaffe, and particularly the fighter arm, had disappointed him too often. A change-over to the defensive was unthinkable. He would give the Luftwaffe one last chance to justify itself—by a renewed attack on England . . .

"Now came the awful thing, Mano. Up to this point, Goering was relaying this news as if he realised how disastrous it was. Then, suddenly, he did one of his amazing turnabouts . . . The Führer, he shouted, was always right. All our force was now to be concentrated against England. We must strike them such a blow from the air that the English would never again attempt another Hamburg. At this point, the *Reichsmarschall* lumbered impressively to his feet and laid his hand on Oberst Peltz's shoulder. 'I herewith appoint you, by order of the Führer, *Angriffsführer England*, leader of the assault on England!' Poor Peltz. He's an able officer. He doesn't believe in his orders any more than the rest of us do, though no doubt he'll do his damnedest to carry them out. The tragedy is that by supplying him with bombers to pinprick England we must draw off pilots and fighters we desperately need for defence . . ."

Mano asked: "How did the general react, sir?"

"You know our general. He's never exactly silent. This time I believe he was too stunned to argue back. He told me afterwards he thought of resigning on the spot, and the only reason he didn't was that he simply has to believe that the Führer's insane order can be reversed in the light of reason."

"Kiss me Kate" had been to Hamburg on 26 August, the second daylight raid of *Gomorrah*. By this time, the German fighter force was as mad as a swarm of hornets whose nest had been stirred up. And it was as hornets that the Focke Wulfs and the 109s attacked. "Kate" had come back from stoking up the fires of Hamburg with nothing more than a large hole in her tail fin. But on that one trip it had come home to Charles Levitson and his crew that a great many Americans were going to die that summer in the frozen blue skies above the Reich. The German fighters hammered in time and again. As one bomber after another fell out of the formation, it became very clear to all that daylight bombing against a determined enemy could not be supported for long, without one's own fighter escort, all of the way. Fighter escort was what they did not have that day over Hamburg. Two days later, however, things took a turn for the better.

On that date "Kate" tucked up her wheels over the end of her runway in East Anglia and headed out to make rendezvous with thirty-six other B 17s over Great Yarmouth. Further down the coast, another similar sized formation was climbing into position. Seventy-seven bombers in all, split into two tight boxes, each with a different target deep in the heart of Germany—factories at Magdeburg and Kassel-Bettenhausen, both making FW 190s. General Ira C. Eaker could not wait any longer to strike at what he saw correctly as his main enemy, German fighter production.

Up front in "Kate's" glass-house, Charles Levitson knew his men had the heeby-jeebies because he had them himself. They had lost two whole crews over Hamburg who had trained with them in Arizona. Not a man got out of either bomber. Each had instantly become a fireball. Twenty buddies gone, incinerated, blown to shreds, falling in agony in the sub-zero air, with limbs torn off, bellies perhaps ripped open, falling until unconsciousness blotted them out. There were other pictures. A FW 190 just clearing "Kate's" nose with plumes of flame and a glimpse of a helmeted head blazing in the cockpit. One got instant snapshots that were pin-sharp, dead-clear, as if the eyelid had gone click like a high-speed camera shutter. Charles told himself this wouldn't do. "Kate" had as good a chance as anyone else. He called up the crew and told them that this one was going to be a hayride. Today they had a real live escort for the first time—Thunderbolts.

It was true. The barrel-nosed P 47s were coming with them, loaded with extra fuel in the wing drop-tanks. Not quite the equals of those goddam Focke Wulfs maybe, but then the P 47s were lugging seven tons around the sky. Still, they packed a heck of a punch.

"Tail-gunner to captain. There's our escort. Boy, don't they look beautiful . . . nicest goddam aircraft I ever saw."

"Thunderbolts?"

"Yeah, about twenty of them. Some Spitfires, too. Those Krauts are sure going to get a surprise."

"Sure are," Levitson said, then: "Enemy coast ahead. Keep your eyes peeled." How much more reassuring it would be if the P 47s had the range to come all the way to the target with them. He and every man aboard knew that the escort would have to turn back and leave them unprotected once the German frontier was reached. The surviving bombers that made the return trip would, with luck, find another batch of friendly fighters waiting at the same point to nursemaid them home.

It was Charles Levitson's formation on to which Dieter Reh and Pohle were vectored that morning from Hamburg.

Dieter saw the bombers just as the controller had predicted. They were in a tight, gleaming mass at 22,000 feet, about thirty plus. He called up on the Y-set and reported his contact.

Control answered: "Heavy babies have fighter escort. Escort is almost at limit of range. Shadow and attack when escort turns back."

Dieter looked at his gauges. If they waited much longer they would both have to land to refuel.

"We'll take the left group now. One firing pass, straight through them and out below."

"Kate" was centre machine of the left-hand group. Charles Levitson heard his dorsal gunner open up at eight hundred yards and saw the two 109s boring in at them. By the time he had reacted to tell the dorsal to hold its fire, the two fighters seemed about to collide with them. He heard stuff hitting "Kate" and smelt burnt wiring. Then the fighters were gone.

Pouring sweat, Charles called his crew, trying not to sound

266

panicky. "There's a fire somewhere. Investigate and report damage." The engines ran smoothly and she responded sweetly to controls. After a few seconds one of the waist gunners said: "It's Peter, sir. He's dead. Cannon shell in the chest. I'll try to pull him out, sir. But it's kind of a mess in here . . ." He thought he heard the waist gunner throw up. Pete was the youngest crew member, a twenty-year-old from a Montana farm.

He forced himself to ask: "How's the turret?"

"Hard to say, skipper, but I guess the wiring's shot up. When I get Pete out maybe it'll operate manually."

"Skipper to tail gunner. Is our escort still with us?"

"No . . . I mean, yes."

"Make up your goddam mind."

"I thought I saw the P 47s go, but there are eleven fighters just where they were, nearly directly overhead. Christ! They've got bombs under them."

Levitson reacted quickly. They'd been warned about the 109's new bombing tactics and had worked out a drill to cope with them. The 500-pounders the fighters carried were on a time fuse. The attackers therefore had to judge not only height above the bomber formation, but also predict its course. The latter shouldn't have been too hard, since the bombers were invariably flying in a straight line to their target. The B 17s could not afford much deviation from course but they might be able to jink enough to make the bombs miss.

Levitson called his section: "Fighter-bombers above. Turning starboard." "Kate" and the three B 17s in her section turned right ten degrees. A few seconds later he saw the wing tips of the section to port tilt as they too made a small alteration of course in the opposite direction.

Three thousand feet above, the eleven 109s led by Heinz Knoke from Jever exactly matched this evolution and then released their bombs. Five bombs fell well behind. Five burst far below. But one burst right in the middle of the four left-hand bombers. Even at a hundred yards the concussion slung "Kate" sideways. Levitson watched the three B 17s to port appear to stop in mid-air, fused together by a single brilliant flash. Then the wreckage of three bombers and thirty lives slowly cartwheeled in upon each other and were gone in a falling tangle of detached wings, half a fuselage, an engine falling free ahead of all the rest. Later "Kate's" tail-gunner reported three parachutes. Three out of thirty.

"Kate" returned from that one, too. Twenty-two Fortresses did not. With that first big daylight battle had begun what the US Eighth Air Force was to call the bloody summer of 1943.

Kate Bristow got used to seeing Americans around. A squadron of Lightnings had just joined them on the south coast. American controllers were attached for experience in their Ops Room. She was amused and, to some extent, charmed by them. They were so confident in themselves and their technology, in the superiority of their ice-cream almost as much as their aircraft. She hoped they were not in for too much of a shock. Their attitude to women was so different from that of the English. She was at first shaken at being called "Honey" by a GI, a mere private, but since he said it with no disrespect and a Southern accent it must be all right. No denying they had a way with women. Directly you had learned that they made a pass almost as an opening gambit, but were not surprised or disconsolate at a rebuff, they were fun. They were cast in the image that Hollywood had created. Perhaps they were a poorish second best to Gable and Stewart, Cagney and Macrea, but they talked like those idols and others besides, and they brought some of the aura of Hollywood with them. When you saw them jiving they became very nearly the real thing. Though fascinated by these young men, Kate was not, like so many of her serving sisters, bowled over by them. She did, however, agree to see Charles Levitson again whenever they could manage a late pass up to town together.

The second time he met her was the day after the Magdeburg raid. "Kiss me Kate" was temporarily out of action while they repaired the dorsal turret where young Pete had died. Mostly, air crew did not talk about their experiences. She found it strangely touching and confiding that Charles should want to. She sensed that he did not have total faith in the invulnerability of Americans or their technology and that his early experiences had scared him badly. Without putting it into words he wanted her reassurance that everyone, even the British, was often frightened out of his wits. So she told him how she had felt when the fighter-bomber had come roaring in over Brighton front, even though in reality she could not remember. She told him what Peter and others had said about combat fear, embellishing or exaggerating to restore his confidence in himself. Finally he smiled a shy smile and said: "I guess what I'm really asking you, Kate, is: have you heard guys talk like this before?"

"Not many," she said. "Not many are that honest."

Afterwards he took her dancing at the American officers' club. He introduced her to other Fortress pilots and navigators. In their immaculate light fawn trousers and darker service jackets they had an almost pathetic freshness about them. They reminded her of young men in flannels and blazers, perhaps a team sent by their country to compete in some harmless international event, more anyone-for-tennis than anyone-for-Frankfurt or Essen. Some, like Charles, had undoubtedly been to some of these places already. As yet, their faces hadn't acquired the old-young look of their RAF opposite numbers. Normally Kate was too reserved to perform in an extrovert way in public, but the elegant swing of Tommy Dorsey and Glenn Miller was too much for her. So, when a fair-haired young Texan, to whom Charles had already introduced her, took her hand and said: "Come on, honey, let's take-off a little," she found herself on the floor, twisting and turning as her partner directed in a fair imitation of a jive. Woody Herman's "Woodchopper's Ball," coupled with the gyrations of the dance, left little room for ballroom conversations. When the last brassy note had died away she got a round of applause from some of the onlookers.

"That's your first solo, baby?" her instructor asked.

"Yes."

"You got real potential, ma'am." He led her back to Charles.

"Are you a Fortress pilot?"

"Me, ma'am? Now, do I look like a truck driver? I wet-nurse these guys in my little old P 47."

"Look after them and yourself *very* well."

"Thank you, ma'am. I sure intend to. Before I left Texas my mammy said to me: 'Son, mind you fly mighty low and mighty slow' and that's just exactly what I aim to do."

When Kate danced with Charles, he held her in the other American style, cheek to cheek. There was nothing fresh about it, it was just the way they danced with a girl. The tune was "Moonlight Serenade". Afterwards Charles climbed into an air force bus that would take them back all the way to base. He was on stand-by tomorrow. Kate stayed overnight at a flat off Regent's Park belonging to the parents of a fellow section officer.

If the Americans were losing many bombers and crews, the same went for the German fighter arm. The *Erprobungs* flight was self-contained and vaguely autonomous. Attached to a

Gruppe with a new weapon to try out at one base, a *Staffel* below strength at another, the *Schwarm* did not feel the losses in quite such a personal way as ordinary pilots who had got used to finding a face missing at lunchtime, a mess chair empty at dinner. Nevertheless all were keenly aware that the drain and strain were increasing and enormous and that unless the fighters could break the Yanks by day and the British by night it could not go on this way indefinitely. It was the Battle of Britain in reverse, only much more so.

Dieter's *Schwarm* had been exceptionally lucky so far. All had made belly landings or bail-outs since the flight was formed. All had had minor wounds or burns, but no one had been lost. It was something they never commented on lest the spell be broken. In the new single-mindedness caused by his mother's death, Dieter flew and fought with more confidence and aggression than he had ever known. His only regret was that he had no opportunity to shoot down the RAF's Lancasters and Stirlings who came by night. Hamburg owed its total destruction mainly to these. And then the chance came with *Wilde Sau*, Major Hajo Hermann's "Wild Boar" scheme.

Wilde Sau was growing in strength and success. Hermann's idea not only had Goering's blessing—which wasn't surprising since the *Reichsmarschall* was desperate—but General Kammhuber's, which was, since he had built up the whole elaborate system of radar-directed night-fighters. *Wilde Sau* was crude in its simplicity. Hermann, who had once been a bomber pilot, came up with a proposal aimed to bridge the gap until German radar engineers got a set into production that could defeat *Düppel*, or "Window," the strips of tinfoil that had blinded the defences at Hamburg. Hermann argued that the British mass extermination night raids caused such a blaze that a fighter flying above the target could see the attacking bombers silhouetted without need of a radar-eye. He even urged that civilians should ignore the black-out and leave all lights on to increase the glare. Hermann proposed that the job be done with single-engined fighters. He had been ordered by Goering to form a special Wild Boar group. Until he had found enough planes and pilots to do so, he was ready to accept volunteers.

The *Erprobungs* flight had just been fitted with experimental rocket launchers beneath the wings for taking on the Fortress formations. In the spirit of the hour, several squadron pilots were flying on normal missions by day and volunteering for *Wilde Sau* operations at night. Dieter argued that night-fighting experience with Hermann's Wild Boars was something that members of his flight should have. He obtained permission for their one reserve Gustav to be stripped of rocket gear, and fitted with flame-guards over the exhaust stubs and an anti-dazzle windscreen.

On the night of 17 August he stood by for his first night flight since he had been shot down over St Omer. The message to take off came just before midnight. It was an eerie feeling opening up a Gustav on a runway that was black save for a few shielded flare-path lights. He held her against the brakes until she wouldn't wait any longer and shot off down the runway like a stone out of a catapult. He wanted her tail up in the shortest possible time so that he could command some forward vision. He lifted her off by feel and turned away in the direction the controller ordered—Berlin. The British bomber force seemed to be headed for Berlin. He climbed slowly to 15,000 feet. He did not envy the nightfighter boys, but at least there were two, often three of them to share the loneliness. Inside the cramped cockpit of the Gustav there was neither time nor motion, merely space. The steady roar of the engine reassured him that he was actually moving through the night sky; the faint illumination of dials on his instrument panel was the only reference point that established his presence there.

His isolation ended abruptly. The sky ahead was lit by four, ten, then a dozen marker flares. Searchlights rose to meet them. Dieter was no longer a disembodied spirit behind a Daimler-Benz engine he could not see but only hear. The dramatic illuminations ahead gave him space, time, movement, and personal meaning all at once. The RAF pathfinders, Mosquitoes most likely, were staking out the capital for slaughter. Under *Wilde Sau* arrangements, the flak batteries were supposed to limit their fire over Berlin to 17,000 feet. Above that it was up to the Wild Boars to charge in. Some tentative salvoes of flak punched brief stars into the now well-lit sky, a reminder to keep climbing. Bombers should soon begin to show up below in silhouette. He put his safety buttons to "fire". There wasn't going to be much time to shoot once he sighted a target. The first flares were already dying in a falling dribble of magnesium. So far he had seen no bomb bursts, no fires, in the city beneath. A shadow flickered briefly below. As he turned on to an attacking course he recognised the outline. Twin tails. It was one of the hundred and fifty 110s who, together with fifty-five single-engined fighters, made up the Wild Boar pack that night. The last flare died. Flak batteries, as radar-blind thanks to the British *Düppel* as the night-fighters, were still hopefully firing a barrage, but still no bomb-bursts, no fires, in the capital city. It was only after half an hour of fruitless patrolling, during which he twice passed uncomfortably close to two other Wild Boars, that the penny dropped at the fighter control centres. Berlin was a feint, a clever hoax. The controller's voice came through: "All Wild Boars converge Map Square Bertha-Freda-Zero. Target appears to be island of Peenemünde. Proceed north maximum speed."

Dieter checked his gauges. He would have at best twenty minutes over the target. What made Peenemünde an RAF priority before Berlin? The first bombs had fallen when he got there. Already there were intensive fires on the ground. Four blue pinpoints appeared ahead, the exhaust flames of four engines—a Lancaster. He mustn't lose it. He climbed quickly and saw it pinned out like a butterfly against the setting board of the fire-lit sky. Under-estimating his own relative speed he was immediately so close that he could see the British rear-gunner in his turret staring down at the fires below. The bomber crews had got used to being attacked on the way out and on the return journey, but not actually over the target. Dieter throttled back and opened fire. Chunks flew off the bomber's tail. The port inner burnt, then the wing caught. In seconds the Lancaster was a falling torch. As it slid from sight, he saw the rear gunner still in his turret. To starboard, two more bombers were burning. Time to find a landing space. The Wild Boars had vindicated themselves.

Mano had been at his desk all night. The chief of Staff, General Hans Jeschonnek, had taken an unusual step. Convinced at last that Galland and Kammhuber had been right all the time—the fighter defence of the Reich *was* the first priority—he had called for a personal report on the first large-scale use of *Wilde Sau*. By seven a.m. Mano had collected the battle reports and analysed them. He was to take these to Jeschonnek's HQ personally. Jeschonnek could hardly fail to be pleased. At least forty bombers had been shot down and almost the same number badly damaged for the loss of eight fighters. The raid on Peenemünde, however, seemed to have been both heavy and accurate.

The staff car delivered him to the chief of staff's HQ promptly at 0745 hours. Frau Lotte Kersten, Jeschonnek's secretary, received him in her office. "Good morning, *Herr Hauptmann*. You have good news for the general's breakfast, I hope."

"Good in parts, Frau Kersten. Especially if he likes choice Wild Boar served with Lancaster slightly overdone."

The phone rang. "Yes, *Herr Generaloberst*. I'll put you through to him at once." She jiggled with the plugs on her switchboard. "That was Lieutenant General Rudolf Meister, chief of operations from 'Robinson'. I hope he doesn't steal your thunder. I know General Jeschonnek wants your report especially. He instructed me to have breakfast sent in to you in case he needs you to wait and amplify any points later on."

Major Werner Leuchtenberg, Jeschonnek's personal adjutant, came in. "Morning, Mano. How did we make out? Not too bad, I hope. The old man could do with some encouragement. Hope to God he's not too long on that phone, I'm starving for breakfast and he insists on making it a working occasion so Frau Kersten and I always have to wait for him."

A minute later Jeschonnek rang and asked for Leuchtenberg. Mano heard him say: "Werner, go on over to breakfast, I'll follow you."

"I'd better wait in the office," Lotte Kersten volunteered. "Perhaps Hauptmann Rumpler will spare me a cup of his coffee."

Breakfast was brought in by an orderly. There was ample for two, so Mano suggested she eat with him. It was well she agreed for when half an hour had passed there was still no word from the chief of staff.

"I never like to go along to his private quarters, but he's usually so punctual! Perhaps I ought to remind him of his first appointment. I won't be a minute."

Lotte Kersten was in fact several minutes. When she came back she was white and shaking.

"Get Major Leuchtenberg," she gasped. "It's terribly urgent."

Mano picked up the phone and asked for the general's dining-room. He told the mess waiter to ask Major Leuchtenberg to come as quickly as possible.

"Are you ill, Frau Kersten?"

She was sobbing with her head buried in her hands.

"What is it? Shall I fetch the general?"

"Dead, dead, dead!" she screamed. "He's dead!"

Werner Leuchtenberg must have run all the way. He didn't even stop to ask questions but rushed to his chief's bedroom.

Minutes later he was back. "Did no one hear the shot? It's Udet all over again. Mano, come here. Advise me. What do I do with this?"

He held out a plain sheet of paper on which Jeschonnek had written: "I can no longer work together with the *Reichsmarschall*. Long live the Führer."

The young adjutant was pouring Lotte Kersten a cognac and trying to calm her.

"Why? What made him do it?" Mano asked.

"He tried once before. Do you know what he said to me a month or so ago? He asked whether I thought that by sacrificing himself a man could draw attention to a mortal danger that would otherwise be ignored. The mortal danger's here all right. You realise what they're making at Peenemünde—V-weapons. He was increasingly pinning his hopes on them, and now it seems the RAF have flattened the place. It was the last straw. Mano?"

"Yes."

"It goes without saying you must keep this to yourself . . . And now I must tell the *Reichsmarschall* that he's done it once again, and, by God, he can see this note for a start."

Wing Commander Peter Bristow, DFC, sat as a passenger in the co-pilot's seat of a brand new B 17 and wondered for the twentieth time since they had left the USA how these American Fortress boys stuck it. It had been a long slow haul via Labrador, Greenland, Iceland and Ireland, but at least there had been no hordes of Messerschmitts and Focke Wulfs to harry them like there were over Germany, as this crew, fresh from training camp, would soon find out. Peter himself was fresh from training camp in America, too, a conversion course which he hoped would soon help to make the life of the Eighth Air Force daylight bomber crews longer and more healthy. Now he was merely hitching a lift back to RAF Fighter Command to put what he had learned into practice. Peter's job in the States had had a dual purpose: to instruct trainee Fortress crews on Luftwaffe fighter tactics and to learn the characteristics and ability of an amazing new fighter, the P 51, the North American Mustang. When the Mustang arrived in strength in Britain he had little doubt that it would turn the tide. The P 47 Thunderbolt at present escorting the Fortresses was a good machine despite its bulk and weight but, even with drop tanks, it lacked the range to go all the way to the furthest targets with the Fortresses and Liberators and then sheepdog them back. The Mustang could do that. What's more, it could outfly the Focke Wulfs and Messerschmitts, overburdened as they were with extra armour, extra armament, external rocket-launchers, cannon in "bathtubs" below the wings—equipment added to their overworked airframes to help them destroy bombers.

There was only one snag. Delivery of the Mustang in any numbers couldn't take place until the New Year. When that happened Peter was to form the first RAF Mustang formation. Until then he was to act as liaison officer with the Eighth Air Force fighter squadrons. It was a job he greatly relished. He loved the freshness and professionalism of his new comrades-in-arms and he was only too aware of the Fortress crews' fear hidden beneath the gum-chewing and big talk. They all knew that the Luftwaffe, far from being on the floor, was giving the daylight raids an appalling hammering. Even in Arizona, where he had trained, they had heard the story of the ball-bearing works at Schweinfurt when the Germans had hurled 300 fighters at the bomber force, shooting down 60 Fortresses out of 400 and damaging 100 more. It was no secret that any Fortress crew who flew over Germany in the summer of 1943 had a less than even chance of being alive and well to do the same in 1944. The Mustang, Peter told them, would surely change all that. He only hoped to God he was right.

The rocky Welsh coast showed up ahead through the glass-house in the bomber's nose. They were to land at a field in Pembrokeshire.

As they roared in over the cliffs, the bombardier pointed down at a little beach below.

"Look at all them broads laid out to meet us. I'm sure going to like it here."

The "broads" were grey seals basking in a cove. You had to admire optimism like that.

Since the death of their mother Peter and his sister had been closer than before. He had been able to pull a few strings to keep them close geographically, too. As liaison officer with the American fighter squadrons, part of his job, until the P 51s arrived, would be to familiarise his opposite numbers with the Ops Room Control of British escort fighters. Kate had gained quite a reputation for coolness and efficiency. Since he was required to take some key Ops Room staff with him, he requested his sister and, to his surprise, got her.

Kate had been delighted with the resulting posting to Suffolk. Her pleasure was only partly due to the fact that Peter would be around the station. To know he was on operations and even to hear his voice during an engagement on the radio was almost more than she could bear. She consoled herself that he was unlikely to do much actual flying until the New Year. She did not fool herself that he was the only reason Suffolk appealed to her. It was also home to Charles Levitson's Fortress squadron, not twenty miles away. She had increasingly come to appreciate Charles' company, his quiet courtesy, his self-deprecating humour. In a dark, Jewish way, he was good-looking too, though this, she assured herself, had little to do with it. His company was what she needed. He was such a complete contrast to dear, open, English Michael.

Peter had been dimly aware of all this when he had left for the States six weeks before. Undeniably, these Yanks did appeal to the girls.

The B 17 put down its wheels and kissed the tarmac of Pembrokeshire with a squelch of rubber. When they tumbled out of the hatch, a pretty WAAF driver was waiting for them with a fifteen-hundredweight truck.

"Honey," said the bombardier, "all that messing about in the sky was sure worth it. What you doing tonight?"

The girl said: "You're the tenth crew I've picked up today, and they've all said much the same thing. Do they issue you boys with phrase books or something?"

The bombardier wasn't at all put down.

"See you around, honey," was all he said.

In late September, Dieter was due for a week's leave. And yet it was unthinkable that he should quit the battle just when the Americans were taking such punishment. Three Fortresses and then a Lancaster on a second *Wilde Sau* sortie, had raised his personal score to twenty-seven. He had been awarded the Knight's Cross to his Iron Cross. Finally, he compromised about his leave. Liese was in Berlin working with his father. Apparently big things were happening in the aircraft industry. Unlike the murderous RAF night attacks on cities, the American daylight raids were precision operations directed at German aircraft production. They were hitting where it mattered most. To counter their effect, German aircraft production had got itself a new broom, or rather two new brooms—Albert Speer, the brilliant young minister for armaments, and his henchman, Karl Saur, a good party man, first-class at carrying out his chief's ideas. The star of Erhard Milch was waning. Speer saw the need for fighters and yet more fighters, although he, like everyone before him, was handicapped by the Führer's blind refusal to admit that the problems of defence existed. Nevertheless, Speer had the industrial drive and foresight to get round even this obstacle to a very large degree. He began to decentralise aircraft production, to scatter factories so that the American bombers couldn't find them, or at least not all of them. He demanded not only dispersal but camouflage, decoy plants, factories built in woods, caves, bunkers. Helmuth Reh was quick to recognise that Speer was the man of the future. In turn, Saur spotted in Reh a man who could get things done. Without actually showing disloyalty to Milch, Reh managed to place himself more and more at the new big man's disposal. All this meant that Liese worked harder and longer hours than ever and that she hardly ever moved out of Berlin. The RAF's almost continual attention to the capital dictated that a good deal of the time was spent working in the bunkers reserved for key personnel during heavy air raids.

The Inspector of Fighters' Office wanted some firsthand data on the effectiveness of the new 21 cm rocket against Fortress formations. Dieter got the assignment and received permission to extend his reporting time to forty-eight hours. In order not to deplete the *Erprobungs* of a single machine, he borrowed an HQ Bücker Jungmeister and flew to Tempelhof.

Mano had fixed for them to stay at his apartment. Hotels seemed to be either bombed or full of staff officers. Berlin was looking badly knocked about, far more so than when he had last seen it. The stench of burnt wood and pulverised brick rubble, the corpse smell of dead buildings hung in the air. Cinemas remained defiantly open, their garish posters appearing against the battered fabric of the city like badly worn make-up on the face of an aging tart. Dieter was amazed how many different languages he heard on the street—Danish, Swedish, French, Dutch. Were these the vultures who found pickings in the death of their own countries? As always, the gleaming turn-out of staff officers brought home to him that there were two kinds of soldiers who fought two kinds of war. This time he was proud of his bent cap and his Knight's Cross and he thought he saw gratitude and respect on the faces of civilians who recognised him as a front-line fighter pilot. The one thing he did not see in the features of those same civilians was defeat and despair as a result of the bombing to which they were now subjected almost nightly. Liese confirmed this within minutes of their meeting.

When he had kissed her he held her at arms' length and examined her, trying not to show alarm that she had lost a stone in weight and looked drawn and tired. The sirens began to wail. He felt her jump as he held her. The memory of Cologne must receive a jab every time she heard that sound and now never a day or night passed without it.

"Do you want to go to the shelter?"

She laughed. "If we did that we'd spend all our time running up and down stairs. It's probably a false alarm, anyway, they sound the sirens for every recce plane. Nothing much happens during the day. They just come to see how much damage they did the previous night. It's the nights we have to worry about."

"We must spend it in the shelter, then," he said out of consideration for her.

Liese laughed. "The only shelter I want is in your arms."

In the middle of the night they woke to the sound of bombs and gunfire. When a stick fell close, Liese clung to him until her nails bit his flesh.

"Swine."

"Ah, Liese. You used to say we couldn't expect anything else once we'd bombed London."

"I know, but being on the receiving end alters the viewpoint. We used to think that Londoners would collapse under our bombing. Well, they didn't and Berliners are just the same. I can't tell you what a wonderful spirit there is everywhere."

Dieter was thrilled that she seemed to have regained her faith in Germany. He was so ressured that he decided to put his innermost fears to the test.

"Liese?"

"What is it?"

"Those terrible things Heine Müller talked about. The camps. That Polish woman I saw . . ."

"Yes, they're real. They're terrible and they happen more and more all the time. But even I don't find time to dwell on such horrors any more. All that matters now is our survival. The bombing has made it possible for Germans to forget every excess and failing of the National Socialist regime."

"Do you think most Germans know, or care, about what goes on in concentration camps?"

"Some do. Some must. Those that do tell themselves that when they have survived this they'll change things and those people include you and me."

"And the others?"

"The others are at this moment down in their shelters hating the British and Americans and conveniently using this hatred to wipe the slate clean."

Far above, Dieter heard the hum of a single engine and wondered how that lonely *Wilde Sau* pilot was feeling above the barrage and the bombs.

When, on the morning of 14 October, the briefing officer told them it was Schweinfurt again, Charles Levitson took consolation from the fact that every crewman in the briefing room was thinking exactly the same as himself, that he had at best a one in four chance of living to see the end of the day. The Eighth Air Force had raided the ball-bearing works there in August and had left the wrecks of thirty-six bombers behind them. Now it was Schweinfurt again. Schweinfurt without a fighter escort that could go all the way with them, Schweinfurt with the whole German fighter force stirred up and waiting for them.

Recently, "Kiss me Kate" had been lucky, but three more of her crew had not. Radio operator and tail-gunner had both died on the way to Augsburg. Navigator had been wounded on the way back from Münster the week before. So "Kate" carried three new crewmen. Such had been the rate of loss among the Liberator and Fortress formations that, for at least a dozen of the 291 crews briefed that bright October day, it was their first major mission.

The intelligence officer was winding up his briefing: "The German fighters will undoubtedly try *Herausschutz* tactics, cutting a single bomber out of a formation and then concentrating on it. They may also throw everything they've got at one bomber box to break it up. Your tactics must be the same in each case. Stick close together. Cover each other. The P 47s will cover you as far as the Eifel. After that, to the target, you're on your own. I don't have to tell you why we're asking for one more maximum effort against Schweinfurt. A final knock-out blow on the ball-bearing plant there could mean the crippling of the entire German war industry. Good luck and God speed."

"Kate" was waiting for them out in the pale October sunlight. She was battle-scarred and patched. She'd recently had replacement engines and a new rudder. She'd left part of her port wing tip behind in Luxembourg and a flak burst had made a large hole behind her bomb bay. Patient surgery had restored her each time.

Charles Levitson had great, almost superstitious faith in "Kate". He watched his crew climb aboard and lingered outside for a few seconds longer than usual. The English air smelt so good, so full of the bitter-sweet death promise of autumn. He wanted to take more than a lungful of it with him. He wanted a memory load of the sweetness of life. He was so busy inhaling that he almost forgot the ritual of the chewing gum. Ever since his first mission he had parked his gum under the starboard undercarriage housing. So far it had always been there when they had come back, a little hardened by being frozen, a little oily to the taste, maybe, but mighty welcome as a reassurance that you had lived through another one. Charles hoisted himself up through the hatch, instantly changing the heady smell of autumn for the bitch-scent of "Kate." Every pilot knows his own aircraft by her smell. The B 17 smelt of fuel and a lingering acridity from the hundreds of thousands of fifty calibre rounds that had been fired from her thirteen guns. Over all, and indefinably, she smelt of "Kate". Her crew could have sniffed her out blindfold from any other B 17 in the squadron. The port outer coughed into life with a clatter that became a steady roar. Charles Levitson said, as he always said: "Welcome aboard, men. This is your captain, Charles Levitson, speaking. Our destination today is swinish Schweinfurt. Kindly make your pre-flight checks and report. I hope we all have a very pleasant flight."

Today there were no wisecracks in reply.

The general not only approved of the *Erprobungs* flight, he had expanded the idea into a special *Kommando* whose task was to try out the ideas put up by front-line squadrons. Dieter's unit had become a self-contained part of this and now he had a new pilot, his brother Jacob. Some of the anti-Fortress ideas were crazy. Fighters trailing wires. Fighters trailing wires with explosive charges attached. For *Wilde Sau* operations, some lunatic had even suggested that the Wild Boar night-fighters might carry a cat. Where the cat looked, there the pilot should look too. Even in a time of extravagant experiment, this one did not reach the operational stage, but only, as Kolbe said, because there wasn't room for a cat in a Gustav. The *Erprobungs* flight's current task of weapon valuation was reasonably rational. They were to try out a combination of super-heavy armament against individual Fortress boxes. Kolbe flew a special Gustav with an armoured car cannon sticking out of the nose. Each time he tried it in practice the huge gun had jammed after four or five shots. "What do I do with it after that?" Kolbe asked bitterly. "Ram the bloody things with the barrel?"

Willy Weiss carried four 21 cm rockets in launching tubes under his wings: the Hoffman twins a combination of rockets and cannons. Dieter, Pohle and Jacob were armed with four 3 cm cannons. The idea was the heavy artillery should blast the chosen Fortress formation from five hundred to eight hundred yards' range, after which the heavily armed cannon fighters would carve up the survivors. This, as Dieter fully realised, was good theory so long as other German fighters looked after the Thunderbolt escort. Ideally, such tactics should only be used beyond the range of the American escort fighters.

The *Erprobungs* flight were as itinerant as gypsies, landing wherever the last operation had left them short of fuel and ammunition. On the morning of 14 October, they were stranded at old familiar Jever, far too far forward to leave them free from the attention of the barrel-nosed P 47s, if the Yanks decided to come over that day.

The *Erprobungs* flight now considered Jever as their main home. They knew many of the pilots there as if they all belonged to the same squadron, so they were aware of the terrific gaps the daylight battles were tearing in their ranks. These were no novices that disappeared daily, but seasoned veterans. On the wall of the aircrew room belonging to Heinz Knoke's famous 5 Squadron the row of signed photographs on the wall was growing. Each photograph was a memorial put there when a friend disappeared. Neatly printed beneath each one was name, rank and date of death. Some were signed. Others bore a sardonic inscription. The tall, fair-haired smiling Steiger had written across his: "No one ever remained upstairs."

The *Gefechtsalarm* rang. "Scramble! Scramble!" Already seated in his Gustav, Dieter saw the rest of the flight come running. The controller's voice filled the cockpit. "Heavy babies in Dora-Dora. Five Squadron stand by. Roebuck One"— the flight's call-sign—"take off immediately for Frankfurt and refuel there."

The engines of the other six planes were starting. The mechanics had already warmed them up. Dieter opened the throttle and led the flight across the grass. All seven planes lifted their tails as one and rose as easily as a flight of ducks. Thank God, the controller was pulling them back beyond range of the Thunderbolts. With all this artillery aboard, the once lissom 109 was about as manoeuvrable as a coal barge.

None of the three hundred young Americans assembled over the North Sea that bright October day had any wish to die in exchange for a moment of glory, or for that matter for a chance to shorten the war by a week, a month or even a year. Yet many of them knew they were likely to do so. The first Schweinfurt raid in August had caused a crisis of morale inside the Eighth Air Force. General Spaatz had had to ask himself whether such losses could be borne. The White House had told General Spaatz that it had no wish to see its air weapon broken before the time came to use it against Japan. The American bombers were facing exactly the same situation the Luftwaffe had faced over London in 1940. Against resolute fighter opposition, even the most heavily armed bomber force must sustain terrifying losses. Resolute the opposition most certainly was. The Fortress crews had no doubt that the German fighter pilots were fighting with a ferocity and valour that matched anything produced in the history of aerial warfare. They did not, perhaps, realise that their own courage was its equal. General Spaatz saw only one answer—to hit and destroy the German fighter force where its root grew— in the factories. Hence this raid today, 14 October 1943, hereafter known as "Second Schweinfurt".

Peter Bristow was glad to be going with them. As liaison officer he had no difficulty in joining the Spitfire escort wing flying with the Thunderbolt escort. As they climbed up to join the great silver phalanxes of bombers approaching the Dutch coast, he tried to gauge what he would feel if he had to make a head-on attack on that mass. He found it a terrifying prospect.

On the first Schweinfurt raid in August, the German fighters had hung back, waiting for the Thunderbolts to turn for home. Today, the first Focke Wulfs came in straight away, concentrating on one bomber section at a time.

"Kate" and her sisters were spared their first onslaught. Ahead and below, a Fortress fell apart in flame, wings, tail, fuselage all separate and burning. The bomber beside it reared up, stalled, fell on one wing and spiralled down out of sight. No one got out. Charles saw the attackers turning away at long range—rocket-firing 110s. They'd found a daytime use for the out-classed Zerstörer at last.

Peter saw the 110s too. Easy meat. He yelled to his wingman to watch for single-engined fighters and wheeled right, away from the Fortresses, to cut the 110s off. They caught them as they straightened, turning one into a scarlet chrysanthemum of fire, sending a second away with port engine smoking. And then tracer crossed his own wing. He pulled up in a tight corkscrew climb and lost the opposition in time to see the remaining Fortress of the badly clobbered formation falling behind with two engines already stopped. Four 190s were tearing at it like hyenas at a dying animal. Pat Hay had stuck with him somehow. They bored in at the rearmost Focke Wulf, shooting lumps off it until it rolled on its back. The pilot fell clear but neither saw his parachute open. But now the wounded Fortress had gone, leaving silver debris from its final explosion to cartwheel down to join a trail of dead and dying men and aircraft that littered their way across four countries on that October day.

"Kate" was one of the 220 B 17s actually to get to Schweinfurt and unload. Her part of the bomber stream had been lucky so far. Only one out of her box of twelve had gone, to a direct flak hit that had taken the nose right off and left the aircraft to flutter down like a beheaded dragon-fly. Now all "Kate" had to do was to get back.

At Frankfurt, the *Erprobungs* flight had been among the small part of the total fighter force of nearly 400 planes that the controllers had held in reserve. Now, on the American's return trip, they were about to be committed. Dieter kept his small formation in well-drilled order. Kolbe and Weiss and the Hoffmans slightly below as a compact *Schwarm,* a battery of flying artillery. Behind and five hundred feet above, Dieter and Jacob and Pohle acted as collective wingmen to the bombardment group. When they spotted it, the *dicker Hund,* "fat dog", as the German fighter pilots now called the bomber streams, was a very ragged pack of hounds indeed. The B 17s were all over the sky, with stragglers falling behind. These had little hope of reaching the protective screen of the second wave of Thunderbolts flying to meet them, still over a hundred miles away, and no hope of reaching home even if they did. Gaggles of fighters were diving head-on into the *dicker Hund,* firing until the last second, breaking to dive through and away below. As Dieter began his approach it seemed impossible that the fighters could emerge without hitting abandoned hatch doors, bomber fragments, falling men, flak bursts and a trellis of tracer. Many of them did not. Dieter's problem was to find a compact enough target. Then far off, and above, at 24,000 feet, he saw a solid wedge of silver glinting in the sun, a more or less intact bomber box and "Kate" flew in the centre of it. He climbed the formation to get them above and began to overtake, racing alongside the flank of the aerial rout to move into a firing position.

"Kate's" tail-gunner saw them first. "Fighters making port beam attack, twelve o'clock high. Looks like they've got rockets, skipper."

Charles knew about rockets, had seen plenty of their work that day. If only one could judge the moment of firing, or preferably, just before firing, and take avoiding action. He put "Kate's" nose down, taking the nearest three Fortresses with him. A second later he heard the upper and port waist guns hammering.

Kolbe gave the order to fire, holding his Gustav's nose slightly above the target to allow for trajectory. Range seven hundred yards. He pressed the silver cannon button and felt the plane shake as the first shells went. White trails streaking out from six rockets on either side, two apiece from Weiss and the Hoffmans. Blast! Part of the *dicker Hund* had anticipated, was losing height. The heavy cannon he carried fired twice more and then stopped with a familiar clang. Of the seven Fortresses still flying level, one broke in half, a second slanted away with the whole starboard wing beyond the outer engine missing. Eight parachutes opened above the falling wreck. Something, whether his shell or the other's rockets, he couldn't tell, had scored. Tracer coming up and towards. Time to break as planned. Three hundred yards and the other three, covering them with cannon fire. A third Fortress faltering, smoking, beginning to lose height. *Herausschutz.* A certainty. Someone would get it now. Dieter calling, telling the rocket-carriers to stick close. Kolbe swore. All he had now that stupid bloody Big Bertha had jammed was two small machine-guns. He turned away feeling the Gustav with its unnatural load as heavy as a sodden sponge. What a thing to do to a fighter! Kolbe had every good reason to pull out of the fight, go down, clear his gun, refuel, but the thought never occurred to him. The four Fortresses that had escaped the first attack were still together, lower but tight, a worthwhile target. Dieter's voice, mingling with excited American voices, hysterical German voices. For the rest of his life "Shoehorn" Kolbe knew that he would hear these voices in many languages and accents, in elation, in agony, in terror. For the rest of his life! They reformed and came in again. Again Kolbe gave the order to fire and although he pressed his cannon button until his thumb was blue he knew nothing would free the jammed mechanism.

Aboard "Kate", the mid-upper gunner saw the rockets coming and yelled. Charles pulled the nose up this time. It was, in fact, Willy Weiss's rocket, fired just a little too high, high enough to miss had "Kate" not evaded, that caught the engine cowling of "Kate's" port outer, tearing out the cylinder blocks, leaving a twisted mass of silent mechanism that hung from the leading edge. "Kate" shuddered, shook, filled with smoke, started to veer, took correction, straightened, considered whether to fall apart and, by Boeing, didn't.

"Shoehorn" Kolbe saw what he took to be a mortal wound, had nothing to offer to "Kate's" final destruction except two 13 mm machine-guns, but because he had offered nothing so far, kept going when the others broke. "Kate's" mid-upper gunner threaded him as he came in, thinking at first the 109 meant to ram, stitching the Hun from nose to tail. One of his bullets took Kolbe in the groin, passing upwards through his intestines and out of his back to flatten against the armour plate. Kolbe had seconds, maybe a second, to live, saw, as the eyes dimmed, the gigantic tail of the machine beyond "Kate" and, without conscious effort to hit or avoid, rammed, the barrel of that useless cannon tearing rudder from fin, just as he had joked it would. Dieter saw him go, saw the Thunderbolts and Spitfires ahead, called his boys and took them down, shocked by what should have been a commonplace.

"Kate" shouldn't have flown but did. The wind pressure on that tangled mess of wreckage that had been an engine should have torn the weakened wing away. But they built 'em tough in Seattle. Thank God the Thunderbolts were there. And the Spits. Peter Bristow saw the limping Fortress and, though he did not recognise her, recognised her plight. So did the Luftwaffe. The Jever boys were up and at it again, knocking off the stragglers. Up front Charles was too frightened now to care or even pray. He just knew he was dead. Only on the intercom the tail-gunner still talked to him. "Kate" was losing height and likely to lose a wing. Impossible to remember how many times the Focke Wulfs came in to finish them. Just impressions. Blood. Whose? Running forward under his seat. Map shreds torn like confetti. Must be a big hole somewhere to cause such a draught. Sudden realisation that his co-pilot had been dead for five minutes. Smell of fire and smell of his own fear and then that radio operator yelling it was under control—the fire. No intercom left. No telling who was alive, who dead, who still fighting. Cartridge cases and blood swilling around the tunnel of the fuselage but "Kate" still flying with a second engine stopped. Charles sat there and saw the English coast come up, saw the runway come up, saw and felt the ground come up, heard the rasping and tearing, the heat smell of a belly landing and then suddenly the silence save for a faint trickle—fuel. Get out! *Get out!* Crash crew tearing, ripping, using an axe. Tail-gunner and, unbelievably, four of his men tugging him, pulling him out of the seat, dragging him across the tarmac, hurling him down in the grass that smelt of that English autumn smell already a light year away. Charles sat up and saw what remained of "Kate" lying there and wondered how men or machines could ever have lived through it. Second Schweinfurt was over. Sixty gone. Seventeen totally wrecked. One hundred and twenty-one badly damaged. And then, face-down in the wet English grass, he passed out.

Mano was deeply depressed. Mano had no regular girl-friend. He had tried serious love affairs several times in his life. Each had gone wrong because he had not been prepared to give enough of himself to them. His work as a barrister had come first. So he had decided he could do without women though not perhaps without an occasional woman, especially when deeply depressed. He had just sought professional aid in this respect and, as a result, was more deeply depressed than ever.

Mano now regarded his country's defeat as inevitable. One part of his mind even felt that this was just. He had never had many illusions about the monstrous aspects of Germany's leaders. He did, however, have a passionate loyalty to his country and an even more passionate one to the branch of the forces which he served. The Luftwaffe had been disgracefully led, inappropriately equipped, wickedly maligned by the one man who should have inspired it. What was depressing Mano at this moment was that that betrayer, Hermann Goering, had decided that he personally would take over the direction of the daytime fighters against the American raiders. This absurd directive had been issued immediately following the *Reichsmarschall*'s inspection of home defence fighter stations. On this tour of inspection, while dressed like a comic opera count and heavily made up with cosmetics, he had harangued fighter pilots for not giving their best. He had not actually accused them of cowardice as he had in Sicily. But he had made it plain to these men, who were fighting against odds which made the Battle of Britain seem almost a skirmish, that he considered they were not putting their hearts into the struggle. Mano saw the casualty figures and knew that it was not only the novice pilots, fresh from training schools, who were dying —most of them within their first ten operational flights—but also the seasoned squadron and group leaders. To cope with the losses the training period had just been shortened to 150 hours against the estimated 450 of the American fighter pilots. Despite the bombing, Speer, Saur and Milch between them were pushing more and more fighters off the assembly lines. The question was: where were the pilots coming from to fly them? The thing was a vicious circle. The shortened training time not only produced an inferior pilot at the front, it killed far too many before they got there. The training losses were nearly as bad as those inflicted by the enemy. Now, on top of all this, the *Reichsmarschall* had elected to play soldiers and staff officers had been detailed to attend to see how it should be done. Today was Mano's day. Goering had decided to take over direction of fighters at the Battle Opera House at Döberitz, near Berlin.

The atmosphere of these operational bunkers with their shaded lights, illuminated glass screens, rows of telephones manned by dedicated girls, never failed to grip Mano. He felt a desk man's sense of inferiority that he was not up there four miles above the Reich with the fighter boys. However that had been settled long ago when a medical officer had written on his report sheet: "Insufficient visual acuity. Marked cardiovascular instability. Colour-blind." Sitting in the observation benches, as if looking down on an operating theatre, was the closest substitute to participation available to him. His barrister's sense of drama relished the entire performance. The presence of the *Reichsmarschall* as top of the bill made him wonder wryly whether he was about to witness drama or farce. He did not remain in doubt for long.

The *Reichsmarschall*, magnificent in lavender blue uniform and crimson boots—was there a touch of rouge showing on the collar?—made his entrance, as befits the star, a trifle late. Plots had already begun to build up on the board.

A fighter area controller, who had also been summoned to watch the master's display, sat next to Mano and whispered his interpretation of events.

"The Yanks are heading for the Rhineland. It's obvious, we've seen these plots many times. Why the hell doesn't that fat clown do something about it?"

Soon fighter divisions began to confirm this diagnosis. Goering ignored them, saying openly that he distrusted their judgement.

Now a fresh lot of thoroughly confusing plots streamed in. Fighter divisions insisted that the *dicker Hund* was heading for the Rhineland, probably for Düren. Mano heard the *Reichsmarschall* growling, ordering his deputy controllers to remain silent. Goering at last addressed the gallery.

"It is quite obvious, gentlemen, the true objective is in Upper Franconia. I think I can predict that it is Schweinfurt once more."

"Bloody fool," hissed Dieter's informant. "Ten to one they're using *Düppel*, those damn tinfoil strips are such an old trick, you'd think he'd suspect."

Goering had taken action at last. All fighter wings were to

take off to intercept yet a third raid on the ball-bearing industry. No sooner were the squadrons scrambled than reports
began to pour in from the Düren area. Heavy bombing there
from above ten-tenths cloud.

As a man of decision, even the wrong decision, the *Reichsmarschall* gave his verdict. "Bluff. A diversion. The main target is still Schweinfurt."

Within ten minutes, the great man seemed to have his confirmation. The Aircraft Report Service, the German equivalent of the British Observer Corps, reported heavy aircraft
noise approaching Schweinfurt. The *Reichsmarshall* looked
triumphant but after some time no bombs fell there either.
Now the reports spoke of aircraft travelling high above cloud
east of Schweinfurt.

"They're our own bloody fighters," Mano's neighbour whispered. "They've overshot, that's what they've done. They can't
find Schweinfurt with all that cloud."

The Fat One had reached his own conclusions. Was he
sweating, slightly, the make-up running down his cheeks?

"The probable target is now Leuna. All aircraft to proceed
direction Leipzig."

Some squadrons had already been forced to land to refuel
but others were quickly sent up to replace them. It soon became plain there were no Americans over Leipzig either. In
fact, fighter divisions were already reporting sporadic contacts
with them well on their way home. The *Reichsmarschall*,
spurred on by the Aircraft Report Service observations of aircraft noise overhead, finally decided that the objective was the
Skoda works at Pilsen and sent what he could still muster of
the defending fighters there.

Mano's companion was now shaking with laughter.
"There's nothing up there except our fighters chasing their
own tails. The Fat One's made a complete fool of himself.
Now, perhaps, he'll leave it to his professionals."

Mano was watching the met reports. The cloud was breaking up fast, so fast that when the fighters finally got to Pilsen
all they could see in the clearing sky was each other. By that
time the Americans were putting their wheels down in England.

Now that the truth was plain to everyone, the *Reichsmarschall* underwent one of his incredible turnabouts. He had become Jolly Uncle Hermann again, roaring with laughter and
slapping staff officers on the back. At that moment it was impossible not to see that the buffoon had an engaging side. But
the fighter controller next to Mano did not see it that way,

even when Goering sent out a signal to the leaders of all formations congratulating them, and himself, "on the successful defeat of a heavy air attack on the Fortress of Koepenick".

Within days, the raid on Koepenick had become a classic joke throughout the fighter arm. However, other interferences by the leaders of the Reich were not so sunny. Talk everywhere, both within operational squadrons and among the staff, was of "Turbo." Turbo was the popular name for the Me 262, the miraculous jet whose praises the general had sung after flying it nearly a year before. Now with the American daylight raids to contend with and the pinprick bombing and reconnaissance by the otherwise uncatchable British Mosquitoes, OKL had suddenly taken an interest in the 262 again. It had received high development priority. In November, Goering visited Augsburg to see how work was progressing. A staff colonel who had accompanied him told Mano about the visit.

"Do you know what the Fat One asked Herr Doktor Messerschmitt? He said: 'Can it carry a bomb? The Führer wants a super fast bomber.'"

"And what did Willy Messerschmitt say to that?"

"He said: 'Of course, *Herr Reichsmarschall*, any fighter can carry a bomb so long as you don't mind it ceasing to be a fighter.'"

"Did that shut our Hermann up?"

"It seemed to."

Soon afterwards came the really bad news. The Führer had been to Augsburg to see for himself. The 262 had enraptured him. Here at last, he had declared, was his "Blitz Bomber" that would strike terror into the Allies when they attempted their suicidal invasion. Production as a fighter was forbidden. By order of the Führer, the 262 was to become a bomber.

When Mano heard this, he was so depressed that he toyed with the idea of seeking further professional aid in straightening out his sex life. He decided that on balance a bottle of brandy was both cheaper and less depressing.

After Second Schweinfurt, the Eighth Air Force sent what remained of "Kate's" crew on leave. What remained of "Kate" they towed off the end of the runway and handed over to the engineering and maintenance section for spares. There wasn't a great deal of second-hand value left in her. With twenty missions and the long, hot, bloody summer behind him, Charles was due for a rest. Though the Fortresses kept hammering away, with frightful losses, everyone knew that there were big changes coming, changes in structure and command, changes in quality and endurance of escort. As far as the bashed, battered survivors of 1943 were concerned, any change must be for the better.

The other released air crews had no doubt how or where to spend their leaves. Except for those who had, in the British phrase, "got their feet under the table" locally, they headed for London. Charles headed for Kate. He guessed that sexual attraction was part of it but mostly he needed her as a reassurance, as an anchor. He knew that at the end of ten days he was going to have to get back into another B 17, lick another crew into shape, and eventually fly another tour over Germany. At the moment he was by no means sure that he could do any of this. Kate, he knew, could help, just by being with him.

But Kate, unfortunately, was not due for any leave. She had, however, an understanding Queen Bee who took a lenient view of off-duty hours. Knowing this, Charles Levitson phoned Kate and asked whether, if he stayed at a country pub nearby, she would be able to see him at all. Kate at this time worked long Ops Room watches with correspondingly long spells off-duty. Moreover, she had recently regained an old and unexpectedly ally in the shape of cockney Rosie Lee, now a fully fledged sergeant in charge of a transport section whose main task was to ferry aircrews to and from dispersal points. Rosie had achieved her ambition not to spend the war bashing spuds. In servicing the crews she felt that she was at last making a contribution towards bashing Huns. Rosie had greeted Kate with characteristic warmth and assured her that if ever she needed a bit of transport she was sure she could oblige. Thus Kate managed to escape from the base for a few hours most days of Charles' leave and was able to spend four out of seven evenings with him.

Those parts of the day he could not spend with Kate, Charles spent with England. He was more than a little in love with both of them. These twin infatuations had begun in those distant days at university. He now realised that he had returned to America in far-away 1939 thinking of his friend's tall, fair, shy sister as the personification of the country he had adopted as his second home. So now it was enough for him to stay in an English pub with Tudor beams; to eat bacon and eggs for breakfast without that tearing pre-briefing wrench in his guts; to drink luke-warm bitter, to walk along Suffolk lanes between berried hedges, rimed with frost. Even the weather was crisp and kind to him. And when he heard the B 17s and B 24s leave, and more especially when he heard them come back, he tried not to look up, though that he found was hardly possible. He forced himself to live, encapsulated in the here and now. Kate and the soft Suffolk countryside were the reassurance that tomorrow wasn't here quite yet.

They knew they were becoming lovers, yet they did not kiss and barely even touched hands when they walked together. Charles was content that it should be like this. He reckoned his chances of emerging from his next tour of operations as very small. He had no wish to appeal to Kate on the grounds that he was virtually a dead man. For her part, Kate needed a respite from losing lovers; she was too much a casualty herself to invite more personal injury. She felt Charles' gentle presence as something that would help heal old wounds. She did not want to risk it being the means of opening new ones. Each was happy to leave things that way for the moment.

At the end of ten idyllic English winter days, Charles went back to his base and learned that he was to have a reprieve until the New Year. Until then he would train new crews, including his own. They gave him a new B 17E and this one he named simply "Kate".

There were rumours that the *Erprobungs-schwarm*, now part of the larger test unit the general had created—the *Erprobungs-kommando*—was to be switched to flying 262 jets experimentally on operations. But rumours were all they got because there were no 262s to fly.

The general was busy setting up one experimental jet flight at the Messerschmitt works at Augsburg and hoped for a second one that could cut its teeth operationally at Rechlin, outside Berlin. At the moment, these were largely hopes rather than realities. Even so they had to be proceeded with in disguise, as did Speer's vastly increased production plans for more standard fighters. The Führer's ban on defence remained absolute.

Dieter's *Schwarm* stayed under his command, though now responsible to Kommando HQ who fed them the weapons they were to test in action. Meantime they continued to make volunteer flights with *Wilde Sau*.

With the deterioration of the weather as winter drew on, *Wilde Sau* was no longer the miracle cure for night bombing it had once seemed to be. The accident rate among single-seater fighters had risen alarmingly. Iced up, without blind flying instruments, or training, the 109 and 190 pilots frequently could not find a field on which to land and, if they did find one, they frequently piled up.

The Lancasters had now turned their attention to Berlin, a target to defend which *Wild Sau* pilots accepted any risk.

Since Kolbe's death, Dieter Reh flew with an inner conviction that the *Schwarm*'s charmed life was broken and that for each of them it was only a question of time. The RAF were now dispersing their bomber streams, sending them in on a broad front so that the night-fighters had to hunt harder for their prey. The 110 boys had come up with a weapon that at least made a kill more likely once that prey was found. An armourer *Feldwebel* called Paul Mahle had invented a mounting for two fixed 20 mm cannons which pointed upward and forward at an angle of about 70 degrees. The otherwise excellent Lancaster had a blind spot under its belly. If the 110 could make its approach unseen, below, the twin cannon, aimed by reflector sight, had a good chance of doing fatal damage without the Lancaster being able to hit back, or even knowing its attacker was there. Mahle called his invention *Schräge Musik*—"slanting music" or sometimes "Jazz music". It was exceedingly effective and now all the 110 units were clamouring for it. The single-seater "Wild Boars" were on their own with just their flying skill, their eyesight, and, if they still believed in Him, God.

When Dieter took his 190 off from Rechlin on the night of 20 December he was prepared to give the existence of the Almighty the benefit of the doubt, without relying on it too much. For *Wilde Sau* operations he preferred a 190, as did most of the single-seater pilots. Its widely spaced undercarriage at least gave more stability on night take-offs and, more particularly, on night landings.

It was a bad night with heavy cloud up to 10,000 feet and icing conditions above that. The cloud had one good effect; it acted as a ground-glass screen against which the bombers showed up, silhouetted by the fires and the searchlight illuminations.

Dieter found a Lancaster without difficulty and was just about to close when he realised that a 110 was giving it a dose of *Schräge Musik* from below. It burned before he had time to fire and fell away, shedding flaming fragments. Almost at once he spotted a second Lancaster ahead and above. This one was wide awake. The rear-gunner opened up at once. Only the fact that the pilot took immediate avoiding action threw the gunner's first long burst off aim. The bomber went into a corkscrew climb, Dieter following, marvelling at the big machines' agility. At 21,000 feet he was in trouble. Ice formed on his canopy as if suddenly sprayed on. He was blind. The controls quickly became soggy with ice. The Lancaster had gone. So had vision, sense of direction, everything. Apparently the Lancaster, or someone, could see him. He heard the bullet strikes in a wing, in the fuselage. The strikes made a sound like apples drumming on an empty barrel. His pilot's reflexes made him take avoiding action though he had no notion what he was avoiding. The dive felt heavy, with ice on wings and control surfaces. It was an appallingly helpless feeling, falling blind, though dimly, through the ice on the screen, he saw the glow of searchlights. The 190 was dropping through the bomber stream. Wash from a large aircraft buffeted him. He had nearly collided in his fall. Worse, he was in the area at which German flak operated. An 88 mm burst rocked him, but still his one thought was to get below the icing conditions in order to see again. At 8,000 feet he tried to ease out, the 190 responding better. At 6,000, he had her level with the engine still running sweetly. But she yawed about the sky, no amount of trim making much difference to her attitude. She was like a horse playing about on the bit, throwing her head around wildly. Thank God a partial thaw was setting in. Ice had flaked from the windscreen giving him some forward vision. Now came the moment of decision. Bail out as many a *Wilde Sau* pilot had done recently, unable to find a base in the darkness. Common sense told him to do so. But a signal from the radio beacon at Rechlin cancelled out common sense. Every fighter that could be saved was vitally needed. The signal became stronger. With its aid he could find Rechlin. The aircraft was certainly controllable, becoming more obedient as the ice was ripped away by the slipstream in the warmer temperature levels. Below cloud now, he was sure he could make it. The signal was stronger still. He called the field that he was attempting a landing and saw the shaded blue lights of the flare-path glow two miles ahead. Now it should be easy. He throttled back, testing, feeling out what she was like with the power reduced. Like flying a brick, he thought. There was still time to climb again, open the canopy and jump. A stubborn streak of professional pride told him he could make it, should make it. The 190 came in over the end of the runway at an unhealthy speed. When he judged the flare-path lights were only feet below, he cut power and just let her flop. She bounced, rose, hit again and started to run. Only when he applied the brakes did he realise he only had one undercarriage leg down on which the brakes could act. He released the brakes frantically, pulled the lever to try to raise what remained of the undercarriage. The fighter was belly-down on the grass, bouncing and jouncing, throwing up earth, hurling him against the straps, turning a complete circle before finally rearing up on her nose. At the last second, she decided not to overturn and fell back on her tail. Dieter passed out as he hit the canopy roof.

By some miracle, the 190 did not burn. He came to in the state hospital two hours later with concussion, a bullet crease in his calf that he had not even felt, suspected broken ribs, multiple cuts and abrasions. Fifteen single-seater fighters had gone the same way that night. It was the death-knell of the seven-week wonder known as *Wilde Sau*.

1944

The North American Aviation Company's P 51 Mustang was all that a fighter pilot could ask for. It was also all that the daylight bomber crews of the US Eighth Air Force *had* been asking for. Wing Commander Peter Bristow was ready to fly operationally with the Americans by New Year's Day.

It was a lovely big brute of an aircraft that conceded only a little in grace to Messerschmitt or Spitfire. Moreover it was better in combat than the currently overloaded 109s and 190s. It could really go places and the astonishing thing was the places to which it could go. The Mustang could fly all the way to Berlin with the bombers, engage in a dogfight and still be waiting over the target when the Messerschmitt had landed, refuelled and re-armed and climbed up to try its luck a second time. The strange thing was that the P 51 had originally been ordered by the RAF back in 1941. Like the Fortress it had, in RAF hands, been a failure. Not, in the Mustang's case, because it had been wrongly used but because the machine just didn't have enough power in its 1,150 hp American Allison engine. Performance fell off with altitude, just where the 109s were best. The machine that was about to change the whole balance of daylight air war over Germany was a lusty offspring of Anglo-American technology. The engine that now powered it was a 1,650 hp Rolls-Royce Merlin made under licence in the States by Packard.

When the first trial of strength with the Mustangs came early in January, Dieter was still compulsorily grounded by order of the *Erprobungs-Kommando*, though fretting to be up and away. The concussion had proved heavier than the doctors had suspected. Mercifully for him, the bad weather had kept the Americans comparatively quiet.

Willy Weiss came to see him in sick quarters at least once a day. After a few visits Dieter became aware that Willy was in a sense the real invalid. He needed Dieter's company and reassurance. He was just now testing a heavily armed, heavily armoured version of the FW 190 with four cannon and two machine-guns. The idea was to build up a wing of these so-called "Stormfighters" to go in really close to the Fortresses to dish out heavy punishment while absorbing the return fire with some chance of escaping destruction.

"How's it going, Willy?"

"It's like flying a bloody armoured car. I don't fancy the job myself. It's a suicide role."

Dieter touched his bandaged head ruefully. "Anything that happens up there is fairly dangerous these days."

Willy, the tall, smiling young Austrian who had started out with them so gaily in 1940, was now an old-young man with a wound stripe, a Knight's Cross and thirty-one victories. These days he didn't smile much except when playing with Elsa, the Alsatian bitch who had once belonged to their first flight commander, Leo Feuchter.

"Dieter, we've lost, haven't we? What's left of your family and mine? Why should they be sacrificed? Okay, as fighter pilots, it's our job to carry on. But our families! There won't be a city in Germany left standing. Why can't we have peace with some honour now? Dieter, have you ever asked yourself what we've all fought for? What kind of leaders we've fought for?" Willy's voice was trembling.

"Willy, you need some leave."

"Don't dodge the question, Dieter. Has it all been worth it for men like Goering? One hears terrible things . . ."

Dieter dreaded to hear Willy develop his fears, knowing that they would be so much like those he had forced himself to bury. It was his duty to play Willy's superior officer, so he said: "I don't think we should concern ourselves with such matters."

"Very well. If you insist. You realise I was speaking to you just as a friend."

"Understood, Willy. You're one of my oldest . . . How's that young brother of mine?"

"Flying as my wingman. It's his job to keep the Thunderbolts away while I take my flying pillbox in and ram them."

"Tell him from me, I'll have him on the carpet if he doesn't do his job properly."

With a flash of his old humour Willy said, "If he doesn't, I'll be spread all over the carpet myself."

On a dispersal hut nearby the *Gefechtsalarm* rang.

"I'd better go, Dieter, this may be the chance to try my aerial battleship out."

The time was 1200 on the morning of 11 January. Over Germany the 5,000 feet of cloud that had blanketed the country for over a week was breaking up fast.

In southern England, the weather was still cloudy, but General James H. Doolittle, who had taken over the battered Eighth Air Force from Ira Eaker, was in fact about to do a lot. The US bomber commands had been reorganised into USTAAF, US Strategic and Tactical Air Forces. Doolittle commanded the Eighth in England, Major-General Nathan T. Twining the Fifteenth in Italy. These were the nutcrackers between which Germany was to be crushed. Their brief was no less than to destroy the Luftwaffe on the ground, in the factories and in the air. The Allies now found themselves in exactly the position the Germans occupied in 1940. Then the Germans couldn't invade without total air superiority. The RAF fighter pilots had denied it to them. Now the German fighter pilots were doing their damnedest to deny it to the Allies. Just before noon, Doolittle, who had waited for the weather to improve for a week, said: "Turn 'em loose." "Them" were 663 Fortresses and Liberators, of which "Kate" was one. "Them" also included forty-nine Mustangs and Peter Bristow flew one of those. The target was the German fighter production area of Brunswick-Halberstadt-Aschersleben, one hundred miles short of Berlin and on the direct route to the capital. The target, for the first time, was within range of at least forty-nine of the escorting fighters.

It began to go wrong for the bombers on take-off. The cloud which was clearing over Germany still lay thick over England. "Kate" was one of the first off. Charles was only too aware that his new crew, stiffened by only three of his 1943 veterans, were relying on him completely. Only this reliance stopped him from being sick with fear on the first operation since "Kiss me Kate's" write-off after Schweinfurt. He talked to the new boys encouragingly about the fact that the Mustangs were going all the way with them. He hoped he sounded convincing.

"Kate" came out over cloud to find herself practically alone. Well, that was better than finding herself on top of another Fortress. There had been plenty of collisions during bad weather take-offs. Today there were no collisions but a lot of delay. It took the controllers and formation leaders a disproportionately long time to form up their bomber packs over the North Sea and it was this assembling that had rung the *Gefechtsalarm* prematurely at Rechlin. After the bombers had gone, the Mustangs got away without any trouble.

Peter Bristow thanked God for the range of the P 51 as he stooged aimlessly around, burning up valuable fuel while the bomber boys sorted themselves out. The fuel lost in this period was to count later on.

That morning Mano Rumpler had been ordered to report to the Battle Opera House at Döberitz, outside Berlin. In command was an old acquaintance, the multi-talented former Major, now Colonel, Hajo Hermann, ex-bomber pilot, inventor and pioneer of *Wilde Sau*. Now that the Wild Boar had snuffled itself to an exhausted standstill across the night skies of the Reich, Hermann had been placed in command of the reorganised No 1 Fighter Division.

Mano watched the plots thickening, fascinated as always by the chess game. The pawns, the fighter squadrons in the front row, those of No 3 Fighter Division in Holland, were already committed. It was the movement of Hajo Hermann's pieces in which Mano was particularly interested. Hermann's First Division corresponded to the knights and bishops of the rear rank, the heavy boys. Theirs would be the task of dealing with deep penetration if the Americans succeeded in making it. Mano had been sent by the inspector of day fighters as an observer for the very good reason that German Intelligence knew about the Mustang, knew it was only a question of time before it penetrated the heartland as a bomber escort. Today, after a long lull due to bad weather, could be the day.

No 3 Division was hitting the *dicker Hund* as it straggled across Holland, hitting it hard, hitting it in waves, in mass attacks. Already the Americans were losing bombers. So far, the 190s and 109s had only tangled with the expected Spitfires and Thunderbolts.

In Britain, Doolittle saw things were going wrong, realised the bomber force was losing cohesion in rapidly worsening weather, gave the order to recall the second and third waves, leaving only 238 bombers to push on to the target. "Kate" was in the centre of these. This was the *dicker Hund* pack which seemed to Colonel Hermann to be heading straight for the capital. The colonel was a free-chase man. He had no intention of letting the Yanks get near Berlin before he struck them. So, in plenty of time, he scrambled the rocket-carrying 110s, holding back his escorting single-seaters until the Zerstörers were on their way up to operating height. Every drop of fuel counted.

Just after Willy Weiss and Jacob Reh had reported themselves airborne, the pretty blonde *Luftwaffenhelferinnen* placing the new information on the plotting table at Döberitz

298

reported a fresh formation of forty-plus converging on the *dicker Hund*. They were travelling too fast to be bombers, unless they were Mosquitoes, and the British never operated Mosquitoes in swarms. But fighters this far into Germany?

"All fighters in Gustav-Caesar-Eight identify forty-plus hostiles approaching 22,000 from north-west."

It so happened that Willy Weiss and Jacob Reh were nearest to this new threat. Willy saw the pack closing for its rendezvous with the bombers, flipped his radio switch and called: "*Achtung,* Jacob. *Achtung,* Mustangs."

They had been studying silhouettes of the P 51 for weeks. At last they were looking at the real thing.

Willy's instructions were to test the efficiency of the heavily armoured Stormfighter but not to risk it or himself unduly. Far back along the trail of shattered machines stretching back to the Dutch coast a formation of Zerstörers had fired their rockets, scored, smashed a bomber box. Their escorting Gustavs had torn at what remained and had left one Liberator lower and slower than its fellows, but still flying. It was just what Willy and Jacob needed. Their tactics had been discussed and rehearsed many times. Willy would take the Stormfighter in as close as he could and use the lame bomber as a flying target for his four 20 mm cannon. Jacob would cover him. As Willy made his move to come up astern of the Liberator, Jacob watched four Mustangs slide away from the pack to shepherd the wounded bomber. They were fast and beautiful, only the large airscoop under the centre section breaking their lines. He kept his eye on them, turning instinctively to cover Willy, registering as he did so that one Mustang carried RAF roundels, the other three USAAF insignia.

Three of the Liberator crew were already dead, but the rear-gunner was very much alive. He opened up at Willy at six hundred yards. The four Mustangs were coming down. Jacob called Willy Weiss: "Four Mustangs. Closing fast. Break right. Break! Break! I'm with you, Willy."

Fascinated, Willy watched the great slab-sided Liberator come up as large as a wallowing tramp steamer ahead of him. Liberators did not scare him as much as Fortresses. He pressed the cannon button and saw with satisfaction the mass artillery he carried ripping holes in the bomber's silver hull. He was a shark tearing a dying whale apart. The rear-gunner was good and brave and he stayed there, firing, until he was dead. Most of his bullets stopped on the Focke Wulf's armour plate or on its engine and this engine, likewise, was itself in process of stopping. The last burst the American fired took

Willy square in his still boyish, still earnest, still handsome face and left his corpse headless in the cockpit, save for a few shreds of bone and flesh. But by then the shark had, of its own impetus, passed into the cavity it had torn in the body of the dying whale. Wrapped together, killer and victim were already falling to the bottom of a sky-sea four miles deep. Jacob Reh broke and turned to face the Mustangs, firing a long burst at the one with the RAF roundels before it flicked right-left-left again, a silver snipe rising before a man with a shot-gun and successfully evading his fire. The Mustangs were gone. Ahead the Zerstörer packs were lining up at a respectful range to fire their rockets. Above and behind them Jacob saw the Gustav and 190 escort. Willy was dead. Willy was gone. To hell with Mustangs. The Mustangs couldn't be everywhere, even though they tried. Alone, he turned back to cut off the *dicker Hund,* making a solitary pass from the flank that took him through the nearest Americans and out the other side, with his finger and thumb on the gun buttons, kicking rudder like a crazy man to bring his Gustav to bear on anything that offered. Miraculously he came out untouched, glimpsed a Mustang above him, climbed, firing as he did so, saw the American lose glycol, white fuel, gain scarlet fire.

Mano, in the Ops Room at Döberitz, saw it all, heard a good deal more of it. One half of his mind was caught with the excitement and glory of the fight the Luftwaffe put up that day. The Americans had tried it, made their first big blow at the aircraft industry with at least a token of the escort they had long prayed for, and were paying for it dearly. The cooler side of his legal brain told him that Germany and Luftwaffe had reached the crisis of their sickness. The Mustang was here. A few had come. More and more would follow. Early battle reports suggested that nearly sixty American heavies had been shot down at the price of thirty German fighters. But this was only the beginning.

Somehow the madmen at the top who cancelled out all the heroism and sacrifice of the fighter pilots must be made to see sense. He had little hope of this. The general had a plan for saving all the fighters Albert Speer could produce for a single great blow against the Americans. The general argued that there was still time to cancel out the Mustang and turn its arrival into a rout. The general had a plan to mass produce the 262 jet. The general had a plan . . . but then the madmen weren't listening.

"Kate" came back from that bloody day with her new crew members made veterans in one horrifying lesson. From

Spaatz and Doolittle down to Levitson and Bristow, everyone who fought on that eleventh day of January gave testimony that, far from being beaten, the Luftwaffe fighters were more aggressive, better armed, better trained than before the New Year lull. But Spaatz and Doolittle, at least, had no doubt in their minds that this state of affairs would not last for long.

Helmuth Reh had grown to be quite an important man since his wife died with 50,000 others in Hamburg. First Milch, then Albert Speer, the minister of munitions, had recognised his worth. Karl Saur, Speer's able first lieutenant in aircraft production, was a keen Party man which made him Helmuth Reh's man also. The harder things became for the Third Reich, the more ardent Helmuth Reh became in his belief in the military genius of the Führer.

Four days after the appearance of the Mustangs, Speer held a conference. Herr Reh was proud to find himself summoned to it. There were things about the minister for munitions of which Reh did not approve. He made no secret of these to his daughter-in-law. Herr Reh was not at all sure that he entirely approved of Liese these days. She did her job as efficiently as ever, yet he always had the feeling that she worked all the hours the bombing allowed to support Dieter, his son, rather than Adolf Hitler, his Führer, and the Reich the Führer had built. As far as she bothered to do so, Liese covered her lack of enthusiasm by silence. What she didn't say was worse, in a way, than what she might have said. Other women in the ministry managed to look cheerful despite the horror of the perpetual bombing. Liese remained withdrawn. The only person she ever seemed to wish to meet socially was that Staff Captain Rumpler. He was another cynical one; hardly the sort of officer one liked to see in a key position at this stage of the war. Rumpler would bear watching.

Speer strode into the conference bunker dead on time. Herr Reh admired his efficiency, his ability to cut through to the heart of the matter. What he did not appreciate was the minister's scarcely veiled criticism of, as Speer presumed to see it, the obtuseness of the Party leaders. Today the young minister was in no mood to conceal it.

"Gentlemen," he said. "What happened four days ago had been extolled to me as a victory. Just the same, we lost thirty fighters we certainly can't afford. The significance of 11 January was that the American Mustang appeared within a hundred miles of Berlin. If that wasn't a defeat, it's likely to turn into one damn quickly.

"The Americans are soon going to hit us hard. The raid of 11 January showed us what the target will be. They're going for our aircraft industry. If they wipe out our fighter production that's it, the end.

"Gentlemen, we're going to push that fighter production sky high. As far as I'm concerned bombers are a zero priority . . ."

Speer looked round the table at the dozen men seated there. He caught a look of anxiety on Reh's face.

"Herr Reh?"

"I was only going to remind you, *Herr Reichsminister*, that *Angriffsführer* Peltz has only just commenced his offensive against England. He'll need bombers."

"Forget it," Speer snapped. "It will come to nothing. There are enough bombers about already to keep that seven-day wonder going."

Reh tried again. "Surely the wishes of the Führer concerning the importance of keeping up bomber production . . . the He 177, the Ju 188 . . ."

Speer was icy. "Herr Reh, either you are part of our production team . . ."

"Of course, *Herr Reichsminister.*"

"I appreciate your loyalty to our leader . . ." was there a hint of sarcasm? . . . "but you must leave me to worry about satisfying the Führer. Meantime, here are our absolute priorities.

"One: all plans for dispersal of component factories will be speeded. Extra labour force from the Todt organisation will be drafted immediately.

"Two: production of the Me 262 jet is to be given maximum priority.

"Three: arrangements are to be put in hand at once for all fighters waiting delivery to units at factory aircraft parks to be camouflaged and dispersed, wherever possible hidden under trees in forested areas.

"Within the next two months I intend that we raise fighter output to 4,000 planes per month."

A colonel from the secret weapons department asked: "At the expense not only of bombers but of *Wunderwaffen, Herr Minister?*"

"If we don't have fighter protection there will be no wonder weapons."

"Do you include the rocket-powered Me 163 as one of the *Wunderwaffen* to be held in the background?" asked a production chief from Messerschmitt, Augsburg.

"The 163 is a fighter. It gets production priority."

302

The secret weapons colonel was at it again. "What happens to prototype ground-to-air anti-aircraft missiles and to *Natter, Herr Minister?*"

Natter, or adder, was a manned rocket with stubby, token wings. At a speed of 900 mph it was designed to reach 30,000 feet in ten seconds. There it ejected its pilot who descended by parachute. A second parachute returned the costly rocket motor safely to earth. The warhead, steered by the pilot until the moment of bailout, went on to destroy a bomber formation. There were other equally weird and wonderful wonder weapons in the colonel's box of tricks. The *Mistrel*, a pick-a-back combination in which an FW 190 was perched atop a Ju 88 loaded with explosives. The fighter pilot released this huge flying bomb on to the target.

Speer answered: "Your department will continue to develop all the mechanisms you have mentioned, colonel. But no additional manpower or supplies can be diverted to them at present. Orders for factory dispersal apply to your department as to everyone else. Have no doubts about it: the Americans will come looking for our factories any day now."

After the eleventh, Charles knew it was only a question of waiting for the weather over Germany to clear before the Eighth Air Force went back to finish its business with the German aircraft industry. You didn't have to be Napoleon, Clausewitz or even Eisenhower to know that the prerequisite of the invasion of Europe was the obliteration of the German air force, especially its fighter force. The thick cloud layer that hid Germany during the last half of January gave the Fortress and Liberator crews a much needed breathing space. With a forty-eight hour pass unexpectedly thrown his way, Charles phoned Kate and told her he had managed to borrow a Jeep. If she didn't mind a chilly ride, how would she feel about a quick trip up to London for a meal? Kate was off duty the following night. She could get a pass so long as she was back for her watch at 1000 hours the following day.

Charles picked her up at the WAAF officers' quarters in the dark of a frosty January afternoon. Kate felt like a small girl being taken to a Christmas party. The sparkle of frost had something to do with it. She had always found frost evocative of some of the best days of her childhood and the idea of a long ride in a Jeep was like a special, unexpected treat. She hadn't experienced joy in anticipation of a simple pleasure since Michael had been killed. Simple? Perhaps the source of pleasure was more complex than she imagined. Charles' dark, serious face was framed in the raised collar of his heavy Jeep coat. A fleece-lined flying jacket lay on the seat on top of a pair of flying boots. Another American might have slung her the coat with a good-humoured wisecrack; Charles dismounted and held the coat for her while she slid her arms into it. Did he perhaps hold her a second or two longer than necessary as she fastened it? If so, it was most agreeable to be cherished.

"See," he said, "it's got your name on it."

Above the heart was the word "Kate".

"It's a spare crew jacket. I'd like you to have it—the crew would. They all know who the ship's named for. Sometime I'd like you to meet them. They're a great bunch of kids."

She began to protest about keeping the jacket.

"Honey," he said gently, "we're all in the same army. We'd like you to wear it. You're our mascot. The boys all feel you'll bring them luck."

On impulse she put up her face and kissed him lightly, a gesture of gratitude.

He took it as no more than that. "Shall I put the boots on you as well, Cinderella?"

She laughed. "I can manage those. Just see that your pumpkin gets me back to base on time, Prince Charming."

"I have a set of four supercharged Pratt and Whitney mice."

They talked little on the drive into London. The rumbling, bouncing Jeep, dimly feeling out the night ahead with blacked-out lights, became an encapsulated world of safety. The boots and jacket kept her snug. The cold against her cheek was exhilarating. Charles touched her gently only once, to see that she was warm. They were at peace, each, as the other knew, extracting the same assurance from the night around them. Each was sorry when the frost-tinselled trees of Epping Forest gave way to the concrete causeways of Wanstead. A searchlight was stroking the cloud base over Woodford. Charles lit a cigar. While they were driving through the frozen countryside he hadn't wished to intrude a single alien note on the glacial purity of the night. Cigar smoke was something that went with cities. Kate glanced sideways at the strong face pulse-lit in the ebb and flow of the cigar glow. He was unlike anyone she had felt drawn to before. Charles was something only America could produce—part USA, part Assyrian.

Charles, with a cultured American's instinct for the best, had discovered Prunier's. They dined off *Poisson du Jour*, which Kate diagnosed as cod elevated to the Prunier pantheon by a superb sauce.

"So what's wrong with cod?" Charles demanded. "Boston was founded on cod and only the best people come from Boston." He made an inscription to this effect on the menu, and madame herself insisted that they drink a liqueur as guests of Maison Prunier.

Afterwards they parked the Jeep off Brewer Street under the eye of a friendly MP patrol and went off to dance until midnight at the American Officers' Club. At 2100 hours the sirens went for the second time as *Angriffsführer* Dieter Peltz's scratch bomber force did their best to obey the Führer's order to repay terror with terror. The bombing was scattered, to say the least. Yet, when they emerged at five minutes to midnight, on Charles' insistence that she was bound by her Cinderella oath, one of the Luftwaffe's scatterings had effectively scattered their Jeep. The same MP sergeant was sadly contemplating a crater, a collapsed house front and a detached Jeep radiator grill.

"Can we give you a lift anywhere, sir?"

"Suffolk?"

"Afraid we don't go that far, sir. We can offer you a bed, sorry ma'am, *beds*, at our barracks. You'll get a full report on the incident to cover you for the vehicle."

"Thanks, sergeant, we'll manage."

Kate said: "I *must* get back by 1000 hours tomorrow."

"Don't worry, honey," Charles said. "The milk train leaves at 0530. I should know, I've caught it often enough."

"You're sure?"

"Positive. Until then we can sleep in chairs at the officers' club."

"Charles. I have the key to my section officer's flat."

"Okay," he said slowly.

"We could walk it. It's off Baker Street."

The MP sergeant had been listening while trying not to listen. "No business of mine, but if you folks, I mean sir and ma'am, want transport to the station in the morning, we'd be happy to oblige."

"Sergeant, you're a darling."

"You're a bit of a honey, if you'll pardon the breach of regulations, yourself, ma'am. Now if you'll just give me the address . . . Well, I guess we might as well take you home now. Taxis are one thing we have plenty of." He signalled up a white-painted MP Jeep.

The flat was small and easily warmed. There was a bottle of

Scotch in the cupboard and Kate soon had coffee percolating on the electric stove.

When she brought it in, Charles said carefully: "I suppose this is what's known as a golden opportunity."

She put the percolator down and stood waiting for him to continue, her head on one side as if she was waiting for the most interesting information in the world, which perhaps she was.

"It's not that I don't want to try. I wouldn't want you to think that. That'd be kind of insulting."

"I'm not insulted."

"Well, that's great," he said unenthusiastically. "Kate, I guess I'm in love with you."

"But you don't want to sleep with me?"

"You're not angry?"

"No, dear Charles. I'm far from being angry. Later perhaps you'll tell me why you don't want to . . . I might even be pleased to hear."

"Kate," he said. "I want to marry you."

She sat down quickly. "You Americans are nothing if not impulsive."

"That's no answer to a proposal."

"Have I had one?"

"It's no time to make you one. You've seen enough, been through more than enough, to know that."

"It's true that I'm still a little bruised," she said.

"That's exactly it. That's why I don't want to . . . I mean, if I go and get myself killed . . ."

"Charles," she said. "You've come through a lot, too. The worst is over. Peter says that more and more Mustangs are coming in to escort you every day . . ."

"You should have seen those Kraut fighter boys a fortnight back!"

She tried to joke him out of it. "Don't forget I've got the lucky jacket now. I'll even wear it in bed if it helps."

He groaned comically. "Don't even talk about bed!"

They drank a good deal of whisky and then, because it was the only comfortable place, lay down on the bed together, but a little apart. Somewhere, distantly, Peltz's desperate bomber force, whose offensive was doomed to run down in a very few weeks from sheer inertia, unloaded a last random stick.

Charles said: "I can imagine how these Luftwaffe guys are feeling up there. Pretty much the same, I imagine, as the boys who fly with us in the P 47s and 51s."

306

She said sleepily: "I suppose so. I knew one once, an age ago, before the war. You met him at university and at Axeham. I expert he's dead long since." She sighed: "If you really want to marry me you ought to know I've had love affairs."

"Don't be so old-fashioned."

"Who's old-fashioned? You could at least kiss me to see if you like it."

A minute later he said: "I like it."

They lay in silence for a moment.

Then, "Kate, I'm bloody scared."

"Yes. That's what Peter says. What they all say." ·

"Do you think those German guys are scared, too?"

"Peter says if you're not scared you're dead. It must be so for both sides."

"Kate. What'll you do after the war?"

"Get married, I expect. Have children."

"I'd like to be around."

She kissed him. "You will be. I know it."

"Kate, you know there's a big thing coming up for the Eighth?"

"I guessed as much . . ."

"If I get through it, my present tour will be nearly up."

She took his hand. "You'll get leave. I know the ideal place, a farm where I worked in Sussex."

Downstairs someone was knocking.

"The Gestapo," he said. "They always come for you in the middle of the night."

At the front door the MP sergeant was waiting.

They held hands to Liverpool Street Station and fell asleep in the train. Firemen were sweeping up shattered glass on the platform.

Dieter was discharged from hospital on 10 February to learn that the *Erprobungs-kommando* was operating from the Frankfurt area. The news was brought by the loyal Oberfeldwebel Pohle, who flew in to Rechlin to fetch his CO in a Bf G-12. This was a two-seater version of the Gustav, developed to by-pass the genuine article's vicious handling characteristics that had caused so many losses, both of pilots and fighters, in training. There was a great deal of news. A sealed envelope told Dieter that he had been promoted to *Hauptmann*—captain. The Americans had been suspiciously quiet since 11 January. Pohle had a fantastic new girlfriend whom he had affectionately nicknamed after his Gustav, *Die Beule*, "The Bulge". There was a good deal of talk going around about the coming of "Turbo", the wonder fighter, though Pohle, personally, would only believe it when he flew it. An old friend of Hauptmann Reh's had turned up at Frankfurt called Stecke. He had transferred from a *Zerstörerstaffel* to a new "suicide" wing—JG 2 *Udet*—that was being equipped with armoured Focke Wulfs, some said, to ram the *dicker Hund*. Pohle did not believe that the intention could really be to commit suicide ramming Fortresses, since if you'd got close enough to the bloody things you'd committed suicide anyway. He added, that from what he'd seen of Oberleutnant Stecke, he could be the exception. "If you'll pardon me, *Herr Hauptmann*, he seems a bit of a fanatical bastard. He's all *Sieg Heil* and jackboot polish . . ." Dieter had to smile. Rank didn't count where Pohle was concerned. "If you ask me, that sort doesn't last long. He's made one or two trips with us to get his eye in. Being his wingman is a one-way ticket to the cemetery, I can tell you."

"How's Jacob?"

"A better damned fighter pilot, with respect, sir, than you'll ever be. Give him a chance and he'll be another Marseille. Two more Liberators and a Mustang."

"And the Hoffmans?"

"Fritz had to belly-land the other day with his undercarriage shot up and Heinz comes in beside him and forgets to put his wheels down out of sympathy. That's the trouble with identical twins."

"I don't believe it."

"Nor did the CO when Heinz told him his hydraulics had been shot away, just like his brother's."

"What have they got lined up for us?"

"Several things, but the best is a flight of new high altitude Gustavs. They're G5s."

"What's so special about them?"

"They're fitted with a new supercharger, and they carry a drop tank below the belly."

Dieter groaned. "More plumbing to cause drag, I suppose."

"Listen a minute . . . sir . . . The tank is loaded with thirty-one gallons of water-methanol. Pumped in by a nitrous oxide injection system, it's like rocket fuel. For short periods, you can touch 420 mph at 24,000 feet and climb to 41,000. Mind you, total duration's only fifty minutes, but if we can get that high above the Yanks . . ."

"Big Week" was five days long and five long days they were. On 19 February a wedge of high pressure moved south into

Germany from the Baltic. The Eighth Air Force met. Men forecast that the deep layer of clouds that ruled out precision bombing for the past two weeks was breaking up fast. One thousand Fortresses and Liberators, seventeen US fighter groups of Lightnings, Thunderbolts and Mustangs, plus sixteen RAF squadrons of Spitfires and Mustangs stood ready to go. By now they all knew their objective. The orders were clear: "Destroy the enemy air force wherever you find them, in the air, on the ground and in the factories." Though the crews called it "Big Week", the greatest strategic air attack in history had a more official name. It was "Operation Argument". On 20 February, General Spaatz took a deep breath and said for the second time: "Let 'em go."

If you live through a week like "Big Week" events become hard to separate. For Charles Levitson it was ever afterwards a blur of names and targets. The twentieth of February started with the Junkers 88 works at Bernburg and Halberstadt. The Eighth lost twenty-one bombers on that one. Next day it was the Lutter-Miag Me 110 factories at Brunswick. Casualties were still bearable. Next day they went to Gotha, or rather the 1st Bombardment Division did. The 2nd and 3rd Divisions took so long to form up in the bad weather over the Channel that Doolittle, to their intense relief, called them back. "Kate" and over a hundred others carried on. Forty-four went down in flames. Next day the weather worsened and saved them from further operations, but on the twenty-fourth that most dreaded of names went up on the briefing board again—Schweinfurt, Schweinfurt and Gotha. "Kate" seemed to bear a charmed life, though her tail-gunner did not. A Focke Wulf spattered him over his turret so that he had to be lifted out in pieces by the medics when they finally landed. But still they were comparatively lucky. Forty-four of the 477 that set out ended up among the wide path of aerial debris spread across three countries. On the final day, 25 February, target visibility all over Germany was excellent. The two main objectives were the aircraft plants which "Big Week" had so far let off lightly, the Messerschmitt factories at Augsburg and Regensburg. The Eighth sent out 738 bombers from England while Twining's Fifteenth Air Force launched 176 from Italy.

In the Battle Opera House at Schleissheim, near Munich, Major General Huth was faced with two converging streams. He decided to commit his fighters mainly against the southern threat which had, previously, often been unescorted by American fighters. His hunch paid off. Nearly one-fifth of the attacking force—thirty-three bombers—was slaughtered.

The Eighth got off more lightly with thirty-one losses out of 738 but then it had a strong Mustang escort. Peter Bristow flew in that escort. All the way to Augsburg the bomber streams had been subjected to determined mass attacks by packs of Focke Wulfs and Messerschmitts. Every so often, pairs of high altitude 109s would come piling down in one quick firing pass, darting through the Fortress and Liberator formations, to climb steeply again, positioning themselves for a second attack. As the bomber stream turned for home, the Hoffman twins made the second attack that the limited fuel of the G5s allowed them. Peter saw them coming, yelled to his wingman that he was going after them, opened the Mustang flat out and dived beneath the bombers to catch the Germans as they levelled off. He fired at the point at which he judged they would pull out and saw the leading Messerschmitt fly into his burst. It lost some pieces straight away. The pilot was one of the best—Heinz Hoffman. Feeling the strikes, Hoffman rolled and dived, relying on the Gustav's great speed to take him to safety. But the Germans were too fond of that dodge and this time the Mustang was able to stay with him. Desperate, Hoffman pulled up into a wicked right-hand turn and almost immediately flicked into a spin. Now it was easy. Peter watched his first circle, throttled back and fired at the space in the sky through which he judged the German's second complete turn must take him. The Messerschmitt exploded in front of his eyes like a ripe plum. Fritz Hoffman had followed his twin brother down, harried and shot at by Peter's American wingman. When Heinz's Messerschmitt exploded, Fritz lost all concentration, flew straight and level for three fatal seconds in which time the second Mustang hit him so hard that his Gustav turned end over end until it disintegrated. Peter waggled his wings, saw his wingman climb to join him and headed back to escort the harassed bombers home.

"Kate" was coming home with No 3 engine stopped and the blade feathered, with her radio operator, thigh shattered by a cannon shell, sedated with morphine and with every spare flying jacket, except the one Kate Bristow wore that chilly morning, piled on top of him to keep his fading body alive. He had a chance of making it if nothing else happened. They were lower than what was left of their bomber box but there were four Mustangs and a Thunderbolt hanging around to keep the Focke Wulfs at bay. Just short of the Dutch coast, a solitary 88 mm battery opened up. The first salvo was uncomfortably accurate, but to one side. One large shell splinter tore straight through "Kate's" nose, shattering the instrument panel, tearing part of her perspex glass-house away. Fragments of metal hit Charles in the forehead. He felt pain in his right arm and leg. The rush of air pushed him out of his seat. There was blood in his eyes, warm blood filling his flying boot.

The co-pilot got "Kate" back this time and even managed to land her, as her makers had intended, on her wheels.

Kate Bristow saw the first bombers returning. She could tell from their scattered formations, as well as from visible battle damage, that this had been a pretty rough one. True to her pledge, she didn't take "Kate's" flying jacket off until she judged them all landed. An hour later she heard that Charles had received multiple splinter wounds.

"Big Week" was over. Not one stone stood upon another at the Messerschmitt works at Augsburg. It was much the same everywhere else. The German aircraft plants lay in rubble-piled, smoking ruins. Conference followed conference at the German Air Ministry. Milch, Speer, Saur all felt despair, all demanded action. The Allied press was trumpeting the success of "Big Week", yet 200 American bombers had paid the price and with them 2,000 aircrew dead or prisoners. No air force could stand that kind of loss for long. But the job was done. Doolittle said so. Spaatz and Twining said so. The Luftwaffe was one phoenix that could never rise again from its own ashes. Yet just over a week later it showed every intention of doing so. This time, on 6 March, the Americans came with an immensely strong fighter force for Berlin. Their objective was not so much the capital itself as what remained of the German fighter forces. It was a strange reversal of roles played by the opponents in 1940. Then the Germans believed that the British fighters would sacrifice themselves in defence of London. Now, four years later, the Americans believed the same thing about Berlin. In a sense they were right. The general had already prepared his tactics with fighter divisions and *Gruppe* commanders. The fighters, led by three *Gruppen* of the high-speed Gustav 5s, would attack in formations of anything up to sixty strong. Dieter, Jacob and Pohle, the sole survivors of the original *Erprobungs-schwarm*, flew with 111/JG1 from Paderborn on that day. Twice they refuelled and climbed to 24,000 feet to throw themselves on the bombers. The battle lasted four hours. That day there was a significant and frightening change in the Americans' tactics. The swarming Mustangs and Thunderbolts, confident in their superiority, had gone over to free-chase. Shades of 1940 in reverse once

311

again! The Yanks were no longer stuck to the slow-moving *dicker Hund*. They were released to roam the sky, hunting for the German fighters. But still Dieter and his comrades were condemned, not by their general but by the *Reichsmarschall*'s express edicts, to concentrate their attacks on the bombers. And so, this day they found themselves pursued and snapped at by the escort long before they could reach the bomber streams.

By their last sortie, they had a Liberator apiece and a Fortress shared. Dieter had just fired a maximum deflection burst ineffectually into a Mustang and was pulling out, climbing away vertically, when he saw tracer passing his port wing. Surely nothing could outclimb him, but there behind was a Thunderbolt, clambering vertically up the sky astern, actually overhauling him. It was unbelievable. Sweating, he saw the checkerboard markings round the American's engine cowling, the blunt nose reaching for him and the eight wing guns blazing. In another second it would be all over. Where the hell was Pohle? He hauled back on the stick. Inverted, he was almost flung against the cockpit canopy, his body straining at the seat straps. The engine was hit, black oil flowing like treacle over a wing root, coolant and oil gauges going off the clock. He had lost a lot of height and mercifully seemed to be suddenly alone in the sky. The vapour trails of the battle were thousands of feet overhead. A fighter coming up on the left. Pohle calling: "Dieter, are you all right? Jacob got the Jug." Jug was the Americans' slang name for the tubby Thunderbolt and, typically, Pohle had picked it up. "Bail out. You're in trouble. Engine's on fire. You've lots of time. Jump!"

Dieter could feel the heat, had opened the side panel of the cockpit to let some air in. He strained at the canopy release catch. But one of the Thunderbolt's fifty calibre slugs had jammed it. He cut the engine and pushed the Gustav into a vertical dive in the hope the flames would blow out. At four thousand feet he levelled and felt no more heat. The fire had died. Now to look for an airfield. Pohle beside him yelling: "Jump, for Christ's sake."

"Can't. Canopy jammed."

"Try to make the field. It's only five miles ahead."

"Losing too much height. Going to start the engine." It might explode. He had to take that risk.

Dieter put her nose down, pushed the switches, saw the prop spin, heard the engine catch with a death-clatter. Pohle, unable to fly slowly enough to keep with him, was circling the field ahead, showing him where to land. The temperature gauges were going mad again. If the engine didn't burn or explode it must seize soon. It seized with a mile still to go. Never make the runway. Ploughed field below. Must be soft there. Over the hedge, two small woods rushing by. One fifty miles per hour. One twenty. One hundred and the Gustav throwing up clods of earth like a runaway plough.

Thrown forward against the straps, feet braced against the rudder bar, Dieter waited for it to stop or else to die. "I'm getting used to this sort of thing," he thought. The Gustav had stopped. That hot smell again. He was going to burn after all. One last wrench at the jammed canopy. The damned canopy had gone, perhaps torn free by the violence of the belly landing. He did not remember getting out and throwing himself into a ditch half-filled with water. He only knew he was still sitting there when Pohle came for him twenty minutes later in a scout car.

Helmuth Reh believed in the Führer, which meant, even at this late hour, that he couldn't possibly afford to believe in defeat. The reports had all come in after the Americans' "Big Week" and pretty sinister reading they made. But things were humming and Speer was the man to make them hum even more. Moreover, Reh's own particular star, Party Member Saur, was in the ascendant. On 1 March, Speer called a conference to which Helmuth Reh had once again been summoned. There was to be a complete reorganisation from the top. Fighter production was being taken away from the Air Ministry which had always been bomber-orientated. Now Speer's Ministry of War Production was to have its own "Fighter Staff" with the energetic Saur in charge and the energetic Saur wanted production leaders like the energetic Reh to serve him.

Already Speer and Saur were driving the surviving staffs of the key aircraft plants to scratch around among the debris. Some incredible things were being unearthed. At the Messerschmitt works at Regensburg, the vital machine-tools were found virtually undamaged beneath the piles of rubble. At Erla, near Leipzig, 160 Junkers 88s were salvaged from the devastated workshops and found to be repairable. Yet this was only a start.

Albert Speer's directness and almost open criticism of the regime shocked Herr Reh considerably. The minister told the conference in no uncertain terms that the whole German war industry would run down, and defeat become inevitable, if fighter production couldn't be boosted to stop the American daylight precision raids. He was giving Saur's fighter staff a new labour force, top priorities for materials and fuel. Nothing else mattered except to get the fighters rolling off the assembly lines. By May he intended that they should be turning out at least 2,000 a month.

While Speer and his aircraft production chiefs worked round the clock, they received an unexpected bonus. Allied air command, apparently convinced that they had done the trick, suddenly relieved the pressure. The bombers still came in droves every day but their targets were no longer aircraft factories. Both British and Americans seemed to believe that there were no more plants worth bombing left. On the afternoon of 6 March, Mano Rumpler phoned Helmuth Reh to tell him that news had just reached him that Dieter had been shot down and injured in a forced landing. Reh senior prided himself on his objectivity and patriotism, so, having assured himself that his son was not mortally wounded, he simply required to know when he would be fit to fly again. Germany, he told Mano, needed all its experienced fighter pilots. Mano rang off.

Pohle came to see Dieter in hospital. He saluted formally and then threw himself down on the bed.

"That Jug," he began. "The one that nearly got you. The one Jacob shot off your tail."

"What a rate of climb! I had the methanol-water booster in but I still couldn't get away from it."

"We had a look at the wreckage. It had a new kind of propeller. Like nothing we've seen before. Four short, stubby blades like canoe paddles. The engineer officer thinks that it was the prop that gave him that fantastic climb."

Dieter said: "Those damn Yanks. They get better all the time. Meantime whatever we do to hot up the 109 and 190, we know we're really flogging dead horses."

Pohle grinned: "Don't worry. I came to tell you the rumours."

"Never believe rumours, *Oberfeldwebel*."

"Ah, *Herr Hauptmann* . . ." the pair were far too close as comrades for any rank-pulling, but they sometimes played this game of formal rank swapping . . . "I got this one from a close friend of yours. Major Rumpler . . ."

"Mano's been promoted?"

"Yes, apparently. About time those idiots in Berlin started recognising real talent."

"Never mind that. What did Mano say?"

"We're to be taken out of action. They say we're earmarked to fly "Turbo". So you'd better get out of bed, *Herr Hauptmann*, as soon as you can damned well hobble. The *Erprobungs-kommando* thinks that our original *Schwarm* has been so carved up that they might as well preserve what talent they've got left for a week or two. We're to go on leave, maybe until the Turbos are ready."

Decentralisation was the order of the day and so fighter staff itself had decentralised. To date, Hamelin had been untouched except for a stray bomb or two, so Helmuth Reh had taken his personal headquarters there, using the old Reh house as the nerve centre for his production group, rather than the factory which might yet be bombed out of existence.

Dieter and Jacob Reh came home to Hamelin at the beginning of April and found the old city torn and forlorn and its citizens more so. Dieter's head still throbbed from the concussion caused by his second belly-landing. The part of his brain that throbbed was glad to be out of the fighting for even a short spell, but the rest of him ached, like a system suddenly deprived of drugs. When he heard the Fortresses go over at 25,000 feet and saw the con-trails of the fighters escorting and pursuing them he felt an overwhelming sense of guilt that he was not up there with them. He found he yearned for the sounds and smells of a fighter airfield: of fuel, hot oil, engines coughing and starting in the morning darkness.

Nevertheless, it was wonderful to be with Liese. She had aged, not so much in looks but in outlook. She no longer queried and questioned. She seemed just to accept that she was a fragment on the vast, ebbing tide that was Germany. She did not even try to persuade him to ask for extended leave from flying, for he was certainly in no state of health, either mental or physical, to go back into fighter action straight away. She knew that it would be useless, that like her he felt that the violence of the forces ranged against them was so gigantic that one had no choice but to resist them, to lessen their impact in any small degree possible. Every American or British bomber shot down might be one German family saved and this was now all that mattered. At night she made love to him with desperate passion, as if willing him to impregnate her.

On the third day of their leave they got news that Jacob had been awarded his Knight's Cross and so, of course, there had to be a party to celebrate. An important man like Herr Reh could still drum up a few luxuries. He urged his hero sons to parade in front of his workmen with their decorations, but both firmly declined. If there had to be any sort of celebration, then let it be a quiet family one. So they drank wine and schnapps and ate real frankfurters and sauerkraut while Liese played Schubert *Lieder* on the piano and a few friends dropped in. The friends included Heine Müller's sister, Heidi. Heidi wore a black arm-band, a common enough thing these days. Heine was dead, killed flying a Heinkel 111 on the Russian front.

They drank to Heine's memory, dear, kind Heine who had never been cut out for war, let alone for flying a bomber. It was only as his sister was about to leave that she took Dieter aside and said: "Heine always trusted you, so I feel I can tell you. The official explanation was an accident, but his wireless operator parachuted before the crash and came to Hamelin three weeks ago to seek me out.

"They had been hit by anti-aircraft fire over the Russian lines. Heine ordered the crew to bail out when he got back over German-held territory. Then he kept on flying the crippled bomber alone. There was very little chance of landing it safely. Its undercarriage was damaged and there was a five-hundred-pound bomb stuck in the bomb bay. He flew the machine, not to a German airfield, but to a certain sort of camp kept for Russian prisoners and others thought undesirable. There he deliberately crashed the plane on part of the camp used as a crematorium . . ."

The girl's dark eyes were filled with tears. "You know, of course, that the Müllers have Jewish ancestry. Heine would have liked you, who have given so much for Germany, to know what he did and why he did it."

The front door slammed and she was gone.

Helmuth Reh came hurrying out into the hall. "Better shut the door. The black-out. The RAF is still quite active. Who was that who went out?"

"Heidi Müller, father."

"A strange girl. Don't let it get around, but I suspect the Müllers might have Jewish blood."

Mano Rumpler did not doubt that the war was irrevocably lost. A realist at all times, he knew that he should wait cynically for the end, and so was surprised to find that he was unwilling to become totally defeatist. The general's ardour was partly responsible for this. The general was determined that it was still possible to strike the American daylight raiders one colossal blow, and his enthusiasm affected everyone around him. On the face of it, there was little reason for optimism. It was now April. Since the year began, over 1,000 fighter pilots had died in battles with Fortresses and Liberators. With them had gone many of the veterans, the *Gruppe* and *Geschwader* leaders. The Americans roamed the sky above the Reich, almost at will, their bombers escorted by an equal number of fighters. Their main targets now were the railways and bridges, goods trains and engines. The Allies were out to paralyse the transport system. Every now and again they got an unpleasant shock when some Fighter Controller managed to hurl in a mass assault of a hundred or more Messerschmitts and Focke Wulfs. But the numerical odds favoured the Americans at around seven-to-one. Each pitched battle cost the German fighter arm anything from thirty to fifty machines and at least half as many pilots. The general and the minister of munitions, Albert Speer, saw eye to eye. They agreed that the last moment had come to turn the tide. Speer's production plans were already bringing results.

In April, Mano received orders to attend as his Inspector's *aide* at a conference with the *Reichsmarschall* on the Obersalzberg. Mano did not expect to be admitted to the inner sanctum, but he was well briefed on the agenda. Speer and Saur, backed up by the general, were to put before the *Reichsmarschall* a streamlined production plan that virtually cut out bombers and concentrated on vast numbers of fighters.

Outside, in the ante-room, Mano could hear the rumble of voices. Saur's level tones as he explained his chief's production schedules. The heated interruptions of the *Reichsmarschall*. A passionate tirade from the general. A banging of fists on table. At last a deathly, embattled silence. After half an hour the general emerged. He looked wild-eyed. Speer held his elbow and Mano caught the minister's words . . . "Not necessarily final. Leave it to me . . ." The general stamped out to his waiting staff car. Later, driving back with his own chief, Mano heard what had happened. The *Reichsmarschall* seemed to have made up his mind to turn down Speer's plan in advance. More likely he had had his tottering mind made up for him—by the Führer. Goering had insisted that fighters were not the main priority. Instead, he expected 900 heavy bombers to come off the assembly lines each month. Well, the inspector told Mano, they might come off the assembly lines, but they'd be lucky if they ever reached an operational unit before Allied bombs reduced them to scrap. And if they did so, there would soon be no fuel left with which to fly them.

The Americans were already turning their attention to the synthetic fuel plants and oil refineries. Without hordes of fighters to oppose them, they'd make a bonfire of the Reich's fuel supplies.

Mano said: "Then the position is totally hopeless, sir?"

The inspector of day fighters said: "I wouldn't bank on that. Our general is not one to take things lying down. Speer's a pretty sly dog, too. Between them they'll find a way round things somehow."

Mano's chief was right. During the next month, Speer's production figures gradually crept up. During May alone, three months after "Big Week", 1,760 single-engined fighters and 627 twin-engined fighters left the factories. Though the Führer had expressly forbidden any more fighter squadrons being called home from the Russian front for defence of the Reich, the general had found a way round this, also. He was steadily withdrawing single fighter flights rather than squadrons and attaching them to existing formations in Germany. He had even talked the *Reichsmarschall* into the idea of building up a reserve of pilots and machines. By the beginning of June, the general's reserve, held in preparation for one big blow at the Americans, had reached nearly 500 machines.

Charles Levitson spent a month in a hospital outside Cambridge. The flak burst had caused superficial damage over a fairly representative area of his body. The lump of metal that had been instrumental in filling his right flying boot with blood had caused rather more than surface damage, removing a largish piece of calf muscle. So when he was discharged in early May, it was conditional on his taking three weeks' sick leave, after which his future as a Fortress pilot would be revised. Kate had anticipated Charles' convalescence by keeping her own week's leave open and available. She had written to Tom Roland who replied immediately begging her to bring any friend she chose. In view of the fact he had so ardently wished her for his daughter-in-law, his reply could hardly have been more generous.

There was no Jeep and no Rosie to provide transport this time. On the train journey the tall American, hobbling with a stick, attracted a good deal of sympathy and attention. Kate was pleased and proud about this. In some quarters there was some resentment against the Americans with their inflated rates of pay, their nylons from the PX and their success with British women. Few people outside East Anglia knew or particularly cared about the frightful losses the Eighth Air Force had suffered.

As the train drew near to the coast, she found herself increasingly sensitive about Tom Roland's reaction. Would he think that she had picked up a Yank just to obliterate the memory of Michael? Within minutes of stepping off the train she was ashamed at having underestimated Tom. He kissed her heartily, insisted that Charles wait while he drove the old Austin right alongside the platform so that he didn't have to hobble far. His welcome could scarcely have been warmer had it been Michael that Kate was bringing home.

The farmhouse had not changed, except that it was rather more orderly than when Kate had last seen it. A large motherly Land Army girl cook was the reason for this.

"Got four of them. Land Army girls, I mean. A positive harem. I'm thinking of marrying this one. She's worth it for her apple crumble alone." He slapped her backside as he might have slapped a horse. The girl giggled happily. "Mr. Roland's not serious," she said. "I almost wish he was."

Tom had tactfully given Kate and Charles adjoining rooms. When he had shown Charles to his, Tom followed her into hers and said. "Everything all right, my love?"

She laughed. "Tom, it's not like that."

"I want you to know I shouldn't blame you if it was. He's a nice fellow. Had a bad time, too, I daresay."

She wondered if he were thinking "like Michael". She said quickly: "That wouldn't be a good enough reason . . . I never do things unless I mean them."

"I know you don't, lass. Well, come down when you're ready. That strapping wench of mine will have high tea ready."

The May weather was kind to them. Charles' leg strengthened with daily walking on the farm; on the third day he was able to make the high bank of the inner sea wall, a quarter of a mile away. They lay down in the grass and looked out over the grey Channel. A squadron of Marauders escorted by Spitfires droned high towards the French coast.

Charles said: "I wonder what opposition they'll meet. Not much, with any luck. I expect they're pounding the airfields. The invasion can't be far off now."

"Charles. You're not going to have to fly any more, are you?"

"I've got three more missions to complete my tour."

"But you don't have to do them now."

"No," he said slowly. "I don't suppose I do. But somehow it

would seem like unfinished business if I didn't. Lots of guys have flown in worse shape than me."

"Supposing I asked you not to. On medical grounds alone you could . . ."

"I'll give it some thought, I promise. If you promise to give some thought about marrying me when all this is over."

They lay in each other's arms, each drawing comfort from the other. Only once more, on their last evening, when they were alone together in Tom's living-room, did Charles broach the subject.

"Kate, you don't think I don't want to make love to you, do you?"

"I don't."

"It's just that I don't want to start anything I can't finish." She kissed him. "There'll come a day."

"There sure will."

Before they left next day Tom took Kate aside. "He's a great lad. You couldn't have found better."

"Thanks, Tom."

"Kate, I've no one to leave Rife Farm to. If you don't mind, I've decided to leave it to you. I hope you'll keep it going."

"Tom, you've got centuries yet!"

"Maybe. I'd just like you to know, that's all."

As April dragged on, Dieter became increasingly irritable and nervous. He was still forbidden to fly. Jacob had reported to Rechlin, where the Me 262s were supposed to be waiting for them to start their conversion course on jets but, owing to production blockages and the Führer's express and personal order that all 262s were to be turned into "Blitz Bombers", no jets had arrived. Jacob, it seemed, had managed to commandeer a G10 and with it had scored his fortieth kill, a Mustang.

Dieter was sleeping badly again. Now that there was no action into which his nerves could discharge their erratic voltage, the dreams had returned. The victim of murder in the Polish railway station was now Heine Müller. Another time Heine crashed his Heinkel on to the train but he overshot and missed. The SS men stood by laughing and then dragged the woman out and shot her. The woman was once again Liese. There was a new dream in which Liese and he stood in the centre of the city square in Hamelin. An air raid was taking place, though there was no sound of falling bombs. The square was a sea of fire, drifting like liquid. Liese stood on one island in the fire, Dieter on another. She did not appear to

320

notice it creeping closer, and though he called and called, she did not hear. Gradually the fire encircled her until she went up in a gush of flame like the last Fortress he had destroyed. He woke with his teeth chattering. She was already awake, cradling him.

"There, there," she said, as if to a sick child.

"God, I had an awful dream. Fire. You were on fire."

"Well, I'm not. I'm here. Safe and sound."

"Liese. You must stay here in Hamelin until the end of the war. You're completely safe here. Whatever you do, you mustn't go back to Berlin."

"We're probably safer there than anywhere. We work and sleep in deep bunkers."

"I'd like you to stay away."

"And I'd like you to stop flying."

"You know I can't."

"And you know I can't desert your father."

"Father doesn't seem to realise what's happening to us all. He thinks Germany can still win."

"I'm not sure that's true."

"Then what keeps him going? Personal ambition?"

"I'm not sure that's completely fair, Dieter. Perhaps he's much the same as the rest of us, determined to go down fighting. The bombing has given us all that kind of determination in common."

"I suppose you're right. All I know is that I've got to get back into a cockpit as soon as possible or go crazy."

It was a mystery to Peter Bristow. There was practically no opposition all that week. Great hordes of Fortresses and Liberators, of Marauders and Mitchells, had been continually pounding the Channel coast from the Pas de Calais to Cherbourg. Coveys of Mustangs, Thunderbolts and Spitfire Mark Nines shot at transport, aircraft on the ground, even individual men, in fact anything that moved. The truth was that the German air force on the invasion front had eighty serviceable fighters belonging to JG 2 and JG 26 to oppose more than 7,000 aircraft available to the Allies. All that week the British and Americans hammered away at road junctions, pillboxes and at airfields that did not appear to contain a single German plane. Then, on the morning of June 6, on the dawning of a grey, rough day, Wing Commander Peter Bristow found himself leading his Mustangs out over an armada of grey ships ploughing into a grey, rough sea. He took his wing inland shortly after first light above the piled and bloody chaos of

Omaha beach where the Americans were dying in helpless piles, north to where the British were driving ashore with less resistance at *Gold, Juno* and *Sword* beaches. There were targets galore for the Mustangs on the ground, but none in the air.

Peter kept a sharp look-out for the Messerschmitts and Focke Wulfs that the Jerries must have been keeping somewhere in reserve and for the German jet they had heard so much about, the 262. Nothing! Not a German fighter challenged them, though flak came up in increasing intensity as the surviving defenders recovered from the 5,000 tons of bombs that had been dropped on them since the previous night and the shells that screeched in from the warships offshore. But still there were no fighters. Unbelievable!

Out of ammunition, Peter was about to lead his section home, turning southward and climbing to escape the overkeen attentions of the Allied navies, who, not unnaturally, fired at anything that flew. As he turned he caught the familiar flash of wings. Two Focke Wulfs had dived out of thick cloud, flattened above the British beach at *Sword* and streaked across the landing-craft, flat out, with all guns firing. It lasted a few seconds, then the two 190s were gone, disappearing into cloud with every ship in the fleet hurling anti-aircraft fire at them. In the 190's cockpits, Colonel Joseph "Pips" Priller, *Kommodore* of JG 26, and his wingman, Heinz Wodarczyk, could hardly believe the size and meaning of the target they had just attacked. Alone of the entire Luftwaffe, and alone they were to remain all that D-Day, they had seen and attacked the Allied invasion of Europe. They had only witnessed it because they had decided for themselves to find out what the confused reports that reached their *Geschwader* were really all about. It was almost a repeat performance of the RAF's belated action on the German navy's Channel dash. When they landed and told their story, such was the confusion of bombed and disrupted communications that no one at OKL would believe them or act upon their information. The invasion had been expected for weeks and yet it had taken the Luftwaffe completely by surprise. It wasn't until that night that a few Ju 88s backed up Priller's virtually single-handed effort by dropping a handful of scattered bombs on the invasion beaches.

Mano caught the backwash in Berlin. For weeks past the fighter force had had its plans cut and dried for dealing with the invasion. Mano had worked through many nights to complete the clockwork-timed scheme by which nearly 600 fighters, from home defence units as well as from the general's treasured reserve, would be transferred immediately to the invasion front. Each unit had its prepared forward airfield equipped with food, ammunition, fuel and a ground staff to receive it. But now, on the morning after D-Day, the phones never stopped ringing with conflicting reports. Such-and-such a field had been made unusable by bombing. A few hours later came the report that the field was intact but the fuel supplies had been destroyed. It was impossible to get a clear picture of anything.

The only fact that emerged was that everything was being clobbered by the non-stop bombing. Often, before orders could be got to a unit to switch destinations, their new airfield had been cratered into unserviceability. In Berlin the general fumed. He wished desperately to hold his fighters back until the position stabilised. But the *Wehrmacht* was crying out, as the British Army had cried out at Dunkirk, and the cry was: "Where is the air force?" Already the old accusation that the fighter arm had let the Reich down was formulating in the *Reichsmarschall*'s disordered mind. And so, on the morning of 7 June, on orders from OKL, Mano started pushing the buttons that sent the precious home defence reserves towards the Channel front.

In fact, about half the fighters never got there, or if they did, never saw action. The refuelling fields en route were full to overflowing. Landing conditions at touch-down points claimed their share of write-offs. The reserve pilots were not trained in cross-country flying. Some did not find their way to their allotted fields and force-landed, often with considerable damage and sometimes with fatal results. American and British fighters intercepted and shot down many others en route. Those that did arrive frequently found their selected bases destroyed or under attack as they came in. Losses were incredible. Units became inextricably mixed up. From Berlin, Mano and the entire fighter staff were powerless to check, let alone to produce any sort of order out of the chaos.

At Lechfeld, where the general hoped to form his test *Kommando* of jets, Dieter, Jacob and Pohle fretted throughout early June. The promised 262s had never materialised. The Führer had blocked supplies. The miracle "Turbo" was still to turn the tide at the invasion front, yet not one "Blitz Bomber" had seen action there. From Mano, Dieter learned how the general was risking his political neck, with Speer's backing, to try to get a trickle of 262s diverted to the fighter arm. But nothing happened, except that the general's stock daily sank lower with the *Reichsmarschall*. In his present personal vacuum, Dieter was surprised to find that he had no wish to press for a posting to the Channel front. From ferry crews returning to the Messerschmitt works at Augsburg, nearby, the three pilots of the former *Erprobungs-Kommando* heard of the losses at the front but, worse, of the bitter fall in pilot morale among the squadrons. It was not only the total superiority of the Allied air forces that had caused this, but the realisation that, through no fault of their own, the fighter pilots were being reviled by the ground troops for having betrayed them when they were screaming out for protection. These days, Dieter, Jacob and Pohle were all realists. They were not prepared to be shot to pieces or burn to death to no good purpose, for an ideal that no longer existed and for leaders who clearly no longer believed in the valour of the fighter arm, if they ever had done so. They were not prepared to risk their lives until the High Command produced some plan on the Channel front that made dying there worthwhile. To be strafed on one's own airfield before one could take off; to have to hide one's fighter in a wood between missions only to have the entire wood carpet-bombed; these things made the effort totally futile. However, all three saw the continuance of the fight against the American strategic bombers as eminently worthwhile. This was defence of the homeland. It had nothing to do with Aryan purity, *Lebensraum,* the Master Race or any of the labels in which, ten years, or even five years, previously, they had so thoroughly believed. This was a fight for survival for what remained of families and homes. The *dicker Hund* was something tangible on which to focus all one's professionalism, all one's fear and hate. It was an enemy which you could still hit to good purpose. At first it seemed that the opening of the second front would take the pressure off Germany's tortured cities. So, for perhaps the first fortnight, it did. In a short while, well before the end of June, it became clear that the Allies could afford to cope with both the demands of their invasion and the insistence of General Spaatz that the attack on Germany's oil and fuel plants should continue with full fury.

Dieter called Mano in Berlin and asked him to use his influence to get the three of them temporarily attached to the test unit at Lechfeld. Mano had, at that moment, received orders to report with the inspector of fighters, Hannes Trautloft, to the invasion front. It was the same Trautloft who as *Kommodore* of JG 51 had led Dieter on his first sorties in the Battle of Britain. On the invasion coast, the inspector, together with the special communications staff to which Mano

324

was attached, were to try to make sense of the utter chaos and to report recommendations to the general personally. Before he went, Mano assured Dieter, he would try to clear the wires for the two brothers and Pohle to fly with the Lechfeld unit. There should be no difficulty about providing them with machines since Lechfeld was, after all, the test airfield for the Messerschmitt factories. Mano was as good as his word. Within twenty-four hours, not only had their attachment been confirmed, but three brand new 109 G5Rs were ready to be handed over to them. The G5Rs were yet another version of the old workhorse, fitted with a wooden tail unit to save metal which, because of its heavier weight, necessitated the fitting of a block of lead as counterweight under the oil tank. It was just one more example of what the poor 109 had to suffer to stay in service.

On 16 June the Americans made their intentions very clear. They attacked Hamburg and fuel plants in central Germany with 1,000 bombers, escorted by 800 fighters. Four days later they came again in even greater numbers and this was the day on which Dieter and his companions rejoined the battle. This time, the German controllers got their limited defences into the air in good time, in well consolidated packs, and they met the bombers head-on. Whatever might be happening on the invasion front, the result of this battle was enough to put new heart into a fighter pilot. Out of 1,361 bombers sent on the mission, forty-eight were shot down and 468 badly damaged. Of these Dieter and Jacob accounted for a Liberator apiece and shared a Fortress. Pohle settled for a Mustang and Thunderbolt before having to bail out himself with his wooden tail unit shot away. His was one of the twenty-eight German fighters shot down on that day. Unlike the precious reinforcements incinerated in the furnace of the invasion, these fighters were not sacrificed in vain. The Americans went home to lick their wounds and to report a temporary loss of air superiority over the Reich. As for the general, he became more than ever convinced that, if only OKL would give him the chance to build up a large fighter reserve, he could still strike the daylight raiders a great blow that would give them pause to think.

Kate Bristow had prayed that the doctors would turn down Charles' request to return to flying. She knew that the thought of flying more missions over Germany kept Charles awake at night, but she knew equally that he would ask to fly again. He was not consciously heroic in this attitude. He could not tell her precisely the reason for his compulsion to finish his tour

with only three more flights to go. The nearest he could come
to an explanation was to say that he didn't like unfinished
business; that unless he rounded off his tour, he would feel for
the rest of his days that he hadn't completed the job he had
come to do. Though he never said as much, he was, perhaps,
one of the few airmen she knew who still saw the war against
Germany as something of a crusade. If so, the explanation
could be the simple one that Charles had Jewish blood in his
veins. Her brother Peter certainly didn't feel like this any
longer. Whenever she met Peter nowadays she sensed an utter
weariness, a desire simply to have it over and done with. He
did not appear to feel hate, and certainly not pity, for his outnumbered opponents. They were just Germans who had to be
got out of the way so that they could all pack up and go
home. He did not even seem to feel elation that the British
and Americans had almost complete air supremacy. He
shrugged it off by saying: "Well, the other bastards shouldn't
have joined."

It was a week after D-Day when Charles phoned her at the
base.

"Honey, I've got news for you which I guess you may not
dislike too much. The docs have turned me down for flying
duties for a while."

"For good, Charles?"

"It's nice to hear that anxiety in your voice, Kate."

"That not answering my question. You know I'm anxious.
It's so near the end now it seems ridiculous to go asking for
trouble . . ."

"Hey, wait a minute. We've a fair way to go yet. The
Krauts haven't exactly welcomed us over there, from what I
hear."

"Are they going to let you fly again?"

"They said maybe in three months or so. I have to go for
another medical board in October. Meantime they're making
me—you'll never believe it—intelligence officer with my old
bombardment group."

Kate let out a sigh of relief.

"Good to hear that sigh, honey. Meantime we'll be able to
see quite a lot of each other."

"Yes," she said carefully.

"Don't you like the idea?"

"Of course I do, darling. It's just that I've been asked if I'd
like to go across the other side with the fighter Ops Room
staff as soon as things get a bit more stable."

"Now who's sticking his neck out? You say 'no' from me."

"I'm afraid I've already said 'yes'."

Mano Rumpler had always experienced a sense of guilt that he was unable to share the dangers of the fighter pilots whose destinies he, to some extent, controlled. As a member of Oberst Trautloft's staff he now came very close to doing so. Conditions on the forward airstrips opposing the Allied bridgehead were frightening in the extreme. Not that the airfields were all that far forward. In order to find some protection from constant bombing and low-level attack, and to provide the squadrons with an adequate ground organisation, most of the fighter fields were to the north and north-west of Paris. This, however, was no bar to the Mustangs, Spitfires and Thunderbolts, the Marauders and even Fortresses who strafed and bombed continuously.

Trautloft drove from squadron to squadron as if the enemy air forces did not exist. Twice they ended up in a ditch. The *Herr Oberst's* sense of timing seemed to extend to knowing the exact moment a Thunderbolt fighter-bomber would release its load, the precise pre-second at which a Spitfire pilot's thumb would descend on his cannon button. But then the *Herr Oberst* had many times performed these same actions from up top himself.

The hot summer, which stank of dust and death, became for Mano an endless unedited film in which one incident followed on another without connection or explanation. Yet all were connected, all were part of the same drama. The story of the tragedy being enacted was only too clear. Everything he saw in those weeks spoke of the futile destruction of a once fine fighting force. Some impressions dominated. The redoubtable Heinz Knoke, the veteran who had invented the technique for bombing Fortress formations back in 1942, confessing that every time he closed his cockpit canopy, he felt as though he was shutting the lid on his coffin. A replacement 190 coming in at a hastily contrived forward airstrip, its pilot failing to notice a telegraph pole and cutting a wing off. The thing Mano remembered about this fatality was the horrible silence that followed the crash. Another pile-up was by no means so silent. Trautloft had insisted on visiting a single flight of 190s operating from a cornfield. The landing place was a hastily cut strip in the centre of the growing crop. Three planes had landed safely, each one generating a choking cloud of yellow dust. The fourth, flown by a young NCO on his second mission, came in too fast and high. Instead of opening up and going round again, the pilot still tried to get in, hit the standing corn at the edge of the strip and slewed diagonally towards the surrounding stone wall. There the fighter somersaulted and fell on its back. Inside the cockpit they could all see the pilot fighting to free himself. Ground crew and other pilots were running to help him. Petrol was leaking into the corn. Suddenly, miraculously, the pilot was out and running through the sea of aviation fuel to get away from his machine. He had made perhaps ten yards when, with an explosion that seared the face at one hundred yards distance, the petrol ignited. When they dragged the boy from the blazing corn his features were barely recognisable. They appeared to have dissolved like melting rubber. He screamed for fully three minutes until a needle brought him peace and, happily, death. Five minutes after they drove away from the cornfield, Mustangs found it and incinerated the remaining three planes on the ground.

Perhaps what Mano afterwards recalled most vividly was a captured British Spitfire pilot saying to Trautloft: "I'll say this for your chaps. They show a damn sight more guts than skill."

It was true. After three weeks, there was only one possible recommendation for Trautloft to make his general: "Pull as many of the squadrons out as you can and build up a reserve back in Germany."

The general had already made up his mind to do just that.

There were still a few men in Germany who believed that the war was not yet lost and one of these was Helmuth Reh. The evidence was all around for him. Despite all that the Allies had done to the German aircraft industry, production was booming as it had never boomed before. Speer and Saur had attained this between them with considerable help, of course, from men like Reh. Reh did not doubt that his part in Speer's great dispersal and production plan would be adequately rewarded. He had great faith in the Führer and the Führer's sense of justice and loyalty, as well as his military infallibility. The Führer would yet turn the tide.

And then on 20 July came the unbelievable, inconceivable news. An officer called Stauffenberg had carried a bomb in a briefcase into the Führer's staff conference at Rastenburg. The room had been demolished, others killed and yet, miraculously, the Führer had been preserved. It was further proof, if proof was needed, that this was still Germany's man of destiny. The story was that the Führer had demanded that every last plotter be wiped out and the ring-leaders hung like cattle on piano wire from meat hooks. Well, serve them right.

In Berlin, Mano Rumpler sniffed his long ascetic nose when he heard the news. He kept his thoughts to himself. Many things had been said about the Luftwaffe but so far no one had accused its officers of being mixed up in plots. Rumour had it that well-known faces were disappearing, with the help of the Gestapo, from civilian as well as from army high places. No doubt old scores were being paid off in a way that would become increasingly and sickeningly familiar but, thank God, the Luftwaffe wasn't involved. It had troubles enough without adding political intrigue and murder to them. If others liked to settle that hash, well and good. The only pity, he said to himself, was that they had made such a hash of it.

Troubles the Luftwaffe most certainly had. The general had been buzzing around the squadrons in the west in person for the second time. He had returned convinced that, never since Sicily, had fighter pilots been asked to sacrifice themselves in such suicidally useless conditions. Aircraft losses at the front were running at the rate of 300 per week. And yet the wonder was that industry was more than making good these losses. The flying training schools were turning out nearly one thousand pilots a month. On the invasion front these would disappear like icicles in a heat wave. Yet, carefully nursed and battle-indoctrinated, they could hold their own with tolerable losses against the American daylight raiders.

The first thing the general did on storming into the office was to demand to know the strength which the reserve of fighters had reached. Mano had the end-of-July figures pat: just over 700 fighters and pilots, many of whom still needed about another fifteen hours before they were ready for full combat duty. The general stubbed out his cigar with satisfaction. "Now, we're getting somewhere at last," he said savagely. "If only the fools at the top"—he was careful not to mention names—"will let us double those figures, we'll knock those Fortresses out of the sky. What I want is one great blow."

Three days after he had said this, the Allies broke out of the Normandy bridgehead, at Avranches, and the race for Paris was on. Almost immediately the orders came from OKL. "Commit the entire fighter reserve to stabilising the battle in the west."

Fortunately Mano never heard what the general said when he received this order. He did hear, however, that he had instantly demanded to see the *Reichsmarschall*. The *Reichsmarschall* could not see him because he felt "unwell". The general had then sought out the one man he felt he could trust, Albert Speer.

Helmuth Reh was with Speer when the general called on the security phone. He heard Speer say, "If the *Reichsmarschall* won't act, then it's my duty to do something immediately. Come to the ministry as quickly as you can, *Herr General*. We will fly to see the Führer at the Wolf's Redoubt immediately."

Thus was Helmuth Reh on the fringe of great events. He confided as much to his daughter-in-law later that morning. "Those dastardly assassins haven't affected the Führer's energy or zest. Mark my words, something very big is afoot. He's just sent for the minister and the general of the fighter arm."

Which wasn't entirely true since it was the minister of munitions who had, in desperation, asked for an audience with the Führer.

It wasn't until much later that Mano was able to piece together, from conversations with a certain staff captain who had been at Rastenburg during that meeting, what actually took place.

Hitler, according to his account, was in a manic state to begin with. Perhaps this was hardly surprising, since it was barely a week since he had survived Stauffenberg's assassination attempt.

Speer, sensing that he was handling a time-bomb, approached Hitler with more deference than usual. He began to explain with careful, cool reasoning, backed up by production figures, interlarded with frequent *"mein Führers"*, why it would be fatal to send the vital fighter reserve to the western front, that it would be swallowed up as had been the first and smaller reserve. He had just begun to expound on how a revived fighter arm, kept at home, could yet save the Reich's war industries, when Hitler dashed at him, practically foaming at the mouth.

"Look after the war industries, Speer! Leave the conduct of the war to me. I've no more time to waste on either of you. Get out of my sight."

Both the general and Speer had wanted to return to Berlin immediately, if only to let the situation cool. But, as they were about to leave for the airfield, the staff captain was sent running after them to say that they were required to stay overnight; the Führer wished to see them again next day. The general hoped for a reprieve, but Speer cautioned him against undue optimism.

When they marched in next morning, Hitler was in his most icy mood. A reprieve for the fighter reserve was far from the Führer's thoughts. He had received a letter from an impartial observer, he said, that made it clear the German fighter pilots in the west were bailing out rather than accepting battle with a superior enemy. The general rushed in to defend his men, but Hitler silenced him.

The staff captain who recounted all this to Mano said that Hitler's frenzied screaming had been clearly audible beyond the closed door of the conference room.

"How dare you make excuses! I intend to dissolve the fighter arm. Air defence will be entirely in the hands of flak batteries from now on. Speer, you are to switch production immediately from fighter planes to anti-aircraft guns. Silence, both of you! Speer, you will have a revised production schedule in front of me within ten days."

Then they were dismissed. Mano's friend the staff captain reported that for the first time the general looked grey and despairing. Only Speer seemed comparatively calm. In the communications squadron Heinkel on the return flight to Berlin, he had counselled the general not to be too depressed.

"Don't worry. During the next few days I'll produce figures that will convince even him that a change-over from light aircraft alloys to heavy steel for guns is impossible. If he insists on more flak batteries, then we can switch the material from the locomotive building programme."

Speer was right. Once he'd delivered his report, there was no more talk of disbanding the Luftwaffe. But the order to pour the second reserve of fighters into the melting pot of the retreat across France still stood. Eight hundred fighters took off. Over half of them crashed on the way, fell into enemy hands, or were destroyed by their own ground crews in the retreat ahead of the Allied break-out. When all the battle returns were in, Mano calculated that in exchange for the 400 lost fighters, the now squandered reserve had accounted for not more than twenty-five enemy planes.

Liese was pregnant again. A forty-eight-hour leave back in June had done the trick. Now she concentrated everything upon the child in her womb. She no longer had any hope for Germany and she dared not entertain any hope for her husband. She knew that he was flying daily against the ever intensified American attacks on the German oil and synthetic fuel plants, and regarded it as only a question of time before she received the news that he had been killed. Their baby was the symbol of the new Germany that must one day emerge from the self-inflicted wounds and mutilation of the past five years. For the child's sake she dutifully went to the deep shelters every time the bombers came over. For herself she did not care. Though she no longer had sympathy with, or heart for, the pursuit of her country's hopeless struggle, she served her father-in-law loyally because it was the only way she could show loyalty to Dieter. Luckily for Liese, she was more snowed under with work than ever. Buried in her contempt for the regime and its masters was an unbounding admiration and pride for what German civilians had suffered and achieved. That month, September, had seen an output of aircraft that had not been exceeded throughout the entire war—4,103 machines, mostly fighters. Whereas, when she and Dieter had made their propaganda tour of the aircraft industry in 1942 there had been just twenty-seven major works making practically everything, Speer had dispersed manufacture into 729 small and very small plants. These were in caves, mines, forests, ravines, even disguised as barns in country villages. Speer's master plan had worked and Liese did not deny that her father-in-law's organising ability had played no small part in the success. She also recognised that Helmuth Reh was not a man who could handle success well. It sent him into a state of nationalistic euphoria which clouded his judgement.

Liese had no such illusions. It was not a question of whether Germany would disappear in a final political and military earthquake, but *when*. She was close enough to the centre of events to feel the shiftings of the ground beneath her feet, just as vast sliding plates of rock are said to shift along the major fault-lines of the earth before a seismic cataclysm. Germany, in late 1944, was one vast fault-line and the shiftings in her case were shiftings of power.

In a less sensitive way, Herr Reh's personal seismograph had recorded these also. As far as he was concerned, the danger was that he would place the wrong interpretation upon them. In olden times, the appearance of a comet was said to presage the coming of great events, usually calamities. Herr Reh was very apt to attach himself to the tail of the latest comet in the political sky. Liese noticed that the picture of a new Party leader had recently joined the Nazi pantheon on his desk—that of SS Chief Heinrich Himmler.

In the inspector of fighter's department Heinrich Himmler's

name was a dirty word. On 23 September the general had come stumping back from a meeting at the Führer's HQ at Rastenburg spitting fire. As the squashy, fat sun of the *Reichsmarschall* stubbed itself out low down on the horizon, Himmler's star was rising in the blood red sky. The SS chief was making his influence felt where he was least expected or wanted.

The conference had been about a project which the general, Trautloft, Mano, everyone with any experience or grey matter, knew to be utterly lunatic—the *Volksjäger*, the "People's Fighter", a conception about as suitable for aerial warfare, and certainly not as useful, as the prewar people's car. For months past, the Air Ministry had been inviting aircraft manufacturers to come up with a design for a simple, cheap, easily flown jet fighter. This very description was a contradiction in terms. The general had told everyone concerned this from the outset, in his masterly, tactless and direct fashion. Only in a Germany descending fast into anarchy, defeat and dissolution could such an idea have been taken seriously. At Rastenburg, Saur, chief of fighter production, *had* taken it seriously. Moreover he had obviously gone out on a limb for the *Volksjäger* because he knew that he had powerful and dangerous backing. Himmler! Without any knowledge or experience of aerial warfare, the little SS chief had seized upon the people's fighter as a political tool with which to move in on Goering's crumbling preserve.

Because Speer had, of his own accord, stopped production of the out-dated Heinkel 111 bomber, indeed of all bombers save the jet Arado 234 B, the Heinkel factory had time and workmen on its hands and was well placed to get the contract. The winning design, the He 162, was about as simple and unsophisticated as a flying bomb and just as lethal to its pilot. It was economical of materials because it was largely built of wood. Its crews would be expendable, because—and here was the bit that really made the general blow his top—they were to be drawn from the *Hitlerjugend*, after a short preliminary training on gliders. Imagine it! Kids without powered aircraft experience, let alone jet flying time, being ordered into this flying coffin and told to save the Reich at the eleventh hour. The general had let everybody at the conference table know what he thought of the idea and, by not very subtle inference, what he thought of those who supported it.

In a calmer moment, the general had tried to persuade the conference that such a hare-brained scheme could only detract from production of the two machines that now mattered, the Me 262 and the rocket-powered Messerschmitt 163, the so-called "Power Egg".

Goering had virtually ordered the general to shut up. "This is fantastic," the *Reichsmarschall* had moaned to everyone present. "The general of fighters stands here and tells us he doesn't want a jet fighter plane that can be produced by the thousand within months."

Worse had followed: within an hour of the conference ending, the Führer had got to hear of the general's stand and had demanded from him his reason in writing for turning the *Volksjäger* down.

In a moment of troubled confidence, Trautloft told all this to Mano next day. "From now on, they'll all be gunning for our general. You watch. Once that kind of thing happens, they'll pull his seat from under him. He's spoken out once too often. The bloody *Gauleiters* will be taking over our business from now on. They'll do everything except the flying and dying."

Two days later Mano was summoned to attend Karl Saur's production conference at the Ministry of Munitions. Even the level-headed Saur had caught the general hysteria. "I tell you, with Himmler's backing we'll turn out hundreds, thousands, tens of thousands!"

Deeply depressed, Mano went round to see Liese afterwards. Helmuth Reh caught sight of him in her office. "Come in, my dear Major Rumpler. Isn't the news tremendous? We've won the day with the *Volksjäger*. Now we'll really see some sparks fly! Did you know that production and training is to be in the hands of hand-picked special *Gauleiters?* I hope you won't think me immodest if I mention that I am to be one of them."

"Congratulations," said Mano drily. He pointed to the picture of Himmler now displayed well to the forefront on the desk. "I'm delighted to see that you are backed by such a well-known patron of aeronautics."

The day of the *Gauleiters* had indeed dawned.

Yet, even in this mad-hatter's world, all was not completely insane, though one came to doubt whether even the sane decisions weren't just the haphazard ravings of madmen. Whatever their origins, one had to be thankful when they turned up.

Though the general's influence was waning rapidly, though he was little more than tolerated as the German armies fell back to the Rhine, OKL had surprisingly agreed to one long-standing plea. Even Goering backed it. The general was being permitted to conserve Speer's astonishing output of fighters rather than waste them on the new Rhine front. OKL, even

Goering, had at last listened to him when he asked for between two and three thousand fighters to strike the American raiders one great blow.

It may have been the time of *Gauleiters*, but it was also the time of slogans. OKL had latched on to the general's phrase. Everyone was now talking of the "Great Blow".

Despite all the difficulties, the Me 262 jet test unit at Lechfeld had begun to score successes against the American raiders. It was a frustrating business. At best there were six jet fighters in service. Dispersed about the airfield, however, were up to sixty 262s being converted into Blitz Bombers—the Führer's dream weapon. The Reh brothers and Oberfeldwebel Pohle looked upon this scene with despair. No fighter pilot, even those like themselves who were earmarked for jet service, was allowed to touch those machines. The three of them had to be content with flying piston-engined Messerschmitts. Their job was to protect the Blitz Bombers on the ground and to provide landing and take-off cover for the handful of jet fighters that were permitted to fly against the daylight raiders.

The total absurdity of the situation was vividly illustrated one autumn day when the Fortresses and Liberators once more turned their attention to Lechfeld and Augsburg. General Spaatz had become increasingly worried by intelligence reports about the numbers of 262s revealed on these two airfields by photo reconnaissance. The three 109 pilots got the order to scramble in good time. Their job was to look out for Mustangs or Thunderbolts who might try to ground-attack the airfield. This time there were no low-level American fighters. Dieter and his two companions, flying at a few thousand feet to cover the take-off of the six Lechfeld jets, met no opposition. The six jets successfully fastened on to the last box of Fortresses and destroyed three. By that time the bombs dropped by the rest of the Americans had wrecked practically all the 262 jet "Blitz Bombers" parked on the airfield. The general used the disaster to pound on OKL's door once again. If only half the destroyed, so-called Blitz Bombers, had been ready as fighters, he argued, there might have been thirty American bombers shot down instead of three.

This time, unpredictably, someone was listening. In October, the *Reichsmarschall* suddenly saw the light, though it gradually emerged that the man who was holding it directly in front of his face was none other than Heinrich Himmler. Goering sent for the general and told him that he had decided to allow the formation of a squadron of jet fighters to be built round the test unit at Lechfeld. He explained grandly that he had finally persuaded the Führer to release one 262 for fighter service in exchange for each of the new Arado 234 B bombers that went into bomber squadrons. But he had needed the backing of SS Chief Himmler to go even this far.

Breaking the good news to Mano, Günther Lützow, inspector of day fighters, said: "I suppose we shouldn't complain who helps us, but no one really wants those SS swine interfering in our business. They're just using us in their own power game." He gave an ironically exaggerated Nazi salute as he cried: "Heil Himmler."

Kate Bristow got her wish. She crossed the Channel with key Ops Room personnel. There was no longer any object in fighter staff staying behind in Britain. Mustangs, Thunderbolts, Spitfires, Typhoons and Tempests; they were all operating from bases spread across northern France, Belgium, Holland and virtually up to the German border. When the Eighth Air Force bombers flew from England now, the Europe-based fighters met them with full tanks that gave them latitude to wander at will over the Reich.

Peter flew from Brussels almost daily. Kate knew that her brother could have pulled out; he'd more than earned a senior job on the ground. But like Charles, sick and tired as he was of the whole business, Peter could not call a halt now. He had to keep flying almost as a conditioned reflex. Though he told his sister that the risks were getting smaller every day, he knew that this was far from true. The Luftwaffe showed some nasty signs of rejuvenation. God knows how they did it. New packs of 109s and 190s would appear from time to time and give the bombers a hammering. He'd seen the jets go through a Fortress formation, slicing it in half as if with a cheese wire, and he'd realised that the Mustang he sat in, so recently the most sophisticated fighter that flew, was already old-fashioned. You couldn't lay a glove on the German jets. Thank God there were only a few of them! As that bitter European winter tightened its grip on the armies, Peter and those who flew with him felt an unutterable G-force of tiredness pressing them down. It was so bloody cold. Arnhem had gone by in disaster. There seemed no hope of shortening the war, just a long slogging match until the inevitable end came. By then, how many of his colleagues would have bought it? Many, many, many. It was time they all went home. But meantime there was the engine to be started in the freezing dawn, the crawl into the cramped cockpit, the low level sweep and the high altitude escort to meet the bombers. Everyone was just tired to bloody death of it. Why didn't the bloody Huns know when they'd had it?

In East Anglia, Charles felt the same despair in the bomber crews he debriefed. Flak and fighters were still knocking them off. For what? Did it matter now how many tons of bombs they dropped on each square yard of Germany? Mere bombing didn't seem to make any difference. And now the jets. So far they were just bad luck for those who had tangled with them. But there'd be more and more coming if the war didn't stop soon. And even if the bomber crews survived Europe, what had the Army in store for them? They'd be sent to Japan to get killed bombing Nips.

As intelligence officer, Charles heard all this and more. He didn't underestimate the German jet threat, nor did his superiors all the way up to, and including, General Spaatz. Charles was still forbidden to fly, but as IO he had to know what was going on. On the pretext of having a first-hand look at the jet menace, he hopped a lift in a short-handed Fortress going to Leipzig. They didn't meet any 262s but they were set upon by a suicidal group of FW 190 Storm Fighters who pressed their attack to within twenty yards' range, and picked off six of the twenty-five Fortresses in the smaller tighter formation they now flew. One of these 190s was flown by Gerhard Stecke. No, the Luftwaffe fighter force was far from dead. Charles, in the co-pilot's seat, was shit-scared all the way there and all the way back. But his crew and plane survived without a scratch, and that only left two more to get his tour completed.

A Mustang pilot who had force-landed at Brussels reported having seen Kate there. Charles toyed with the idea of writing and telling her that he had made another trip, but decided not. No need to worry her. He had only two more missions to fly to get the set. Then he could relax.

Mano sought out Liese whenever she was in Berlin on business with her father-in-law. She was the one sane person to whom he could really speak his mind. Mano, who had never been able to form warm permanent attachments, except to his parents, was aware that for the first time in his life he really cared about at least two people. Dieter and Liese Reh. Or rather three people, since soon there would be the child. In focusing all his regard in their direction he was doing much the same as Liese herself. If only the Rehs could be allowed to survive they were the material of which a new, different Germany must be made when all the madness was burned out to ashes. About Dieter's survival he could do nothing. Like Liese, he privately rated his chances as very small. Losses even among the most experienced pilots were tremendous. Now there was a trickle of jets going through, one of which Dieter would most certainly soon be flying, but jets in themselves were no guarantee of immunity. Mano was only too aware that there were operational hazards and teething troubles even with the miracle 262.

Mano had business at the Air Ministry with Helmuth Reh that dreary November day. He had no heart for the discussion. It concerned fixing a date on which the inspector of day fighters might expect to witness the first demonstration flight of the *Volksjäger*, the He 162. The inspector was as disgusted and uninterested in this crazy product of crazy and ignorant official minds as anyone else. Like the general, both Mano's bosses, Johannes Trautloft and Günther Lützow, wished to see this string-and-sugar-box, do-it-yourself jet fighter consigned to the scrap heap, and the men and materials wasted on it channelled towards 262 production. With Goering behind it, and Himmler behind him, they had at least to go through the motions.

Helmuth Reh greeted Mano effusively. It was noticeable that since his elevation to *Gauleiterdom*, he had become more expansive towards Mano in a rather patronising way. Mano remained bland and unruffled, simply asking himself how it was possible for such a pipsqueak of a father to have sired sons like Dieter and Jacob.

"My dear Major Rumpler. You've heard the good news?"

"You mean about the formation of a 262 squadron at last."

"No, no, no." He brushed this aside as if it barely mattered. "The *Volksjäger*. It's going to be ready to fly within the month. Imagine it! Only two and a half months since the meeting at which we agreed to take this historic step. I tell you, the Heinkel 162 will change the course of the war."

Mano looked at the photograph of the beady-eyed SS Chief on Reh's desk.

"Remarkable," he said drily. "When can we expect a demonstration of this wonder machine?"

Reh senior's eyes were shining. "I have just been talking to Heinkel's chief designer this morning. He's confident enough to propose a flying exhibition for you experts at the end of the first week in December. For secrecy's sake and to keep the People's Fighter away from prying American eyes we're proposing to unveil it at Vienna-Schwechat. I hope you'll be attending, Major."

"I wouldn't miss it for worlds, Herr Gauleiter Reh. Do you mind if I take your secretary out to lunch?"

Herr Reh was already on the phone. He broke off. "Liese? You won't find her very good company, I'm afraid. You'd think she'd be happy with the baby coming."

Berlin was like an old battered skull, grey, full of ghastly, grinning gaps, its skyline a crenellation of burned-out buildings like stumps of dead and broken teeth. Even so, there were still one or two cellars where a staff officer, at least, could find something to eat. It was incredible how the city still lived on after the pounding it had taken, a beating, Mano was convinced, that would go on and on until the last flicker had been exterminated.

"Come," he said guiding her down the stairs into the shattered and patched *Bierkeller*. "I have half a bottle of cognac to tip into our delicious cabbage soup."

She laughed for the first time. "The baby won't like that."

"Nonsense. Cognac is made from grapes. It's very healthy."

When they had found a seat, he said: "Liese, why don't you give up your job and get out of this city? Dieter would want you to, for the baby's sake."

"I'm hardly five months' pregnant yet."

"Even so, spending half your time in this hell-hole and the rest tearing about with the *Gauleiter* is no good to either of you."

"Mano, what news of Dieter?"

"Good news, my dear. Now the general's got permission to form the Lechfeld 262 test unit into an operational squadron, Dieter will be one of the first to get a jet. You know what that means?" Mano wanted it to sound as safe as a job in a bank. "First of all, he'll have to do a conversion course, so he'll be off operational flying for at least a month. By then the war might even be over."

"You mean lost?"

"Yes, lost. Since we can't win it, it's only a question of when we actually lose."

"What makes us go on?"

"Who do you mean by *us*? There are many different sorts of *us*. If you mean our magnificent leaders, the answer is because they have no choice but to drag everything down with them. If you mean people like Dieter, you and me, then it's part national and professional pride and part, I honestly believe, because many of us feel in our hearts that we deserve what's being handed out to us. Even Goering once said that the bombing was being borne by the German people like a retribution from God. What God? Wotan? We're seeing a real life twilight of the gods—all gods. Berlin itself is like a huge film set for *Götterdämmerung*. I've always detested that bore Wagner."

"Give me Mozart."

"Style and elegance, yes. That's what our leaders have sadly lacked."

She laughed. "But not you, Mano. You come from an elegant baroque city, remember."

"Ah, Dresden! I'm glad you mentioned that lovely place. Liese, early in the New Year you'll have to stop working anyway. When is the baby due?"

"About the third week in March."

"Good. Then I want you to promise me to go to my parents in Dresden in January."

"I shall work as long as I can."

"Very well, but you must promise. I can arrange transport somehow. You'll be safe in Dresden. There's nothing to bomb it for."

"We'll see."

"My mother would love to look after you."

"I'd like that."

"I'll take that as a promise, then."

"We'll see."

For the next ten days, Mano had no time to visit Liese, who was staying on with Helmuth Reh in Berlin. Things were moving fast. The general had got his way at last. Everyone, from chairborne warriors at OKL to secretaries on Albert Speer's fighter production staff, talked of the "Great Blow". It really was quite staggering what German aircraft workers had achieved. The general's reserve had built up until it consisted of nearly 3,000 109s and 190s, some of the latter being the new long-nosed type, the Ta 152, with the twelve-cylinder inline engine. There were pilots for all these fighters. There was no shortage of young men, even at this late hour, to volunteer as fighter pilots. Perhaps most of them weren't very experienced, or even very competent, but it was far better that they should fly, and if necessary die, in aircraft that were battle-proven, if now out of date, rather than crash in Heinrich Himmler's and Karl Saur's orange crate, the People's Fighter. In acknowledging the triumph of the German workers, Mano was not blind to the untold thousands of Jews, prisoners and political undesirables whom Speer's ministry had worked

340

sometimes literally to death and often in appalling conditions to rebuild bombed plants and set up new ones. No thinking man could forget that part of it, but what choice was there but to plunge on and atone, if possible, later?

By mid-November, the general's plans for the "Great Blow" were ready. Mano attended a briefing for all *Kommodores* and squadron commanders at Treuenbrietzen. There, strategic details were worked out down to the last move. The general was at the top of his form, almost feverish in his intensity, puffing away at his famous cheroots, leaping up to emphasise points on the map. Watching him Mano thought: "Here is a man playing his last card, with his last mark and knowing that, unless someone's been dealing from the bottom of the pack, he must win this hand."

The "Great Blow" was to be everything the general and the fighter arm had dreamed of. Two thousand fighters in eleven combat formations would hit the American bomber stream as it made its approach to the target. A further 650 fighters would attack the *dicker Hund* on its run in and as it turned for home. Every fighter that could be refuelled and rearmed would harry the survivors back as far as the Allied escort permitted. German losses of 400 aircraft and 150 pilots would be acceptable in return for an American contribution of at least 400 bombers. It would indeed be the largest and most decisive air battle of the entire war.

By 12 November, 18 *Geschwader* with 3,700 aircraft and pilots stood ready. All that was required now was for the treacherous winter weather to co-operate. Knowing what was at stake for his beloved fighter arm, Mano bit his nails almost up to the elbow. But still the weather refused to relent. The general, like the good poker player he was, played it cool. Each day the Americans came in greater numbers. To scramble the "Great Blow" in conditions that made it impossible for inexperienced pilots to form up for the essential mass attacks would be like a boxer hitting at empty air. Surprisingly, almost suspiciously, everyone, even the *Reichsmarschall* and OKL, kept cool heads.

The weather must surely change soon, but conditions of heavy cloud and icing continued well into mid-November.

Suddenly the blow, but not the "Great Blow", fell. The general was summoned to Goering's medieval hunting lodge at Karinhall and told to prepare the entire fighter force for a great and final land battle in the West. Someone *had* been dealing from the bottom of the pack after all. The general reasoned and then raved, but by now his influence was so small

341

that nothing he did or said mattered. He argued that his pilots had never been trained in a ground support role because petrol supplies hadn't permitted; that most of these youngsters had a fifty-fifty chance of surviving their first few missions in defence of the Reich, but none at all against hedge-hopping Mustangs and Thunderbolts, flak, not to mention Tempests and Typhoons: that squadron strengths of *his* "Great Blow" had been built up to seventy aircraft, a formation much too large for any forward airfield to handle. At last he understood that he had been cheated, that the great blow for which he and Speer had created their third and final reserve was not *their* "Great Blow" and never had been. It was the Führer's.

On 20 November the general received his orders—to transfer all those precious fighters to the army in the West. Only two wings, plus a few jets, were to be allowed to remain behind in the Reich. Even then Goering did not condescend to tell him exactly why OKL had turned all his plans upside down. He wasn't to learn what it was all about for nearly a fortnight yet. Meantime there was another farce to be played out.

For the big occasion Helmuth Reh had got himself a new pair of rimless glasses. He fancied they gave him a more than superficial resemblance to his new Party idol. Heinrich Himmler could not be at Vienna-Schwechat airfield that tenth day of December. No doubt he had other things on his mind. The Reich needed his disciplinary guidance at this moment when faintheartedness and even treachery was likely to take advantage of a temporarily adverse military situation.

The SS was well represented, however, too well represented for Mano Rumpler's taste. The bastards were everywhere these days. Helmuth Reh arrived in the third car of Karl Saur's entourage. After some careful elbow work he managed to get into the second row of VIPs behind Saur and Heinkel's chief designer.

The He 162 looked as smart as new paint. It stood neat and small on the concrete apron on its tricycle undercarriage. The features that struck Mano's eye immediately were the dihedral angled tailplane with fins and rudders at the extremities; the large jet engine, not unlike the stove-pipe ram-jet of a V1, only more streamlined and perched on top of the fuselage, behind the cockpit.

The *Volksjäger*, he had to admit, was a quite amazing production seeing that it had been born in under three months. Heinkel's chief test pilot Flugkapitän Peter wriggled his way into the narrow cockpit. Mechanics closed the streamlined canopy over his head. The turbo-jet started with the now familiar ear-piercing scream. The People's Fighter certainly looked good. It took off with the minimum of fuss and climbed away smoothly, leaving a black streak in the December sky. As it faded quickly out of sight, Mano saw Saur talking enthusiastically to the Heinkel chiefs, Helmuth Reh's new glasses were fairly gleaming with ecstasy. The *Volksjäger* was coming back for its first low-level pass across the airfield. Even Mano felt quite carried away by its appearance and sound. It was traveling at around 450 mph when Flugkapitän Peter pulled its nose up steeply into the start of a loop. At once the starboard wing began to flutter and pieces break off. In a second the aileron and the whole of the leading edge had torn away. The *Volksjäger* disintegrated in the air and hit the ground in a mushroom of black smoke just outside the airfield. The silence when the engine stopped was almost more shocking than the explosion which followed. For at least ten seconds not one of the distinguished spectators broke the silence.

The 262s had arrived, three of them, of which one was allotted to the former members of the *Erprobungs-kommando*. To learn to fly the jet, Dieter soon discovered, one had almost to go back to school. The tricycle undercarriage had solved the problems of take-off. The tail was now in the jet stream from the moment you opened the throttles. Landing, however, called for precise judgement since the thing insisted on making its approach at 150 mph. The Jumo 004 jet engines were not exactly reliable, especially when being started and at take-off. Initial take-off acceleration was sluggish. Unless handled exactly right the engines had an uncomfortable readiness to blow back and catch fire. They were liable to compressor stalls on landing. Once airborne, the plane was a miracle. As the general had said eighteen months previously: it felt as if angels were pushing. Air fighting tactics had to be learned from scratch. The Lechfeld test commando pilots had quickly found that the accepted head-on attack on Fortresses was useless. With a combined closing speed of over 800 mph, firing time was far too short. It was back to the stern attack, diving down at sub-sonic speeds which gave the American gunners a nearly impossible mark, then shooting under the *dicker Hund* to pull up well ahead in order to climb and position oneself for another pass from astern. The 262 was so ridiculously fast that one could literally run rings round the bomber formations. This did not, however, mean that a jet pilot could

343

afford to ignore the escort. Though 125 mph faster than a Mustang, the 262 had little manoeuvrability by comparison. Any conventional piston-engined fighter could turn on a six-pence compared with the jet and it didn't do to forget this simple fact. Straight speed and, for that matter, speed *straight* was the recipe for avoiding unwelcome fighter attention. At the most a turn through a quarter of a circle was all that was safe with Mustangs around. Another fact that soon became clear was that the trusty *Schwarm* of two mutually protective *Rotten* was out. The jets needed too much individual airspace for close formation flying. Come to that, they needed a fair amount of ground space, also. Most runways were too narrow to allow four 262s to take off together. So it was back to the almost forgotten three aircraft *Kette* of pre-Mölders days. It was incredible how an advance in technology called for an apparent retrogression in technique. If feasible, three jets took off together. They made their attack together, deadly as a *Staffel* of three times three. But they seldom contacted each other once the firing pass had been made. Speeds were too high for there to be any question of wingmen and mutual cover. Nor did they bother to form up once the attack was over. They relied on sheer speed to get them out of trouble, individually. The Mustangs and Thunderbolts soon cottoned on to the fact that the 262s were most vulnerable when joining the landing pattern at their home airfield and this was how the first jet wing commander of them all, Walther Nowotny, met his end.

On that winter's day, Dieter was not flying. Fifteen minutes earlier his brother Jacob had taken off under Nowotny's command in the only available 262 to attack some American heavies headed for the jet base at Achmer. It was a special day for young Jacob. For one thing it was the first time he had been permitted to fly in combat with the brilliant twenty-three-year-old Austrian who had been picked by the general to form JG 7, the first jet fighter wing authorised by Goering's special dispensation. As far as character and leadership went he had inherited the mantle of Werner Mölders. He equalled Marseille for sheer panache and spirit. The general had often been heard to say that Austrians had the ideal temperament as fighter pilots; they had style combined with seriousness of purpose and dedication. Every time Dieter heard someone quote the general on this score, he thought sadly of the gallant Willy Weiss. Nowotny, holder of the Diamonds to the Knight's Cross, victor of 258 air battles, was what Willy might have become if he had lived.

It was a special day not only for Jacob Reh who flew with his jet *Kommodore* but for every pilot on the base. The general had invited Generaloberst Keller, an officer chosen for a key post in the defence of the Reich, to witness in person what the 262 could accomplish against the American bomber streams.

Orders for off-duty flying personnel were perfectly clear. Immediately a raid was reported they were to take to the shelters. Pilots were too precious to risk having them killed on the ground by American heavies or fighter-bombers. Like many pilots, Dieter preferred the open air to die in, if dying was the order of the day. So he shared the slit trenches at dispersal with his ground crew. On this morning he shared this precarious protection with the faithful corporal, now sergeant, Streib and with Elsa, Leo Feuchter's Alsatian bitch who had followed him equally faithfully from airfield to airfield.

Above the six-tenths cloud they could hear the drone of the heavies. They were up at 20,000 feet or more. Lower down the rattle of machine-guns and slower plop of cannon fire told Dieter that the fighters had met with American escort opposition. He wondered whether the jets had reached the *dicker Hund* or if they were tangling with the Mustangs. Possibly the dogfight was between the Mustangs and the Focke Wulf *Gruppe* sent up to cover the jets' take-off and landing. The issue wasn't left long in doubt. The whine of an approaching 262 blotted out every other sound. A jet in trouble was coming in, trying to make the field under an umbrella of light flak. Dieter's first fear was that it was Jacob. The 262 was obviously in difficulties, with one wing low: a stalled engine. Behind came a pack of Mustangs. Suddenly the jet reared up, flicked over and dived vertically into the airfield. As the fuselage flashed briefly into the black cloud of the explosion, Dieter glimpsed its markings. Nowotny. Walther Nowotny was dead.

When Mano Rumpler got the news of where the fighter reserve was going he couldn't believe it. The general had only been let into this military secret on 14 December, a couple of days before the battle opened, and he couldn't believe it either.

Nothing made sense or mattered any more now. These, assuredly, were madmen he had to serve. They had treated him like a stooge. Perhaps that was all he was. The reserve of 3,000 fighters that he and Speer had so laboriously and lovingly built up were about to be poured down a drain. And the drain was called the Ardennes. As long ago as July, it seemed, the Führer had decided to gamble everything on one last throw. Some of the chips to be squandered on this personal Zero were all that remained of the Luftwaffe fighter arm. Hitler had promised the army strong air support and the general's precious reserve was it. No one knew better than the general that flying close-support was a highly specialised job. Had not he himself done just that in a Henschel 123 in Spain and then in Poland? But these lads. Not one of them had had the training that such an exacting role demanded. And as the Wehrmacht prepared for its surprise attack on the Americans, the weather was about as bad as it could be. Snow, ice and high freezing winds. Not weather for ground support. The reserve would be swallowed up more surely than it had been during the retreat across France, and to as little purpose.

For the general, all sense in continuing the struggle finished at this point. The general was too good a soldier to let his mood spread to his colleagues. But desperation did not need a carrier among the fighter staff. As New Year 1945 approached, conditions were right for the spread of what, in terms of loss of morale, amounted to a black plague of the spirit.

The German offensive in the Ardennes knocked the gaiety out of New Year's Eve celebrations in the RAF mess at Brussels. Peter Bristow was aware that he should have felt some elation. This year, soon now, the war must end and then they could all go home. They should have been celebrating the last Christmas of hostilities. Instead the pilots found themselves wondering gloomily how long it could go on. The damned Huns didn't seem to know when to give up. This Ardennes business was simply the living or maybe the dying end. Instead of being able to relax, they had been flying up to three sorties daily. Peter had lost five pilots from his wing that very day. Three shot down by light flak. One had hit a house in a snow squall while shooting up German armour moving through a village. The fifth had fallen to a long-nosed 190. Tomorrow it would the the same story all over again. You would have thought that after the hammering the Germans had taken they would have had nothing, neither planes nor spirit, left to fight with.

After dinner Kate came over from the Ops Room to see the New Year in with her brother.

They raised their glasses to each other.

"Happy New Year, Peter."

"*Happier* New Year, Kate. How's Charles? Keeping out of trouble, I hope."

"He's still not allowed to fly, thank God. I only hope he's got the good sense to take advantage of the fact."

"Are you going to marry him?"

"Yes. Do you mind?"

"Mind? I'm thrilled. It's time you settled down."

She smiled. "Yes. I feel like that, too."

Peter looked shifty. She knew the look from when he was a little boy. It meant that he had some confidence he wished to impart but didn't quite dare. In the old days she'd have teased him into telling her. Now she just waited, smiling.

At last he fished in his wallet.

"I was turning out my gear today, Kate. I found some photos in the bottom of an old kit bag, stuffed in a battle-dress pocket. Do you mind if I show them to you?"

It was her turn to say. "Mind? Why should I?"

He held out a heavily crumpled print showing two young men proudly holding guns in front of half a dozen dead rabbits laid out on the grass.

At first she didn't recognise either of them, the photograph was so badly creased. Then she saw that one was Peter. She was so used to his burned face now that she had almost forgotten what he had looked like before the war.

Peter saw her puzzlement and said: "You remember. That German chap who came to stay with us. The one you were so keen on."

"Dieter," she said, without a pang. "Dieter Reh. I wonder if he's alive now. I suppose not. He was in it at the beginning."

"He probably bought it during the Battle of Britain. They lost an awful lot of their regulars then. It's all a long time ago now, but I thought you might like to see it before I chuck it away."

"No, don't do that, not after keeping it all this time. It's a bit of the past. It's so far away I can hardly seem to remember it."

A gang of Peter's pilots came barging over.

"Hey, you two. What the hell are you so serious about? Break it up! Come on, Katie. Let's dance. The weather's so bloody awful that, with luck, ops will be cancelled tomorrow."

A squadron leader turned the radio up. Glenn Miller was playing the New Year in on the American Forces Network. The tune was "Long Ago and Far Away."

The orders were baffling, yet that was normal these days. At Achmer, Dieter, Jacob and Pohle still shared one 262 between them. More were promised daily. In this one jet Jacob had already scored his first kill—a Liberator—his forty-fourth. The two who were not flying the jet on any given day operated as part of the Focke Wulf conventional fighter cover for the airfield. But now, just before New Year's Day, these orders had been changed. Part of the Focke Wulf cover *Gruppe,* including Dieter and Pohle, had been told to report to a forward airfield in Holland. They flew there on the morning of New Year's Eve in conditions of low cloud, snow flurries and icing. It was the sort of weather in which only the most experienced cross-country pilots would attempt such a flight. There could be no question of trying to keep a large formation together in such muck, and so they flew by *Rotten.* It was no surprise to either Dieter or Pohle to learn on touching down that three of the eighteen 109s and 190s that had left Achmer hadn't made it. What was more surprising was the number of fighters dispersed about the airfield. As well as long-nosed and radial-engined FWs, there were many variants of 109gs, including some new to Dieter with the so-called Galland Hood, a more streamlined cockpit canopy with vastly improved visibility. There were night-fighters, 110s, 410s and Ju 88s, as well as a pair of the new bomber version of the 88, the Ju 188. Immense care had been taken to hide as many fighters as possible. Because of the persistent snow of the past week, ground staff had even sprayed all camouflage nets white.

Pohle said: "I didn't know we'd got this much air force left."

They struggled in out of the cold and reported themselves landed.

"One of your chaps bailed out on the way. Two are down in the polders out of fuel, both written off, one dead."

"What's it all about?" Dieter asked. "It can't be the Ardennes, we're too far north."

"Sorry, can't tell you. Briefing at 1800 hours. Until then, no one leaves the dispersal huts to which they've been allotted."

The briefing came as a complete surprise. It was given by a senior wing commander whose reputation was a by-word. The weathermen promised a clear, cold day tomorrow. At first light, aircraft would take off by units as detailed. They would form up over an assembly point north of the Zuider Zee where they would be joined by other formations of fighters making a total force of 300 strong. The target for fighters from this field would be Brussels-Evère air base where photo recce reported Spitfires, Mustangs, Tempests and Typhoons drawn up as if on a parade ground. Navigation of the whole formation would be in the hands of a Ju 188 that would lead them to within five miles of the target. To defeat enemy early warning systems, they would fly at nought feet. Surprise must be complete. At almost the same moment, similar mass formations would be attacking airfields in the vicinity of Eindhoven and the American forward bases beyond Venlo. Twenty-seven Allied bases would be struck all told. It was to be the "Great Blow" that would wipe the Americans and British from the air above *Herbstnebel*, "Autumn Fog", the Führer's personally chosen code name for the offensive in the Ardennes.

"Good luck, gentlemen," said the wing commander. "And, if you take my advice, you'll get some sleep tonight, New Year's Eve or not."

Outside the briefing room, Pohle caught Dieter's sleeve. "Take care tomorrow," he said. "This is just the kind of party where you can stop one through no fault of your own."

Dieter clapped him on the back. "Just you stick close to me, old friend. At least it's something to be attacking once again."

1945

No one slept well. The faithful "blackmen" had been out at the dispersal points running up the parked fighters' engines every half hour. It was the only guarantee they would start when needed in the sub-zero temperatures. The pilots were called an hour and a half before first light. They shuffled down to the mess cursing, to drink some *ersatz* coffee and snatch a hot breakfast. For once the cooks had made a special effort.

Streib had the 190 ticking over when he climbed into the cockpit. *Jesu!* It was cold. Automatically he made his cockpit check and switched on the radio. It was still dark enough for the blue exhaust flames to be blinding. To port he saw Pohle giving the thumbs up sign. A *Schwarm* of 109s from JG 3 swung off the perimeter track ahead on to the main runway, their propellers kicking up a blizzard of loose, fine snow. The dawn was coming up dirty grey as if reluctant to show its face on New Year, 1945. Streib was closing his cockpit canopy and banging on it to wish him good luck. *Hals- und Beinbruch!* It was a long time since anyone had had the spirit to give the traditional airman's parting wish for good fortune. The tower was calling his formation number for take-off. Dieter opened the throttle, saw Pohle turning beside him and a few seconds later was clearing the airfield boundary with his wheels already up.

Day began to come up, tinting the snow fifty feet below flamingo pink. It was beautiful at first, quickly turning to an angry blood red. An omen? Little time for such reflections while hedge-hopping across a landscape which was virtually featureless, a white-out. Rendezvous point coming up now, into a gradual left-hand turn, watching for the others, waiting for the pathfinder Ju 188 to come through on the course that would take them to their target. The mixed gaggle of Messerschmitts and Focke Wulfs fell in behind the 188 in loose formation. No crowding. Just the right distance between *Schwärme*. These were old, picked hands. At the edge of the Zuider Zee, two more large packs joined them. Everything dead on schedule and now the elephant-grey waters, scarcely marked with a ripple this still and frozen New Year's Day, sliding beneath their wings.

There was no one to see them. No one to give the alarm. A Taylorcraft Auster, artillery-spotting north of Eindhoven, nearly fell out of the sky when he saw a familiar formation heading across the frontier at nought feet. About the time Dieter Reh, palms sweating, was lining up on the control tower at Brussels-Evère, the observer in that Auster was radioing frantically: "At least 200 German fighters flying low on course 320." But by then it was too late for Eindhoven also.

Peter Bristow had just left the Ops Room at Brussels with a favourable met report for the day and an unfavourable hangover from last night's celebrations when the first Focke Wulf came in flat-out over the main runway. He threw himself flat as he heard the cannon open up, saw the flickers on the German's leading edge and the mushrooms of fire opening up along a line of parked Spits. One, two, three, they exploded and collapsed in crimson balls. The second Focke Wulf, Pohle's, passed so close that he could see the oil streaks on its belly behind the engine cowling. Cheeky bastards! And then he thought: "Where the hell's my vehicle? Must get to dispersal in case there are any more about." Peter got up and began to run, looking for a fifteen hundredweight and a duty driver. The next few seconds were confused. He had the impression that the ground all around him, even beneath his feet, was spurting dust. The sky was full of aircraft, all of them Jerries. The place was going mad. A lorry passed him out of control, the driver dead, a Focke Wulf giving it a squirt until it turned aside into an already burning, parked Dakota. Now the Bofors were opening up. Three Spits had tried to get airborne. He saw the leader, caught in the crossfire, slide sideways, scarcely having gained airspeed, taking the left-hand machine with him into the ground. Then a Jeep slowed beside him with one of his flight leaders driving. "Come on, Peter, for Christ's sake. The bastards have jumped us." He clambered aboard with one thought: to get the hell out of this inferno in a Mustang as soon as possible—if there was a Mustang left to fly.

The first two passes had been easy, but Dieter still had ammunition left. Brussels-Evère was like a hornets' nest now into which someone had stuck a great big boot. He had ammunition and there was still a line of fighters on the perimeter track unattended to. Five miles south of the field Dieter turned. "Going in once more. Take the east of the field. Right down on the deck. Are you with me?"

"With you," he heard Pohle answer.

Ahead a long-nosed 109 hit a haystack, hurling it up in a great incandescent cloud of fragments. Tempests! Some RAF Tempests had somehow got airborne from the shambles. One levelled out in front of him. He saw the great greedy airscoop below the nose, the knife-edge of the long wings, the twelve-foot disc of the propeller. Now that *was* a fighter. He fired as he lined up for his final run in. The Tempest never knew he was there and went straight in through the ice of a frozen lake.

Dieter bunched himself in his cockpit to make himself as small as possible. They came in six feet above the boundary hedge and the flak was ready for them. Lazy blobs of Bofors tracer that suddenly speeded up unimaginably fast. Yellow Oerlikon, 20 mm stuff. Fifty calibres. The lot. Two 109s colliding in mid-field. A 190 ahead had got in first, blowing up the group of Spits on which Dieter had had his eye. He kicked right rudder, nearly digging his wing into the ground, brought his guns to bear on a Dakota which burst into flames amidships and collapsed like a toy. Nearly out now but a glimpse of a tall tail hidden behind a sand-bagged bay. Back on the stick and then nose down for a final burst and a Fortress in a maintenance area burning under the last of his cannon fire. The click of breeches slamming shut on empty space. Shot out and still alive! Bathed in sweat, Dieter looked round for Pohle, saw him stuck to his tail like a shadow.

"Okay?"

"Okay."

"Let's get out of it."

"Watch out for Tempests."

They were going home. The "Great Blow", at least Goering's "Great Blow", had been struck. It had been five horrifying minutes to remember. Five glorious, fantastic minutes to remember. Though none of the survivors knew it then, it had also been the final blow that killed the Luftwaffe fighter arm.

When all the reports were in that night it seemed certain that they could not have destroyed fewer than 300 Allied aircraft. But at least 100 German fighters had failed to return and about 200 more were irreparably damaged. Half as many experienced pilots had died on that New Year's Day and sixty of those were irreplaceable veteran leaders.

For a week, the skies above the Ardennes battlefield were empty of British and American machines. But only for a week. Goering's final fling had been, like almost everything else the *Reichsmarschall* did, nothing but a wild extravagance.

The general had been sacked, relieved of his command, told to go on leave until a job could be found for him. The reaction in the Inspector of Fighters' Office was that of being stunned if not surprised. Whatever happened now could only be disastrous. It simply depended what form disaster would take. There were many alternatives. The SS could move in. The *Gauleiters* might demand fighters attached for the defence of their individual cities. The frustrated senior bomber command officers might well try to muscle in on the fighter preserves. The time of the long knives was here and not a few of them would be ceremonial officers' daggers.

The upright Oberst Lützow talked freely to Mano: "It can't go on like this a moment longer. After New Year's Day there's unrest right through the squadrons. That outrageous recorded message by the *Reichsmarschall* was the last bloody straw."

Goering had delivered the message personally to fighter leaders at the headquarters of Air Fleet Reich near Wannsee, just before the "Great Blow". He had intended to exhort them, but instead the *Reichsmarschall* had lost control, screaming insults and abuse, making accusations that had first been uttered in 1940 that the fighter pilots lacked moral fibre and fighting spirit, that they had let their country down. More than this: he had had his ravings recorded and ordered the recording to be played at all fighter stations. Thank God the general had ignored this ludicrous order, but now the general was gone.

"The man's mad, sir," Mano said.

"Precisely. That's why we intend to go straight to the Führer. Oberst Trautloft is with me. So are many of the senior *Kommodores* and squadron leaders."

"Please include me, sir."

"Thank you, Mano. It's got to be done according to the book. A delegation. This is not a mutiny."

In his bunker office at the Air Ministry, Helmuth Reh received the news of the general's sacking with restrained pleasure.

"A fine fighting man, no doubt," he said to Liese. "No one can doubt his courage. But steering a Messerschmitt in a dogfight is not quite the same as steering the complex affairs of an entire command."

Liese had little time for tact these days.

"He was too honest, that's all. Ask the pilots. Ask Dieter what they all think of him."

"You don't understand what's needed in these difficult days. He opposed the *Volksjäger* all the way."

"After what happened at your famous demonstration, he was obviously right."

"Teething troubles, that's all. Every new aircraft has them. We're getting them right. In a few weeks now they'll be pouring off the secret assembly lines. Look at these figures from Thuringia and Westphalia. Little factories hidden in barns, in old mine shafts, in cottages, turning out wooden parts almost faster than we can put them together."

"I hope the glue is stronger this time," Liese said scathingly.

Examination of Flugkapitän Peter's wrecked People's Fighter had revealed that the synthetic resin adhesives used in the wooden construction had failed under stress.

Dieter and Pohle got back at Achmer to find the 262s had arrived. Hardly had they taken delivery of their new aircraft when the order came to scramble. After the positive throttle response of the 190, it took discipline to remember that the jet had to be accelerated gradually to get it off the ground. But once airborne they climbed with a freedom and speed that caught them, tired and combat-battered as they now were, in a wild elation. There was the familiar frightening *dicker Hund* at 22,000 feet, ten miles in front. In a piston-engined fighter they would have had to get ahead and then turn in to the attack. But now they soared up astern, gaining so fast it was almost laughable.

"Look out. Mustangs above and to port."

"About twenty Thunderbolts closing, starboard, at three o'clock," Pohle reported.

"Don't worry. They'll never catch us."

Dieter levelled off five miles behind and two thousand feet above the bombers. The closing rate in a 500 mph dive was fantastic even when overtaking. Difficult to judge the moment to fire. At five hundred yards, the twelve 30 mm cannon of the three jets opened up. Within seconds the enormous weight of metal had turned Dieter's bomber into a fireball. Pohle's exploded and Jacob's spiralled down with one wing missing.

When they climbed and came in for a second attack, the Thunderbolts had got into a firing position but the speed of the jets beat them and only two were able to open fire, harmlessly, at maximum range. Pohle chopped down another Fortress on the second run.

When they landed all said the same thing. "If only we'd had these kites a year ago, there wouldn't be an American left in the skies."

The Führer had turned Lützow's request down. He was too busy with other matters. For a moment it looked as though the determination they had all worked up would simply fade away. "If we don't get our case over to the Führer," Lützow told Mano, "the fighter arm will simply collapse into anarchy."

A day later, the incredible happened. The *Reichsmarschall* himself announced that he would see the delegation.

"Waste of time," Mano suggested.

"It's worth a try," his chief said. "It seems we've got friends in high places. General Koller has put pressure on the Fat One to listen to us."

Koller was the last chief of staff the Luftwaffe was to have. He had accepted a post nobody else would take on the unlikely condition that he got a free hand.

"It's fixed for Friday morning. At the *Haus der Flieger*. The *Reichsmarschall*'s called for all fighter *Kommodores* that can be contacted to attend. You'll come as one of my *aides* please, Mano. For my sins, I'm to be spokesman. I'd like you to work late tonight to help me draw up my memorandum. It needs your legal brain. Here's the draft of the main points to be covered. Just run your eye over it."

Mano read the document written in Lützow's neat, firm hand. When he had reached the last numbered point he whistled.

Lützow waited, eyebrows raised. "Well?"

"A bit hot, isn't it, sir?"

"It's a hot situation."

"Pardon my mentioning it, but aren't you personally taking a bit of a chance?"

"I merely present it. It bears all our signatures. I'm there to elucidate, if necessary."

"May I study it for a bit, sir? Perhaps we can find a more diplomatic phrase or two while still making the same direct points."

"We're not in the mood for diplomacy. These are intended to be in the nature of demands, Mano."

When Lützow had gone Mano read the inspector's list carefully. It was dynamite. Point one: the Luftwaffe fighter pilots had suffered appalling losses but had continually been accused of cowardice by their leaders. Point two: the bomber arm was gaining too much influence in fighter affairs. Point three: the dismissal of the general had been a serious error at this point in the war. Point four: the equipping of bomber units with Me 262s was a mistake and must be cancelled at once. Point five: many high-ranking Luftwaffe officers must be removed from their posts . . .

This last one made even Mano feel hot under his uniform collar. All the officers named were known to be Goering's particular cronies.

The final sentence jumped out of the page at him.

"The fighter arm considers that the *Reichsmarschall* is being ill-advised by his staff and is of the opinion that all officers without long war experience should be removed and replaced by experienced fighter commanders."

When they sat down together that night Mano succeeded only in persuading his chief to soften a phrase here and there. When the memorandum was finished and typed it lay on the desk, gleaming like a 1000 kilo bomb whose fuse only needed arming. He had little doubt that the arming would be done the moment this blockbuster was dropped in front of the *Reichsmarschall.*

Mano had many times seen the *Reichsmarschall* in the distance at parades and official functions, but never from closer range than twenty yards. Standing a pace behind Obersts Lützow and Trautloft in the *Haus der Flieger,* and in front of the little group of *Kommodores* and *Gruppe* leaders summoned for the occasion, Mano had an excellent view from no more than three yards. His first impression was that this wasn't the real man at all, but an actor with somewhat the same physiognomy playing the part. Goering looked shrunken, his jowls loose. His gross body seemed to have been poured lumpily into his lavender uniform, like wax into a mould, wax that hadn't set properly. The idea that this was an actor standing in for the real thing was heightened by the amount of make-up on the face. He was using perfume, too, and the pudgy hands that held the grand marshal's baton shook. Mano reflected that Goering had been a drug addict for years and was said to be on at least twenty pills of various

356

kinds a day. "Caligula," thought Mano, "or perhaps Nero. A genuine monster."

General Koller opened the meeting in a surprisingly forthright way.

"*Herr Reichsmarschall,* you have told us to speak frankly. These officers who have asked to be allowed to put their views to you, a fellow fighter pilot, feel, in a word, that you have not been taking the personal interest in their problems that the situation demands."

Mano could hardly believe his ears. The *Reichsmarschall* had suddenly become jovial. As Koller spoke, Goering nudged him in the ribs with his baton, laughing roguishly and saying: "Ah well, general. Don't worry. I promise to be a good boy in the future."

This completely unexpected aside caught Koller off balance. He was unable to repress a laugh. Even Mano found Goering's switched-on charm disarming, as no doubt Caligula's had been. Koller, determined to get back to business, said sternly: "These officers, veteran fighter leaders to a man, have prepared a memorandum which Oberst Lützow will now present to you."

Mano handed the document to Lützow who took two paces forward in parade ground style, saluted, and gave the typed sheets to Goering.

"The 1000 kilo bomb," Mano thought, "is now not only armed. It is on its way down, aimed directly at our heads." He waited for the explosion.

Koller signalled to the delegation to be seated while the *Reichsmarschall* digested the contents of the paper.

Mano watched Goering's pallid face, saw the colour rising from the neck towards the cheeks, saw the flaccid lips begin to twitch. Lützow was watching, also. Mano had never admired the man more than at that moment. Before Goering could speak, Lützow was on his feet, all military etiquette brushed aside.

His voice was subdued: "*Herr Reichsmarschall,* in the name of my comrades, I must ask you to give me fifty minutes of your complete and silent attention while I explain our problems. Otherwise the purpose of this meeting will have been wasted."

Goering was on his feet too. "What insolence! Have you the impudence to suggest I didn't build a strong Luftwaffe?"

Lützow looked him squarely in the face. "You did, *Herr*

357

Reichsmarschall, and it won you many victories. But lately you have gone to sleep."

Goering slumped back in his chair. For a moment he seemed too shocked to reply. Then he jumped up, banging the table with his baton.

"This is mutiny! You have all plotted mutiny! Lützow, I'll have you court-martialled." He flounced out of the room before any of the delegation had time to rise to their feet. At the door, behind Goering, Koller stopped and spread his hands as if in despair, a gesture which at the same time seemed to be imploring them all not to regard this as the end of the affair. Nor was it.

Mano didn't sleep that night. He went back to the office and took out a bottle of brandy which he drank slowly. Trautloft looked in once and said: "Well, we did our best."

Oberst Lützow, normally an abstemious man, shared some of the brandy with Mano. Around one in the morning he said: "I don't suppose it is any use waiting here for the Gestapo. I might as well go home to bed."

Mano phoned Liese. But the Mosquitoes were visiting Berlin again on a nuisance raid and the lines were busy or cut. So he walked several blocks to seek professional aid with his sex life only to find that the RAF had got there first. A thousand-pounder had demolished her apartment block. He strolled sadly back to the office and slept in his chair, to be woken just after eight by the phone. The office chief of Luftwaffe personnel was on the line. An urgent call was being put out for the general. He was to report to the personnel department immediately he could be contacted.

At nine, Mano shaved and sent out for some coffee and rolls. At ten-thirty Oberst Trautloft came bursting into the office and flung down a teleprint message on his desk.

THE GENERAL OF THE FIGHTER ARM HAS BEEN RELIEVED OF ALL DUTIES AND ORDERED TO LEAVE BERLIN WITHIN TWELVE HOURS STOP HE WILL REPORT HIS WHEREABOUTS TO OKL STOP HE WILL HOLD HIMSELF IN READINESS TO BE CALLED UP STOP HE IS TO COMMUNICATE DIRECTLY WITH NO FIGHTER UNITS STOP INFORM ALL COMMANDERS TO SQUADRON LEVEL

"The witch-hunt is on, Mano. The general had nothing to do with our memorandum but the Fat One will never believe that. He's out to get him."

For the next forty-eight hours, Mano knew what terror

meant. He had often been frightened by the enemy but to be made sick with fear by what your own side might do! He was not scared so much for himself. He was but a minor figure in the so-called mutiny. His fear was for the men who really mattered, for Günther Lützow, Hannes Trautloft and for the general most of all. The memory of 20 July and what had happened after Stauffenberg's bomb plot was too fresh in everyone's mind. Thank God, Goering wasn't a Hitler in terms of power or wish for vengeance. But the *Reichsmarschall* was a sick, vindictive man whose personal ship was sinking fast and he wouldn't hesitate to drag others down with him.

On the second day after the fatal meeting, Goering made his malice known. The orders were sent in clear over the open wire.

Lützow was to be exiled from Germany, to command a squadron on the Italian front. Trautloft was dismissed his post to await further posting.

Mano was almost in tears. He appealed to Lützow. "Who do I work for now? What's the use any more?"

Lützow put his hand kindly on Mano's shoulder. "There's no use hanging on here. The place will be run by a lot of damn commissars and *Gauleiters*. Come as my adjutant. The only worthwhile place from now on will be with a front line squadron."

Mano said: "It'll be chaos here. Someone had better stay and try to make sense of things."

"All right, Mano, but the moment you've had enough, get yourself posted."

During the next twenty-four hours, rumour and panic ran the headquarters departments of the fighter arm. There was no one and nothing else to fill the vacuum left by the banishment of its three strong men. Most of the rumours were horrifying. Himmler was taking over the Luftwaffe in person. Speer had been sacked. Goering had decided to fill the role of general of fighters himself. These were so outlandish as to be credible. The rumour that the general had defied the order to leave Berlin and was back in the city was the rumour which Mano was least inclined to believe and yet it turned out to be the only one that was true. The truth of the story was confirmed when an adjutant from Hitler's Luftwaffe staff phoned Mano to ask if the general's exact whereabouts in Berlin were known to the inspector's department. The general was wanted at the *Reichskanzlei* immediately.

To judge by the talk in the higher echelons of the US Eighth

Air Force, the Allies might actually be losing the war. As a bombardment group intelligence officer, Charles Levitson took part in a good many of the middle level discussions. The Ardennes offensive was at last being rolled back, but its vigour and near success had persuaded some Allied commanders that the war wasn't going to be won quickly. The air forces had been compelled for nearly a month to divert the strategic strength they would normally have used against the Reich to tactical support for the armies in the Ardennes battle. During this enforced bombing lull, the American General Anderson argued, German aircraft production had recovered and was now actually soaring. And when he said aircraft production, everyone knew what aircraft he was talking about—the Me 262 jet.

The thought of the jets increasingly haunted everyone concerned with the daylight offensive, the crews as well as the men who sent them out. Charles had seen Top Secret intelligence reports estimating that at least 700 262s had already been built. There were also rumours of a mass-produced jet on the way from Heinkel. If the Germans were able to flood the skies with these machines, then the entire daylight operation might founder even after the enormous sacrifices of aircrew that had been made. General Arnold, commander of the American air forces, had sent a letter to senior officers asking for ideas and suggestions. It expressed a distinctly gloomy view. "Either," the general wrote, "we have been too optimistic in our conception of the possibilities of raids or we have made a fatal error in calculating the effect which the destruction would have on the German war machine."

On 11 January, the Allied air chiefs met at Versailles to consider the course their air strategy should take if the war lasted, as they feared, a long time yet. But no one could come up with anything better than an intensification of the present bombing programme, an all-out offensive on fuel supplies, transport, civilian morale, aircraft production and above all the jets, the accursed jets.

Shortly afterwards, Charles Levitson attended a command conference on the growing menace of the 262. One fighter major had a solution in which he believed passionately. This officer, a Thunderbolt pilot of outstanding courage and success, stood up and said: "Has it ever occurred to you that it takes nearly as long to make a jet pilot as it does to make a jet? A pilot who bails out to safety can always climb into another jet next day. The answer, gentlemen, is therefore simple. Shoot down jet pilots as mercilessly as you shoot down jets."

The thought, of course, had been in everyone's mind long before the major brought it into the open. There had been many rumours that parachuting airmen had been shot at by both sides. But if they were true, then only as an act of personal reprisal, never as official policy of the two air forces. Galland had told Goering he would consider such an act murder as long ago as 1940, back on the Channel coast. After a long silence, a colonel said quietly: "There is no official sanction for such a course, major."

"Maybe not," said the major, "but work it out for yourselves. There are ten men in a B 17 or B 24. In one mission last week I saw a single 262 shoot down three Fortresses—thirty American lives."

"There's no sanction for such a policy," the colonel repeated. "Apart from anything else, it could result in reprisals against American aircrews who might also bail out."

"Have it your way, colonel," said the major and sat down leaving little doubt what his way might be.

"Have we really come to this?" Charles asked himself as he left the meeting. "Yet isn't he right? What's chivalry at this stage of the game?"

Goering had tried to keep it quiet, but of course he couldn't succeed. There were far too many people on the general's side to hush up a good story like this. Mano got it within a few hours from a major on Goering's staff. The *Reichskanzlei* had found the general after his illicit return to Berlin without too much trouble—mainly because he wasn't hiding. When he reported to the *Reichskanzlei* one of Hitler's personal air adjutants told him that the Führer had been completely unaware of his banishment and had given an order that "This nonsense was to stop at once."

The best bit of all was that Goering had summoned the general to Karinhall a few hours afterwards. Apparently, no one had thought of telling him that the Führer's decision had already been made known to the general. So Goering played the part of the stern judge relenting at the last moment.

"In view of your past services to the fighter arm," he had pronounced, "I have decided to take no further action against you. Instead, I intend to give you the chance you have been asking for continually for the past eighteen months—to prove that the Me 262 is all that you say it is against the American daylight raiders."

Mano could imagine the general's attempt to hide his amusement and delight, especially when Goering had added:

"And I advise you to start by recruiting all the recalcitrant and obstinate fighter leaders who have just conducted this unheard of demonstration against my authority. I have already recalled the leader of the mutiny, Lützow, from Italy. Now you may dismiss."

Confirmation of this outlandish story wasn't long in coming over the teleprinter in Mano's office.

FORMER GENERAL OF FIGHTERS COMMANDED TO FORM A SPECIAL UNIT OF ME 262 FIGHTERS DESIGNATION JV 44 STOP THIS UNIT WILL HAVE NO CONNECTION WITH OTHER FORMATIONS STOP JV 44 WILL BE COMPLETELY INDEPENDENT FOR OPERATIONS

Mano laughed outright. What it meant was that the general's unit had officially been put in quarantine. All the so-called mutineers had been penned up together where they couldn't infect others. No doubt the *Reichsmarschall* considered his proposal one which might eliminate the "mutineers" most effectively, by putting them in a virtual suicide unit. Mano saw JV 44 as something quite different—a group of the finest fighter pilots in the world flying the finest machines in the world. How the general must be chuckling.

In the closing days of January, Dieter managed a quick twenty-four-hour leave to Berlin. Dieter just had to see Liese, to find out about the baby, to make arrangement with Mano for getting her to some place of comparative safety for the birth. Mano had promised and he trusted Mano implicitly. Nevertheless he wanted to see for himself. The reason he could get leave at all was a depressing one. They were suffering from shortage of jets at Achmer. The Americans and British had perfected a technique for shooting the 262s up when they were at their most vulnerable, in the landing circuit over their home airfield. Several had been lost in this way. They were not easy machines to fly. Inevitably, there was a high percentage of write-offs due to pilot error. So, for the moment, there were not enough jets to go round. Dieter was sour with frustration when he arrived at Mano's office.

Mano hadn't seen his friend for some time and was shocked at his red-eyed, drawn appearance. Dieter had suddenly ceased to be a young man. He was continually restless, moving things on the desk, tapping, getting up, walking a few paces, slumping down in a chair again.

"It's not a bad thing you're not doing much flying just now."

"Why?" The tone was unusually aggressive.

"Because, dear boy, you're obviously dead tired. You've had enough for a bit."

Dieter didn't attempt to argue. "I daresay you're right. We most of us have. But there's not much chance of a let-up, is there? About one day a week we're operational in a 262. The rest of the time it's flying landing cover in a 190 amidst packs of Mustangs and Thunderbolts and now Tempests. It's not exactly a nerve tonic."

"Agreed. That's why you should have a spell on the ground."

"Then we all ought to have a spell on the ground. There's no other course but to plug on. Besides, I'm not as edgy as this once I get my wheels up."

"Heard of JV 44?"

"The general's supposed to be forming a jet outfit, isn't he?"

"Yes, he's looking for hot pilots."

"I expect he's got all he needs."

"He's getting them. Trautloft, Lützow, Steinhoff . . . Steinhoff's in charge of retraining pilots. He's getting Barkhorn, Barkhorn with a score of 300 on the Russian front. He's even persuaded some of the old hands to climb out of hospital beds . . . Krupinski is one of them, so is Schnell . . ."

"What about machines?"

"I don't think this particular outfit will have much difficulty. The general always spoke well of you. If I could pull a string or two, would you like to join?"

"Is it as easy as that?"

"Frankly, Dieter, things are so chaotic everywhere at command level, you can fix almost anything and no one will argue, provided you're not pinching a perk that one of the big fish wants for himself. Not many of the high command want to risk dying in a jet fighter at this stage of the war."

"We don't see it like that. But there's one thing. If it can be fixed, I won't go alone. It's the three of us, Pohle, Jacob and me, or nothing."

"If jet pilots come in ready-made *Ketten* so much the better, I imagine. Another good thing about it is that it will give you a week or two's breathing space. JV 44 won't be ready to start operations quite yet."

"Well, they'd better be quick, or the war will be finished."

"It'll last a bit yet, Dieter," Mano said gently. "But I don't think many people realise how near the end we are, and I'm damned certain, if intelligence reports are anything to go by, that the Allies have no conception just how close to collapse Germany is."

"I must go and see Liese, Mano. How is she?"

"Very pregnant. It's time that I arranged for her posting."

Like every other German woman exposed to the continual bombing, Liese's face showed intense strain. Beyond that she looked well. Though she was ashamed of the fact, her father-in-law managed to get her luxuries of diet denied to others. She told herself the baby was what mattered. Never mind if some of the food was coming from the black market of a corrupt and rotten regime she despised. The baby must survive to be born into a new Germany.

She clung to Dieter for a long time, crying with gratitude because he was safe and well. She had heard nothing from him for ten days. The posts had become totally unreliable as the result of Allied air attacks on communications. She never dared to think that he was alive and unharmed but when she saw with her own eyes that he was, it was too much for her.

He asked after his father.

"Gone back to Hamelin."

"He knows you're going to stop working soon?"

"He knows it, but it's as if he won't recognise that it's got to happen."

"He's *got* to release you. I'll go and tell him so myself."

"No need. When the time comes, I shall just pack up. He can't make me carry on. I've only done so this far for all your sakes. But now he seems so . . ."

"So what, *Liebchen?*"

"Possessed. Almost crazy. He's pouring all his energies into the *Volksjäger.* He really believes it can still turn the tide. He also really believes that boys from the *Hitlerjugend* can fly it."

"Then he *is* crazy. Flying a jet is only for very experienced pilots."

"Like you."

"Like me."

"Dieter. Can't you stop flying now . . . ?"

She knew the sort of smile he would give, half mocking, half kind.

"No," she said sadly. "I suppose not."

"Mano's going to work it so that Jacob, Pohle and I get

transferred to the most elite unit in the Luftwaffe. You've heard of JV 44?"

"The bad boys," she managed a laugh.

"Exactly. There's one good thing. If he pulls it off, I won't be flying for a week or two. JV 44 is only just forming."

"Thank God. It may be over before you're ready." She clung to him, kissing him passionately, the curve of her belly awkward against his uniform. "I'm sorry I can't get any closer, darling."

"You get the baby born safely first. There'll come a day."

"Please God," she said.

Mano was as good as his word on every count. At the end of the first week in February, Dieter, Jacob and Pohle received instructions direct from the Inspector of Fighters' Office to proceed to Brandenburg-Briest, JV 44's base.

On 6 February, Liese officially informed her father-in-law that she intended to stop work because of her pregnancy and that Mano Rumpler had arranged train tickets to take her to his parents' home in Dresden.

"You'll be safe enough there," Herr Reh said, almost as if he was accusing her of cowardice. "Meantime the rest of us will have to stick it out, turning out fighter planes."

"Yes," she said, "we must all do what seems most important at this time. You'll forgive me if your son's child dominates my life at the moment."

Before she left to catch the train on 12 February, Herr Reh showed some signs of concern for her condition. He pressed a last-minute package of food into her hands, kissed her, and reminded her that it was his son's baby she was carrying and to take good care of it for the future of Germany.

She thanked him gravely, saying that this was how she felt herself, and went down to the waiting car that Mano had provided.

Mano saw her into the train, made sure she had a comfortable seat, told the guard to look after her and to see that she arrived safely in Dresden.

"I can't guarantee that we'll arrive on time," he said, "but the main thing is that we'll arrive somehow."

"God speed, Liese." Mano kissed her warmly. "Give my fondest love to my dear parents and thank them from me for looking after you."

Train-busting was no joke. A train should be a lumbering, defenceless thing, unable to turn round, go anywhere else, con-

365

demned simply to travel back or forward or stay where it was. In fact it did not always work out like that. If you surprised a train that was often how the train turned out to be—lumbering and defenceless. But German trains these days carried plenty of light flak and if the train knew you were coming it could stop in its tracks to give its gunners the steadiest possible platform from which to defend themselves. The volumes of nastiness a train could throw into the air had to be seen to be believed.

Train-busting was now a priority for the Mustangs, Tempests and Typhoons. If the trains could be stopped, then so could Germany's flow of men and materials. Peter Bristow did not enjoy shooting up trains for several reasons. The first was that it was very dangerous, as the loss of several good pilots in the last few weeks had proved. The second was that he occasionally had pictures of what it must be like inside a railway carriage when the cannon shells came smashing and splintering into the compartments. Some of these must hold servicemen, but more often than not there would be women and children as well. Bombing from 20,000 feet as the Fortresses and Lancasters did, was one thing, but an attack on a train was just not impersonal enough. You could see your cannon strikes on carriage doors and windows.

Peter spotted this train south of Berlin before the train spotted him. It was rattling along at a fair rate which meant that it wasn't alert to any particular danger. At head, rear and in the centre of the carriages there were flatcars mounting several multiple 20 mm flak guns.

Peter called his section. Leaving four Mustangs up top to look out for Focke Wulfs, he stalked the train carefully in cloud cover, then pushing the stick forward came out of the low cloud in a split-arse shallow dive that would give the train no time to think.

He came over a small pine wood at a little more than treetop height to see the train a mile ahead. As always, Peter picked the engine for himself. Without engines trains couldn't run. His first burst sent the boiler up in a tower of steam. He saw the driver drop to the tracks and go spinning. The train must have been doing sixty. Then he kicked left rudder to give the leading flak car a burst as he turned away.

Liese, in the carriage immediately behind the flak car, was thrown on to the floor as the engine blew its boiler. She was still there when the tail end of Peter Bristow's cannon burst ripped through the roof of the carriage. Then everything in the compartment was on top of her as the guard applied the emergency brakes. Until some naval ratings lifted her out ten minutes later she didn't realise that the man who had fallen on top of her was dead.

She sat by the side of the track in the shelter of a haystack while they brought a new engine up for the train. All that time she thought of the night in Cologne when she had felt her baby's life oozing away between her thighs. From time to time she felt her belly and reassured herself that there was no haemorrhage. Though she saw Allied planes several times, there were no further attacks on the train. Trains standing still are alert trains. After three hours they were told to get aboard again.

An official came along the corridor. "We can't go on to Dresden. We're returning to Berlin."

The relief train brought Liese back to Berlin early on the morning of 13 February. She phoned Mano from the station. True to form he remained unflappable. When he had made sure that both she and the baby were all right, he sent a staff car for her. He insisted she had a meal and a rest in his apartment. Then he phoned the Air Ministry. Was there any urgent mail awaiting Special Gauleiter Reh's attention? There was? Good. Herr Reh was back at Hamelin? Excellent, then he had a staff car going to Hamelin that evening. He would have the mail collected and delivered to Herr Reh personally.

"You see," he told Liese, "you can do anything these days with a little influence. There's no one to stop you. We might as well not be here. The individual fighter wings have given OKL up and who can blame them? They're still fighting like tigers and like tigers each one is running its own piece of jungle. It's magnificent but it's not war, as some Frenchman or other said. All we can do here is to try to ensure enough planes, pilots, ammo and fuel reach them, and of all these fuel is our real problem."

Mano kept talking to steady Liese down until the sleeping pills he had given her took effect.

She said drowsily. "It's a long way to Hamelin. How on earth did you get the petrol?"

"Didn't you know staff officers always have their own private store to escape with before the final retreat? Seriously, I've made the trip an official one. Sleep now, my dear. I'll have you woken at four. You'll travel at night to escape the unwelcome attentions of the gentlemen who so discourteously stopped your train. The Mustangs even shoot up individual cars these days."

When Liese was safely on her way, Mano returned to his

desk. He had a day's paperwork to catch up with. Shortly after 2200, the teleprinter began to tap out the news that Dresden was under attack by a force of at least 1,000 bombers.

Peter Bristow occasionally found time to wonder how the German fighter pilots were feeling. He knew how his boys felt because he was in precisely the same state himself. At least his side was supposed to be winning. The signs on his own pilots were plain to see. When he told his section to follow him down on the look-out for ground targets, they began to zigzag as if every flak battery in Germany was after them. He couldn't really blame them. Who wanted to end up as a trophy for some square-headed flak gunner just when the war was practically won—or was it? To watch the lads in those long-nosed Focke Wulfs you'd think it had only just begun. Only the day before he had got his section into a dog-fight with four real professionals. One bastard, who'd got too close, had tried to do a barrel roll right round him and when he'd throttled back to catch him out, the Hun had just slid away into cloud, and had banged two 20 mm cannon shells into his fuselage that had wrecked his radio and left some of the instruments hanging out of the control panel by their smouldering wires. But today beat all. They had been detailed to escort a Fortress formation on its way to Dresden. The Yanks were following up a large-scale night raid by the RAF with two daylight attacks. Why Dresden? The beautiful city had slept immune through nearly four and a half years of war. Now when they were still sixty miles away, free-hunting on the flanks of the Yankee bomber stream for Hun fighters, they could see the funeral pyre of the baroque city rising ten thousand feet into the air. Why Dresden? But then why anywhere any more?

Suddenly the radio was alive and crackling with a new sound. Music. *Deutschland, Deutschland über Alles*. A woman's voice shrieking: "Remember German wives and children murdered by the American air pirates."

Peter's No 2 shouting: "Look out. 190s up-sun. Christ, they're diving into the Fortresses!"

Two 190s exploded in the crossfire from the Fortress box. In the second *Rotte*, Gerhard Stecke saw the oil-spattered tail of a Fortress growing larger in his windscreen. His cannon hammered away, knocking chunks off the monster but this time cannon were not to be enough.

Stecke had reached the logical, final conclusion of the Storm Fighter ideal, the heavily armoured 190 that went in close. Now as a member of the *Raubvogel Gruppe* of *Sonder-kommando Elbe* he was ordered to go in closest of all, to ram. The music in his head-set was the last thing he heard as his propeller chewed its way into the B 17's fuselage.

Five rammed Fortresses were already falling when Peter, throttle through the safety gate, caught the only 190 to escape and transformed it into a spewing cloud of burning fuel.

He'd witnessed one of the few recorded suicide attacks of the air war in Europe. Christ. What kind of people were these?

When the picture became clear, Mano shut himself in his office and sobbed his heart out. For such an apparently unemotional man, it was a shattering experience, shattering and cathartic. He could not recall when he had last wept, certainly not since he was a small boy, but now he cried not only for Dresden and his parents but for Germany and all her sons who had been thrown away by madmen. The news from Dresden was catastrophic. The Allies appeared to have decided to obliterate it almost at a whim. Untouched throughout the war, his native city had been attacked by a thousand-bomber RAF raid on 13 February, followed by two mass daylight assaults by the Americans on the fourteenth and fifteenth.

The city had been packed with refugees fleeing ahead of the advancing Russians. The horror even of Hamburg hardly approached what had now overtaken Dresden. First estimates said that over 100,000 people had died in the firestorm, that probably the total death roll would never be known.

That his parents had died was certain. They were old and did not move around very much. Their house had been in the very centre of the worst hit area. Only one thought lit Mano's despair. By a miracle, Liese had been spared. Now, whatever else happened, she and the baby must be kept safe to the end.

Kate Bristow received regular mail from Charles. He was still forbidden to fly, she thanked God. She longed for the peace and security of Charles' presence now more than anything she could remember. He wrote telling her that because of his wounds and length of service he was unlikely to be sent to the Pacific when the war in Europe was over. What he did not tell her was that he was still collecting his full set of thirty missions. He had made it up to twenty-nine with a nice quiet trip in a Marauder to bomb some German airfields that had turned out to be unoccupied. On this raid, ten long-nosed 190s, the first Charles had seen, made a brave attempt to

369

break through the Thunderbolt and Mustang screen. Outnumbered five to one, they lost four of their number. Charles was scared rigid in the old familiar way. It was not so bad when you were flying the ship, but sheer hell when all you had to do was to observe the state of the game. On this occasion, too, the jets he hoped, but feared, to encounter failed to materialise. The limited resources of JG 7 were busy elsewhere and JV 44 was not yet operational.

Kate longed to see Charles again but she had forced herself to turn down leave since she had first landed in Europe. She could not exactly define why. Partly it was a commitment to the fighter crews she served, a desire to see the job over and done with; but, also, it was a private certainty that Charles and she were in a state of suspended animation until it was all over. Arnhem had held out a hope that the war would be finished by Christmas. That was now part of history. The Ardennes and New Year's Day—she had been there when the Focke Wulfs had shot up Brussels-Evère—had wrongly convinced everyone that Germany was far from beaten. Every Tempest, Spitfire and Mustang pilot who returned from an operation confirmed this.

The winter had been bitter and prolonged, its disappointments many. By mid-March Kate had used up all her reserves. A wandering virus pneumonia bug found her and nearly did what bombs and cannon fire had failed to do. Peter came to see her in a Brussels hospital. She had had a close call but now the antibiotics were in charge of the situation. It seemed certain that her war was over. As soon as possible they were going to fly her back to convalesce in England. When Peter had left the ward, she fell into a drugged doze. Her dream was a confused one. Many young vanished faces passed before her. One of these was a dark German face who had picked her up gently and laid her on a bed of pine needles above the Weser a thousand years ago.

JV 44 was ready by the end of March. On the early morning of 31 March, the jets flew in superb formation from Brandenburg-Briest to Munich, over three hundred miles in forty minutes. Compared with Steinhoff, Krupinski, Barkhorn and Hohagen, Dieter, Jacob and Pohle felt comparative novices. Yet they were all *Experten*, the best. The universal badge of the unit was the Knight's Cross. It was the greatest imaginable honour to fly in such company.

No sooner had they landed and dispersed their jets under superbly contrived camouflage than six Typhoons shot up the

370

runway and exploded a fuel bowser. One of the Typhoons hit by ground fire flew straight through the wooden supports of a flak tower killing the crew that had shot him down.

Mano often had the impression he was taking part in a novel by Kafka. Hardly a day passed without some new faceless nonentity being appointed, or appointing himself, as overlord. Because they were now all the rage, the control of the 262s became a prime Tom Tiddler's ground. It was the time of commissioners, *Gauleiters*, special ambassadors to the Führer, the lot. Goering had appointed a special commissioner for jet aircraft who was immediately cancelled out by the commissariat of the Führer for jet aircraft appointed by a general of the Waffen SS.

Fortunately those who flew the jets were barely aware of any of this. They just flew and Mano did his best to ensure they had the wherewithal to do so. Jet fuel was one commodity of which there was no shortage.

Berlin was a macabre madhouse. There was little doubt that those with any sense, influence and foresight were preparing to pull out. The Russians were coming, the Yanks were coming, the RAF and Eighth Air Force came almost daily. The buildings were gutted and sightless. It was a hell scene complete with devils; poor devils of civilians waiting for God knows what; genuine devils, SS officers on the make; junior fiends, nine- and ten-year-olds, *Hitlerjugend*, their scrawny necks sticking out of uniform and greatcoat collars made for men; old devils, ancient civilian warriors dredged up from the last war, their scrawny necks sticking out of greatcoat collars made for younger men. There were no young men left. The ministries, it was said, were getting ready to evacuate. Evacuate to where? The Führer at least was standing firm. Magnificent! He had nowhere else to go either. By early April there was nothing and no one to keep Mano. He posted himself to Munich as Oberst Trautloft had suggested. He had no doubt JV 44 could use a good admin man. But first he had a duty call to make. He summoned his driver and told him to prepare for a long journey and to bring all his petrol authorisations. They were leaving Berlin.

"Thank God for that," said the driver.

Just as Liese had done, they drove through the night to Hamelin. There were road blocks and armoured patrols everywhere. Twice their way through a town was blocked by an air raid. They arrived at the Reh house in Hamelin shortly after daybreak. At first, Mano feared the once handsome now derelict place was deserted. But Reh's old secretary, Gertrud, suddenly emerged from the cellars.

She held her fingers to her lips.

"She's down there, sleeping. A boy. A fine boy. The image of his father."

"When?"

"Last night. In the middle of an air raid. But she's safe down below. Herr Reh had the cellars reinforced by the Todt organisation."

Mano woke Liese gently. The baby lay close at her side, its small face crumpled in sleep.

"How is it, *Liebchen?*"

She smiled. "Fine. The baby's fine. Gertrud has promised to look after me. She'll stay with me. We've got plenty of food. My father-in-law stocked the place for a siege. Dear Mano, why have you come? How did you get here?"

"Never mind that. I'm here. Now listen, you're safe in this cellar. Whatever happens, stay here. The Americans or the British must arrive before very long."

"Not the Russians?" she asked fearfully.

"Not the Russians," he reassured her.

"Dieter, is he . . ."

"Don't worry about Dieter. That's where I'm going now, to join him. He'll be all right. It can't last long now."

Mano picked the baby up and kissed its forehead. Then he kissed Liese. He went upstairs to find Gertrud.

"You'll stay with her now?"

"Naturally."

"Good. Then, when the Allies come, hang up a white sheet. If there's any fighting, stay in the cellar until it's all over."

The Reh house had one final surprise for him. A Mercedes was standing outside. Herr Reh, apparently oblivious to the fact that he was a grandfather, was loading luggage into it.

"Ah, Rumpler," he said, as if seeing Mano there was the most natural thing in the world. "You are aware of the powers conferred on me as a Special *Gauleiter?*"

Mano stared at him, expecting him to say that he was making arrangements for Liese's and the baby's safety. Instead, Helmuth Reh flashed some documents at Mano.

"See these? Know what they are? They were delivered to me personally by the ambassador of jet aircraft production to the Führer. They entitle me to call on immediate fighter protection for factories producing the *Volksjäger.* I therefore order you, Major Rumpler, to arrange immediately for an entire *Geschwader* to be posted, under my direct control, for safeguarding of people's fighter production in the Neuruppin area."

Mano wanted to burst out laughing, the idea of a fighter wing tied to local protection of a factory and controlled by an ignorant civilian was so utterly ludicrous.

In the circumstances there was nothing to do but to appear to comply, so he clicked his heels and gave his first Nazi salute for years.

"*Jawohl*, Herr Gauleiter Reh."

He turned smartly about and got into his own car.

"We're going to Munich," he told his driver. "It's a long way and I want to arrive in one piece, so keep an eye open for enemy aircraft."

Even the overwrought, overtired mind of Peter Bristow became almost obsessed with the fact that the Luftwaffe fighter pilots were putting up an impossible resistance. One way to break this was to destroy them at their most vulnerable, on the ground. But the *Staffeln* now lived like gypsies. They switched from airfield to airfield, seldom staying more than a few hours or at most a few days. They landed in the early morning or late in the evening to find skeleton ground crews with petrol and ammunition waiting to service them. They were hard to find and harder still to hit. Perhaps gypsies was an unfortunate description, also a rather bitter one.

According to reports, all the gypsies in Germany had been long ago put into gas-ovens. The *Staffeln* were more like bands of highly organised guerrillas. Peter's thoughts were running like this as he led his wing on an early morning sweep looking for occupied fighter airfields. He switched on his oxygen to clear his brain. Even a month ago he would never have allowed his thoughts to wander like this. Lack of concentration for a second was all that was needed. He waggled his wings to clear the blind spots, and make sure that in his moment of aberration he hadn't missed anything. To reassert his grip on the situation he told his No 2 not to straggle. New No 2s always did. The airfield he had allotted his section was definitely not occupied. Floods of relief. The amount of light flak down below was unbelievable. He was just looking for an alternative target, perhaps a convoy along the Berlin-Hamburg *Autobahn*, when a flicker of changing light caught his eye. An aircraft travelling very fast was overtaking him almost directly below. It trailed a grey streamer of vapour. Jet! If it was a 262 he knew he'd never catch it. He lifted his starboard wing to get a better look. The jet was slowing, flaps down, apparently coming in to land on a long straight stretch of the *Autobahn,* where it came close to Neuruppin lake.

"Stick close to me," he yelled, knowing that his No 2 would be too scared to do anything else.

He caught the jet just as the pilot lowered his wheels. Then for the first time, he saw the jet engine on top of the fuselage, aft of the cockpit—*Volksjäger,* He 162, People's Fighter. He was closing to firing range when a red Verey light shot up ahead beside the *Autobahn.* A warning to the jet to sheer off. A black cloud of unburned jet fuel as the 162 tried to open up to climb away out of trouble. The nose of the *Volksjäger* tilted skyward briefly. Evidently the engine hadn't responded. The strange-looking kite stalled and spun in. There was no need to fire. Peter got the hell out of it in a tight climbing turn. So that was it. The bastards were using the *Autobahn* as an experimental runway. No doubt there were scores of 162s hidden all around. With luck, the Marauders would now plaster the place. Or the Typhoons. But not Mustangs. Please God, not Mustangs. There'd be every flak gun in the shrinking Reich waiting down below.

From the control tower on a camouflaged bunker Special Gauleiter Reh saw the 162 crash and rang the *Kommodore* of the nearest fighter wing demanding that a *Staffel* be ordered to land on the *Autobahn* as protection immediately. Fortunately the line went dead before the *Kommodore* could reply.

Mano, Dieter, Jacob and Pohle lay in a slit trench at Munich-Riem watching some Marauders bomb the railway station a couple of miles away. Mano said: "Even though it may save our lives, I have a peculiar loathing for this particular piece of Germany."

Mano had been warmly welcomed at HQ JV 44. There was nothing very irregular about his self-posting. From all over fighter command, officers were suddenly appearing and asking to join. Like every other officer, even pilots, on the station, Mano's first task had been to dig his own slit trench. Colonels, majors, even their own real live lieutenant general, they had all dug their personal life insurance policies against the Mustangs and Thunderbolts that made their life a daily hell. Mano had dug with a strange joy and fervour. At last, at the fifty-fifth minute of the eleventh hour, he was sharing the life of the fighter pilots. So he had dug a system of slit trenches that would accommodate three with ease, four at a squeeze. At the end of this labour he had had to agree that JV 44, the

Experten, had gone to extremes in their choice of airfield as in everything else. They had chosen the stoniest landing ground in Germany.

Charles Levitson knew that the top brass believed it was nearly over. Already the plans were ready for the whole of the Eighth Air Force to be transferred to the Pacific for the final blow against Japan. Charles had been told officially that he would not be going. It was clear that if he wanted to complete the thirty trips that meant so much to him he didn't have much more time. On 10 April he judged that he had the last real chance. Over 1,200 bombers were to attack not only Berlin but the bases of the German jets. Charles thought of Kate. She had written that she was returning to England to convalesce soon, that as soon as she was fit enough she would go to Rife Farm to get completely well. He almost persuaded himself that it was crazy to risk getting himself killed at this very last minute. Only a few days previously German jets using rockets, twenty-four per jet, had chopped down an entire box of fifteen American bombers. But the leader of one of the bombardment groups was short of a co-pilot and accepted Charles' offer with such real enthusiasm that there was no turning back.

Dieter, Jacob and Pohle had already flown one mission that morning, shooting down a Marauder and a Thunderbolt. They had sneaked back under cover of the flak lane, an entire *Abteilung*, a battalion of guns that could cover the jets' landing approach with a fire-power of 250 shells a second. Not many Allied fighters risked diving into such a barrage any more. But this morning the danger was not from fighter bombers. It soon became clear that the American heavies were headed directly for the jet fields and that Riem was unlikely to escape.

They scrambled at the last possible minute. The ground crews dragged off the camouflage nets. Streib gave Dieter the thumbs-up sign. The jet engines were screaming and they were off.

Charles had wondered all these weeks what a German jet really looked like at speed. Now at last he knew and could hardly believe what he saw. One minute his bomber box of twelve aircraft was sailing untroubled up to their target. The next, three Fortresses were burning and one twisting down with its tail completely shorn off. Charles heard the waist-gunners blazing away but knew instinctively that they were shooting too late simply to bolster their own morale.

Dieter pulled his *Kette* out in a shallow climbing turn. Fantastic! Now they would go in again. It was then that the six Mustangs caught them, cutting across their turning circle. Jacob, on the outside, received a burst in his port engine. Dieter saw him trailing smoke, bright flame licking his wing root, and shouted: "Bail out, Jacob. For God's sake bail out."

He eased the throttle back, cutting his own turning arc, risking that there might be a Mustang or Thunderbolt inside him. The main thing was to get back to cover Jacob. Out to starboard, Pohle hadn't anticipated Dieter's sudden move and was swinging wide. For once Dieter wished he was in a 109 but at last he was round. Jacob's 262 had plunged straight down, streaming smoke but, thank God, a parachute had opened. His brother was floating down. He'd be okay.

It was then that the Thunderbolt came boring in. It may just possibly have been after a Focke Wulf that flicked suddenly into its pilot's field of vision. Jacob was certainly in the direct line of fire between the two machines. There was just no telling whether the act was deliberate or not. It was enough for Dieter that he saw the flashes along the Thunderbolt's wings and that, in the same instant, his brother's parachute shrouds were cut. The chute fluttered, streamed out, and Jacob fell like a stone.

Pohle's wide turn had put him on the Thunderbolt's tail. The big, barrel-nosed fighter exploded and was gone in a cloud of fragments. Ahead, the *dicker Hund* was still easily catchable. Nothing mattered now but to kill and kill. He and Pohle went through the bomber stream from end to end and when they came out two Liberators had gone and a Fortress was burning, and the Fortress was the one in which Charles Levitson flew.

It was the old familiar nightmare. The smell of burning insulation. The freezing blast from gaps in the fuselage. The moans from wounded men. The stream of blood on the cockpit floor. The tinkle of spent brass cases. The stench of cordite and above all the voices of terrified men. Eight Mustangs had closed in to nurse them back. That at least was better than the old days. The fire was out but so were two engines. The controls felt like lead and over the Rhine she plainly had not much further to go and the captain said "jump". Charles had often wondered what it felt like to jump. It was soft and quiet, almost like passing out after an accident. But on the way down there was no one to shoot at him and four of them made it into the middle of a US transport company. Alive.

After they landed Dieter was still unable to believe what had happened to Jacob. Murdered in cold blood by a fellow airman. He recalled Liese's words: "Once it starts . . ." For Dieter it had now ended. He would fly as long as the general asked him, but he had no heart for it any more. When the second lot of Marauders came that day he lay in his slit-trench staring up at the sky, scarcely flinching at the terrifying shriek of the bombs and the nauseating concussions. Feuchter. Brandis. Willy Weiss. The Hoffman twins. Shoehorn Kolbe. Gentle Müller. Fanatical Stecke. Now Jacob and so many thousands more. All gone and for what? For what had they died? Earth spattered down on his face and he heard Mano calling: "You all right?" He didn't answer but Pohle answered for him: "Yes, he's okay. The bastards missed us again." Dieter thought of what Mano had told him about the baby. Liese would be safe. The baby brought him to his senses. When the next stick fell across the runway he crawled face-down into the slit trench as its designer had intended.

Two days later a Dakota ambulance picked up Charles and the remainder of the Fortress crew and flew them back to England. Now for Charles, at last, it was over. There was a letter waiting for him back at base. From Kate. She was in hospital in the south of England. Soon she hoped to go to Rife Farm. He walked over to the mess. Already, in the three days since he had taken off on his thirtieth mission, the operation against Europe was being visibly run down. Faces were missing from the mess, but this time not because they had been shot down but because they were being sent on leave in preparation for the Eighth's next move: to Japan. There was a cold flat feeling about it all at a time when he ought to be glad that he had survived. He lay sprawled in a mess chair while the radio played "My guy's come back". It was as if the huge silent audience were listening: the 80,000 US aircrew who hadn't. Charles could not remember such a desperate sense of depression. What had they died for? He thought he knew and only hoped he was right. He went to the phone and sent a telegram to Kate in hospital. "Darling, how about honeymoon at Rife Farm. Charles." Then he went back to quarters and took the whole bottle of Canadian Club he had been saving for just such an occasion out of his locker. What's more he would ask no one else to share it with him except those he felt were still all around him, those who had gone out of this very hut, laughing and shouting to hide their fear.

On 18 April Steinhoff crashed heavily on take-off and was horribly burned. Two days later the great Günther Lützow set off in his 262 on a mission and was never seen or heard of again. He had simply disappeared into the riven sky just like Guynemer, the famous French ace of the First World War. The squadron of experts was slowly being whittled down.

In Berlin, a fat man was preparing to salvage his stolen art treasures and a madman was announcing that he would never leave the capital. In a few days he would poison his wife and his dog and shoot himself.

At this point, the general called his pilots together and spoke to them as follows: "Gentlemen, the war is lost. No matter what we do here it can't make any difference. Nevertheless I shall continue to fight because flying the 262 has got a hold on me and because, frankly, I am proud to belong to the last fighter pilots of the Luftwaffe. Only those who feel the same are to continue flying with me."

Dieter and Pohle continued.

Now, ironically, they had more 262s than they knew what to do with. Test units, night fighter units, recce squadrons, blitz bomber groups, all were passing their machines to JV 44 just to keep them flying. It was a supply situation for which the general had fought all along but now it was coming true it was far too late. By 26 April, he was no longer in a condition to do much about it. A Mustang caught him napping, shot out one engine and filled his left knee with splinters. Perhaps because he believed in the 262 so much, his shattered jet didn't let him down and got him home to Riem out of mechanical gratitude. He was still protesting when they took him away to hospital.

Lunacy continued to the very end. Luckily there was now a man in the squadron office who had a deep experience of official lunacy. Mano simply tore up the more ludicrous instructions and passed on those which seemed to make some sense. Thus he ignored the order to reorganise at Prague for a last-ditch defence of Berlin but suggested to his new squadron commander that falling back in good order to Salzburg might not be such a bad idea. The Russians were across the Danube at three points, but, with luck, the Americans would enter Salzburg.

So all sixty serviceable 262s flew to Salzburg and there they stayed, uncamouflaged, on a virtually unprotected airfield.

That was the way Peter Bristow saw them when he flew over with a gaggle of American Mustangs and Thunderbolts on the morning of 3 May.

The 262s stood immaculate and beautiful in the sunlight and not one of them made an attempt to take off because they had no fuel and very little ammunition. High above, the Thunderbolts and Mustangs wheeled as free as swallows in the spring air. And, though they had plenty of fuel and ammunition, they made no attempt to attack, principally because orders said the German jets were to be captured intact if possible, but also because the Mustang and Thunderbolt pilots hoped, themselves, to fly the planes that had given them so much anxiety.

Dieter, Pohle and Mano stared up into the sky, watching the victors and realised more utterly than ever before that the war was finally lost.

With hardly a word to each other, the group of pilots broke up. Sergeant Streib was waiting alongside Dieter's machine. As he saw Dieter approaching he emptied a can of fuel into the open cockpit. Then, silently, he handed Dieter a loaded flare pistol. When they had walked to a safe distance, Dieter aimed the pistol and fired. The bright red ball lobbed out and instantly the jet went up in a burst of flame.

Looking down from the Mustang's cockpit, Peter Bristow saw the sixty bright blossoms break into scarlet flower in every corner of the airfield and knew that at last it was time to go home.

Walton-on-Thames
1970-1

EPILOGUE

At the publisher's request, and largely to satisfy his own curiosity, the author employed a talented lady researcher to discover, if possible, what happened to the principal surviving characters of his novel. The researcher's (G. Conway) report is long, detailed and sometimes diffuse. For the reader's interest here are relative extracts from it, necessarily abbreviated.

Extract from preliminary screening by Major G. E. Robinson, R.A. Intelligence Officer, 21st Army Group.

Reh, Helmuth. I interrogated this civilian on June 10, 1944, in the town of Minden. He gave his age as 54. His last wartime role appears to have been Special Gauleiter for jet aircraft production, also an associate of Albert Speer and, in particular, Karl Saur in the Ministry of Armaments and the *Luftfahrtministerium.* Throughout the war, he was a manufacturer of aircraft components and director and principal shareholder of Reh Fabrik, component-makers with factories in Hamelin (virtually intact) and Hamburg (totally destroyed, 1943). He became a member of the Nazi Party in 1942, but this would seem to have been largely a question of expediency and personal advancement. There is no *prima facie* evidence that he employed slave labour and this is probably true since the security risk in the manufacture of aircraft parts—including Lichtenstein radar—would have been too high. Parallel investigations strongly suggest that the Hamburg factory, at least, would have been built with foreign labour but this would have been almost certainly outside the subject's control. Nevertheless, it is recommended that this aspect of his activities be further investigated. His wife, Greta, an active partner in Reh Fabrik, was killed by Allied air action in Hamburg in 1943. Two sons: Dieter, *Hauptmann,* Luftwaffe, believed surviving; and Jacob, killed in aerial combat, 1945.

Researcher's note: I can find no evidence of subsequent action by the War Crimes Commission so it seems likely that "expediency" also applied as far as the Allies were concerned in Herr Reh's case. Or possibly he was genuinely in the clear. His undoubted industrial talents must have been recognised and found useful in the rehabilitation of Germany. Even allowing for this ability, Reh Fabrik can hardly have got on its feet as quickly as it apparently did without Allied (Marshall?) Aid. The attached clipping from a Hamburg newspaper dated July 8, 1950, underlines the speed of recovery.

Reh Fabrik, the Hamelin manufacturers of refrigerators and washing machines, yesterday announced plans to open their newly-built Hamburg factory. Reh Fabrik are moving into the electronics field with a special eye on future development of television.

Researcher's note: There is ample evidence that the newspaper's confidence was justified. Reh Fabrik showed profits of two and a half million *Deutschmarks* by 1962. In 1964, Herr Reh appears to have sold his interest in the business and retired to live outside Hamburg. He died in 1966 leaving ten million DM.

Reh, Dieter. No surviving relatives or friends could be traced in Hamelin although several people remember the family well. Frau Stecke, mother of a childhood friend, had heard that Dieter had emigrated but didn't know where. The German Fighter Pilots' Association was unable to supply recent details but had records of his career until 1955. *Hauptmann* Reh surrendered with the remainder of his squadron (JV 44) at Salzburg to an American tank regiment. As a jet pilot he was subjected to long and careful screening and prevented from rejoining his wife for two months. Like many other pilots, once the war was lost, he agreed to pass on his expertise in jet flying: this appears to have been almost a matter of professional pride. In 1946, he returned to civilian life and probably found employment helping his father (this is assumption: he is known to have been seen in Hamelin around that time). In 1950, he joined the reconstituted West German (NATO) air force and became a jet instructor with the rank of *Oberst* (Colonel). He left the Air Force with a disability five years later. The Air Force and the Fighter Pilots' Association then lost touch with him. Both organisations would be glad of news of his later movements.

I subsequently followed up the clue given by Frau Stecke and made a short list of countries to which he would have been most likely to have emigrated. These included: Argentina, Chile, Brazil, Australia, with former German colonies, such as Tanzania and South West Africa, high on the list. Emigration departments were helpful in almost every case but none could trace him through their records. I then wrote to embassies and eventually received a direct lead from Windhoek, capital of South West Africa, giving an address for a travel agent, D. C. Reh. I wrote to the address and received the following reply.

"I am answering on behalf of my husband who is at present away on business in South Africa. I believe we must be the family you are looking for. My husband, Dieter Goetz Reh, was indeed a Luftwaffe fighter pilot who won the coveted *Ritterkreuz* (Knight's Cross), though for all of us those days are best forgotten. He left Germany after five years back in the air force after receiving minor injuries in a training crash. My husband has always been attracted to the open air life such as a country like this can give, a country moreover which has strong German traditions. We decided to start a new life here in 1951. My husband opened a small travel agency with his air force pension and money loaned to him by his father. I am glad to say that this has prospered. He has a Piper Comanche which he flies purely for business and pleasure. Our only son, Wulf, aged 27, is a ranger for the Conservation Department and is at this moment working in the Etosha Pan National Park.

"On behalf of my husband and myself may I thank you for your interest and kind wishes. I know that he would be glad, for old comrades' sake, if you would inform the Fighter Pilots' Association with whom he is still very proud to be linked.

Very sincerely yours
Liese Reh (Frau)"

Rumpler, Mano. German legal associations made tracing Herr Rumpler very easy. After a distinguished career as an advocate, he became a judge in 1960. Unfortunately he developed cancer in 1967 and died two years later in his native city of Dresden. He never married.

Pohle, Hans. Re-enlisted West German Air Force, 1949, became a senior instructor on *Star Fighters* with rank of Major. Killed in a car crash on the Berlin autobahn, 1970.

Galland, Generalleutnant, Adolf. You might like to have

the current form about him. He was thirty-three when the war ended, the youngest German general in modern times, and the most famous surviving Luftwaffe commander. He was commanding JV 44—the jet squadron—when the war ended. Galland entered commercial aviation after the war, and eventually became Director of Air Lloyd. He is still alive today, living in Germany.

Researcher's note: As expected, your British participants were far easier to trace. Since I live in Sussex, I decided to start with a visit to Rife Farm, which I found almost exactly as described in your novel. I asked for the owner and was greeted by a young man with a slight American accent who introduced himself as Michael Levitson. I realised at this point that I had struck gold straight away. Michael is, indeed, Charles and Kate Levitson's son. Now aged 26 he has been running the farm for the past two years. Previous to that he attended Seale-Hayne Agricultural College and was apprenticed for two years to a farmer called Marston in Axeham Vale in Somerset. His parents are at present living in New York where his father is a successful advertising executive and a vice-president of a large Lexington Avenue agency. Michael Levitson was largely brought up in England and went to an English public school (Bryanston). His father's job has meant that his family's time has been almost evenly divided between living in London and New York. He is an only child. When I explained the nature of my enquiry, he showed me photographs of his father in US Eighth Army Air Force uniform, also one with his mother as a WAAF officer (*very* attractive). He was obviously very proud of them. Then he took me to the large tithe barn and showed me the remains of a German aeroplane found on the flood meadows and supposed to have been shot down during the Battle of Britain. He is keen on restoring as much as possible and trying to trace its history. I told him that I was sure you could help here. I asked after Tom Roland and learned that he died in 1967. Later, I visited his grave in Sidlesham church yard. Apparently he farmed actively until 1965 when the farm was let to a tenant farmer. Rife Farm passed to Kate Levitson on Tom's death and became a natural inheritance for her son who had spent many holidays there and had developed a keen interest in agriculture from childhood, no doubt as the result of Tom Roland's interest.

Michael gave me his mother and father's address in New York and told me that his uncle Peter was alive and well and practising as a solicitor in the West Country. I therefore wrote to Peter Bristow and received a most courteous invitation to call at his Taunton offices.

Bristow, Peter. I found him pretty much as expected. Seriously disfigured on the left side of his face, a frank, open man of 54. He told me that the office where we sat was only two hundred yards away from the house in which his mother had died in an air raid. As the senior partner in a firm of family solicitors, he is obviously very comfortably off. I asked him whether the picture on his desk was his wife and he said that "strangely enough"—the words he used—he had married a German girl he had met during the brief period of occupation following the war. They now had three children, two girls and a boy, Kate (23), Heidi (19) and Charles (17). He is obviously a man of strong family ties. There were many photographs on his office table, including a wartime picture of him in his Spitfire (before he was shot down and burned), a further picture with a fellow officer and a bull terrier signed "Pat" (Pat Hay, a Canadian flyer, apparently); and a recent picture of his sister and her husband, Charles. When I remarked how like him she was, he said in a quite matter-of-fact way that he had been far luckier than she had. As the result of a wartime wound, the sight of one eye had practically gone, though no one would know it to look at her. Apparently a piece of metal, not removed at the time, had shifted and damaged the optic nerve.

He asked me over lunch whether my researches had included anyone on what he called "the other side". I gathered that he meant by this Dieter Reh and told him what I had discovered. He seemed genuinely glad that he had survived and, after some awkwardness and reticence, suggested that if I did get in touch with his sister I let sleeping dogs lie. It seemed to me that he was being excessively cautious, but it is within your competence, rather than mine, to judge.

In making this report I, therefore, append the address of Mr and Mrs Charles Levitson in New York. I felt that you might wish to decide for yourself what you wanted to tell her on this subject—if anything.

Address attached. Extract from researcher's notes end.